Miss Match

7/15

Miss Match

LAURELIN McGEE

St. Martin's Paperbacks

WHITING PUBLIC LIBRARY
WHITING, INDIANA

NOTE: If you purchased this book without a cover you should be aware that this book is stolen property. It was reported as "unsold and destroyed" to the publisher, and neither the author nor the publisher has received any payment for this "stripped book."

This is a work of fiction. All of the characters, organizations, and events portrayed in this novel are either products of the author's imagination or are used fictitiously.

MISS MATCH

Copyright © 2015 by Laurelin McGee.
Excerpt from *Love Struck* copyright © 2015 by Laurelin McGee.

All rights reserved.

For information address St. Martin's Press, 175 Fifth Avenue, New York, NY 10010.

ISBN: 978-1-250-05918-5

Printed in the United States of America

St. Martin's Paperbacks edition / July 2015

St. Martin's Paperbacks are published by St. Martin's Press, 175 Fifth Avenue, New York, NY 10010.

10 9 8 7 6 5 4 3 2 1

For Lisa, who started it all

Chapter One

Personal Concierge, to start ASAP (Boston Area)

*I am a successful businessman looking for a wife.
Due to a busy career and lack of energy or interest
to devote to the process, I am seeking someone to
assist me in my search. I am outsourcing the entire
process, job to start immediately.*

*The perfect candidate will be assertive, with ex-
cellent computer skills and a knack for reading
people. She—I am only seeking women to fill this
position—will be expected to:*

*• Meet me, get to know me. Spend a week or so in
my company to find out my interests, what makes
me tick. During this time she will come to understand
the type of woman I expect to fall in love with;*
*• Do all searching activities on my behalf, including
online, in real life, on social media, networking,
and so on;*
• Once possible matches are identified, provide me

with pictures and, upon my approval, arrange dates for us to meet.

I am attractive and financially secure. I do not have trouble finding women who are interested in me. It is finding women that I deem interesting beyond the physical that is the challenge.

While this job can be done at home, I'd prefer that several hours a week be spent in my company in order to keep a firm handle on what I expect in a love interest. I will have private space available in both my home and office for the right person to work.

Income will be determined initially by the experiences the candidate brings to this project. Additional income will depend on the quality of women found to date me as well as how far the relationship(s) progresses—both emotionally and physically. We can discuss a specific payment schedule during the interviewp rocess.

Serious inquiries only.

Andrea Dawson held the iPad and read the want ad three times before registering exactly what it was Lacy was suggesting by pointing it out. "No way."

Lacy put on her best puppy-dog eyes—the ones that always seemed to get her out of speeding tickets. "Come on, it's totally up your alley."

"No, it's not." *Dear God, please, let it not.* "What's this listed under anyway?" Andy looked at the top of the page for the heading. "Marketing? That's a laugh. I'll stick to the Administrative section, thank you."

"Yeah, and that's working out so well for you." Bitterness dripped in Lacy's tone.

Andy sighed inwardly. Sure, her job search hadn't led to anything—yet—but she wasn't about to settle for match-

maker. It would all be so much easier if she'd finished her
degree. Or if she'd managed to get references from her last
job.

No use moping about what she hadn't done now. Now
was the time to look forward. "I'll find something. Eventually." *Hopefully.* She pushed the tablet away from her.
"I'm not applying for this. Thanks anyway."

"Why not?"

She lifted her eyes to see Lacy's jaw thrust forward.

Uh-oh. Andy was well familiar with her baby sister's
determined look, and that was it.

Well, Andy could be determined, too. "Because this
whole *Personal Concierge* is fancy talk for pimp. You get
that, right? And I may be down and out, but, dammit"—
she pointed at the iPad where the ad still filled the screen—
"I'm better than this."

"Yes. You are." Lacy sat in the chair across the table
from Andy. "But you have to get a job."

"I'm working on it." She ran a hand through her auburn
hair, sweeping it off her nape. She felt bad enough living
off her sister as it was. She didn't need the lecture.

"No, I mean, you *have* to."

Lacy's serious tone drew Andy's attention. *Shit.* It wasn't
just her sister's determined look—it was her desperate look.

Lacy took a deep breath. "I got my hours cut at the
studio."

Andy's stomach dropped. "Oh, Lacy, no! When? Why?"
As a struggling singer-songwriter, Lacy had been lucky to
get a job helping out in a recording studio. It brought steady
income when she was between gigs.

"Not enough work coming in. Darrin cut me two weeks
ago."

Two weeks ago? And not a word until now? "Why didn't
you say anything?"

"I don't know." Lacy kept her focus on her hands. Andy

knew she'd never been comfortable with expressing her feelings. Unless she was singing about them. "You're having such a miserable time, and I guess I didn't want to add to it."

"That's a laugh. You're the only reason I haven't thrown myself under a bus." Andy immediately regretted her euphemism. It was callous to joke about suicide to someone whose boyfriend had died from a handful of pills only a year before.

But the words were already out. "Don't talk like that."

Well, it was a better reaction than Andy deserved. "I'm overdramatizing. I'm sorry. But seriously, Lace, you have been my touchstone through all this mess and it breaks my heart that you've been the one taking care of me when I should be taking care of you."

When Andy had first become destitute and homeless, she'd considered not even telling her sister. Then, besides having no other choice, she realized that moving in would give her a chance to help Lacy cope with Lance's death. Not that Andy had been very helpful. She'd been present, at least. That was something.

"I don't need taking care of." Ever-independent Lacy actually thought people bought the idea that she was *all right*. Maybe most people did. Not Andy.

Yet Andy would let her believe it if that's what her sister wanted. "I know you don't *need* anyone. But I'm supposed to be the older, more responsible, got-my-life-together one while you're the misfit musician. Instead I've been living off you for nearly eight months."

"Nine," Lacy corrected. "But who's counting?"

The gloom of the situation began to settle on Andy. Dammit. With Lacy's hours cut, Andy *did* have to get a job. Like, yesterday. She tugged on her lower lip with her thumb and forefinger. "God, I'm such an awful sister."

Lacy smacked her on the shoulder a little too hard to be called just a playful hit. "Shut up, will you? This is why I didn't tell you. I knew you would make this a reason to shame-spiral. That's not what I wanted."

Wow, the role reversal of older and younger sister went farther than Andy had realized. She lowered her hand and drummed her fingers on the table, needing to fidget while she brainstormed. Her savings account was depleted. She'd used it up in her worthless attempt at suing her previous employer. "Maybe I can dig into my retirement account—"

"Not an option. I'm counting on you to care for me when we retire. Unless I hit it big time, which, at this rate, does not look like it is happening. We'll need that money when we're old."

If it had been a typical conversation, Andy would have resented the fact that her sister assumed there would be no men in their lives in the future. It was understandable that Lacy thought she'd never love again, but what was wrong with Andy? Just because she hadn't had a date in . . .

Okay, that was just depressing. It had been too long for her to even recall. Coupled with their financial situation, it made for a really dreary morning.

Putting thoughts of her lonely bed aside, she concentrated on the matter at hand. "So how bad are we right now?"

Lacy frowned. "Bad. I thought I could manage the shortage by picking up a few extra gigs, but I haven't landed anything that pays very much. I barely have enough right now to cover rent, and it's almost time to renew my T pass or CharlieCard, whatever they're calling the subway now. And have you noticed our fridge is pretty fucking bare?"

They'd had dry cereal for breakfast and lunch the last three days. "Yeah, I did notice that."

"You paid the Internet bill so we're good for a month there."

Andy kept her eyes down. "Uh-huh." She hadn't paid the Internet bill. It had been the last of her savings and she'd spent it instead on a new suit for a job interview she'd had the week before. A job she hadn't gotten. Not enough experience, no references. Same story every time. She hadn't even told Lacy about it, afraid to get her hopes up.

"And I paid all the other monthly bills already, but it's almost the fifteenth and that doesn't give us long before they're all due again."

"God, Lace, I'm sorry. I'm really sorry." Maybe a general apology would cover all her faults, including the missed Internet bill.

"Stop apologizing and get a job!"

"I'm trying!" Except she really wasn't trying that hard. Not anymore. She'd tried in the beginning, but the interview the week before had been her first in almost a month. No one wanted a twenty-eight-year-old who hadn't finished college and had a mostly blank résumé. The only job she'd held for the past eight years was certainly not going on there, not after the way it ended. The search had begun to feel pointless. "I've tried," she corrected. "You know I've tried. I send out résumés every single day. Just because I haven't gotten any other invites to interview yet doesn't mean I won't." She hoped Lacy didn't recognize her lack of conviction.

"Yeah, I do know you're looking. But without a single callback? I also know the probability of you getting a job anytime soon is pretty slim. At least the kind of job you want. So it's time to start looking elsewhere."

"All right. You're right. I need to lower my expectations. But this is really low, Lace. I . . ." She reached for the tablet, drawing it closer to read it once more. There were so many other options—she could try retail or be a hostess somewhere. "Why this job?"

Lacy held up a finger. "Because, number one, it's hiring *right now*. And we need money *right now*. Unless you want to flip burgers, this is the best chance I see at having another paycheck in our hands within the next two weeks." She added a second finger. "And number two, this job was made for you."

"Thanks. I'm glad to know what you really think of my skills." Truthfully, Andy had no skills. At least not the kind that could be quantified or labeled. She wasn't great at computers, still used two fingers to type. The very thought of attempting Excel made her queasy. Her talents were unique and her previous employer had recognized them, shaping her job to suit her. Then she'd gone and screwed it all up. But only after he'd tried to screw her, literally. Her retaliation had felt worth it at the time. Now, with pennies in her pockets, she wasn't so sure.

"I think your skills are pretty damn rare. Not many people have the kind of talents you do. You know that, right?"

Andy shrugged.

"You just have to get some work under your belt so you can get an awesome referral and take those abilities to somewhere fantastic. This is that stepping-stone, Andy. You know you would rock it. You nail anything that has to do with people's personalities. And this"—she pointed at the iPad—"matching-people-up crap? That's exactly what you're best at."

Actually, when Lacy put it that way, it *was* what Andy was best at. "I suppose so. Only—"

"Look, you can still keep trying. Keep sending applications out, but in the meantime, will you please, please, just interview?" She laced her hands together in a pleading pose.

Lacy was good. Really good. When did she get this good?

Oh, who was Andy kidding? She'd always been easily wrapped around her baby sister's finger.

Andy rubbed her hands over her eyes, aware that she was going to give in but not quite ready to admit it. "Just an interview?"

"That's all I'm asking." Lacy's tone was relieved. Excited, even, and Andy had yet to agree. "Go and find out what it all is, how much you'd get paid. *When* you'll get paid. Maybe the guy's a total hottie and easy to work for."

"Not likely. From his ad, he's an obvious douchecanoe. *Much* like the last one." Andy could picture him now—a stiff-collared, self-centered workaholic who found time to get a weekly manicure but couldn't bother putting in the effort to find a date. He might even be attractive, but no one was good-looking enough to make up for being the total ass-hat that the ad portrayed.

"I don't know. Some people don't know how to express themselves in writing. He could be a prince in frog's clothing." They looked at each other for a minute and burst out laughing. "Okay, he's probably a douche, but we need the money."

"You don't even know if I'll get the job." *Please, God, let me not get the job.*

"You will."

"You don't know that." Though Lacy's faith in her was sort of cute.

"I do. But all I'm asking is for you to check it out. Go to an interview." The puppy-dog eyes were out again. Even bigger now.

It was time to give in. Andy had nothing left to argue. "All right, all right. I'll go." She put a hand up to halt Lacy's victory dance. "Just to feel it out, though. I'm not promising anything else." And maybe it wouldn't be as terrible as she guessed.

"Thank God!" Lacy whipped out a folded piece of paper from her back jeans pocket and handed it to Andy. "I already set it up for you. Your appointment's at three. Here's where you're going."

"What?" Andy peered at her sister's pencil scratch. It was an address downtown. "You set something up without knowing I'd agree?"

Lacy offered an innocent one-shoulder shrug. "I knew I'd talk you into it. Eventually." She grinned. "And I didn't want you to drag your feet and find the opportunity gone. We need the money."

"Okay, I get it. Now. I should have realized before, I'm sor—"

"Stop! I don't want to hear that word from you again today, okay?"

"Fine. Fine." Andy laced her fingers and stretched them out over her head. Why did she feel like she'd just been manipulated by a master con artist?

Oh, yeah. Because being coerced by her sister was pretty much the same thing.

Andy ran a hand through her hair. "Guess I better figure out what I'm going to wear." Her new suit would be perfect. But how to sneak it on without Lacy discovering she'd bought it instead of paying the web bill . . .

"Thank the Lord you're finally changing out of those TARDIS PJs. You're starting to smell." Lacy reached for the tablet. "Now I'm taking back my iPad. I have some Internet stalking to do. Darrin said there's a new sound coming out of Cambridge. I need to check it out. See if it's competition." Lacy swiped at the screen. "What the hell?"

"What's wrong now?"

"It says we have no Internet connection. I don't get it. It was just working."

Andy was up out of her seat before her sister had finished talking. "I'm just going to jump in the shower."

She'd made it halfway to the bathroom when Lacy screamed after her. "Dammit, Andy!"

At least Andy didn't have to figure out how to break the Internet news. Now to get a job.

Chapter Two

Andy read the letters on the gold nameplate of the office door for the millionth time since she had arrived. BLAKE DONOVAN, PRESIDENT. Even his name sounded pompous, old-moneyed, and Republican. And if he hadn't been born with money, he certainly had it now. His waiting room looked like it should be featured in an HGTV special— the leather couch she was sitting on had to cost Lacy's whole year's rent. What a waste.

She leaned into the cool material and swung her crossed leg back and forth while she bit the inside of her cheek. She was nervous. Which was ridiculous. Yes, she needed a job and Lacy was counting on her to land *this* job, but Andy had already decided this was not the job for her. She was only here out of consideration to her sister, to show that she was determined to get employment. She'd sit through the silly interview, then tomorrow she'd stop by one of those temp agencies she'd been avoiding.

Besides, even if this job as personal matchmaker was up her alley, she could tell from looking around the wait-ing room of Donovan's office that she did not fit in with

the surroundings, and she didn't mean the environment.
It was the other employees that made her feel frumpy,
underqualified.

The glass walls gave her a perfect view of his staff
outside. They all looked like they walked out of a
commercial—good-looking, perfectly dressed, put-
together, gliding around as if on rails. That was definitely
a count against her.

Strike one: not a model.

The office door opened and Andy looked up from the
book she was reading on her phone. A leggy blonde exited, her eyes downcast. She was gorgeous—tall, model-thin.
Her cheekbones could cut someone they were so sharp,
which somehow added to her beauty. She fit in with the rest
of the runway-ready girls that it seemed Blake Donovan
liked to employ.

In fact . . . Andy glanced around the staff's desks again,
this time looking only at the women. Yep, she wasn't imagining things. There wasn't a single brunette among them.

Strike two: not a blonde. Two strikes and she hadn't even
made it into the interview yet.

Andy pretended to keep reading, but her eyes followed
the blonde as she passed through the waiting room and out
to the main work area before they darted back to her book.
She was starting to feel more than a little insecure, despite
the sharp new outfit. As proud as she'd always been of her
auburn locks, it didn't feel good to think they were a lia-
bility.

A rustle in front of her drew her glance back to the office
door. A man had stepped out to speak to the secretary. Ah,
this must be the illustrious Mr. Donovan. His back was to
Andy so she couldn't see his face, but from behind he
was pretty good looking. Stunning, actually. His shoulders were wide and defined. Even though the jacket covered his butt, she was certain it was equally sculpted.

Then he turned around and her mouth opened in a silent gasp. *Stunning* didn't do him justice. He was gorgeous. Like knees-knocking, panty-soaking gorgeous. His jaw was strong, his cheeks high. His broad forehead and short dark-blond hair accentuated his blue eyes. Piercing blue eyes. Eyes that left a person feeling dazed and confused. Eyes that made a woman do silly things like forget her name or her reason for being in his office or her predetermination to hate him. Those kinds of eyes.

Strike three: Mr. Donovan is hot.

Too hot. There was no possible way she'd get through an interview with a man that smoking. How would she even be able to speak? She might as well lock her phone, grab her bag, and leave right now.

Except she was frozen, caught up in staring at the man who couldn't *not* be stared at.

"Definitely not that last one," Mr. Donovan said to his secretary. "She has man-calves."

And with that, Andy was back to reality. The guy was a chauvinistic ass-wad, and that made everything about him look downright ugly.

As long as she focused on that, this interview would go fine. She hoped.

"Andrea Dawson." He pronounced it *AND-ree-uh*, which made her skin crawl. She followed Blake Donovan into the richly appointed office. It was masculine and modern at once, all clean lines and neutral shades. At least his taste in art and furniture wasn't as tacky as his Craigslist ad.

"It's Andrea," she said to his back. "It rhymes with Leia. Like Princess Leia. You know, *Star Wars*? That's how I tell people to remember it." Jesus, she sounded like a moron. *Star Wars references; way to land that job at the pizza place, Andy!* And he hadn't even looked at her yet. Even as he called her name he'd been studying her application rather than focusing any attention on her. *Ass with a capital A.*

"Andrea. Drea. Drea." He tapped his finger against his desk as he seemed to be committing the correct pronunciation to memory. That was something at least. "You have sufficient computer skills, it appears." Mr. Donovan unbuttoned his Armani jacket and sat down in a gray wingback chair without inviting her to do the same. He began running one finger down her résumé. One long, strong finger.

"I do." She sat in a matching chair and tried not to stare. He continued perusing her résumé, and she continued ogling his body. It was long, and very fit. His chest muscles strained against his dress shirt and, wow, did he have pecs.

Perhaps it was better that he didn't look at her. Then he wouldn't notice her ogling.

And why was she ogling? He was inside-ugly. Total inside-ugly. She had to remember that.

Without glancing up, he asked, "Do you know your way around social media?"

"Yes." Who didn't these days?

He didn't even process her answer before moving on. "Ah, I see you worked for Max Ellis as a personnel consultant."

Andy tensed. "I did." Her voice sounded meeker than it should. Maybe she should clear her throat? No. She'd sound awkward and awkward didn't bode well when trying to appear attractive. Attractive as in a job candidate, not as in the sexual sense, though everything about the man did make her want to check herself in the mirror one more time.

God, why was she still so nervous? She didn't even want the job. It had to be because Donovan was asking about Max. Yeah, that was it. This was the part of the interview she'd been dreading. She didn't want to talk about her past

employment. But it was inevitable. The faster she got it over
with, the faster she could walk back through those pristine glass doors and forget this ever happened.

"Hmm." Donovan continued staring at her résumé,
though Andy was sure he must have read it over three times
by now. "What did you do for him exactly?"

Just keep it simple, she told herself. *And vague.* "I helped
him pick personnel for his key positions." Well, that was
true enough.

"You worked in human resources then?" Donovan
flipped the page.

"Not exactly." *Ah, fuck simple.* She'd go for the truth.
What did she have to lose? "I went with him to business
dinners and events where he was seeking potential candidates, and I'd mingle with them. With the people he was
interested in hiring, I mean. Afterward, I'd give Max my
opinion."

His forehead wrinkled. His mouth may have twisted,
too, but she couldn't see it with his head still down. "Your
opinion? On their job-worthiness?"

"Well, sort of. More like on their personality and social skills. Whether they were married or not. Whether
they were the type to cheat on their girlfriend. Stuff like
that. Max wanted a complete picture of every candidate."
She glanced around the room as she spoke, taking in the
stark details of his office. There was nothing warm about
it. No family pics, no personal mementos. Closed off. She
wondered how he thought someone could possibly make
a love-match for him given how sterile he was.

He cleared his throat and she guessed it was a cue to
say more. "Max would use that to help determine whether
he wanted to hire them."

"In other words, you manipulated them."

Andy grimaced. "I wouldn't call it that . . ." Although
it was kind of accurate.

"What would you call it then?" He paused, but not long enough for her to fill the space with an answer. "Did the candidates know that you were working for Ellis?"

She hesitated, still stuck on the question he hadn't let her answer. What *would* she call the work she'd done for Max? Practical, smart, maybe borderline unethical. Actually, *spying* did seem to be the most correct term.

Donovan cleared his throat again.

Right; he'd been asking her something. "Excuse me, could you repeat the question?"

"Were the candidates that you spied on aware of your position?" He said it slowly, enunciating each word as if she had a hearing problem. Or was just stupid. And at this point she was feeling very much like the latter.

This time she had to clear her throat, awkward or not. "Some of them. Or at least they knew I was with him. Sometimes. Maybe not. I don't know." She felt flustered. That was his intent, she was sure of it. She really hated men like that—confirming their own power by intimidating women.

Donovan scratched a note on her résumé. Andy imagined what he'd written. *Flusters easily, no ethics, total spy.*

"And how did you get to know them, so to speak? Were these candidates always men?"

Uses her feminine wiles to obtain information from otherwise unaware men. She was sure that was what he was thinking even if he didn't write it down. It's what *she'd* be thinking. Might as well just own it. "Mostly. Yes."

Donovan's head rose, and he looked at her for the first time since she'd arrived in his office. His shockingly blue eyes squinted slightly as he tilted his head at her. She stared back, caught up in his penetrating gaze.

"I see."

"What? What do you see?" What the hell was he implying? His voice was judgmental, but his expression showed almost . . . attraction? No, that couldn't be right. Maybe she had something in her teeth? That wasn't exactly the image she had hoped to project, even if this was just a practice interview.

Andy felt unbalanced. Normally she'd have a read on someone by now. Instead, all she had were her own reactions. This guy must be great at poker.

He went on as if she hadn't said anything. "Why you? Why did he care about *your* opinion? I don't see anything listed on your résumé that even remotely qualifies you to choose experts in banking."

Oh, God. This was the part that was always hard to explain, difficult to sell to a new employer who hadn't seen her in action. Or who, as Donovan obviously did, read sexual undertones into the job. She took a deep breath and plunged in. "I worked a temp job for Max as an administrative assistant one summer while I was in college, and—"

"Pursuing a degree in psychology?" he asked, looking again at her résumé.

"Yes. He noticed that I had a 'unique talent for discerning people's true motives'—his words, not mine." Though they were words that always made her smile. She was proud of what she could do, even if it was unusual in terms of job employment.

She swallowed then went on. "He started taking me with him to business functions out of curiosity, and we sort of developed this working relationship. At the end of the summer he offered me a generous amount to continue working for him in the way I described before. He basically created a position for me. So I dropped out—*left* college and kept the job."

Instead of looking skeptical as she'd suspected he would, Blake Donovan seemed interested. Intrigued, even. "You worked for him in this capacity for eight years? Why did you leave?"

She gritted her teeth. "A difference of opinion." That dickwad, Max. It still made her see red to recall, even nine months later.

"And you haven't held a job since?" Again, he sounded more perplexed than judgmental.

Maybe she was reading him wrong. Which meant she wasn't as good at her so-called abilities as she thought. "No job since. I haven't been able to find anything that I'm really qualified for."

He clucked his tongue. "I'm sure that's true. You have a very unique skill set, indeed, Drea. Did Max provide a reference for you?"

Wow. He'd acknowledged her skills as legit. That was a first. Of course, the answer to his last question would probably end any interest he had in her. Not that she cared. "No references. And really, it's Andy."

"Then I'll make a note to call him." He scribbled on the top of her résumé.

"No, don't!" She nearly jumped out of her chair. Which was embarrassing. She hoped he mistook her heated cheeks for enthusiasm.

He stalled with his hand on the receiver.

She took a second to calm herself, sliding back into the chair and making a conscious effort to smile naturally. "Please, Mr. Donovan. Max and I didn't part on the best of terms."

"Oh?" He sat back in his own chair.

Thank the Lord.

"I'd rather not discuss that if you don't mind." Andy crossed, then uncrossed her legs. That hadn't come out as smoothly as it had sounded in her head. She would have to figure out a better way to deal with this question in her future interviews.

"I do mind." His tone told her that he had no qualms about ignoring her request.

She held her breath while he stared at her, willing him to speak first.

"But since you aren't my employee—yet—I suppose I'll have to abide by your wishes. Let's discuss my needs, shall we?" he finally rejoined.

His needs? If he kept looking at her with those devastatingly blue eyes, they'd have to discuss *her* needs. Not that she was entertaining the idea. Blue eyes were just generally disarming. Especially when attached to a tall, muscular man in an expensive suit. Shame about the personality.

And shame on her for thinking about him as anything other than disgusting. Or at the very least, unappealing. Or mostly unappealing. Inside-ugly! "Yes, let's discuss your needs."

Please, please let that have come out less seductive than it sounded to my ears.

If he registered the want in her tone, he ignored it. "I'm a very busy man. I built this IT business from scratch. It's expanded worldwide. I often have to travel to New York, Los Angeles, and Chicago. Occasionally Japan or Germany. I work long hours, catering to clients in different time zones. When I finally leave the office, I head home and typically continue working there. Obviously, this leaves little time for anything else."

Ah, the married-to-his-work type. But he was so attractive. He had to get it on sometimes. She couldn't stop herself from asking. "You don't date or . . . anything?"

"You mean do I have sex?"

She blushed at his bluntness, refusing to acknowledge that that was indeed what she had meant. Was this appropriate to discuss in an interview?

Turned out he didn't need her confirmation and felt it was relevant. "I have plenty of sex. When I'm in the mood, so to speak, I simply go find what I need."

"What you need . . . ?" The conversation had her lower belly tightening in a way that made her both aroused and uncomfortable.

"I believe the term is *cruising*, Drea. I go by myself to a club or a bar, and I don't leave alone."

"It's Andy. And how often do you do this?" She was starting to get a read now. *Narcissist, control freak, misogynist . . .*

Donovan leaned forward, grabbing her eyes with his. "*Very* often, Drea."

She shivered at his low silky tone, at the way his gaze held her captive. When he looked at her like that, she wanted to be one of those women he picked up in the bar. Even though the idea should make her feel gross and slimy, it made her feel hot and bothered instead.

Blake continued his piercing stare. "Did you think otherwise?"

Andy shifted in her chair, not sure how to answer or even if she should because at that moment she was afraid her response would be to climb in his lap and lick him from head to toe.

Donovan decided for her, breaking their eye contact to brush an invisible piece of lint off his sleeve. "These rendezvous never last more than one night, however. It seems the women waiting to be picked up by men in bars are not the type of women I'd like to spend any real time with."

Thankfully, Blake's inside-ugly statement broke the spell he'd had over her. Well, mostly. She still found herself morbidly curious, about to ask the question she couldn't believe she was going to ask—the one she had promised herself she wouldn't. "What exactly would the ideal woman be, Mr. Donovan?"

He was quick with his answer. "About five-seven, five-eight. Between one hundred five and one hundred twenty pounds. I prefer the exotic look—dark-brown eyes, near-black hair."

God, the man was a pig. And not just because the look he'd described left Andy's five-foot-five, 147-pound frame out of the running. In fact, she had never been more proud of her light-auburn locks and hazel eyes. She'd hate to think she made it onto this disgusting bastard's wish list.

At least, that's what her brain was saying. The pulsing between her thighs said differently.

Snap out of it, Andy. He's a filthy man-whore. Stay focused and get through this farce of an interview. "That's a very specific type, Mr. Donovan."

"What can I say? I know what I want."

The office full of blond women came back to her. "Interestingly, I didn't see anyone fitting that description on your staff."

His lip rose in a smug smile. "Best not to surround oneself with temptation."

Andy tried hard not to let on how repulsed she was with that statement. So many things about it turned her off—the idea that women could be lumped together based on their physical appearance; that looks were a more important factor to job placement than ability; that Blake Donovan believed his attraction to a woman was the only factor in the get-laid equation.

The last might be true and that was what bothered Andy the most.

Swallowing her loathing, she plunged into scary waters. She'd already committed to seeing the interview through, after all. "What about her personality?"

Donovan's brows creased. "What do you mean?"

"I mean, what type of personality are you looking to spend your life with?" Did he really not get the question? "Will she be funny or sweet or—"

"Quiet," he said, decisively. "I don't want to be bored with talk of shoes and soap operas. Sweet is good. Perhaps *submissive* is a better term."

Now that Andy thought about it, calling Donovan a pig was rather unfair to the noble swine.

Andy ran her hand through her hair and scanned the office one more time. Certain there were no hidden cameras, she had to assume the man was for real. "What about long-term goals? I'm guessing you plan to marry this life partner. Do you want children?"

"God, no." He was silent for a moment. "Maybe one. I'd hate to see my cousin or, more accurately, his wife get their grubby hands on my money after I'm gone. As for marriage—yes, with a prenuptial agreement. And nothing fancy as far as the wedding is concerned. A simple ceremony, no reception. There is no reason to invite anyone but close family. Even that is questionable."

Unbelievable. "I see." It was Blake's turn to narrow his eyes and contemplate exactly what it was she meant with that statement. *Well played*, she told herself, chalking a point under ANDY on her mental scoreboard.

"What about a profession?" She had no idea why she was even bothering to pursue the conversation. It was almost like watching a train wreck. She couldn't turn away.

"For the woman? Certainly not. If she's working now I'd like her to give that up when we marry. Part of the reason I want a companion is to have someone to come home to. A woman with a profession cannot be counted on for that."

Why doesn't he just hire a housekeeper? Or get a dog.

"Okay. So you'd like *someone*"—she specifically avoided saying *me*, like hell was she taking this job—"to find women that fit this description and then . . . what?"

"You'd show me her picture to make certain I find her

attractive. If I do, you set up a date for us to meet. If it works out, I'll give you a bonus and you're done. If it doesn't, then you start searching again." He leaned back in his chair and smiled slightly.

Knowing it was at the prospect of ordering a date like a restaurant meal kept Andy from returning it. "Where would the searching take place?"

"Wherever you choose. Facebook, dating sites, the grocery store—I leave that up to you. That's why I'm hiring you. To do the research for me."

"Right." Because that's how people met and fell in love—by being *researched*. Max Ellis and this jerk could be great friends, although all of the women in Boston would be worse off for that match.

"Any other questions?" His tone suggested he was surprised there'd been any questions at all. As if the whole transaction was everyday.

Well, it certainly wasn't *her* everyday. And even if the pay was beyond excellent, it would be an impossible task. There could not be a match for Blake Donovan. She believed it wholeheartedly. Time to shut the morbid game down. "Nope. I think I have a grasp on the job."

"Good. Although you should never assume you have a grasp on the job from one interview. Your employer will think you're oversimplifying or are conceited."

Her conceited? Wasn't that the pot calling the kettle black?

"Now let's test your skills, shall we, Drea?"

"It's Andy." Her patience was wearing. "Or Andrea, if you prefer."

"I prefer Drea, thank you." He leaned forward, his elbows propped on his desk. "Suppose Max Ellis were looking to hire me. What would you tell him?"

She almost laughed. "Oh, let's not do that."

"Let's do. And I expect the truth."

"Honestly?" It was awfully tempting . . . "You don't want to know."

"No, I do. Be brutal. I can take it."

She hesitated. Telling him would put an end to her candidacy for the position. But did she care?

She did not.

Sorry, Lacy. "Okay. I'd tell Max that you are a devoted businessman with the commitment, hunger, fortitude, and ambition to succeed."

The edge of his top lip curved upward slightly.

Then she went on. "I'd also tell him that you are lacking in common social skills, particularly humility, kindness, and decency. You're sexist, arrogant, and, basically, a rich pompous ass. I also noticed all your very expensive, very monotonously black pens are lined up ruler-straight. On the *right* side of your desk. That indicates you are both rigid *and* boring. Probably a conservative. Don't even get me started on your shirt. That shade of mauve screams *Desperately hetero and hip.* Nothing could make you farther from either." *That felt marvelous.*

"Very good, Drea. Very good, indeed." He stared at her as though he, too, was making an assessment of *her* character.

Huh? That was her move, and it made her squirmy to see him employing it.

He sat back in his chair finally, a smirk playing on his lips. "And tell me, would Max Ellis have hired me based on your input?"

"Yes. Unfortunately, he probably would have."

Blake laughed out loud. It was the only thing he could think to do to dislodge the strange warmth he was suddenly feeling in his chest. Please let it be heartburn and not a fondness for the potential employee in front of him.

Andrea's eyes blazed at his outburst.

"I apologize," he said, composing himself. "Thank you, Drea. I appreciate your candor."

"It's Andy."

He was finding her obvious annoyance more than a little amusing. This whole interview was exactly the opposite of what he'd expected. It was almost enjoyable.

Not almost—it *was* enjoyable.

He regretted now that he'd played a total asshole since she'd arrived. Most of it was exactly his true colors, but he'd amped up his arrogance. It helped weed the women who'd shown up only to sign up to *be* his bride, from the ones who wanted to *find* him a bride. Sadly, there had been few of the latter.

When this one had walked in, though, he was immediately on edge. It started with her bizarrely sparse résumé, something that screamed backstory to him. Blake liked a good mystery. Then there was that completely unprofessional lingering gaze they had shared. That had led him to be even nastier than usual. He just wasn't used to not having the upper hand.

Now that he'd deduced Andrea Dawson was sincere about her job application, he decided he could dial it down a bit.

"Andy." He tested her nickname on his tongue. "It doesn't fit. It's too boyish. And you are definitely all woman." She wasn't even remotely his type—between the curves and the all-American coloring, not to mention ambition. Ambition in a woman had always struck him as one of the least attractive things on earth. Probably because his money-grubbing stepmother had run his father into the ground, all in the name of "ambition."

But the woman in front of him didn't put him off as he might have expected. Despite her flaws, he had to admit there was something distinctly sexy about Awn-dray-uh Princess Leia Dawson. Really, a *Star Wars* reference?

"I . . . thank you, I think."

He settled farther into his chair, reveling in her discomfort. "You're welcome. Drea."

She, in contrast, sat up, squaring her shoulders. "My name is Andy, Mr. Donovan. I've never gone by Drea. It's always been Andy or, when my sister's mad at me, Andrea."

"Fine. Andrea it is. Perhaps it's best since I suspect you will frequently anger me." Did he just wink at her? That was strange. He never winked.

He rubbed his eye, hoping she'd believe his wink had been a twitch. "And you may call me Blake. You'll need to get to know what makes me tick and I think that requires a first-name basis, don't you?"

"What? Excuse me, but—are you actually offering me the job?" She looked completely shocked.

He was a little shocked himself. Normally Blake preferred his employees to treat him with a certain level of deference, but something in him said that Andrea Dawson was *the one*. "I am."

"But—"

"But we haven't discussed pay yet. That's right. Here's what I think your beginning skills are worth." He grabbed a Montblanc and a fresh sheet of stationery from the desk and scribbled a figure. Folding the paper once, he handed it to his new hire, who opened it rather suspiciously.

"Oh."

"I expect that's reasonable."

"It is, but—"

"As I mentioned in my ad, there will be an increase dependent on how the relationships progress. We can discuss that further if you accept the position."

"Sure, of course. I appreciate the offer—"

"Don't answer now." He interrupted, suddenly nervous he'd scared her off before she even started. Or maybe the number he'd written down wasn't high enough. "You should always take your time replying to business offers even if you already know how you're going to respond. If you say yes, you'll look desperate. If you say no, you'll seem ungrateful for the opportunity. Never appear ungrateful. Call me by close of business tomorrow with your answer."

"Uh . . . Okay."

He stood and reached for her hand. That was what one did at the end of a business meeting, after all, but he knew it was an excuse to see if her skin was really as soft as it appeared.

She seemed startled at his outstretched limb. It took her a second to put her palm in his. When she did, when their flesh touched, Blake could swear he felt a spark. Not like the shock of electricity from rubbing your feet across the carpet, but a mingling of energy. The warmth traveled through him, spreading into every part of his body.

He was too stunned to let go.

Blake met the eyes of his soon-to-be employee. Their already dark shade seemed darker, and the small part of her mouth suggested a silent gasp. That meant she felt it.

Andrea was the one to break the spell. "Excuse me, I do have another question now."

Sprung back to reality, Blake dropped her hand. Probably a little too eagerly. "Yes?"

Drea bit her lip. "Why are you offering the job to me? Am I the only person who applied?"

He considered telling her it was her qualifications, which was partly correct. It would be the nice thing to say, the honorable thing. It would be appropriate, too.

He'd never tell her the real truth—that she intrigued him and beguiled him and he couldn't imagine letting her walk out the door, never to be seen again.

He settled on another answer, no less true, and decidedly dickish. "You're the only applicant who hasn't offered to be my wife rather than search for one. And from our interview here, I gather that filling that role doesn't hold any interest for you." The last comment should ensure that passing sparks and longing gazes did not occur in the future.

"No, it doesn't."

"Excellent." And it was, but she didn't have to look quite so horrified at the thought.

Chapter Three

Andy paused outside the heavy wooden doors of the temp agency and smoothed down her pencil skirt. After a long night of practice-interviewing with Lacy, she felt more than ready to nail this. Temping for a few businesses would provide the references missing on her résumé. Not to mention the networking opportunities. She hadn't exactly been Max Ellis's most popular employee. Because of the nature of her position, everyone assumed she was spying on them and reporting everything back to the boss.

Everyone was right.

Still, it had stung when not a single co-worker had reached out in the aftermath of her departure. It also confirmed that she wouldn't be using any of their names on her résumé. Hence the rigorous paces her sister put her through planning just what to say to explain her gaps.

She threw back her shoulders and stalked into the office with confidence. A pretty brunette looked up from behind the desk and smiled.

"Welcome to Spencer and Colt Staffing Solutions. How may I help you?"

"Yes, I'm Andrea Dawson, and I have an interview with Denise at nine."

"Have a seat, Ms. Dawson. She'll be with you shortly," the brunette told her. "Can I offer you some tea or coffee?"

"Coffee, please. Thank you. I didn't have time to stop on my way over."

The receptionist stood up, revealing a slender figure in a slim-fitting mauve sheath. She was tall, even without the strappy heels. *Donovan would love her.*

Oh, God, what am I thinking? Andy shook her head. The whole scene yesterday had left a bad taste in her mouth. All the more reason to rock this preliminary interview and start getting matched up for jobs.

"Here you are, Ms. Dawson, and Denise will see you now. If you'll follow me?" Andy collected the steaming cup and her leather notebook case, stood up, and trailed the woman back to a small conference room. It was cramped, and standard—the exact opposite of yesterday's luxurious surroundings. She felt more comfortable already.

"Ms. Dawson. Have a seat. Close the door, Evelyn," said the woman at the head of the table without bothering to rise.

"You must be Denise. It's nice to meet you. Call me Andrea, please," Andy said, setting down her things and extending her hand. Denise ignored it. She removed the reading glasses perched on the end of her nose and stared silently. Andy stared back, smile fading, unsure of what was happening. The woman in front of her was angular and sharp, graying blond hair scraped back into a severe bun. She looked pissed. Andy wondered if she wasn't supposed to have brought her coffee into the room. She sat slowly, two seats down from Denise.

"Denise *Thornton*, Ms. Dawson." She said her last name as if Andy might know it, but she'd never met the woman in her life. Perhaps it was simply the power of her position talking.

And since there was power to Denise Thornton's position, Andy wasn't above butt-kissing. "An absolute pleasure to meet you. You have a very lovely name."

Denise narrowed her eyes almost to the point of scowling. Maybe she wasn't fond of her name. Andy had better stick with Ms. Thornton then.

"You've been out of work awhile," Denise said, glancing at Andy's résumé. "Tell me, what kind of position are you looking for?"

"An office setting." Except she didn't want to be the person who emptied the trash and watered the plant, so she added, "Administrative."

"I see."

The woman took no notes, which bothered Andy in the same way it bothered her when a waiter didn't write down her order. Invariably, the food came out wrong, her side salad missing the extra croutons or her sandwich layered with tomatoes when she specifically said to leave them off. Andy hoped this wouldn't prove to be a similar situation.

Denise tilted her head and scowled some more—something she was rather good at. "Exactly what do you think qualifies you for an administrative position, Ms. Dawson?"

Andy had already written this all out on her paperwork, but she answered as she had when practicing with Lacy. "I have above-proficient computer skills. I'm organized and detail-oriented. Plus, I have a knack for reading people and determining their benefit or hindrance in a corporate setting. That's what I did for a number of years in my previous job, as you can see from my résumé."

Denise's eyes remained glued to Andy's. "Oh, yes, I know. My husband, Bert Thornton, is an associate at Ellis Investments."

"Oh." Things were starting to click. And her stomach, along with her hopes, was starting to sink. "Oh," she said again, this time with less surprise and more dread.

Bert Thornton was a good guy. A great guy, even. He spoke of his wife and two sons often. The boys, twins, were blond, handsome, and star soccer players at the local high school. The wife . . . Andy hadn't paid much attention to his stories about her, except to note that it was awfully cute to see a middle-aged man dimple up like that while speaking of his wife of twenty years. He was obviously happy with his life.

The problem was just that, at Ellis Investments, happiness was not considered a valuable trait. Three times during her tenure, Bert Thornton's name had come up for a promotion. Three times, Andrea Dawson had recommended that he be turned down. Bert Thornton wasn't hungry enough.

Kevin Weber, who showed up before the secretaries to do research each morning on new accounts, who occasionally was found to have slept at his desk to complete a project, who had a mild heart attack at age twenty-six that prompted him to give up smoking, but not eighteen-hour days—that guy was hungry.

JJ Ballon, the guy who openly discussed his love of high-end escorts with junior partners because dating would have taken time away from his career—that guy was hungry.

Hannah Wang, the radical feminist and PETA activist who frankly scared the shit out of the entire firm with her zeal to prove women could work harder, faster, and better than their patriarchal oppressors—she was hungry.

Each time Bert Thornton's name was raised, Andy had recommended one of the others instead.

So the great family guy, avid Red Sox fan, and two-time winner of the HOA lawn award was left behind as the younger, angrier, more driven associates moved up. It sucked, but that was the culture at Max Ellis. And everyone knew that culture was bolstered, if not built entirely, on Andy's suggestions.

Now here it was to bite her in the ass.

"I'm afraid, Ms. Dawson, that with your lack of real credentials and real-world skill set, I can't offer you any positions in a corporate environment."

Fuck. Okay, get a read on her and figure out how to make it work. Deference. She's in charge here, just take a little abuse and let her get it out.

"That's fine, Denise. Mrs. Thornton. I'm willing to work my way up. I can start in an administrative assistant capacity, it's something I've done before . . . how are your boys, by the way?" She received a cold stare in response.

"Jason and Steven were both accepted to Ivy League schools. Due to financial concerns, they both chose to attend community college for their first two years and deliver pizzas to help bulk up their college funds for their undergraduate studies. It's also helped to have them contribute to the household."

Andy had no idea what to say that wouldn't make this situation even more uncomfortable, so she wisely said nothing. She felt like she'd been punched in the stomach. Never, ever during her time at Ellis had she considered the real-life ramifications of her recommendations.

Maybe it wasn't Max that was to blame for her bad karma, but herself.

"As I was saying," Denise continued, "I do have two positions open at current that would suit your résumé. The first is at Skybar."

The exclusive Pierce Industries club downtown? It's not an office, but I could hostess for a bit, if I get to hobnob with the clientele they pull.

"Their second-shift bathroom attendant is on maternity leave."

It was impossible for Andy to keep the look of contempt off her face.

"No? All right, the only other position I need an un-skilled laborer for is with a local landscaping company. You would be required to do a moderate amount of physical labor, as well as work unusual hours and weekends. Is that something you could handle?"

Andy took a deep breath. She could quit her hot yoga classes and save that money while still getting a workout in. Maybe learn a thing or two about growing plants instead of just killing them. "I believe I can handle that, ma'am."

"Wonderful." Denise Thornton smiled a wolfish grin, and played her trump card. "Mataya Landscape and Design's primary client is Ellis Investments. You can report to the building at four a.m. tomorrow. Won't it be nice re-visiting your old stomping grounds? I imagine you'll run into quite a few former co-workers. Wear blue jeans, you'll receive a company T-shirt as well, the cost of which will be deducted from your first paycheck."

Andy's eyes widened. This woman was *good*. Would have far outranked her husband, if she'd worked for Ellis, in fact. Unfortunately the balance of power was rather different right now.

"If neither of these options feels . . . *suited to your profile*, of course you are welcome to take your résumé to an-other temp agency. I have personally taken the liberty of sharing what I know about you with every staffing solution business in town that caters to Boston's high-end firms. We are a very supportive community, you know."

Andrea was not at all happy to discover that Blake Don-ovan's Order-a-Bride offer had suddenly become her most appealing option, and yet it was a relief to be able to as-sure Ms. Thornton that she had decided to accept a differ-ent offer, and could see herself out. Not that anything was going to make her feel any better about herself at this point. She'd always thought Max Ellis was a shitty human being. It had never occurred to Andy that she was as bad as him. It was only out of love and respect for Lacy that she was able to keep the tears in as she called her sister to report back.

That lasted right up until she heard her sister's voice, then she lost it.

"Andy, calm down. I can't even understand you. Did you not get in with the agency?"

"I have twenty emergency dollars in my purse. I'm buying french fries and ice cream," she sniffled in response.

"How could things possibly have gone that badly, good God! We *practiced*. We practiced *all fucking night*. What the hell did you say to them? Wait, did you say french fries?"

Halfway through the best meal the girls had enjoyed in a week—the handfuls of crispy fries perfectly salted, cherry ice cream eaten straight from the tub—things started to look up.

"Look, Andy. You know how desperate this is. But it hasn't been totally fair of me to ask you to start supporting us with no notice, either. I can look for something else part-time, too. I still remember how to bartend. It's been the lot of musicians forever, not to mention good song fodder." This time Andy's tears were of gratitude.

"No, Lace, I'm not going to let you work multiple jobs while I sit around. I can suck it up and take the Donovan job." Ouch, it hurt to say that.

"No way . . . From what you told me, you're way too good for him. Just because we need the money doesn't mean you need another Ellis in your life. No one treats my big sis like that. Well. Not anymore."

"Thank God, you agree." She detested the idea of working for that man. Thinking about it made the fries and ice cream in her stomach want to come back up. She would have taken the position, though, if Lacy had insisted.

But she hadn't.

"Hey, remember how you got our rent lowered the time you told the landlord he was taking his divorce out on the female inhabitants of our building?"

"Yeah." That had been a gamble, but one that had been worth it. The landlord in question has postured big, but when Andy read him like a book—a heartbreaking book, but a book nonetheless—he'd teared up, apologized, and, instead of raising the rent by thirty percent as threatened, lowered it by a hundred bucks a month. That paid for two weeks' groceries, with no more work than a simple Freudian analysis.

"Or when you convinced Mom and Dad to let us spend that spring break in Florida without them?"

"Probably my finest moment, Lace." That one had been inspired, Andy had to admit. Knowing how adamant their parents were on college, Andy had woven a story about self-reliance, common sense, and adventure that had their strict parents practically falling over themselves in their haste to send the girls off to Panama City Beach.

That they had spent their vacation vomiting and wishing Mom was there was beside the point.

So Lacy wasn't going to force the Donovan job, thank goodness.

Andy would take another one of the less desirable options before her, which, compared with working for Blake Donovan, seemed like an exec position at The Boston Consulting Group. "Then I can wait tables while I look for something permanent." She squirted some mustard into her ketchup and stirred it into an orange puddle with a burnt fry. "That might work better anyway. We need cash before two weeks from now if this isn't going to be our last hot meal until then."

"Sad days when a couple cones of fries becomes a hot meal, isn't it? Tell you what. I'm playing backup for Lua Palmer tonight at the new hipster wine bar place that opened up across from the studio. It's all trendy and young and too cool for school. Why don't you come with me? We can split my comped drinks, and maybe talk to the manager about picking up a few shifts. We haven't worked together since high school. Remember the good old days at the Steak Buffet?"

Andy flicked the end of her fry at Lacy's face. "Oh, I remember that all right. I remember doing all your side work while you flirted with the tattooed cook, what was his name—Olaf? Bjorn? Something as Scandinavian as it was fake. I served his mother one night, and she told me it was really—"

"Georgie!" Lacy shrieked. "I totally stopped flirting with him after you told me that. Besides, he sucked at guitar, and that was so not hot."

"But then you immediately transferred your attentions to Salvadore, the buffet attendant who didn't even speak English. So I was still bussing your tables and refilling steak sauces while you batted your eyelashes and pocketed the tips."

"Salvadore taught me Spanish guitar, and that music is a universal language," Lacy said primly.

"So is French-kissing, judging from the scene I witnessed in the walk-in."

"Passion is a key requisite of flamenco, sis. I was merely seeking authenticity."

It was a breath of fresh air to see Lacy's smile reach her eyes. Andy couldn't remember the last time she'd seen her sister relaxed and genuinely happy besides when she was onstage. Since before Lance died, for sure. Which was why she rarely missed Lacy's gigs, even when she'd rather be home soaking in the tub with a glass of wine.

The fact that she couldn't afford a cheap bottle of Beringer played in Lacy's favor.

Lacy licked the fry salt off her finger. "So we're decided, then? What are you going to wear tonight?"

"Don't think you'll catch me doing your side work these days, little sis. What *does* one wear to a hipster wine bar, anyway?" How sad was it that she wasn't even thirty and she had no idea what was *in*? The Ellis bubble hadn't left much time for real life.

"How about keep the pencil skirt, and wear my gray sequined tank? I have a pair of oversized lensless glasses and a fedora you could wear, too."

If that was what was *in* these days, no wonder she hated going out. "How about *you* wear that, and I'll find something else. I think I'm too old for hipster chic."

Blake stared at his monitor, fingers steepled beneath his chin. He was well aware that the pose made him look slightly villainous, and had cultivated it to keep unwanted visitors from popping into his office and interrupting him. The ad had been taken down nearly as soon as Andrea Dawson had closed the door, overly firmly, behind herself. Yet the email account he'd set up to receive answers was still getting messages, 242 and counting. He could have delegated it to his secretary, of course, but this was a delicate matter. Best to handle it personally. Blake wanted to delete them all, but since Drea had left a message with his secretary an hour before politely declining the job, he knew it wasn't wise.

Maybe he should forget the whole damn bride idea. Except that would be admitting defeat, and Blake Donovan never admitted defeat. When he'd hit his thirty-fifth birthday nearly a year before, he had achieved everything on his five-year plan except marriage. He firmly believed then—and still did now—that a wife was necessary for various reasons, such as hosting social engagements, appealing to clients who were more family-centered, and having an automatic plus-one at all the charity and business functions he attended. Also, the sex would be more convenient than his current method of cruising the local bars. And though he'd never say it aloud, he found returning home after a long day at work to an empty house was lonely. Silly, yes, but true.

He'd thought finding a wife would be an easy enough task. First, he went to his colleagues to set him up. But after several horrible blind dates and with his next birthday approaching quickly, he felt a professional was needed to find the woman for him. So Blake had joined Millionaire Matches online. That turned out to be another big fat failure. Perhaps Blake made a mistake by sleeping with and then dumping the CEO. Her parting words to him as she closed his account were, "You couldn't pay someone enough money to find a bride for you in this town." He couldn't let that challenge go undefeated, now, could he?

Blowing air through his pursed lips, he considered.

Drea was his choice for the job, hands down. Who else had the precise background and skills to seek out and vet his future wife? By and large, the other candidates who had shown up in his office wearing too much makeup and perfume were only interested in wedding him themselves. And the few serious inquirers had résumés filled with skills such as "social media ninja." What the hell was that supposed to mean? He wasn't about to hire someone like that to perform the most important task he was going to assign this year.

And there was that something else about Drea. Something he couldn't quite put his finger on. Her brash approach was usually a turnoff in an employee. Perhaps it was that she'd turned him down—no one said no to Blake Donovan, after all. It couldn't be that, though—he'd sensed the *something* even before that.

He struggled to put a name to it. Underneath her obvious dislike and disrespect for Blake and the job he was proposing, he sensed . . . what?

A connection, that's what. An understanding that few people had of him.

It was both terrifying and thrilling.

He had to explore it further. Completely in a working relationship form, of course.

So how to convince her to change her mind? He was willing and able to up the starting salary. Calling her to tell her that would make him look desperate, though, and Blake Donovan would not be seen as desperate. His shoe tapped the floor rapidly. He pulled up Google and typed her name into the search field. Several hits came back from various society pages, photos of Drea in evening gowns on the arm of Max Ellis.

He noticed two things immediately. The first was that for a girl who had absolutely nothing in common with his ideal, she looked more stunning in each photo. The second was that in each picture, Drea was leaning slightly away from Ellis, while he was either leaning closer to her or gripping her waist. Blake smiled. He'd bet money he had just discovered the root of her tight-lipped silence on the subject of her former employer.

That was a relief, because in truth he *was* a bit disconcerted about her lack of a referral. That it was due to an unwanted attraction was something he could deal with.

Among the glamorous pictures of charity balls and banking events was one he almost overlooked. Drea in jeans, grinning widely at the camera, arm around a taller, blonder version of herself. The caption indicated that the tall girl was named Lacy Dawson, an up-and-coming singer-songwriter. Had to be her sister. Intrigued, Blake changed the name in his search field.

Lacy came back with a lot more hits than her sister.

Although far from successful, she had tons of gig listings, studio bios, and even a Facebook fan page. Blake felt most musicians were fairly shiftless, but he could tell this was a girl who worked hard. That reflected well on Drea. The proud, supportive sister. The type to show up to all of Lacy's shows.

Blake clicked on a link listing Lacy's upcoming performances, and wrote down the address he found there. He smiled for the first time all day.

Chapter Four

"So is it *mandatory* that I wear a trucker hat?" Andy asked her new boss, Zeke. They were at a corner table in the brick-lined bar discussing terms of employment.

"The thing about trucker hats is that they are so *out* that they have become ironic all over again. So you'll probably want to hit a thrift store and grab a couple. We love irony here at Irony and Wine. It's sort of our thing, as you may have gathered. You have no idea how hard it is to stay up to date on facial hair trends for our male staffers." Zeke sipped his Malbec and glanced around the still-calm early-eveningb ar.

Lack of confidence leading to overcompensation in beardage. Andy loved being able to comfortably work out people's issues. She could do this.

"Your bar is obviously super successful. I can't wait to be a part of it." She played to the strength she perceived: his ego.

His lip quirked beneath the thick coating of ginger hair. "You know, Andy, I think you'll be a nice fit here. Why don't we plan the rest of the night to be a working inter-

view. Are you comfortable sliding behind the bar and helping Brax out this evening?"

So her initial read had been correct. Thank goodness.
As unmarketable as her skills may be most of the time, she
relied on them to guide her through social interactions as
much as business. She still had it.

"I can't say I'm much of a sommelier"—she was impressed with herself for knowing the correct wine term—
"but I'd love to learn more, and Brax seems like he knows
what he's doing. Thank you, Zeke." One of those sentiments
was genuine, anyway.

Who cares? New job, new Andy. Trucker hats and thrift
stores, okay.

Brax the Waxed Stache, as she immediately dubbed him
in her head, grinned at her as she flipped up the partition
that divided staff from customers. His handlebars were
amusing enough to keep the smile on her face even as he
began his rundown on the wines she ought to be suggesting to various patrons. Evidently Chardonnay was the first
suggestion to be made to women, unless they were wearing graphic tees, which entitled them to Cab Sav. Then with
couples, they were to be talked into obscure German blends
because they'd spend extra to have a bottle they couldn't
pronounce. Dates always spent a lot to impress each other.
Men alone were to be Italian-ed.

Andy's head was spinning at the wine details, but her
heart rate kicked up a notch at the psychology. Good
Lord, this job had written itself for her. Meet people and
determine what they'd like? She couldn't work out why
bartending hadn't made her list of life options previously.
Who cared that she didn't know the difference between a
Merlot and a Zin? She could fake that. It was perfect.

You could call literally any wine at all "well balanced,"
or mention the "nice finish." She realized pretty quickly
that telling customer their glass of white had notes of pear,

or apricot, or apple would never get her called out. You just picked a fruit and watched them nod in agreement.

"Hey, baby, I'd like a glass of red, with a shot of you on the side."

Oh, no, no. The proposition came from a guy in a plaid button-down and Brax was at the opposite end of the bar— *typical.*

She wasn't about to fall for that shit on her first non-shift. She took a deep breath, trying to recall what wine Brax recommended for overly aggressive flirts. "We have a lovely Cabernet on special tonight, almost as spicy as I am." *Cabernets can be spicy, right?* "You'd like a glass, but love a bottle."

A cheeky grin and a popular blend silenced the wannabe lumberjack just as she'd hoped it would. Mayhap this job would be the thing she'd been waiting for.

Or so she thought, until he'd killed the bottle and was giving her the lusty side-eye again. What a dick. Luckily, the polite older gentleman sitting in front of her was rambling on about his favorite books, so she could pretend to be engrossed in conversation. She hadn't heard of a single one he mentioned, but he didn't seem to mind. Or notice.

A couple young enough to have Andy double-checking their IDs sandwiched the older guy and started hugging and talking at once. There went her protection from old lusty-eyed. Also, she noted, the regulars here were shockingly friendly, considering Zeke's snootiness. The couple ordered a bottle of Sauvignon Blanc apiece and then requested straws. Andy hesitated, thinking it was likely a no-no of some sort, but Brax slid past her with a pair of Krazy Straws for the two.

When in Rome.

"Hey. Hey, are you related to that girl with the guitar?" Lumberjack had finally taken his eyes off her long enough to let them land on Lacy.

The desire to protect her sibling lost to bubbling pride. "My sister." She beamed as she grabbed a bar towel and started polishing glasses to hand to Brax.

"Seriously, you guys totally look alike. Do you get that a lot?" Lumberjack swiveled back and forth on his bar stool to ogle first one, then the other.

"Uh, yeah. We're sisters." *Idiot.*

"Do you guys ever, like, I mean, two sisters would be so hot—" The stool wobbled precariously.

"Let me stop you there with an emphatic no." Yeah, she should have kept her mouth shut about their relationship. The idea that this guy was thinking disgusting thoughts about her baby sister . . . *and* her . . . Uh, gross.

She wasn't sure she was allowed to deny service to anyone, but she decided she was done with Lumberjack. "Hey, if you need anything else, Brax here can take care of you." She could have sworn he mumbled something rude, but decided it wasn't worth it.

Onstage, Lacy was tuning her guitar as Lua Palmer set up a mike stand. Lua wasn't a good friend or anything, but she and Lacy performed together fairly regularly. Andy poured what seemed like a decent white into two glasses and brought them to the little wooden stage. There wasn't time for more than a quick *hello* and a *break a leg*—the place was filling up fast.

Back at the bar, Brax had her setting out little bowls of roasted garbanzo beans and olives. She was just thinking how much more swank that was than peanuts when a hand gripped her wrist. *Shit, who gave the lumberjack another bottle of wine?* Yanking her arm away, she glared at the guy, who just grinned back. She pushed down the anger that was starting to build. *Not the time to throw another sexual harassment fit.*

"Hey, Brax, this dude in the plaid shirt is getting a little inappropriate."

"You'll have to narrow it down a little more than that. Every second dude here is in plaid. Including me." He followed her gaze to the lumberjack. "Oh, no, Steve? I love that guy! He's hilarious. Don't worry about him."

So much for professional courtesy.

A glimpse of someone familiar and out of place shot past her peripheral vision but a customer cut her off as she strained to see who it might have been. The customer was a guy about her age, wearing all gray and sporting disheveled blond hair. She thought he could be cute if he didn't look so downtrodden. He ordered a bottle of Riesling—a wine Andy had never heard of—and began to eavesdrop on the book fan's monologue to the young couple.

As Lacy began to strum onstage, Andy got caught up in the rhythm of the bartending dance. She took orders from customers and servers, suggesting wines by how the sounds of their names matched the personalities of the patrons. She must have guessed well, since she collected a decent amount of tips. Pausing to blow the hair off her hot forehead, she listened with half an ear to the morose guy—whom she'd decided to refer to as Eeyore—complaining about the book fan under his breath. Apparently no one was reading classic literature anymore. Salinger would be rolling in his grave.

"Because that shit sucks. Just watch the fucking movie, dude." Steve the Lumberjack was suddenly in front of her, lips stained purple and eyes drooping.

"You are what is wrong with this country." Eeyore's green eyes suddenly blazed.

Steve sat up straighter. "And you're what is wrong with this bar."

"Illiterate lowlife." It was the most spark Eeyore had shown since he'd sat down.

"Old man."

Andy started to get a little worried a fight was coming.

So was Brax, it seemed, because he was already frowning as he headed down the bar.

"Who served this guy?" He gestured to Eeyore.

"I did." Andy bit her lip at Brax's disapproving scowl. "Is that—was I not supposed to? He had ID."

"Pierce is a recovering alcoholic."

The guy in gray was already standing up. "I'm leaving anyway. I have to feed my pet rabbit." It was impressive how much dignity he injected into that statement, considering that he was no longer wearing pants.

What the hell is wrong with this bar?

"You're welcome for getting rid of that loser. So you wanna go make out in the men's room?" Steve leaned across the bar. Andy turned to Brax, but he was already gone.

"Fuck you, no. And I happen to like the classics." She'd actually hated *Catcher in the Rye*, but no way was this dude getting the satisfaction.

God, did she really want this job? She was fine suggesting drinks and clearing tables but dealing with half-naked alcoholics and crude lumberjacks wasn't worth the handful of tips in her apron pocket. Blake Donovan's find-a-bride service sounded a little less dreadful than it had an hour ago. At least she'd be dealing with women. Online, if she liked. And she could wear her slippers all day and no one would notice.

But too late for that. She'd already turned down that job. *For the best*, she reminded herself, as a memory of the attractive bastard flashed through her mind. *Back to work*.

She turned to see what Brax wanted her working on next, when Lacy caught her eye from the stage, nodding to her empty glass. Relieved to have an excuse to take a break, Andy grabbed the bottle reserved for the performers and started weaving her way through the crowd.

*   *   *

Blake watched Andrea's hips swivel as she pirouetted through the onlookers to reach the stage. With an effort, he wrenched his eyes up to her tousled auburn locks. That was rather inappropriate of him, the rear-gazing. It's just that she was so graceful, he told himself. He almost believed it, too. Observing her behind the bar, he really had been impressed with her grace. That one customer had actually dropped trou and she barely batted an eye. She was exactly the right person to screen his future brides—nothing fazed her.

He thought she'd noticed him before the pantsless gentleman sat down, but she hadn't looked his way since. That was good; he hadn't exactly figured out a way to make his professional interest in her look less like stalking. He sipped the Shiraz he'd ordered from the bartender with the peculiar facial hair as she was dealing with other customers.

Wooing her into his employment would have been much easier if she hadn't actually found work here. In his half-assed fantasy, they would have spoken more about his offer, which he would have quietly raised over a bottle of Sangiovese. As Andrea's sister serenaded them, she would have accepted his offer. After apologizing for her earlier refusal, of course. He assumed she'd have regretted that almost immediately. Evidently not.

Something plaid landed on him like a falling tree. It was thanks only to his own grace that Blake was able to keep the wine in his glass from sloshing all over his pristine white T-shirt. By the time he'd recovered enough to deal with the drunken asshole who'd staggered into him, the guy had already lurched off. He lost him in the crowd, so Blake decided to let him go. Then he returned to his observation of Andrea, only to realize she'd been covered up by the plaid guy. Blake was already shoving people out of the way when he noticed the lout was trying to cop a feel on his future employee.

Reaching the pair quickly, Blake overheard her using some rather creative phrases to dissuade him. His smile faded before it was half formed when he saw the reason for her colorful language—that fuckshovel had one hand on her breast, and the other was roughly pulling her by the arm toward the back door. *Oh, hell no.* Future employee or not, that was not how you treated a woman.

"Is there a problem?" Blake steeled his voice into his best boardroom tone.

"Blake?" Drea's face went from shock to relief to confusion in a rapid sequence the drunk guy obviously wasn't going to follow.

With glossy eyes, the drunk attempted to square his shoulders, his grasp still firmly on Drea. "Back off, dude, I saw her first."

Blake couldn't remember the last time he'd been in a bar fight. Oh, that's right—never. But he wasn't about to let on. "I think, *dude*, that you should be the one to back off. The lady is clearly uninterested."

"Oh, she's interested." He punctuated his declaration by squeezing Andrea's breast.

She struggled to free herself. "I'm *not* interested."

"You're interested." The drunk inched closer to Drea's mouth.

She cringed, possibly as much from his bad breath as from the unwanted assault. "Nope."

Blake's free hand, the one not still holding his glass, curled into a fist at his side. Strange, because he'd never strike first. But he had to do something.

An idea came. "She's mine." His voice cut through theirs.

"Fuck you, man, she's—"

With one easy tug, Blake pulled Andrea to him. He encircled her waist with his free arm and pressed his lips to hers. They were stiff at first but relaxed almost right away. His heartbeat sped up and his entire body hummed as she melted into him like ice cream on a hot day. Time seemed to stand still as the guy's droning voice faded into the rushing of blood in Blake's ears.

The feeling of her soft lips on his, parting slightly as he nudged his tongue against hers, made everything else in the world go away. She tasted like the first day of autumn— clean and cool and refreshing. One of her hands came up to tangle in his hair. She had to have noticed his intake of breath, but if she hadn't, she'd definitely feel the way her kiss was affecting the fit of his pants. Blindly, he set his wineglass down on a nearby table to pull her closer.

With both hands on her waist, he could feel her heat through the thin fabric of her shirt. She was warm. So warm and so soft. He tightened his grip, unable to resist.

He groaned into her mouth. The sound brought him back. What was he doing? This was an incredibly inappropriate way to convince her to work for him. As he pulled away, he cleared his throat slightly.

In his periphery, he saw the drunk guy standing there gaping. "I guess she wasn't interested," he muttered as he swayed off.

Drea's eyes never wavered from his. In them, Blake thought he saw a flicker of desire. But he must have imagined it because next thing he knew she was shoving him away with more force than she'd used on her attacker.

"What the hell was that?" she demanded, as if she hadn't given her all to that amazing lip-lock. Maybe she was a better actress than he'd supposed, though. Even the best thespian couldn't fake the flush of her cheeks.

The kiss really had felt like *something*.

But that was impossible, because it was nothing. He'd gotten carried away, that was all. Nothing more. The adjustment he would need to make soon beneath his belt was just a fluke. A reaction to the wine, perhaps. He was normally more of a scotch man.

Refusing to meet her eyes again, Blake focused on the crease of her forehead. "He won't be bothering you again. You're welcome."

"Yeah, okay, I could have dealt with that myself. And what the hell are you doing here, anyway?"

His practiced speech left him, and he was forced to be blunt and to the point. "I came to offer you that job." So much for the schmoozing he'd planned.

"Didn't I turn you down once already today?"

With her hands on her hips, eyes flashing, Blake could see why Max Ellis had been so intrigued by this woman. She wasn't Blake's type, he had to keep reminding himself, but she was always a surprise. He'd expected a bit of gratitude, if not for the position he'd offered, then for saving her from the ass who'd manhandled her only a minute before. Instead she was scowling and accusing and, the worst, denying the moment they'd shared.

Well, he wouldn't stand for her dismissing it so easily. "Didn't feel like you were turning me down just then." He located his glass again and took another sip. Watching her blush was almost as fun as kissing her had been.

She opened her mouth and shut it. Then opened it again only to slam it closed once more.

"What the hell was that?"

They both turned toward the heavily bearded redhead. Drea redirected her fluster toward this man who was obviously unhappy about something.

Uh-oh. Was this Drea's real boyfriend? It had never occurred to Blake that she might have one, but of course, why wouldn't she?

"Very uncool, Andy," the man said. "I asked you to do a working interview for a bar, not a cathouse. You're supposed to be helping Brax, not making out with your boyfriend. What will the customers think?"

Thank God, Blake almost sighed audibly. The hairy

fellow was only her boss—and not even her boss, if he heard correctly. *Interview* meant *not yet hired*. So he still had a shot. He stepped back to watch the situation play out.

"Zeke, he's not, oh hell. Not my boyfriend. He's a friend, well, he's—he was rescuing me from a customer that was getting too handsy." Drea was growing more muddled, smoothing down her shirt as she babbled.

"Really, Andy? Because all I saw was the two of you getting handsy with each other. In the middle of my bar. Part of the job of being a female bartender is to appear available. The male customers like the fantasy. And no one wants to see their server sucking face with some . . . some . . . *businessman*." He practically spit the word out, as if he wasn't a small-business owner himself. Indie cred, maybe.

Also, Blake had been fairly certain he looked cool in the white tee and black slacks. What had given him away? His perfectly polished wing tips winked up at him. Oops.

"I apologize, Zeke, but Mr. Donovan here"—her eyes darted to him—"Blake, I mean, was simply trying to stop Steve—"

"Steve? I love that guy! He's a riot." The bearded man clearly had poor taste in friends. "Don't tell me you're blaming this on him."

"I . . . well, yes. Yes, I am blaming him, if you'd just lis—"

Zeke didn't wait for her to finish. "Take off your apron, I think we're done here."

"Are you firing me?" Her lip trembled.

Blake would feel bad for her if he wasn't too busy thinking about how good that lip had tasted.

No, that was *not* what he was thinking. It couldn't be. He refused to think about that lip again.

"Technically, I hadn't hired you." Zeke held his meaty

paw out. "I'm going to need your tips back along with the apron."

Andrea's hands were shaking as she untied the strings and threw the apron at Zeke's face. She pulled a wad of cash out of her back pocket and threw it into the air. As bills rained down among them, the bar's patrons dove and grabbed at the free money. Zeke glared, but Drea's glare was harder.

"Fuck you, Zeke." She stalked off. Then she turned back around for a parting shot—"Your giant beard makes it pretty obvious you're compensating for a small dick, by the way."

Blake snuck a look at the stage, where her sister was staring in disbelief, impressively without missing a note. Then he followed after Drea. His long stride had them even by the time she reached the back entrance.

She turned the knob and pushed it open, pausing in the frame. "Oh, and fuck you, too, Donovan! Way to stick up for me back there."

He jumped ahead to avoid her slamming the door on him. He half feared she'd jump into one of the cars in the back lot and drive away, but she stopped, back to him, her head down.

Blake cleared his throat. Again. If he kept this up, she was going to think he had some sort of excessive drainage issue.

She didn't turn around, but her shoulders tensed, signaling she was aware he was behind her.

"I should apologize, Drea."

She spun toward him. "Go right ahead, then." Her hands were on her hips again, voice echoing in the alley behind Irony & Wine.

Oh, the irony in this moment.

He folded his arms, wanting to appear as firmly grounded as she. "I said I *should*, not that I was planning to."

Even in the dim light he could see her eyes flash.

He ignored the jolt that this sent to his groin and focused on his objective. "I want you to work for me. You were working for someone else. That person chose to unemploy you right in front of me. Things were working out in my favor. It would not have behooved me to stick up for you, as you call it. Some might say that I was sticking up for you when I rescued you from that lumberjack fellow." He took a step closer.

She took a step back. "Sticking up for me? You forced yourself on me and got me fired."

"My job offer still stands, Drea. As for forcing myself, I don't believe that's a point you can truly argue."

Her eyes narrowed, but she didn't retreat any farther.

"As for the job, please don't try to tell me that these"— he gestured to the bar behind them—"are better working conditions than I'm offering. This is not an appropriate use of your skills, and you know it. It also can't pay as well as I can. I'm prepared to add another thousand to that monthly figure I gave you before."

After a long silence, she sighed. He knew what she'd say when her shoulders slumped.

"I accept your job offer, then. But you owe me for this. I lost a whole night's tips to your antics. You can pay me back in cash up front."

He pulled out his wallet and peeled off a few bills. "I'll do that now, as a show of good faith, and I'll buy you a drink, too, if you'd like to stay on for the remainder of your sister's performance." Why he'd made that last offer, he had no idea.

Drea's eyes widened. "How did—?" She shook her head, changing her mind. "You know what? I don't even want to know how you knew Lacy was my sister. Let's get one thing straight, Mr. Donovan. Blake. I think you are a fairly deplorable person right now. I'm accepting your job offer, but we are not going to be friends. No drink. Just cash. And the cash for the drink you would have bought. I'll see you at nine Monday morning."

Blake bit back the smug expression that he knew was playing on his lips. It was Wednesday—he really should give her until Monday to start, but he couldn't stop himself from correcting her. "I'll see you Friday at nine." He simply wanted to get a start on their new venture. Or he wanted to have the last word, assert his authority. It wasn't like he couldn't bear going the weekend without seeing her.

"Fine," she said tersely. "Friday, then."

When she pocketed the bills and headed out of the alley, he decided it would be prudent to wait a moment before following. Just to make sure she got to the lit street safely, of course. Not because he wanted to hold on to that moment in the bar any longer.

Chapter Five

"You look like an employed person. Is that a business suit? Or did you just suddenly figure out how to match clothes?" Lacy set down her cereal spoon to grin at her big sister.

"I *am* an employed person. What's that supposed to mean?" Andy poured herself a bowl as well. Brand-name cereal. With actual milk, no less. Employment was even better than she remembered.

"That you've looked homeless for some time now. This look is working for you. Do you want to look nice for your douchebag boss? And before you deny it, remember I saw him. He's hot with a capital *hot*."

"Lace! Don't be disgusting." Though the mention of her hot weasel boss brought an unexpected flutter to her tummy. First-day jitters. That was all it was. "I just want to make a good impression. All the chicks who work in that office are size zeros with cheekbones like razor blades."

She stopped pouring her milk at half an inch less than normal at the thought. Then she thought again, and added the rest. *So what if Donovan is a great kisser. I'm moving into Friendzone, specifically into the neighborhood of*

Workville. Not that she could imagine ever being friends with the man. He was just so, so . . .

Whatever he was, she couldn't dwell long on it without feeling her cheeks flush.

Forget the boss, focus on the work.

Abandoning her breakfast after only a few bites, she positioned herself in front of Lacy, then buttoned and un-buttoned her blazer. "Which looks better?"

"Are you really going to ask *me*? I base my outfits on a bar's diviness versus holes in my jeans. How would I know what the white-collar crowd does?" Lacy stuck out a tongue colored by marshmallow bits as proof.

It was effective.

Andy retreated to her bedroom to double-check the fit of her slacks in front of the full-length mirror. Were pant-suits too 1990s? Too butch? She took off the pants and threw them on the growing pile of rejected clothes on the floor. Her room was starting to resemble the aftermath of a Black Friday sale. She was seriously regretting not going to Mar-shalls with the last of Donovan's money instead of buying groceries.

She settled on a skirt that she'd already rejected twice because it was maybe just a touch too short, which brought her to another standstill—hose or no?

"This is definitely not just about the first day at a new job."

Andy startled at her sister's voice. She turned to see Lacy leaning against the door frame, her arms folded across her chest.

Andy rolled her eyes, dismissing the accusation while hating the feeling that her sister may have hit the nail squarely on the head. "I'm not going through this again." She decided no hose, slipping her feet into a pair of stylish black pumps. She kicked them back off and put on ballet flats. Kicked again and went back to the heels.

"Stop for a second, will you?"

With a sigh, Andy pivoted to give Lacy her attention. "What?"

Lacy approached her, settling her hands on Andy's upper arms. "You look great. You are a good worker. You will not burn the office down. You got this."

Andy giggled, the reassurance from her sister releasing the knot of tension in her belly.

"And if you're worried about the impression you're going to make on your hot boss," Lacy went on, "no need. You've already impressed him big time. I saw the look on his face before he went after you in the bar."

"I'm not concerned about that in the least." Her voice wasn't quite as convincing as she'd hoped. She turned to the mirror to apply a final swipe of mascara. "I'll admit he's . . . attractive." *Sexy as hell* was more like it, but she'd never admit that out loud. "Only on the outside, though. Trust me." Except his behavior the other night had removed him from the total-douche category. Now he was only somewhat of a douche. Medium douchiness. Average douche-dom. Boss material.

Lacy leaned her chin on Andy's shoulder and met her eyes in the reflection. "The worst sort of contradiction Mother Nature can provide, isn't it? Lucky for you he's got the looks. It will make your job easier."

That was an excellent point, Andy decided. Thank God for his looks or her job would be impossible. Anytime the recall of his handsome face made her insides flutter against her will, she'd remind herself that this was his one and only selling point and revel in the effect he had on her—or, rather, the effect he had on women in general.

With her plan of attack in place, she thanked her sister, threw her purse over her shoulder, and headed out the door toward the nearest subway station.

Even with a stop for coffee, Andy still got to the building a good twenty minutes early. She was a little peeved that she'd been made to start before Monday, but less so than she should have been. It was her first day and she didn't know how long it would take to get there—that had to have been the reason she'd gotten there before she needed to. Not because she was eager to get to work. Or see Donovan. Especially not that.

Afraid that her earliness would be mistaken for something else, Andy decided to linger before going up. Luckily, the lobby had a newsstand, and she still had some change left from the Donovan signing bonus. She was perusing the gossip rags when she smelled a familiar, expensive scent. *Blake's scent.*

Andy was frozen to the spot, not able to turn and see if her guess was correct. She knew it was. And she wasn't ready to see him—she had yet to pop one of the breath mints she'd just purchased. Not to mention the absolute trash she was reading—what an impression to make.

"Drea."

At the sound of her name that wasn't really her name at all, her thighs began to quiver and her entire core tensed. Man, what was with her body and its mixed signals? She understood why she immediately felt like punching him, but the tingle in her legs was completely ridiculous. Neither reaction was in line with her new plan to make the best of the situation.

Pull yourself together, Andy.

Taking a deep breath, she put on her most cordial smile and turned to greet her new boss. "Blake."

"You're early. I didn't expect to see you for another quarter of an hour."

It was impossible to keep her eyes from flickering to his lips as he talked. *Dear God, please let him not have noticed.* Forcing her gaze to meet his, she said, "I mistimed the T. First day and all."

"Oh. That makes sense." He glanced at the magazine in her hand but, thankfully, didn't poke at her choice of reading material. "Well, I'm about to go up. Would you like to accompany me or should I meet you up there?"

If Andy could read people—and she could—she'd say the man seemed nervous. But that didn't make sense. Why would Blake Donovan be anxious about orienting a new employee? She obviously was still rusty with her skills. After all, she'd actually pinned the bar job as a potential career move.

What she was certain of was her own nervousness. But delaying the inevitable was not going to ease her in any way. Plus, she was still working on that make-the-best-of-the-situation thing, and surely that included being nice to her employer. So, widening her smile a fraction of an inch, she said, "I'd be happy to accompany you."

"Very good." He glanced at his watch even though he'd only a second ago noted the correct time. "They should be finished setting up your space. Shall we?" He gestured toward the elevators, inviting her to proceed before him.

Andy twisted her lips as she walked past him. He'd indicated in his ad that she would be spending a week or so getting to know him, but after that she assumed she'd be able to get at least some of her hours in at home. Having a space set up for her in the building didn't bode well for working remotely. And her job was of a personal nature—why was she stationed at Donovan InfoTech anyway? What was she supposed to say her title was? Surely Blake didn't want his entire company to know the real purpose of her presence. She made a mental note to clear those questions up first thing.

They caught the elevator just as it was about to go up. It was crowded, and in order to get everyone in, Andy had to press closer to her boss than she would have liked. Or maybe it was exactly as close as she liked. The shudder that ran through her at the touch of his body pressed against her back seemed to suggest as much.

He leaned into her ear. "Are you okay?"

His breath skated across her neck, sending yet another chill down her spine. Unwilling memories of the night at the bar invaded her mind—the taste of his lips, his body melding into hers, the unmistakable bulge pressed against her hip. A third shiver rolled through her limbs.

Dammit.

"I'm fine," she snapped before he could ask again. "Cold. It's cold. I'm cold." Yeah, he'd buy that. It was only seventy-five degrees outside and the air-conditioning hadn't been turned on, at least not in the elevator. She gestured to the skirt that now seemed obscenely short under his gaze.

"Maybe I should warm you up."

Did he really just say that? And if he did, did he mean it the way it sounded? She pivoted toward him. "What was that?"

He cleared his throat, something he seemed to do frequently. "I said that maybe some tea would warm you up. Or coffee, if you're not a tea drinker. We have both in the employee lounge. My secretary could get some for you, if you like."

She raised her near-empty coffee. "I have some already. Thanks." Then she turned away from him, hoping he hadn't noticed her flush. Of course he hadn't said what she'd thought. She was ridiculous for thinking that he had.

Andy spent the rest of the ride admonishing herself. She really had to get a grip if this job was going to work out. First of all, she didn't even like the man. Her body simply kept reacting to an unfortunate encounter they'd had nearly thirty-six hours ago. It was physiological, that was all. It meant nothing.

Second, she was supposed to be finding a match for Blake Donovan, not daydreaming about *being* his match.

Third, why did he smell so damn good anyway? It just wasn't natural.

By the time they arrived at their floor, the crowd had thinned and Andy was no longer pushed against her boss. It made thinking considerably easier. That would be the answer to making their relationship work—no contact. Simple as pie. She had no plans to touch him again anytime soon.

They walked in silence through Donovan InfoTech toward Blake's office. Andy wondered if he would send her to HR or if he would leave her with his secretary. Or would he handle her paperwork himself? She looked at the cubicles as they passed. Would one of those spaces be hers? Again, the notion of matchmaking while her co-workers wrote strings of computer code at the desks next to her seemed strange.

His secretary stood as they approached. "Good morning, Mr. Donovan."

Blake didn't return the greeting. "Put together some paperwork for Ms. Dawson. She'll be a contract employee."

The woman nodded, not seeming to notice or care that he'd neglected to use a *please*. "Will you want it under the business account or personal?"

He considered for a moment. "Business." He nodded for Andy to follow him to his office.

After sharing a sympathetic smile with the secretary, she tossed her cup in the trash and joined Blake at his door. It was shut and evidently locked since he pulled a key from his pocket and inserted it into the knob.

Sure to not stand too close to him, she took the moment to ask her first question. "You're running my employment through the corporation? How are you justifying that?"

He glanced at her as if the answer was obvious. "I told you I needed a wife for public appearances. That justifies qualifying you as a business expense."

"So romantic," she muttered under her breath.

Her words didn't escape her boss. "Practical, Drea. Practical." He opened the door and swept his arm out for her to enter.

Andy bit back the urge to argue and headed in. Then she stopped abruptly, causing Blake to crash into her and send goose bumps racing down her skin.

So much for no contact.

"Sorry." She stepped away from him and gestured toward the sight that had halted her—a small mahogany desk sat opposite Blake's large one. A desk that hadn't been there three days before. "What's this?" She feared she already knew the answer.

"It's your desk," Blake said matter-of-factly.

That was what she'd been afraid of.

"My desk is in *here*? With *you*?" She tried to keep her volume down, but really, she didn't try that hard.

His forehead creased. "Is there a problem?"

"Is there a problem?" She echoed his phrase and inflection, dismayed that he couldn't see it for himself. "Yes, there's a problem. We'll be together. Alone. Behind closed doors."

Blake nodded as if understanding. "You're worried about what will happen between us."

"Wha—no!" She was mortified. "Your employees will think things are going on that aren't. That's not the kind of reputation I want floating around about me. There will be rumors!" If the rumors were true, on the other hand . . .

No, there is no other hand. This is the only hand.

Blake shook off her concern as he walked to his desk. "There are hundreds of rumors about me. If I cared about squelching every single one of them, I'd never get anything done."

"But there aren't hundreds of rumors about *me*." Well, after what happened with Max Ellis, maybe there were.

Which made it that much more prudent that there weren't any new ones. However, she wasn't willing to explain that to Blake, so she conceded. "You know what? Fine. Just fine." She walked to *her desk* and deposited her purse in a drawer. "I won't be spending much time at the office anyway."

Blake frowned at her from across the room. *God, he was even beautiful when disgruntled.* "Why not? Of course you will."

"For a week or so. That's what you said in the ad." She wouldn't get alarmed just yet. He couldn't mean long-term.

"Yes, I did." Still standing, he opened his top drawer and threw his keys inside. "For a week, I need you to spend time with me so that you can get to know what I'm looking for in a woman."

She tried not to roll her eyes. Did he even care what a woman might be looking for in him? How on earth was she supposed to find someone for this man? The task was impossible.

No, she wasn't going to think that way. She could do this. Either she could search for a woman equally as shallow or she'd have to search for his humanity. The latter sounded perhaps more difficult, but also more beneficial to the world in general. If she could discover something redeeming about Blake Donovan, something maybe even a little lovable, that was how she'd advertise him when searching for his match.

But to make that happen, she needed to be in control of her schedule.

Placing her palms on the surface of her desk—*the* desk, she wasn't going to think of it as hers—she braced herself for her next question. "Then after that week, my hours can be performed outside the office. Correct?"

"Correct."

She started to let out a sigh of relief.

"Except on Monday, Wednesday, and Friday. I want you in the office those days."

Her back straightened, rearing for a fight. "In the office? But you didn't say that in the interview."

"I didn't not say that in the interview."

She gaped, not sure if she was more surprised by his working terms or that Blake Donovan would use a double negative.

When she got past the surprise, the denial set in. She could not work with him in the office every day. Could. Not. Between his inside-ugly and his outside chiseled perfection, he would drive her to drink. And even with what he was paying her, she couldn't afford the amount of alcohol that she'd need.

Besides, it was impractical considering her assignment. "How am I supposed to find you dates if I'm in the office all the time?"

Blake unbuttoned his jacket and sat. "You won't be in the office all the time. You'll be here Monday, Wednesday, and Friday. You can use Tuesday and Thursday to do your *shopping*, so to say."

She pinched the bridge of her nose, hoping it hid her cringe at his choice of words. "And what will I be doing when I'm here?" She sounded like a petulant child, but, seriously, what did he expect?

He seemed happy to tell her. "Work using social media and the like. You can conduct phone interviews with potential dates. Plus, the more time you're with me, the better you'll get to know me, effectively helping you to find appropriate matches. I also need you around so I can report how each date goes. Having you here is convenient."

Andy was getting pissed. Blake had said the search process was up to her and he was taking that away. She told him as much.

He waved his hand dismissively. "I'm not taking

anything away. I'm simply telling you when you'll be in the office and when you won't."

"But . . . but . . ." She couldn't think of what should follow that *but*. He had made some valid points, and if it weren't for the fluttering and stuttering that he seemed to provoke in her, she'd have volunteered for that schedule herself. Just discussing the time she'd be spending with him made her throat tight and her palms sweaty.

Another excuse flickered through her mind and she grabbed onto it like a life raft. "Don't you meet with people in here? I'll be in your way."

Blake straightened a stack of papers that already seemed straight to Andy. "Don't be silly. I'll schedule meetings when you're not here. Or I'll use the conference room."

Andy teetered on the line between acceptance and full-out *fuck no*. She chewed on her lip as she evaluated her choices. No matter what she said he was going to have a counter. She knew that about him this early in their acquaintanceship. It was part of his egotistical, narcissistic nature. And arguing with her employer probably wasn't the best way to start a new job.

"Fine," she snipped, conceding but not without a huff. "You're the boss."

"I am the boss. And you'll do best to remember that." He waved her over to his desk, as if she were a pet. "Let's start, shall we? Come have a seat and I'll give you a history of myself."

"Fine." She was saying that word an awful lot. Ironically she felt far from it. "Just let me grab another cup of coffee from the lounge and I'll join you."

Blake watched Drea's hips swing as she walked out of the office. Stomped out was more like it. He couldn't really blame her. He was shocked at the way he was acting himself. Normally he was rigid and on-task, never deterring from a preset plan. Today he was changing things on a whim.

The desk for Drea? He'd come up with that at seven that morning. Before that, he'd planned to set her up in a cubicle somewhere. After several phone calls and a hefty sum of come-in-early-bribes, he located an extra desk in payroll and was able to get the janitor to move it in his office pronto.

Now, why on earth had he done that?

He also hadn't originally intended his matchmaker to be in the office on specific days. He expected that the job would require networking on and off the computer, and he certainly didn't need to be present for either. But the moment Drea suggested she wouldn't be in the office at all, he panicked.

Oh, and that remark he'd made about warming her up—whatever had made him say something as arousing as that? Thank God he'd recovered.

He had to stop going off book. Yes, the woman had the cutest little dimple when she scowled and her lips were so damn kissable that he couldn't stop staring at them, but she was obstinate and ballsy—both major turnoffs. The semi he'd been sporting since she pressed against him in the elevator was merely a standard male response. That it had only seemed to grow more uncomfortable when she got feisty meant nothing, either.

This was about taking back control. She would do what he told her to. He, Blake Donovan, was the boss. He needed to behave like one. Even if it meant behaving like kind of an ass. He squared his shoulders as she reentered.

"Here's a pen and paper," he said, handing her his desk pen and a pad of legal paper. "You'll want to take notes."

He watched as Drea sat and adjusted her short skirt. She certainly had delightful legs. Long and lean, her calves shapely. How had he not noticed this before?

"I'm ready," she said when he hadn't spoken.

He blinked, looking up to find her poised and ready to write. "Yes." He cleared his throat. *Stop doing that.* "Very well."

Blake settled into his leather chair, the new position making it harder to see Drea's gams, and thus easier to concentrate. "I was born, thirty-five years ago, to Ralph and Sylvia Donovan in Fall River. My mother passed away when I was three. My father and I moved to Boston when I was seven. He remarried when I was eight. They both passed in a car accident when I was seventeen, leaving me nothing but a handful of debts and a beat-up Chevy. Not the one they wrecked, obviously. Fortunately, I earned a scholarship to MIT or I wouldn't have been able to afford school. I got my bachelor's degree in electrical engineering and computer science and followed that with a master's in business from Boston University."

Blake continued to recite the details of his life, highlighting the building of his company and his rise to the top of the IT industry. While telling her about the Hyland industry award he'd won three years running, he noticed she'd stopped writing in her notebook. He halted midsentence. "Drea, you aren't taking notes."

She took a deep breath as if she might be counting to three before speaking. "I don't need to write this down, Blake."

He tried not to bristle. "This is my life story. It's relevant. Are you planning on memorizing it?"

She shrugged. "I could regurgitate any of it if I needed to. But I don't need to. You're giving me a résumé. I can find most of it online. The rest is superfluous. And it's boring."

"I beg your pardon?" And he'd let her use his prized Montblanc. The nerve!

"I didn't say *you* were boring. Necessarily." Her addendum drew a frown to his face. "But this information is definitely boring."

He didn't like that. Didn't like that at all. "It's not intended to inspire you. It's intended to attract a potential wife."

"But this"—she pointed to the few notes she'd taken—"doesn't attract anyone. Except maybe the author of *Who's Who in America*."

Blake pursed his lips and leaned forward, his eye threatening to tic. "You need to get to know me, Drea. Did you think that you'd simply sit at your desk and learn about me through osmosis?"

"Kinda, yeah." She shifted in her seat, her skirt riding up a centimeter—yes, he noticed. "How about we try something else? Let me ask some questions for a while, will you?"

"Uh . . . sure." He didn't know why the idea of her questioning him made him uneasy. What could she possibly ask that was so difficult to answer? "Go ahead."

"Okay, we'll start easy. What kind of music do you listen to?"

This was why he was uneasy. There was no way he could answer this question truthfully. He swallowed, as he straightened a pile of papers for the second time that morning.

"Music?" He was stalling for time, trying to come up with an artist that wasn't as embarrassing as the Whitesnake CD he currently had loaded in his player. A slew of other favorite bands ran through his mind: Def Leppard, Poison, Guns N' Roses—each was as humiliating as the last.

"Yes, music. You know that sound coming from my sister at the bar the other night? That's called music."

He narrowed his eyes but didn't verbally acknowledge Drea's sassy statement. He was too busy focusing on the thickening of his tongue and the sudden dryness of his throat. And was it hot in here? He adjusted his collar and tried to swallow back the panic.

Why was he panicking anyway? It wasn't as if he were attached to a lie detector machine. He could tell her whatever he wanted. He could lie. Maybe he could say he listened to jazz. But with his luck, Drea would be a fan of the style and would want to compare favorite artists.

Finally, he said, "I don't listen to music." That was a good answer. "I listen to NPR. And the BBC. Sometimes I'll put on the classical station." Yes, that was very good indeed. No potential match was going to take him seriously otherwise.

Drea frowned. "Okay. How about movies? What kind of movies do you like?"

Another question he didn't want to answer. He'd never admitted to anyone his love of sweeping historical dramas. He'd snuck into the last one he'd seen, *Anna Karenina*, hiding in the back row in case anyone he knew was in the theater.

Drea was waiting for his answer.

"Documentaries," he lied. "And before you ask, I don't watch television. Ever." That should keep her from discovering his addiction to *Downton Abbey*. God, he'd never paused to consider how much potential humiliation resided in his personal life.

Again, Drea scowled. "There has to be something interesting about you," she muttered. "Do you read? Besides the *Wall Street Journal* and the *Boston Herald*, I mean."

"Of course, I read. Biographies, mostly." Which was true. He read those as well as other things. But he wasn't about to tell her about the stack of old detective books he had next to his bed.

"Biographies?" Her dull tone said that she was unimpressed.

"Yes. Understanding the great businessmen of our time is very beneficial to my job."

"Of course." She let out a slow breath of air, but wrote down his answer. "Do you have any pets?"

"No." Blake shuddered at the thought.

She looked up from her pad of paper. "Why? Are you allergic?"

"Not that I'm aware." He'd wanted a pet once. A rabbit he'd seen at the local pet store. He still remembered the extreme softness of its fur and its adorable nose that constantly sniffed and wiggled. His stepmother had put her foot down at the request. It was her words he spouted to Drea now. "Pets are nasty creatures. They're time-consuming and expensive."

"Hmm."

"Hmm?" he repeated. The hum in her throat had vibrated through Blake. The almost pleasant sensation irritated him. Particularly when he realized it was likely a form of judgment. "What does *hmm* mean?"

"Nothing. Just . . ." She twisted her lips as if considering if she should share whatever was on her mind. With a reluctant sigh, she said, "My nana used to say, 'Never date a man who doesn't know how to care for a pet. If he can't love a simple animal, how could he possibly love someone as complex as you?'"

Their eyes met, and he remained captured in her gaze for several long seconds. A strange sequence of emotions overcame Blake. First, he was moved by the tenderness in Drea's tone as she spoke of her nana. Then he felt a stab of interest, as if he wanted to stop talking about himself and listen to more about her complexity. That led to confusion, because he'd never felt anything like that before. Finally he was pissed—he didn't like to be confused. Or moved. Or interested.

And did she basically say he wasn't good enough for her because he'd never owned a hamster?

Screw that. It didn't take a pet to know that he was good enough for her. He'd be the best damn thing she'd ever known if they were together. Which they weren't. And wouldn't be.

Why did that cause a wave of disappointment?

The latest emotion renewed his fury. No matter that the fury was with himself and not her. With gritted teeth, he said, "It's a lucky thing then that you aren't dating me, isn't it?"

"Yes, it's a lucky thing indeed."

Is my disappointment mirrored in her eyes?

No, of course not. That was ridiculous.

Whatever it was he'd seen, it flickered away as quickly as it had come. In its place was resignation. "Look," she said, "this isn't working. You're right that I need to get to know you. Not like this. This is not genuine. I need to spend time with you where you aren't showing off what you have. I need to observe on my own." She held up her hand as if he might interrupt. "You said you recognized that I had skills. I can only use them in my own way."

"Fine. I understand. How about you spend the rest of the day working with my secretary on the new-hire paperwork? There are a few orientation videos to watch as well, about teamwork and sexual harassment, and all that." He wasn't sure why he mentioned the sexual harassment video. Perhaps because the thoughts that kept entering his mind every time Drea crossed her legs in that short skirt of hers did not comply with the company's code of conduct.

Then, for the umpteenth time that morning, he went off plan. "And tomorrow, we can spend the day together. You can observe whatever you'd like."

Her forehead crinkled in confusion. "Tomorrow's Saturday."

"Yes, it is. You can take off a day next week in exchange. You need to see me in my home environment. It's the perfect opportunity." Or maybe he just couldn't stand the idea of two days before seeing her again. Infuriating as she was, he sort of liked her company.

It was another reason why it was imperative he found a wife. He was lonely. Why else would he choose to spend any time with a woman such as the maddening one in front of him?

Chapter Six

"Ms. Dawson?" The pale-faced elderly woman who answered the door must have been prepped on Andy's arrival. "Mr. Donovan is expecting you. He's upstairs in his office."

"And you're . . . ?" Andy suspected she was facing an employee of Blake's, but something about her grandmotherly air made Andy question her assumption.

"His housekeeper, E llen."

So her first guess had been right. She extended her hand. "Nice to meet you, Ellen. You can call me Andy."

The housekeeper's gentle features crinkled into confusion. "Oh, I thought he said it was Drea." Andy swallowed back a curse as Ellen turned and called over her shoulder. "This way."

Ellen led her through the foyer past a large living area toward a sweeping staircase.

"Do you mind if I just . . . ?" Andy didn't finish the question, afraid that permission to look around would be denied if she asked, and instead peeked into the living room before heading to the stairs. A shiver ran down her spine.

It felt as cold and industrial as the office at Donovan Info-Tech. She'd hoped that was only the spirit of the front entryway, but it continued to the main room. There was no sense that anyone actually *lived* there. It was pristine and perfect and sterile.

And this was what she had in her arsenal to attract a bride?

Forget it. The place was like a museum. Except museums at least had gift shops with cheerful volunteers. There was no cheer here, and certainly nothing she'd like to bring home. *The Donovan Mausoleum*, that was more accurate.

She felt Ellen come up behind her. "Does Mr. Donovan spend much time here?" Andy gazed at the expanses between couches in the massive living room. Blake definitely didn't entertain much. People would be shouting from one distant seat to another, too afraid to sip their wine in case a stray drop of red landed on the immaculate marble tile. The mental image made her smile. She caught the housekeeper's eye and quickly dropped the cheer.

"Most of the time he's in his office, though occasionally I think he reads down here after I'm gone for the day. He often leaves a book perched on the side table."

Those boring biographies of businessmen and dead presidents seemed to fit the environment. Andy had known she'd get a better picture of her boss by seeing his house but also had hoped that it would be a prettier picture.

With the sweetest of smiles, the housekeeper asked, "Are you ready to continue up?"

"Of course." Andy frowned as she trailed behind Ellen. Each step farther into the house felt drearier and drearier. At least Ellen was a ray of sunshine. Otherwise, Andy feared the place would collapse from the weight of the drab.

They continued up the stairs. At the top, the hallway extended in both directions. One side ended in a set of closed

double doors. Andy looked the other way and found another set of double doors—this time with Blake Donovan
standing in front of them.

"Drea, you made it." His tone suggested that he'd been
waiting for her, as if she were late. "Thank you, Ellen. I'll
take her from here."

Andy nodded to the housekeeper then checked her watch
before starting down the hall to meet her boss. Nope. She
was totally not late. Maybe early was Blake's preferred time
of arrival. When she reached him, she opened her mouth
to ask, but he spoke first.

"Here we are." He threw open the double doors and gestured for Andy to step inside.

She sucked in a breath and immediately forgot all about
her plans to harass him into opening up as she took in his
inner sanctum. It, like the rest of the house, was way too
freaking big, but—

"Thank God." *Oops. That was out loud.*

"What does that mean?" When they'd entered the room,
Blake had seemed calmer, but now he was glaring again.

She placed a hand to her chest, in somewhat dramatic
fashion. "Honestly? I was wondering how I was supposed
to convince any woman who saw your fortress of solitude
here that you were human and not some sort of business-
droid. Then I was wondering if I was actually convinced
of that myself. And then you showed me your office, and—
thank God."

He looked as surprised as her at the giggle that came
out of his mouth at that.

He brought the back of his hand to his mouth, recovering quickly. "You like it, then?"

Like it? She loved it. Huge windows took up the far wall
of the office, filling it with soft sunlight. The desk was over-
large, but it was beautiful. An antique, Andy thought, but
that was as much as she could guess. There was an actual

rug on the floor, and it didn't even look expensive. It just looked warm. There was a cushy chair by the window, and a decanter of amber liquid on the table near it. A spider plant—probably the perfect plant for a man like him—hung from the ceiling.

In short, there was some humanity in here. *This* she could work with.

"Yes, Blake. I like it."

His smile held an air of satisfaction. "Good, I like to work here better than the office, so we can plan to set you up in here as well." He was definitely relaxing now, striding over to his desk with looser limbs than had greeted her.

He sank into his office chair that creaked with the sound of long use. "So—you really think my house is like an ice palace?" Blake kept his eyes downcast, as if he were completely uninterested in the answer, but the fact that he'd asked at all meant he was in want of her opinion.

Andy was flattered.

She quickly attempted to talk herself out of that. *Don't make too much of it, you're probably the only girl he knows who ever gave him an honest opinion.* The vacant-eyed models in his office sure wouldn't tell him what they thought he wouldn't want to hear.

Tucking a loose strand of hair behind her ear, she said, "Firstly, I'm impressed that you actually got that reference, Mr. I-Only-Read-Biographies-and-Watch-Documentaries. Second of all—yes, yes I do."

"Now, Drea, what sort of business tycoon would I be if I hadn't studied Lex Luthor?" Blake's eyes actually twinkled a bit.

"Well, what a surprise." *A delightful one at that.*

"I contain multitudes." Was that a hint of a smile? If it was, he quickly hid it away. His jaw tightened. "Is this . . . *problem* . . . with my home something you feel capable of fixing?" His words came out strained, as if they were hard for him to say.

"I'll have an easier time with your house than with your arrogance." Had she really said that? It wasn't quite fair to be in the man's own house and insulting him. She quickly redirected. "We can start with just a few touches to make it seem more lived-in. Maybe more plants, some throw pillows."

Blake's eyebrows were furrowed. "Why would I throw my pillows?"

She started to roll her eyes until she realized he was serious. "That's just their *name*, Blake. You throw them on the couch, so people feel like they are welcome to sit there. Right now your living room is incredibly uninviting."

"It was professionally designed."

"That in no way translates to lived-in."

"It was expensive." He was getting defensive.

But she wasn't backing down. "Obviously. Still not inviting."

"I don't like knickknacks."

She threw her hands in the air. "For Pete's sake! You asked me if I could fix it and I'm telling you how. Why do you have to argue with every single thing I say?"

"I don't argue with *everything* you say. Just the ridiculous things."

Why did it seem like the tables had been turned, and it was now Andy that was being wound up?

Manipulative. Even the throw pillows can't hide that.

"Case in point. Why don't you go about your work and I'll just settle in with my notebook and jot down some thoughts." She was already drifting toward the chair by the window.

As she sat, a closed door behind his desk caught her eye. It was in an odd spot to be a closet. "What's in there?"

"What's in where?" His gaze was shifty, his hands fidgeting.

Andy nodded to the door. "There. Behind you."

Blake paled. "Nothing. Storage. A copy room. Closet, I mean."

"If you say so." Obviously he didn't want to tell her what was really behind that door, which only piqued her interest. What could Blake Donovan be hiding? A vault? A private washroom? A sex dungeon?

She giggled to herself at that last one. Hardly likely. Knowing Blake, it was probably something lame that only rich people had—like a safe room. He was paranoid enough. That had to be exactly what it was.

With the matter settled in her mind, she let the thought go and concentrated on her job. Several minutes later, she'd decided the situation wasn't all that bad, despite giving up her Saturday. The beginning had been rocky, but now, sitting in a patch of sunlight, taking notes on a guy who was incredibly sexy as long as his mouth was closed, it was more than tolerable. Her mind wandered to the interior design—*I bet his budget for that is hefty. I'm going to all the little boutiques I've ever window-shopped in Cambridge. I'll channel every HGTV show I've ever seen and transform this place into the envy of every woman in Boston. There'll be an accent wall. Unusual details. All Anthro everything.*

Blake's voice nudged into her fantasy. "I'm going to have to think about the house thing for a little bit. I like modern lines. My wife should, too. Besides, they're easier for her to clean."

Andy crashed back to earth.

She wrote her bitter thoughts in broad strokes across her notepad so as not to say them aloud. *Stupidest job ever. Worst boss ever.* He was certainly unmatchable. Could she muzzle him on dates?

She took a cleansing breath and put on a grin. "Maybe we can revisit the subject when you're beginning to feel closer to inviting a date home." She was rather pleased with the calmness of her reply. *See, I'm not as easy to wind up as you thought I'd be.*

He stared at her for a moment longer than was necessary. Though it was also true that she hadn't looked away, either. Why did Andy keep getting that nervous read from him? This dude probably didn't know the definition of nervous. *He's just acting weird because I'm invading his personal space. He obviously doesn't really "do" personal.*

"Perhaps a drink?" Blake rushed over to the decanter and poured a splash into two crystal glasses before she even agreed.

That's totally what it is. I'm cramping his style, and it was his idea and he doesn't know how to deal. She beamed internally as he handed her a glass, satisfied with her conclusion.

After swallowing and refilling his own glass, Blake's swagger was starting to creep back in. He plopped down behind his desk and promptly began to work as if Andy were invisible. She took a sip of the strong amber liquid, curled her feet under her, and began to take notes, narrowing her perceptions of him to single words.

Confident. That was a good trait. *Condescending.* Not so good.

Persuasive. She'd call that another good one. *Manipulative. Domineering. Stubborn. Closed-off.*

She sighed.

Letting her pen fall to her lap, she sat back in the chair and watched him work. For a man sitting behind a desk, he was in constant motion. He balanced a cell phone and a landline, and alternated between two computer screens and a tablet. It was pretty cool to watch him go, she had to

admit. This was the tireless energy that had built his company from the ground up, into the beast it was today.

The sunlight glinted off his olive skin as he rolled up
his shirtsleeves. Even in his home office on a Saturday, the
man looked like an Armani commercial. He was barking
into the office phone but grinning at a text that had come
through. *Sexy.*

She almost added that to the list.

Then she reminded herself that he was not some sort of
Greek god, but a jerkface that earlier talked about how his
wife should clean his house.

Chauvinist, she wrote instead.

Well, that wasn't helpful. If she wanted to frame him
in an attractive light, she'd have to concentrate on his better
attributes. She crossed out *Chauvinist*. And *Manipulative*.
And *Domineering*. And all the other less-than-delightful
words she'd given to him.

Then she added, *Sexy.*

When she looked up their eyes caught again, and he gave
her the full benefits of that wicked grin. Maybe she better
make that *Sexy as Hell.*

She definitely did not want to be as aroused as she was
by that smile. Definitely not.

Blake had completely forgotten that Drea was in the room.
Between the relaxation from the scotch and the normal
adrenaline of a day filled with meetings and decisions and
the other thousand little details he liked to personally over-
see, he'd forgotten the little detail of her. Until he glanced
up from a text and saw the way the sun was highlighting
her auburn hair as she gazed at him. If he didn't know for
a fact that he infuriated her, that look on her face could
almost have been misconstrued as desire.

Her lips slowly curved and he realized he was still grinning like a demented person. Well, so what. He was allowed

to have a positive emotion, at least once a week. As long as no one else saw. The matchmaker hardly counted. Only, she did look awfully nice in his chair.

Of course, it was a great chair. The windows looked out over the pool and the manicured garden. There was a freaking gazebo in the background. The sun was perfect and summery. She had worn a nice dress-thing. Anyway, that was probably the niceness.

Not the memory of holding her pressed against him while the sounds of her sister's guitar floated past.

That was nice in a cringe-y sort of way. Like the hung-over memories of a party that was fun until the host found you in the coatroom with his girlfriend. Actually, it was the girlfriend that had spoiled that one. All that buildup, and she was pretty blah in bed. In coat?

He digressed.

He was still grinning at Drea. This was getting uncomfortable. "Do you need anything?" *That should cover it.*

"Thanks, but I'm fine observing."

And what exactly *was* she observing? Blake considered demanding her notebook to review but immediately decided she would fight him. Perhaps she'd use the restroom and he could peek at it then. He should refill her drink. It wasn't even lunchtime, though, and forcing scotch on an employee, even an annoying one, even when it was really good scotch, was still bad form before noon.

She was still staring at him. Okay, perhaps she was in love with him. He *had* been told he was an excellent kisser.

"Blake, we have to find a way to make you look less arrogant."

Oh. Maybe not love, then.

He straightened his collar. It was a Saturday so he'd gone sans tie, leaving the top button of his dress shirt undone. He'd given himself a good glance in the mirror before she'd arrived, and had been pleased with his appearance. "I look good, thank you."

"No, you don't. I mean, you literally look good." Her eyes clouded momentarily. "*Really* good." Then she shook her head. "I mean, you know, or whatever."

Finally, he'd flustered her. *Fun.*

She placed a hand on her forehead, eyes closed. "It isn't your physical presence that is the issue, Blake." Her lids popped open, her gaze missing the fog from a moment before. "It's your general attitude that I'm troubled by. It doesn't matter how dumb, submissive, and bland a girl I find for you—you are scary. I think I can make you a human. Or—maybe that's harsh?"

It *was* harsh.

She blew out a stream of air. "I'll think more on it." She rummaged in her bag and pulled out an iPad mini. "Meanwhile, what's your Internet password? I need to get online."

He returned his focus to his computer screen and, without thinking, answered, "PinballWizard. Capital P, capital W, no spaces."

He felt her eyes on him, heavy and questioning.

"What?" Her expression was incredulous. "PinballWizard?"

Dammit. He should have offered to enter it in for her. "Yes. It was set up by someone else. My IT guy." That didn't sound like fumbling, did it?

Andy kept her gaze pinned on him. "You *are* an IT guy. You have someone else handle your IT?"

He brought his hand up to fiddle with his tie before remembering he wasn't wearing one. "Yes. Is that not okay with you?"

She shrugged. "Just strikes me as unusual. I guess I never thought about it."

He really did have an IT guy. He had the know-how to set up the White House with a secure Internet system; it was a poor use of his time to set up his own. The password, though, had been his decision. No need to share that with nosy Andrea Dawson. "Is that all then?"

"I'm connected to the Internet, so yes. Thank you."

Blake watched her for a few minutes as she scrolled through pages on her iPad. Then, with a bit of effort, he refocused on the matters at hand. Another IT company was trying to underbid him for a couple of contracts. The text he had allowed himself happiness over had involved his personal detective finding some discrepancies in the accounting of his rival. Time to deal with them.

He wrote a strongly worded email to the CEO of the other firm, and allowed himself another grin at its completion. One more problem off his plate. Then there was the small matter of an employee of his that he suspected of spying for the other company. Although Massachusetts was an at-will state, he felt certain the guy would fight a termination. Besides, anyone who committed treason against his company was not going to get unemployment under his watch. Surely they could come to some sort of solution. Blake began to review his employee files.

The office phone rang. A board member was planning to resign. Blake dropped everything for half an hour until he determined that it truly was for personal reasons, and nothing indicative of problems in the board. Emails rolled in, questions were answered, scotch was refilled as a quiet celebration when the other CEO withdrew his bids.

"Blake?"

Drea's voice knocked him out of his work mode. He'd actually forgotten she was there *again*. Odd that he was so comfortable in her presence. "Yes?" He glanced at his watch. "Oh, is it lunchtime?"

She shook her head, her auburn hair catching the light in a way that was quite mesmerizing. "It's a little early still for me. I wanted to go over some things with you, if you don't mind. When you have a few minutes."

He blinked, shifting his gaze from her locks to her eyes. She'd asked him something . . . what was it? Oh, yes. "Certainly. Now is fine."

Her face lit up. "Great." She stood and crossed to him, iPad in hand. "I put together some pictures of things I think we could do to warm up the house." She set the tablet on the desk in front of him and pointed to the screen. "Here. I made a folder in Pinterest and pinned some things that could work."

"Pinterest?" Whatever the application was, it was easy to use. He was already flipping through pictures of expensive houses such as his. The shots Drea had chosen were specific—close-ups of square couch pillows, lamps, rugs, several wall hangings.

Her voice fell over his shoulder. "Pinterest is social media for sharing pictures. Sort of a virtual corkboard. Don't worry, it doesn't have your name attached anywhere."

He nodded, pleased that his new hire actually did have social media skills. Continuing to scroll through the images he noted that she also had good taste. His designer could have used these suggestions, though Blake had been adamant about what he wanted at the time. If his expert had even tried to show him these items, he would have refused to look. Perhaps he'd been a little *too* obstinate.

When he reached the bottom of the page, he clicked a button at the top that said ANDY D. This took him to a set of folders, two of which said BLAKE DONOVAN. The first seemed to contain the images he'd just seen. The other . . . He clicked on it to find several pictures of beautiful women with near-black hair and slight body frames.

He clicked on one of the more attractive girls, a gorgeous young woman with a sparkling smile and Asian features.

"You want to put this in my living room? That certainly would warm the place up."

Drea leaned closer, peering over his shoulder. "Oh, that's the other board I want to show you." She reached over and clicked the screen back to the full page of images. "I'm aware of your personality preferences, but I want to make sure I understand what you're looking for physically. I found some pictures of models and actresses that I thought you might find attractive. If you could just tell me if I'm on the right track."

Her hair swung to tickle against his cheek, and he caught her pleasant scent of perfume mixed with apple blossoms. Must be her shampoo.

He had to remind himself to move his eyes back to the tablet instead of letting them drift to the woman leaning over him.

Again, he scrolled through the images. Again, he had to admire Drea's taste. The women she'd picked were absolutely gorgeous. "Hmm." He meant that appreciatively. "Hmm." Was it odd to be ogling attractive women with a beautiful woman looking over his shoulder?

Beautiful? Where had that adjective come from? Though, he had to admit, with each passing moment Andrea Dawson was more and more of a pleasure to look at.

He continued to scroll, landing on a particularly enticing model. A *naked* enticing model. "Oh, I wasn't expecting that." Even with her body contorted to hide her private parts, the image was quite erotic.

"Uh, yeah." Drea shifted nervously next to him. "Those models. Sex sells, they say."

Without realizing what he was doing, Blake clicked on the image, making it bigger. Then again he clicked and suddenly he was on another website.

Drea put her hand on his shoulder, her fingers digging nicely into his muscle. "Oh, don't do that. That takes you off the Pinterest site to—" Her voice cut off as the screen filled with another image of the same naked model, this one not so modest. "Oh, my."

Blake swallowed past the lump in his throat. "Wow." The image changed again, apparently part of a slideshow. This time the model was wrapped around a naked man, her head thrown back in pleasure with his mouth anchored on her bare breast.

Drea gasped behind him. Blake felt that he should do something, get off the website they were on, but he was frozen in place.

The next picture came up. It featured the same man and woman now curved around each other in a position that seemed near impossible to get into. That had to be listed in the advanced version of the *Kama Sutra*.

"How do they—?" Drea leaned in to examine the image further.

The pressure of her body on his arm, her overwhelming scent, her auburn curls swinging against the bare skin at his collar, all while looking at what could only be called erotica—it wasn't any surprise that Blake's pants suddenly felt tight.

"That's . . . wow." But he wasn't looking at the tablet anymore. He was looking at the real live in-the-flesh woman next to him.

As if sensing his gaze was on her, Drea's eyes flicked to his. They were warm and hazy and alluring. Had he noticed that before? He couldn't remember. And her lips—they were full and plump and rosy, close enough that he could kiss her if he just moved in . . .

"Uh, maybe we should get back to the photos I selected." Drea took the iPad from his hands.

"Yes." Blake cleared his throat, hoping that would clear his mind from whatever it was he was just thinking. Because the thoughts that had been filling his mind were of

Andrea in the place of that female model, and him in the place of the male. So wrong and yet so . . .

No, they were simply wrong. That's all. He needed some fresh air. Needed some space. Needed to be done with looking at near-pornographic pictures with his employee. "I mean, no. You don't need to get back to your photos. I've seen enough." He rolled his chair back and to the left, distancing himself from Andrea. And he definitely didn't meet her eyes. "Those women fit my tastes to a T. The ones you picked. Not the other . . ." He waved his hand, not able to voice what the other pictures had been. "Well, you know."

Drea seemed to need the same distance. She was already halfway back to the armchair. "Good. Then I'll start finding some dates and setting things up."

"Perfect." It was perfect. Funny that he had to tell himself that. "And the home items—order whatever you wish. I added you to my business account." He stood and walked to her again, wishing he'd remembered to give her this when she'd been near him. He stopped at a long arm's length away. "Here's a card. You can use this to buy items for the house or to make reservations at restaurants when necessary. Or hotels."

Why had he said hotels? Was he trying to make this more awkward than necessary?

"Right. Hotels." Her tone was curt as she took the card and placed it in her purse.

God, she had to think he was a complete man-whore. "Later, of course. Not yet. Anyway, good job." Everything he said seemed to increase the uneasiness. And there was still the matter of his semi pressing in his pants. Had she noticed? It was eye level from where she sat in the chair.

Maybe *completem an-whore* was an accurate label.

He pinched the bridge of his nose. "If you'd like, you may spend the rest of the day working on this from your home. You obviously have the information you need from me. No need to keep you here longer than necessary."

"No need at all."

He tried to read her tone—was she eager to be leaving? Or disappointed to be dismissed? He couldn't tell. He wished he could.

But why does it matter? The question flooded his mind as he watched her gather her things. "I'll see you to the door."

She waved him off. "I can find my way. I may stop and look around your front room a bit more before I leave, if you don't mind. Take some pictures for reference."

"Go ahead."

He stared at the empty doorway long after she'd left, her scent wrapping around him as if she were still there. Finally, he shook himself from his trance and returned to his desk.

What was it about the woman, anyway? Time and again she seemed to affect him in ridiculous ways. Maybe her perfume was one of those pheromone scents—the type meant to attract a man at a primal level. Yes, that had to be it. Tricksy woman. Simple enough to deal with. She was gone now. He would find some Lysol from his housekeeper to cover any traces of her. Next week he'd make sure to have the janitor put an automatic air freshener in the room. That ought to take care of things.

He emailed the janitor immediately with his request. But he didn't end up asking Ellen for Lysol. He tried to tell himself it was because he was too focused on his work, but he couldn't lie anymore—he liked the smell of Andrea Dawson. Whatever that was about, he didn't know, and he was sure he didn't want to dwell on the matter. For one day, though, he could live with her scent in his office. He'd even let himself enjoy it.

Chapter Seven

Andy shuffled around the apartment, not caring that she was already probably going to be late for work. It wasn't that she was nervous about going in—actually, that's exactly what it was. She was shaking-in-her-socks nervous and she couldn't even begin to say all the reasons why.

After she'd left Blake on Saturday, she'd spent the rest of the afternoon racking up charges on his business card with purchases for his home. That had felt good. She'd never realized how much fun it was to spend money, never having had much of it herself. Although she'd certainly imagined it enough times.

But after she'd finished with her shopping spree, she'd been at a loss as to what she should do next. She was certain she had a grasp on the type of woman Blake wanted to date, only where to find her? Should she take out a Craigslist ad as Blake had? She imagined the headline—*Wanted: Attractive, preferably Asian, woman to date sleazy bachelor and ignore his lack of humanity in exchange for an account at Nordstrom. No personality desired. Serious inquiries only.* Her gut told her that wouldn't attract any-one decent. Well, gut *and* brain.

She'd scoured her own social media accounts looking for anyone local who might fit the bill. No one. Besides, did she really want to submit her friends to Blake's arro-gance? Not if she intended to keep her friends.

Saturday night she'd tagged along with Lacy to a gig hoping she'd find a suitable candidate there. Not even close. She'd gazed around the room at various women and ruled them out one by one. The one with blue streaks in her hair? No, she obviously enjoyed attention too much to be sub-missive. The flawlessly beautiful brunette standing by the stage? Oh, just threw her undies at Lacy. This one, too hip, that one, too hippy. The show was a complete bust.

Sunday she'd tried one of the mega churches, standing outside the doors while the parishioners filed out on their way to brunch. Here she'd spotted several women with potential. Approaching them, however, was a whole new problem. How the hell was she supposed to sell a date with Blake to passersby? It was hard enough figuring out how she was going to allure dates when she had the time to build him up. Perhaps if she held up a sign with his much-too-gorgeous-for-his-own-good face and the words WANNA DATE? She'd put that on her mental list of possi-bilities for the future.

Sunday night she refused to think about it anymore. By Monday morning, she had a headache and a case of cold feet. She was already so much of a failure in her own eyes. She really didn't want to fail this too. Yet she was begin-ning to think it was inevitable. So could anyone blame her for not wanting to hurry to her job?

There was another reason for her hesitancy—one much harder to admit. It could be boiled down to two words: Blake Donovan. Not only had her visit to his mansion enlightened her on the women he was attracted to, but now Andy was also pretty sure she knew the kinds of things he'd like to do with those women. She'd seen his tight pants after looking at those explicit pics and if she hadn't been sure then, his comment about hotel reservations made his intentions crystal clear.

It was to be expected; he was a man after all. Looking at extremely erotic images would surely pique his *interest*. Standing next to him, leaning on his firm shoulder as his musky scent filled her senses, even she'd been aroused. Because of the pictures, of course. For no other reason. It was an overall arousing scenario. Surely, if she were a man, she'd also have become *interested*.

But for some reason, witnessing his . . . *interest* . . . in other women bothered her. Bothered her a lot. It was psycho, because this was ultimately her job. She was supposed to find the woman that interested Blake to no end. Why did that thought tug so uncomfortably in her chest?

Best not to answer that.

"Aren't you going to be late?" Lacy called groggily from where she'd passed out on the couch the night before.

Andy grabbed some pumps to toss into her bag then slunk into the armchair to tie her sneakers. "Maybe." Definitely.

Lacy squinted open her eyes just enough to send a scowl across the coffee table. "You've been there less than a week. Tardiness—"

"Oh, shut it, Lacy. I'm not in the mood."

"Your mood doesn't count. It's keeping that creeper boss of yours happy that pays the bills." She pulled a pillow over her face. "Did you at least make coffee?"

Andy pretended not to have heard the muffled question. If she'd gotten up instead of hitting SNOOZE, she could have made the coffee. Instead, she had pushed the button and closed her eyes, then proceeded to lie there fuming about the day ahead of her instead of enjoying the extra ten minutes. Then she had done it twice more. So now she was riled up *and* undercaffeinated. Freaking Mondays.

She closed the apartment door behind her just as Lacy's pillow hit. "Missed, sucker!" she called through the door as she locked it. She was still smiling to herself when she turned around and saw a gorgeous Asian woman standing in front of the neighbor's door and staring at her.

"Are you looking for Mrs. Brandy?" The words were out before Andy remembered that wasn't the elderly next-door neighbor's real name. "I mean, Mrs. Brando."

The woman looked at the envelope in her hand. "Yeah. I got her mail by mistake. I'm in the same apartment, but the next building over." She knocked for what couldn't have been the first time, judging by the toe-tapping.

"She's out of town for two weeks. I've just been stuffing her mail under her door." Andy took the mail from the other woman's slim, manicured hand and crouched. "Getting a bit of buildup, I see. Just give it a little—push—ah! There we go." She wedged the envelope past the jam triumphantly then looked up to see the woman's expression.

"She asked me to. I didn't just decide to do that randomly," Andy reassured her. The woman's face relaxed into a stunning smile.

"Thanks for the tip. If I end up with any more of her mail, I know what to do. So . . . Mrs. Brandy?" They fell into step heading for the stairs.

"That's what my sister and I call her. She's a bit of a drinker."

"Ah. Clever." The woman's heels clicked smartly down the steps ahead of Andy.

She couldn't help but notice how fit her new acquaintance's legs looked stemming down from her skirt. Particularly her calves. She'd always wished for that kind of definition herself, but didn't have the willpower to acquire it.

"Her name's basically begging for it, isn't it?" Andy was impressed with how well she was performing at small talk. She usually didn't articulate anything very well before at least four ounces of coffee.

"That or some Marlon Brando joke. Is she very manly?"

"Actually, she is . . . I'm Andy, by the way. Andy Dawson." She stuck out a hand.

The woman's grip was firm but not overbearing. "Jaylene Kim."

Ah, Korean. Andy was starting to formulate a plan. And a read. "You said you're from next door?"

"The next building, yeah."

They reached the front door, which Andy held open. "God, I have got to get better about knowing my neighbors."

"No worries. I'm the same way." Jaylene flashed that smile again, made even more glorious in contrast with her bright red lips. The woman's makeup was flawless.

"Are you headed—" They stepped out into the warm Boston morning.

"To the subway. You?" Jaylene paused for Andy's answer.

"Me too." Though she had considered grabbing a cab—it was the only way she'd make it to the office on time. But if she could snag a date for Blake out of this chance encounter, the tardiness would be justified. With a possibly too-wide grin, Andy said, "So what do you do, Jaylene?"

"I teach at Boston University Academy."

Andy watched as Jaylene spoke, mesmerized by the way her lips moved and how precise and articulate each word was. "You're a professor?"

"Not quite. It's a private high school on BU's campus. I teach English."

English at a private high school? How girlie could a woman get? *Feminine, demure.*

Jaylene wiped a hand across her dry brow. "I'm a little embarrassed that I'm taking the train."

"Do you usually walk the whole thing?" Andy was impressed. Physical exertion of any sort was not her cup of tea. She suffered through the yoga but wasn't about to take it any further.

"I don't. But only because I run seven miles before I get ready for work." It was amazing how she didn't even sound like she was bragging. As if it were the norm. "Running to work would be a little much. Plus, sweaty."

"Oh, yeah. Me too." Andy pinned her eyes to her cross trainers—the ones that still looked as pristine as the day she'd bought them a year ago since they hadn't gotten much action. *Dammit. I never grabbed my heels.* "I mean, I exercise before work because, sweaty." *Lies.*

"So you're off to work as well?"

"Yeah. I'm, uh, a personal assistant for an IT executive." Andy swallowed, preparing to make her move. "Hey, can I ask a totally forward question? Are you seeing anyone?"

"Um . . ." The other woman's steps slowed.

"Not for me. For someone else. A guy." Andy realized she was likely not making the situation any better, but charged ahead anyway. "I mean, I'm not hitting on you. I didn't think you were a lesbian, if that's what you thought. Not that I wouldn't be interested if I was, that's just not— if you were thinking that's what I meant."

"Actually, I didn't know what to think. I still don't."

"Of course not. I'm going about this all weird." God, pimping was so . . . awkward? "It's for my boss. He's decided to get out in the field and though we just met, I have to say, I really think you'd mesh with him. His name is Blake Donovan—"

"Blake Donovan of Donovan InfoTech?" Jaylene's right eyebrow lifted.

"You've heard of him?" Andy couldn't help the surprise that sounded in her voice.

"He's the toast of Boston's business scene." Jaylene fanned her face with her hand. "Who hasn't heard of him?"

Until she'd met him the day of her interview, Andy hadn't, that's who hadn't. "Yeah, exactly. Who hasn't."

"If I remember right, he's a hottie."

"Yes. Yes, he is. I have a picture." Andy was suddenly grateful for the doldrum hour on Saturday that she had filled snapping shots of Blake on her phone unbeknownst to him.

Jaylene took the phone, her eyes brightening as she took in Blake's picture. "Yummy."

Though pleased with Jaylene's assessment, Andy couldn't help feeling a little bit stabby that someone else recognized how attractive Blake Donovan was. It was honestly the most absurd feeling she'd had in, well, ever. She dismissed it as a side effect of the no-coffee-plus-walking thing.

Jaylene handed the phone back to Andy. "And you think he'd want to go out with me?"

"I'm positive. He asked me to set him up, in fact." *Not a lie.* "Would you be interested?"

"Maybe." Jaylene's tone said there was no maybe about it. It was yes all the way.

"Tell you what—are you on Facebook?"

She nodded so Andy opened her phone and entered Jaylene's name in her social media app. When her profile came up, she sent a friend request. "I just friended you."

Jaylene's own phone buzzed from the side pocket of her purse. She pulled it out and flicked her fingers across the screen. "And I just accepted."

It took all of Andy's strength not to happy dance right

there in the station. "I'll show Blake your profile, if you don't mind, and see what he says?"

"Yeah. That sounds . . . great, actually. Thanks."

There was a moment of semistrange silence between them which Andy filled with unnatural grinning and staring at Jaylene's daintily polished hands. Thankfully, the moment was interrupted by the arrival of a train.

"Well, this is me," Jaylene said with a shrug.

"Great meeting you." *Was that too eager?* "I'll get back to you soon."

The women waved and parted.

With Jaylene out of sight, Andy let out a sigh of half relief, half elation. She might have a grip on this ridiculous job of hers after all. Although extremely tardy and under-caffeinated, she couldn't help thinking, *I'm awesome.*

Two days in, and his matchmaker was already late. How could he have been so wrong? Blake was rarely off on his assessments like this. Her first working days seemed to have been going extraordinarily well, despite all his best efforts. He still cringed at the thought of how Drea had derailed him so much in the elevator.

Now that she was showing her true colors, he was feeling far more in control. Once that unruly hair popped around his door, he was going to give her a piece of his mind. He was going to put her in her place, and then he was going to sit down in his place, and get in the B-Zone. He was going to show Andrea *and* Monday who was boss.

But when she peered around the jamb with such a delighted sparkle in her eyes, he decided to wait and hear just what had her all riled up before laying down the law. And when she started hopping back and forth from one foot to the other while gushing about the date she'd just interviewed, he decided that her neon-orange cross trainers were actually the worst part of what was happening here. After all, she *had* been working. He knew he hadn't been wrong about her. Blake Donovan was rarely wrong. Andrea wasn't the only one who was an astute reader of people.

He let her words flow past his ears as he studied her, trying to decide why he was finding himself so unexpectedly charmed by this display of enthusiasm. Probably it was because most of his employees played their cards close to the vest. Probably it was just the novelty of it. Probably nothing.

He tuned back in as she collected a few folders and printouts and marched over to his desk. "So I tentatively scheduled you for Thursday evening. I figured you'd want to approve it, obviously, but this also gives you a little time to make sure that jives with your schedule. Okay, these are the latest batch, and I'm not telling you which one I've spoken with." She slid the small stack over to him and fanned them.

He gave the head shots a cursory glance. At first look, he thought two were decent, one was doubtful, and one was perfect. He slid one of the maybes back at her. "Tell me about this one."

"Amanda Delgado. Retail clerk at a high-end boutique. Has an associate's degree, no plans to further her education beyond that. Hobbies include shopping and horses." She waited for his reaction. Blake considered. There were a few things that gave him pause about her profile, brief though it was. He'd never liked horse people, for one. Creeped him out. And shopping? Was she going to be a shoe person? He sent another disapproving look in the direction of Drea's feet.

The thing that he was silently debating was the education bit. It was true that he didn't like ambitious women, and those with degrees tended to be. Many educated women also tended to have opinions, and those simply would not stand when his spouse was entertaining business associates. On the other hand, and he had Drea to thank for this, he was beginning to realize that women with opinions could simply be more *interesting*. Blake was torn, and he didn't like that feeling.

"Pass," he said. "This one?" He pointed toward the doubtful girl. There wasn't anything wrong with her per se, but something about the arch of her brows and the sharpness of her nose said *total bitch*, even with the smile she was wearing.

"Mina Mizuki. Works in a nonprofit animal shelter, active member of PETA, enjoys cooking."

"Pass. Absolutely not. No way." He was shaking his head before she'd finished her spiel.

"Why? She's skinny and brunette, and already has a pet charity. That's kind of perfect for the stay-at-home wife of a gazillionnaire." Of course she was going to argue about this.

"It isn't *any* charity, Andrea. PETA is for vegans. *Vegans*, Andrea." He felt pained at the very thought. "Do you think I plan on dating this woman at salad bars, because the menu at Del Frisco's offends her?"

"I suppose you don't look like the tofu type, no. But she cooks, didn't you want that?" She still looked hopeful. This woman was impossible. Why was he explaining himself to an employee?

"PETA is also an organization that prides itself on celebrity endorsements. If I start dating this person, I'll be her ticket to landing a big name for the next ad campaign. Her cooking or not is beside the point. I'm not interested in being used for my name or status." Andrea pressed her lips together and held out her hand for another folder.

The other maybe skidded in her direction.

"Melissa Carswell. Dancer. Not very talkative, but seems nice enough." That sounded promising.

WHITING PUBLIC LIBRARY
WHITING INDIANA

"She's a possibility. Pull up her home address on Google Earth."

Drea stared at him in disbelief, but he was not joking. Location, location, location—it wasn't just a real estate mantra. Where people chose to spend their time said a lot about them.

Once she had located the address, he leaned over her. "I know that neighborhood. Lots of bars. It's a party area. She's obviously a drinker. Pass." He was close enough to smell her shampoo, but also to hear the choice words she muttered about him. He pulled back.

"That leaves us with Jaylene Kim," she said in her normal voice. He leaned back in, ostensibly to study the picture, but she smelled really nice. Blake idly wondered why he didn't find excuses to smell her more often.

"Because that would be inappropriate," Drea was saying.

Oh, dear. Had he said that last thing out loud? "Excuse me?" Please don't let that have been out loud.

"I was saying it would have been inappropriate for me to have informed your secretary about your date already, but you clearly don't have many choices left if you plan on meeting anyone this week. Try and keep up."

"Is Jamie a carnivore?" He picked up the woman's picture and studied it more closely. She was a stunner. An apple-scented stunner. Wait—that was Drea's shampoo again. Either way, it left him pleasantly dizzy while he drank in the dark-haired beauty on the page.

"It's Jaylene, and I believe so."

"Book Jamie and I a table at Del Frisco's for Thursday. I'm suddenly in the mood for prime rib." Blake was back in the B-Zone, confident as hell, stalking around the office and ticking off items on his fingers. "Deal with those shoes. They clash horribly with your skirt. You can have Friday off, since you came in Saturday. We can discuss the date Monday." He paused. That would be a three-day weekend without seeing Andrea. "Plan to bring me another batch of candidates on Saturday, at my home."

"Blake." He faced her, the questioning look on his face a contrast with the stormy one on hers. "Her name is Jay-lene. It doesn't matter how good the steak is, how sweet and submissive the date, no woman will ever want to be with you if you can't remember her name. Try to have a little respect. For you, a wife is an accessory, but you're expecting to be someone's whole life. Also, I forgot my heels, so."

Even the confidence of the B-Zone couldn't keep that from stinging. And now he'd have to look at those stupid orange shoes all day. He felt himself deflating. This was unacceptable. He'd have to find a way to gain his control back.

Chapter Eight

Andy awoke with a start when Lacy burst through her bedroom door at—she glanced at the clock—seven forty-three in the morning. Seven forty-three on her day off.

"What the hell, Lacy? I'm sleeping." Andy pulled the covers up and started to snuggle back into her pillow.

"Your phone, which you left out on the coffee table last night, has been ringing nonstop for fifteen minutes." Lacy was obviously none too happy about it, too. "When it wouldn't stop, I answered it. Here—take it."

Andy sat up and took her cell, wondering who on earth would call her at such a god-awful time of the day, and why her sister didn't just silence the phone instead of answering it. She glanced at the number on the screen—it was one she didn't recognize—before putting the cell up to her ear. "Hello?"

"She was gay," the male voice barked into her ear.

"What?" Andy wasn't awake enough to register who the caller was let alone the meaning of his words.

"Gay. As in lesbian. As in not fond of men. As in likes to get it on with other women."

"Blake?" The high-pitched frenzy in his tone didn't sound quite like her boss's voice, but the words he was spewing could only belong to Mr. Donovan himself.

"I don't understand why you would set me up with a gay woman," he continued without verifying that it was indeed him.

But Andy was sure now. She should have expected this actually. Jaylene had stopped by last night after her date with Blake and already given Andy an earful. Turned out the couple weren't a match made in heaven as Andy had hoped. They weren't even a match made for the moment, the pairing had been so ridiculously awful.

Andy took a deep breath. "Jaylene wasn't gay, Blake."

"Ah, she had you fooled as well," he muttered. "Then it was a purposeful snow job. Obviously she was after my money. Or at the very least, a free meal. No more first dates at expensive restaurants. Write that down."

If she'd been more awake, she may have thought it was comical that Blake thought she carried a notebook around at all times, ready to jot down his latest candidate preferences. But she wasn't awake. And it was her day off. A day that she'd meant to spend sleeping until noon.

"Blake, Jaylene isn't gay. She's a feminist." It was a fact Andy hadn't realized until the night before. Definitely not the right woman for Blake, but how the hell was she supposed to have figured that one out? None of the dedicated feminists she'd ever encountered had ever had such traditional women's jobs—nor did they spend so much time on their makeup.

The fact that Andy had only known one die-hard feminist in her lifetime was beside the point.

"A feminist?" Blake said the word with equal exclamation, equal questioning. "God, that's even worse."

"How in the world is feminist worse than lesbian in terms of bride-finding? You know what—don't answer that." Andy rubbed at her sleep-crusted eyes. "This is my day off, Blake. Perhaps we can discuss this further on Monday."

"She drank Sam Adams. She follows baseball. Drea, she had a bob." Apparently the conversation couldn't wait until Monday. "I thought in the pictures you showed me that her hair was just up. Nope. It was a full-on bob."

Andy sifted through the comments lining up in her brain and picked the one least likely to get her fired. "You've never mentioned long hair as a prerequisite for your dates, Blake."

"I would have expected that to be obvious. You did say you had a handle on my preferences."

That was it. She was not having this conversation. Not on her day off, not without coffee. "Okay, Blake, I'm done now. I'll talk to you more about this on Monday."

"She owns a cat, Drea. A diabetic cat." Blake spat the word *cat* as if pet-owning were the worst thing he could imagine about a person. "No cats. That's a rule."

"I'm jotting it down," she lied. "And I'll jot down more on Monday. Talk to you later." She'd moved the phone away from her ear when she heard him call back to her.

"We'll talk tomorrow. The new files you bring had better be more appropriately aligned to my tastes."

"Got it. Have a great day, Blake." She clicked END before he could say anything else. After saving the number to her contacts so she'd be warned the next time he called, Andy turned the phone off and fell back into her bed.

Dammit, she hated her job. No, scratch that, she hated her boss. Well, she hated her job *and* her boss. And she hated mornings. But, dammit again, she was awake now. Besides, she was suddenly worried that the files she had were not appropriately aligned to Blake's tastes. Which meant she had work to do, namely finding more candidates

before she stopped by his house the next day. Well, she'd
show him she could find candidates, all right.

Within an hour, she'd showered, dressed, and laid out a
plan of where to search for potential brides. Both the coffee
shop in the Asian American Civic Association and the
Italian Cultural Library seemed like good places to meet
exotic women. But even if her scouting for suitable dates
was successful, she still had one very huge problem: However would she make Blake Donovan suitable for dating?

Fortunately, she thought she just might have an idea to
solve that as well.

"Your sister's worried about you, you know." Lacy's boss
glanced over at Andy from the driver's seat of his van.

"Oh, my God, Darrin, I have told her over and over that
I am not going to screw this one up. Will you please attest
to what a great employee I am being?"

His glance traveled over her skeptically. "Well. You are
definitely a dedicated employee. Unusual, even. Great . . . ?
Jury's still out." He chuckled. "I'm pulling for you, Andy."

"Oh, shut up." She glared out the window. Despite
her words to the contrary, her confidence in the job was
somewhat lacking at the moment. She had found some
brilliant women on her scouting mission the day before, but
she still feared that none of them would succeed in wow-
ing Blake if she didn't manage to soften him first.

That fear was what led her to her plan. Today's plan. A
glorious plan, she hoped. Though she had the feeling Blake
might not see it that way.

No time to doubt herself. According to her Google Maps
app, they were almost there.

She nodded to Darrin. "Left here."

His muscular, tattooed arm flipped the turn signal on.
For a guy who perpetually looked like he was on his way

to meet Sid Vicious for a bender, Darrin was a surprisingly careful driver.

"I've been worried about her, too, of course." His tone grew serious. "Having to cut her hours on top of everything else made me feel like a complete asshole."

"Oh, no. We all know music is a precarious business. There are ebbs and flows in the work. You have to keep the studio open. She'd rather have a part-time job than no job at all. Seriously, D, she understands." He smiled, but hardly looked convinced. "Really. I'm hoping a little less time playing songs for other people will give her a chance to work on some songs of her own. I don't think she's done much writing since Lance."

"I don't think Lacy has done *any* writing since Lance. Much as I agree with her that you are out of your mind half the time"—he shot a look toward her lap—"I have to say, the fact that she's worrying about you is an improvement. For a while it was all I could do to get her to show up to work with her hair brushed. She's starting to get involved with the world again and not just go through the motions."

Andy sighed. Darrin was more than a boss to Lacy; he was a good friend. When Lance died, Andy froze. She didn't know what to do or say, and Lacy pretended none of it was necessary. If Darrin hadn't stepped in, Andy knew there was a chance she could have lost her sister as well. She'd owe the guy for the rest of her life for that. Which was why she let the crack about being out of her mind slide.

"This is it." She pointed him into a winding drive.

"This place? It's a mansion. Shit, girl." He craned to see through the windshield.

"Did I mention my boss owns the company?"

"Does he have any use for sound recording?" Darrin was still staring openmouthed. Personally, after seeing the coldness of the place, she'd reserve the dropped jaw for its owner.

"Not likely." She put her hand on the door handle. "Okay, I need to go in there first and talk to him. I'll be back in twenty minutes. Wait here, please."

"Jesus H, are you kidding me? This was not part of the plan."

"I know, I know, but I can't just walk in there with this. I need to prep the situation. Please, give me just twenty." *Puppy eyes, engage.* "I'll make it up to you. Lacy will work half a shift for free."

"Don't make deals you can't keep, you little brat. Your sister is going to kill you." He looked sort of delighted at the thought, and Andy knew she had him.

"So you'll stay?"

"I'm leaving if you aren't back in fifteen. Your time starts now."

"Fine. And thank you, Darrin." *Puppy eyes for the win.*

"Hey, don't be trying that feminine wiles stuff on me. It won't work. I'm doing this because I'm a friend, is all."

Andy rang the doorbell and was again greeted by Ellen, the housekeeper. "Good morning, Drea. Nice to see you. Mr. Donovan didn't say you were coming by today."

Uh-oh. He'd forgotten. Maybe the situation needed more prepping than Andy had hoped.

Then she thought about the time limit Darrin had given her and the present she had waiting in his van. Perhaps this would be one of those occasions that baptism by fire was the appropriate route.

But first, the housekeeper. "Yes. I have some files for Blake. And something else. Could you hold the door open for me a moment?"

Without waiting for Ellen's response, Andy handed her the stack of folders she'd been carrying and ran back to the van to retrieve her gift. With a wave, she signaled Darrin could leave and returned to the house.

Andy set the surprise on the floor and motioned for Ellen to shut the door behind them.

Ellen then raised an eyebrow skeptically at the gift. "Good luck," she said.

"Do you think it's a bad idea?" It was too late now to change her mind even if it was.

"Not at all. I think it's an excellent idea." Ellen smiled encouragingly as she handed the files back to Andy. "But I'm still saying good luck."

"Thanks." Andy tucked the files under her arm and headed for the stairs. Luck wasn't what she needed. She needed a goddamn miracle.

Blake sat at his desk, trying to remember what it was he'd forgotten. He knew it wasn't a conference call. His secretary would have alerted him if he'd missed something like that. His phone was charged—wasn't that. Rolling his neck around, he decided the niggle would come to him eventually. In the meantime, it *was* Saturday. Maybe a long jog outdoors instead of the usual prework treadmill session?

As he rose from his desk to change into gym shorts, a noise came from downstairs. He jumped a mile. Who the hell?

Then, with a rush, he recalled Andrea. Considering he'd completely forgotten about her, the sudden thrill that rolled through his body at the realization she was here took him by surprise. Especially when he realized she'd been the cause of the niggle.

And yet nothing could possibly prepare him for the surprise that came tumbling through his door instead of the woman he expected. A waddling, clumsy, chubby little thing. It was horrifying. It was hideous.

It was a fucking puppy.

"It's a puppy!" Drea exclaimed the obvious, bursting through behind the creature with a Cheshire-cat grin on her face, her arms stacked with files. "Isn't he the cutest thing?"

"He's disgusting." Though, really, it was kind of cute, in an odd way. "Why is it sniffing me? These shoes were rather pricy and I don't want them drooled on."

"It's just a little puppy slobber. It won't hurt anything." Drea's face was softer than he'd ever seen it, her eyes warm. Because of a four-legged creature?

Perhaps there was benefit to having an animal around.

But then . . . "Is it—is it *peeing*? On my *desk*?" Blake's moment of consideration returned to alarm. What was happening to his fortress of solitude?

Drea dropped the files on his desk and bent to pet the thing. "Oh, little sweetie! I should have let you go while we were outside. Silly me." She peered up at Blake. "It's only a little puppy piddle. Wipes right up."

Puppy slobber and *puppy piddle* were not phrases that made the fact that animal bodily fluids were being emitted around his office any cuter. The distracting view of Drea's cleavage that her crouched-down position gave him didn't make the situation any better, either.

Well, maybe it helped a little.

But then she stood and reached to the hook behind him. "Can I use this?"

"Wait, that's my suit jacket, don't—" It was too late, as a thousand dollars' worth of Ralph Lauren's finest gently absorbed the puppy piddle.

"Isn't he sweet?" Andrea was flushed, holding the furball to her chest and appearing to be utterly charmed by the filthy little thing.

"*Sweet* is hardly the word I would use to describe it." *Nuisance* was more appropriate. *A maker of messes.* Perhaps, a little charming, but not, well . . . "What is it?"

She lifted her mouth from where she'd had it nuzzled in the pet's body. "It's a corgi, can't you tell? Look at those big fox-ears! He doesn't have a tail. Good grief, do you know nothing? Come on, pet him. He's so soft."

Before he had a chance to protest, she'd taken his hand and placed it on top of the ball of fluff. The soft texture of the animal was pleasant under his fingers, but nothing compared with the delightful shock that traveled down his body at the feel of Andrea's skin on his.

Her gaze drifted up to his and the spark he found there shot an arrow of warmth to his chest.

What the hell was that about?

It was the damn puppy. It had to be. Fuzzy, cute things always seemed to have that effect on people.

But Blake Donovan was not *people*. He had to regain control.

Breaking their eye contact, he drew his hand back with a snap. "I am hardly concerned with its breeding or the feel of its fur. I am curious as to why you would bring your needy little dependent into my office, where it has thus far attempted to ruin everything it comes into contact with."

Blake could feel his eye twitching a little. Judging from where Drea's now less-delighted eyes were riveted, he guessed she noticed as well.

"It isn't my pet; it was my plan." Despite the waver in her voice, she maintained eye contact.

Damn, this girl was good. He was definitely going to hire her on at the company when she was done with her current contract.

"What plan? The one where I have to have my desk refinished?"

Her eyes narrowed. "The plan where you become a man, albeit a real jerkweed, but still a man, and not a machine."

He bit the inside of his cheek to keep from smiling. *Jerkweed?* "I fail to see how unleashing this small beast upon my home will make me more of a man. If anything, it will make me more of a tyrant."

"So you admit it!" The sparkle was stealing back into her grin.

So much for regaining control. "I can be stern, and a bit aloof," he corrected. "*Tyrant* isn't the word I would have chosen, but it is bandied about the office a fair bit."

"The queen of England keeps corgis. The breed is very distinguished. It fits into your lifestyle and yet warms you up. And believe me, Blake, you need warming up. You need the puppy." She thrust it in his direction.

He kept his hands at his sides, hating the thoughts that flickered through his mind at the idea of Drea warming him up. "I need no such thing." Though he wasn't sure whether he was referring to the dog's warmth now or Drea's.

"You need the puppy! Look at the puppy. You want the puppy." Again, she attempted to jam it into his arms. He took a step back. She took a step forward. Another step back—he'd been put on the defensive, and he hated that position. How had everything gone so wrong, so fast?

He firmed his stance, refusing to move again. "I do not want the puppy. Keep the puppy away from me. Doesn't it have a kennel or something?"

"Why would you kennel this little bundle of joy? This is exactly my point, Blake. Even if you have only a shriveled blackened lump where your heart should be, this little critter will melt any woman unfortunate to end up here with you." She was getting cheekier and cheekier. How was someone who treated him so flippantly going to sell him to the prospective dating pool?

Oh.

"Look, Andrea. I know you meant well, but I am not interested in adding another member to my household that cannot operate a can opener."

Her face fell. She frowned down at the scrap of fluff in her hands.

"It *was* a good plan, you know. Now I'm not sure what I'll do. You are just incredibly difficult to get to know. If I could *find* a redeeming quality in you"—she held up the puppy—"I wouldn't have to buy you one. Why won't you work with me a little on this? For the woman you plan to marry—you're going to have to let her in, too, at some point."

Watching her standing there, absently petting the big ears attached to the furball while she blinked at him, he almost could imagine letting *her* in.

For his future wife, of course. He supposed she might be right about that bit. But it was too soon. For either of them. He desperately needed that run, now. Time to cut this off.

"Drea, I think we had a nice moment here. You got the chance to run your idea past me, and you've certainly given me plenty to think about as per my privacy preferences." The corgi looked up at him with sad eyes that matched those of the woman who held it. "You can leave the animal and its information here. I'll deal with the drop-off. You may take the rest of the weekend for yourself. Thank you for your insight."

"Am I fired?" Drea demanded, suddenly back to the furious temperament he'd seen too many times from her already.

All this emotion was exhausting.

"No, Drea, you are not fired. I just think we're done for the day. After all, I now have the files I asked you to bring. I'll look them over on my own. Put"—he waved at the ball of fur—"*that* down, and I'll see you on Monday." After he had time to regroup. Time to figure out how he could give Drea what she needed from him without exposing any of his weaknesses.

He watched her with as much detachment as he could muster while she lovingly set the creature in the chair she'd occupied the other day—the upholstery would be covered with hair!—gathered her stuff, and walked out without a good-bye.

Was he truly so inaccessible that she required drastic measures to make him attractive as a spouse? If he was being honest with himself, then the answer would be . . . maybe. Maybe Andrea *did* know what he needed.

But good God, really? A puppy?

Chapter Nine

Blake glanced at his watch for the third time in two minutes. Drea had warned him that anxiously watching the clock while on a date did not leave the best impression, but frankly, he didn't care what effect he had on the woman in front of him. The impression *she* left on *him* was appalling.

All right, maybe that was an exaggeration. Drea would want to know why he didn't want to go out with her again, so he attempted to form a reason. He studied her features as she sipped her dessert coffee. Like all the women he'd been set up with in the last month, she was pretty enough— her skin was pale, her frame slight, her straight hair so dark it was nearly black—exactly the type of woman he was attracted to for the most part. Drea had gotten his preferred look down, that was certain.

At least, it *had* been his preferred look. Now he wasn't so sure. Her knobby bones couldn't be comfortable to embrace. He imagined hugging her would be like hugging a skeleton. He couldn't even think about what it would be like to have sex with her.

In fact, he hadn't been able to imagine having sex with any of the dates. He'd tried to kiss one of them once. Even that had gone badly. When he leaned in, she'd lifted her eyes to meet his and he was startled when her big browns weren't the green-flecked that he'd been imagining, so he'd aborted the attempt. Which was absolutely ridiculous. He didn't even know anyone with green-flecked eyes. Except Andrea.

He looked at his watch again. Two minutes later than the last check and he still didn't have a reason he could quite articulate for why the woman in front of him wasn't right. He'd been unable to explain why the others weren't for him as well. Well, except for Jamie the femi-Nazi. Simply put, they were just . . . *wrong*.

Perhaps it was him that was wrong, though he'd never admit that aloud. And if it was him, he couldn't say what it was he was wrong about. He looked good for his dates. He followed Drea's social advice, mostly. The dates were all ones he'd approved of by photo and résumé. What was the problem, then?

He caught his date smiling at him over her coffee cup. Her teeth were so perfectly straight and white, it almost seemed unnatural. He wondered if he should attempt conversation again. Drea had suggested, though, that talking about himself was not the best way to attract a woman. *Listen to them instead*, she'd said, or ordered, rather.

The problem with that advice was that this woman didn't speak. At all. She *hmm*'d and *ah ha*'d, but that was the extent of her conversation. Even when he asked a question, he'd receive only a giggle in response.

She should be the perfect woman—attractive and quiet. And bland.

Maybe he didn't want a quiet woman after all. Though Andrea argued with him at any chance she got, at least she was entertaining. Often over the last weeks, he'd actually looked forward to seeing her in his office. Her opinions might be overbearing, but her insight was also usually spot-on.

Andrea also wouldn't expect him to order for her, as all the other ones did. What was that anyway? A test of some sort? How was he possibly supposed to know what she'd want when he'd never met her before that very evening?

He'd tell Andy about that the next day. She'd get a kick out of it.

Now why did he just refer to her as *Andy*? *Andrea* was more suited to her looks. Admittedly, the more he'd gotten to know her, the more *Andy* seemed to fit her personality. But it was a hell of a lot of fun to see her feathers ruffle when he called her *Drea*.

The waiter came then to ask if there'd be anything else.

"No, just the bill." Blake said that a little quicker than he should have. Andrea would have disapproved. "If you would, please," he added, hoping to soften his obvious anxiousness. Actually, being in charge of the meal meant he *could* just demand the check like that. This was exactly why he continued to do the ordering for dates.

There. That was better. Andrea would be proud. He was nice-ish, *and* making sound business decisions.

Blake paid the bill and looked to his date—what was her name again? Sally? Cindy? Cinnamon? No matter, he'd simply leave it out when addressing her. "Are you ready then?"

"Hmm," she replied.

It had to mean yes since she put her napkin on the table and rose from her seat.

Blake followed, a small smile gracing his lips at finally ending the miserable charade of a meal.

It wasn't until later—much later—when he was tucked into his bed and he'd completed a chapter in his latest noir detective novel that he realized he'd spent the night thinking more about his matchmaker than his proposed match.

He needed to get it together.

Andy paced the office waiting for Blake to arrive. She rarely got to work before he did, but today she was anxious to hear about his date the night before. It wasn't even her day to be in the office, though lately she'd spent most of her days there whether she was required to be or not. Today she wanted to be there to catch up with Blake first thing. Cynthia, the woman she'd set him up with, was *the one*. Andy was sure of it. Cynthia fit his profile to a T—slender, quiet, submissive. If this wasn't the perfect bride for Blake, then she didn't know who was.

Of course, she'd thought that about the last several women. Sure, there were a couple of misfires in the beginning—the loud one with the obnoxious hyena laugh came to mind. And Jaylene. Now, setting Blake up with her had been a genuinely bad idea. If Andy had only taken more than two minutes to screen her instead of latching on to make up for her lateness, she would have realized it. Jaylene was a bra burner, for heaven's sake. And talk about man-calves—Blake wasn't as impressed with her muscles as Andy had been.

Since that first week, though, she had fallen into a groove. She'd found a pool of candidates at the Boston Secretary Association. Each chapter had a weekly meeting, and Andy attended as many as she could in her free time and on her days off. There, in the midst of women who took their careers seriously, she'd found a plethora simply looking for a rich boss to marry. They were the perfect contenders for Donovan—happy to serve coffee and sit on the sidelines as long as the Mister brought home a nice paycheck. That, she could work with.

And yet, Blake had refused to see any of them a second

time. It perplexed Andy to no end. Of course she'd questioned him, prodded for reasons so she could narrow her selection criteria, but she never received any helpful feedback. Over and over, she was forced to return to the same conclusion—Blake Donovan was unmatchable.

Quick-paced steps echoed across the waiting room outside the office door. Andy peered out, recognizing his stride by sound before she saw him. Their eyes met, hers wide under raised eyebrows, his serious, but with a spark to them. Did that spark linger from his date the night before?

Or was it for her?

That was a silly thought. Of course it wasn't for her. He must have had a good time with Cynthia. Sillier was how that knowledge disappointed her. Over and over again. She had to stop with this stabby-feeling thing.

"Well?" she nudged, chewing her bottom lip in anticipation.

The spark in Blake's eyes vanished. "No."

"*No?*" She couldn't hide her shock. Or her annoyance. Or her delight. "But why?"

Blake turned his attention to his secretary, signing a document she'd handed him, then proceeded into his office, past Andy. "What was that?"

She trailed after him, reminding herself of the puppy that she'd left with Blake—whatever had he done with the adorable creature? Hopefully returned it so it could find a happy home, and not just—fired it. She'd have to ask. But now, the pressing question had to do with a human creature and not the four-legged variety. "Why don't you want to see Cynthia again?"

He set his briefcase on his desk and opened it up. "Does it matter?"

Did he really ask that? God! This was her whole job, figuring this stuff out. "Yes! She was perfect, Blake. She perfectly fit your profile. She had the perfect body, the per-

fect temperament, the perfect teeth, for crying out loud—
what on earth could have been the matter with her?"

He answered with a simple shrug.

Andy huffed, throwing her arms out in exasperation. "If
I can't figure out why you don't like them, how am I supposed to find a better one? Articulate, please." This emotional defensive he had her on was exhausting.

Now it seemed it was Blake who was annoyed. "I don't
know, Andy, but that's your problem, not mine."

"It's your problem too if you expect—" She halted mid-
gripe when she registered exactly what he'd said. "What
did you just call me?"

"Drea. I called you Drea." Blake kept his eyes averted,
snapping his briefcase closed and placing it under his desk.
Then, with a clearing of his throat, he met her gaze. "Of
course."

She shook her head. Obviously, she was hearing things.
"Well, this job is impossible, then." She stomped to her desk
and slumped into her chair. How could he not even tell her
what was wrong with her choices? And if she picked so
poorly, why did he continue to have her try again? Jealousy or not, she did have a job to do.

Running a hand over her face, she pressed him further.
"Cynthia wanted to see you again, you know." Andy had
received the email the night before. The message had gone
on and on about how gentlemanly Blake had been and how
they'd totally clicked. *Clicked*, she'd said. That was part
of the reason why Andy had been so sure she'd found *the
one*.

Maybe if they'd kissed? Maybe Cynthia would have
seen the passion Andy noticed in him while he was making big business decisions. Of course, they had to have
kissed. There was no other way he could have monotone-
monopolized the date and left her wanting more. Thanks
to the Jaylene debacle, she knew full well how dates went

if Blake wasn't interested. So. Cynthia and Blake had shared a moment at the end of the evening. That shouldn't make her stomach sink. She had matched him with a woman that clicked. She should feel good about that. So why was her stomach in knots?

Blake flipped through some papers seeming to only half care about their conversation. "Does she? I can't imagine how you know that seeing as how the woman has a vocabulary of two words. And I'm not even sure you can call those words."

"Two words?" That was odd. Though Andy had never spoken to the woman, Cynthia had seemed eloquent and well spoken in her emails.

Blake swirled his pen along one of the documents. "She barely spoke the entire evening."

"You did ask for quiet." There was significant amount of snark in her tone, even for Andy.

"I didn't think *quiet* was synonymous with *brain-dead*."

Andy fought her instinct to say something even snarkier and instead tried to evaluate the bit of information that Blake had given. "Maybe she was nervous. I'm sure she'll loosen up with time."

"It doesn't matter because I don't want to see her again." His declaration was final. "Try again."

Andy growled. It really wasn't fair. Almost all of the candidates had requested a second date and time and time again Blake said they were wrong. What was she missing? If Andy hadn't so expertly picked his dates, she'd understand. But she had, and they'd been exactly what he'd asked for. Why would a woman think that an evening had gone well when the man did not?

He must be an excellent kisser. Well, she knew he was an excellent kisser. But she hadn't wanted to go out with him afterward. What she was missing had to be subtle. Unless it wasn't.

They'd all been attractive—Blake had approved of their pictures beforehand. And all the women had been more than pleased with Blake's appearance. So if the women were interested, and Blake was attracted, they were all kissing—the only reason she could think that he wouldn't want to see them again was that he'd already . . . wait.

Oh, no.

Please, God, no. The kissing must have led to more. More that she *knew* he was capable of. He'd told her himself, hadn't he, when he said in her interview that he had sex anytime he wanted.

Pure fury swept through Andy, driving her from her chair and over to Blake's desk. She pointed an angry, shaking finger at him. "You did, didn't you?"

He looked up at her, his brow furrowed in confusion. "I did what?"

"You slept with them." Her words were a harsh accusation, but she knew in her bones they were accurate. "All of them. You had to have. Why else would they be so smitten with you? I know you, Blake. You don't easily smit women. Not once you open your mouth, that is. And yet, one after another has said they've clicked with you. *Clicked?* That's a euphemism for 'screwed,' isn't it?"

He frowned with apparent indignation. "That's insane. Why would you assume—?"

She swept past his denial, the puzzle pieces slipping completely into place. "And you! Like a typical man, once you've slept with them, you've gotten what you wanted. No wonder you don't want to see them again. God, how could I be so foolish? I'm a glorified pimp!"

Blake stood and reached a tentative hand toward her across his desk. "Drea. Calm down, would you?"

She stepped out of his grasp. Balling her fists at her side, she stomped a foot—a little childish, perhaps, but she was pissed. "I will not! How could you do this to me? You're purposefully undermining my work. Were you finding cruising too time-consuming?"

"What? No. I'm sincerely looking for a bride."

"You expect me to believe that you didn't sleep with them?" Did he think she was a moron?

Blake straightened and with what sounded an awful lot like sincerity said, "Yes, I do expect you to believe that. Because I didn't."

God, he was good. If she weren't so entirely convinced otherwise, she may even have believed him.

Her nostrils flared as she drew in an angry breath, deliberating her next move. If he'd just admit what he'd done and promise not to do it again, she felt certain she could redeem the situation. She'd have to start with a new pool of women—the secretaries surely talked with one another and no one wanted to marry a player—but she had some ideas of where to look. Except if he was going to repeat his actions, a new pool was pointless. Her entire job was pointless.

Swallowing past the strange lump in her throat, she made her declaration. "If you aren't going to be honest with me, then this isn't going to work, Blake. I quit." Did she really say that? She did. "I'll collect my things. I'm sure your secretary can mail me a final check."

She spun back to her desk, keeping her face down as she grabbed her purse from the bottom drawer where she kept it so that he couldn't see the tears forming in her eyes. If she were crying because of the loss of employment, that would be one thing. But the sadness she felt was tied to something else entirely—something she couldn't quite name. She knew that he'd slept with the women, was convinced beyond a shadow of a doubt, and the images that brought to her mind stung with a bitterness that raged through her entire body.

The name of the emotion hit her with sudden force—
it was jealousy.

Well, shit.

Blake stood with gaping horror as he watched his personal
concierge gathering her belongings. What had just happened? He'd come in that morning with a spring in his step,
not because of his date the night before, but because he
hoped he'd be spending the day with Drea. Then when his
hope had been realized, well, he was pleased to say the
least. Though he hadn't figured out all the intricacies of
his emotions regarding the woman, he'd realized that he
had some sort of attraction to her. While this strange pull
was a roadblock on the path to securing a bride, he felt sure
it wasn't insurmountable. He'd planned to devise some way
to deal with the situation that day, but before he'd even
had time to settle in at his desk, here she was accusing him
of things he hadn't done and stomping out of his office.
Out of his life.

That certainly wasn't the answer to his problems.

"Andrea, wait."

She stood from her crouched position, her eyes glisten-
ing. "What? Are you going to admit you slept with them?
Are you going to tell me the truth?"

"I am." He took a deep breath, planning to tell her the
real reason he didn't want to see any of the women again—
the reason he hadn't slept with any of them—was because
he couldn't stop thinking about *her*.

But before he could figure out how to phrase it, Drea
seemed to make her own assumptions as to what his statement was affirming. "I knew you slept with them! Thank
you for at least admitting it. Why would you do that, Blake?
Screwing them on the first date sabotages a potential
future. I know you know this. I mean, I get that they'd be

interested in you—you're quite an attractive man, what with your solid chest and that sharp-angled jaw. And those eyes—God, those eyes—" She ran her tongue along her bottom lip as she stared at him hazily.

Was that lust he saw clouded there? And the way she'd described him physically, did that show interest on her part? Was it possible that Drea was as attracted to him as he was to her?

The thought stunned and gladdened him.

Then, with a shake of her head, Drea's eyes cleared. "But couldn't you control yourself? Leave a little something for next time?"

Again, he opened his mouth to protest, to explain the true nature of the situation, when all of a sudden he saw a door open. Perhaps he could get what he wanted—what he *needed*—from Andrea without having to admit an actual interest. If he could just get this *thing* out of his system, he could regain some semblance of control over his life.

Before he could second-guess himself, he went with it. "Maybe that's exactly it—I can't control myself."

"What?" Andrea seemed taken aback. "You're the most disciplined person I know."

"Well, but, as you said, they threw themselves at me." It was easier than he thought to pursue this angle, the words coming to him quite easily. Surprisingly, and happily, considering what a bad liar he was. "How could I resist? Especially when I'm used to getting it so often."

"*So often*." She repeated the phrase as if it were distasteful in her mouth.

He circled his desk, crossing to her with sure steps, his eyes glued to hers. "I told you in your interview that I . . ." He paused to consider how to put it. "Well, that I engaged in physical activity on a regular basis. How am I supposed to suddenly go cold turkey?"

She folded her arms. "I don't know—take care of your-self like every other man, maybe?" She released one arm to sort of flap toward his crotch before trapping it again with a blush.

"That's hardly the same." His eyes flickered to her cleav-age. The woman had incredible breasts. He'd noticed be-fore, but now the desire to touch them tugged at him with increasing urgency.

"Are you saying you can't go for even a short period of time without . . . without . . ." She circled her hand in the air as if she couldn't bring herself to speak out loud what they were both so clearly talking about.

It was adorable. She couldn't say the words.

Well, he could say it. "Without *sex*?" He couldn't stop the smile from forming on his lips when a shiver ran through her at the word. "That's exactly what I'm saying."

She opened and closed her mouth several times.

Good. He had her flustered.

Finally, she recovered enough to ask, "How the hell is this bride-seeking supposed to work then?"

"I see your concern." He pursed his lips, pretending to consider. This was his chance to bring the conversation around to where he'd intended it to go in the first place. "Perhaps, if my needs were met another way . . ." Would she understand where he was going?

"Like with your hand?"

No, she didn't understand. "That's not what I was sug-gesting." The conversation alone had his pants feeling tighter. Imagine how turned on he'd be if she agreed? He hadn't realized how completely into her he was until he gave himself permission to pursue it. Now all he needed was her acquiescence. His pulse quickened in anticipation.

"What were you suggest—" Her face suddenly flushed crimson as her eyes widened with comprehension. "Wait. Are you suggesting that *I* sleep with you?"

"*Sleeping* really isn't necessary."

"Oh, my God." Her hand flew to her mouth. "You can't be serious. Oh, my God, you are."

"You don't need to say it as if it's such a repulsive idea." Despite her words, he could sense she was considering it. Desire once again clouded her eyes and her breathing had grown shallow, as if she were excited by the thought.

And that only excited him more.

Still she protested. "Are you kidding me? It's absolutely repulsive. You want to sleep with me—"

"Not sleep," he corrected.

"Fine, *not sleep* with me so that you won't have the urge to come on to the women that you're dating in the hope of finding a wife?" She let her question hang in the air a moment. "Do you hear how disgusting that sounds?"

He shoved his hands in his trouser pockets. "No, actually, I don't."

"Blake!"

All right, maybe it sounded a bit untoward, but his true intentions weren't awful. Maybe he should have approached it another way. Or not at all. Now what should he do? He rarely was in the position of second-guessing himself. It was unusual and uncomfortable. He wished he could erase the last two minutes. "Forget I said anything."

"It's forgotten." Andy sank into her chair. Only a matter of seconds passed before her expression blazed again. "How the hell am I supposed to forget that?"

Blake closed his eyes for a moment. He himself had a feeling it would be difficult to forget her blatant rejection. He threw a dismissive hand in the air. "It was merely a suggestion. You had a complaint. You asked how to fix it. That's what I came up with."

Andy shook her head repeatedly. "You're impossible, Blake Donovan."

"Well, you aren't so possible yourself." He turned on his heels and headed back to his desk.

"Like that's supposed to be an insult?" Her voice trailed after him.

She could never let him have the last word, could she? "It's . . . I don't know what it was supposed to be." He sat in his chair and deeply inhaled to gather his thoughts. He had a feeling an apology was due, and he wasn't very good with those. "I'm . . . I'm sorry, okay?"

Her eyes narrowed. "For sleeping with your dates or propositioning me?"

"Both." Neither, really. Because he hadn't slept with any of his dates and he wasn't sorry for propositioning her. He was sorry he hadn't done a better job of it. He was sorry she hadn't agreed.

She sighed. "It's fine. I guess. Don't do it again. Can you manage that?"

Considering that he hadn't done the one thing in the first place, he was sure it wouldn't be a problem. The other thing, though—he had a feeling that his attraction to Andrea Dawson was nowhere near over. He couldn't promise he wouldn't make another move. So he answered simply, "I'll try."

"It has to be more than try if you want me to agree to stay."

She was seriously maddening. "I'll manage then." Across the room, he locked his gaze with hers. Even with the yards between them, her eyes pulled at him, pierced through him, as if they saw him in a way that no one ever had. He was nearly moved to go to her, to pull her into his arms, and kiss the hell out of her.

But considering she'd just blatantly shot him down, a kiss was probably a bad move. Instead he reached for her with words. "Please, don't quit." He couldn't remember the last time he'd pleaded with someone so sincerely. It made him feel both vulnerable and free at the same time. Their eye contact never broke. It reminded him of the moment they had shared during her interview, the point even then when he knew he was in over his head. This girl rattled him to his core, and he thought she knew it as she watched his eyes beg her.

Drea's expression softened, almost as though she realized how significant his statement had been. "Good. Then I'll stay."

They held their stare for several seconds, until the air felt warm and Blake had the urge to take off his jacket, but didn't dare move for fear of ruining the moment. As if he could convince her to stay through the sheer force of will and eye contact. If she didn't understand how much he wanted her here, it wouldn't be for lack of him showing her. If the eyes were the windows to the soul, his was on display.

It was Andrea who broke the connection. She leaned down to return her purse to its place. "And you owe me a bonus, you know. Several bonuses, in fact. Don't forget that our original deal stated I'd get compensated for how a relationship progressed emotionally or physically. *Physically*, Blake. You owe me."

He'd pay her anything she asked, even if the stipend was based on a lie. Whatever he had to do to keep her near.

Unbelievable. Un-fucking-believable.

Andy couldn't believe that he'd actually suggested that . . . that . . . that *she* should have *sex* with *him*.

She was mortified—the major component of that mortification being that she'd actually considered it. Disgusting. How on earth could any decent person spend a single second entertaining the idea that Blake "Inside-Ugly" Donovan was attractive? He was so inside-ugly that it seeped out through his hatefully perfect pores.

Okay, maybe it didn't, but it should. He was too hot for his own good. So insanely gorgeous that her insides fluttered every time she looked his way. Even after his ridiculous proposition, the flutters remained. They were heightened, in fact, but now they were accompanied with revulsion. Revulsion mainly with herself, but she clung to it. It worked to keep her hormones in check—thank God—because she'd been dangerously close to agreeing to his devil's bargain. Especially after that stare-down. He'd looked honestly desperate for her. It made her warring bits actually *want* to reconcile.

At least the rational bit of Andy had won that little conscience-cage match. *No! If you sleep with him, you'll be out of a job in about a day and a half flat. You know how he is with girls he sleeps with.*

Although the horny, teenage girl part of her had put up a decent fight. *Remember how he kisses? Imagine what else he can do with that mouth! Just the one time. Or seven. Then he'll be satisfied, you can insist on his quick marriage to Cynthia, and you'll leave with a hefty bonus and a glowing reference.*

Tempting. Overwhelmingly tempting. More tempting than it should be.

It was like the battle of the angel and the devil on her shoulders, and the angel's rationalization was barely heard over Andy's rapidly beating heart and the *whoosh* sounding through her ears.

But then Big Girl Andy grabbed a megaphone and trumpeted above all the other noise. *He does not respect women. The second you jump into his bed, you confirm everything he thinks he knows about them. You won't get the bonus, or the reference, and quite likely not the orgasm, either. He's too selfish to satisfy you first.*

With that her mind was made up.

Unfortunately.

Though she hadn't actually said no. It was Blake who withdrew his offer. If he hadn't, would the desire surging through her veins have won?

It didn't matter now. The conversation was over. But it was far from forgotten.

Sitting at her desk now, the idea played over and over through her imagination in vivid detail. Blake, running that sharp tongue of his, down her neck. Blake, drenched in sweat as he hovered over her. Blake, pushing in and . . .

No, no, no. She had to stop this. For God's sake, he was sitting across the room. What if he could tell what she was thinking? Surely her flushed cheeks were a good indication of the dirty movie playing in her mind.

Andy scrubbed her hands over her face and attempted to concentrate on the horrid situation that had led to his proposition in the first place: Blake had been sleeping with his dates. Oh, whoops, not *sleeping*. Sexing them up. Giving them a good time. Introducing them to the other Mr. Donovan.

Since she'd turned him down, did that mean he'd continue to be unable to control himself? At this rate, he was going to burn through every potential candidate in Boston before the year was up. *I'll be forced to mail-order dates from Ukraine.* Did the man even want to get married? Sure didn't seem like it.

So what does he want?

That one sat her back on her figurative heels. What *did* he want? She knew the reasons he'd spouted off to her, but none of them seemed particularly genuine. They sounded rote, things he thought he should say and so did. But the look on his face, that seemed as real as anything she'd ever seen from him.

"Blake?" she ventured, even though she could see from the set of his jaw that he wasn't super interested in talking to her right now. Well, she'd forced an actual apology from him—he was probably licking his wounds.

"Yes?" His expression, when he looked up at her, was actually open. Maybe he was just tense from all the drama of the morning. Maybe she was a hack who had no idea how to read anyone. Who knew anymore?

She sat back in her chair. "We've never talked about what happens beyond the wedding, and subsequent rewriting of your will."

"What's to discuss? It's done and then it's done." His eyes were full of genuine confusion.

There it was, then. *He wants a wife because it's what he thinks he should do.* She was certain that just as he had no idea how to treat a date, he had no idea what made a successful marriage.

Well, that had to be addressed. She searched for terms he could understand. "When you form a merger with another company, does it end at the contract signing?"

"Hm. I see where you're going with this. Obviously not. The signature is only the beginning. What sort of . . . maintenance . . . does a marriage require?" The puzzlement was fading into intense concentration. For all his faults, Blake certainly always liked to be the best at everything. Maybe she could train him into a decent husband after all. If only he'd kept the damn pup, they'd be going through obedience school together.

She stifled a grin and started to educate her clueless boss. "There will be an obvious restructuring, just as you would do with a company you take over. In that case, it's purely clinical. In this case, there will be emotions involved. Deciding whose home to live in—"

"Mine."

She went on as if he hadn't interrupted. "There's the question of whose things—how do you merge two households' worth of furniture and household goods and kitchen appliances and books and—"

"We keep mine."

"*Blake*. This is exactly what I am talking about." She rolled her neck, trying to release the new layer of tension that was building. "If you treat your wife—her things, her *life* without you—this callously, she'll have that sucker annulled before you even consummate it. It doesn't matter how submissive a girl you end up with, you cannot treat her like an acquisition. At least, not to her face."

"But I'm being logical. My future wife needs to be logical." He pointed at her open notebook. "Write that down. It's a new requirement."

Andy was going to lose her temper. Again. "Logic has nothing to do with it. You have to compromise. Marriage is a series of compromises. You live in your house? Fine. But she gets to put her pictures on the walls. Keep your furniture? She gets to buy new bedding. It's give-and-take. How do you not know this? Don't you have any married friends?"

The puzzlement crept on his face again. "I know a lot of married people, yes. From work. I don't really have a social circle."

Of course. Of course he didn't have any friends. Where would he fit them into his busy schedule of working, working, cruising, *not* sleeping, and working some more? Business dinners were probably his only real social outlet.

Andy felt inexplicably sad at this revelation. Everyone needed friends.

Granted, she didn't have a ton herself, but at the very least she had Lacy. Always Lacy. Someone to celebrate her successes with, to help her pick up the pieces when things went to shit, someone to talk to at three in the morning about absolutely nothing—*Oh, God. Lacy is my wife!*

Note to self: Make more friends.

Perhaps friend number one should be Blake.

No, that was going a bit too far. But she could at least continue with the friendly advice. "Well. It's likely that your business associates wouldn't discuss the finer points of the most complex relationship in their lives with you."

"Oh, I've heard plenty about them." He pushed his keyboard away and directed his full attention to Andy. "We have a few too many drinks, and then someone pulls out a cigar and they all complain. That's why I specified someone submissive. All my associates' troubles seem to come down to overly assertive women trying power plays on the home front. If my wife understands that I am the head of the household, we'll avoid all of that."

"I don't even think you're kidding right now. Good grief, Blake." Andy had no idea how to argue with that. Because the thing was, that *was* logical. Only it made no sense in the real world. And someone who didn't seem to be capable of empathy wasn't going to understand her objection to this. *I am earning this freaking paycheck, for sure.*

"Look, Andrea. I know you mean well, but I don't see you in a successful marriage, either. So you do things your way, and I'll do things mine." The condescension in his tone killed whatever ridiculous sadness she'd felt over his earlier disclosure.

Never in her life had she gone through so many emotions in one day. And every day since she took the job was like this. Beyond exhausting. She was taking her final bonus on a tropical vacation when this was over. *If* it ever ended.

"Just remember me when you've been divorced and need to find a new wife." Andy pouted for a minute. She had to find a way to make him let her in. Otherwise he was going to sabotage every date he went on until he eventually decided she was to blame.

And not just because of that, or even that it was her job

to find a good match, but because it seemed like the right thing to do. It was the closest friend thing she could do without assuming the title.

Glancing up from under her eyelashes, she studied the exasperating man at the neighboring desk. He *was* so gorgeous. On the outside. It was no wonder he was sex-obsessed—who wouldn't be with those looks?

Ignoring the upkick of her pulse at the thought, she wondered—could that be the key to him opening up to her? In a post-orgasmic haze, could she convince him to listen to her? Had she been too quick to shoot down his ridiculous proposition? Was his proposition actually not all ridiculous?

The little war inside her began again: *Worst. Idea. Ever. You don't have any better ideas. It's stupid. It's brilliant. It's happening. It's inevitable.*

Shortest war of all time. Turned out all Andy needed was a little justification for the horny teenager inside to get her way.

Now, how to go about it? She'd just flatly rejected him. It wouldn't work to simply turn around and accept. This called for something more extravagant. This called for a full-on seduction.

No matter that she'd never done one before. How hard could it be?

Chapter Ten

"Let me get this straight. You are asking me to give you a makeover. In order to get your boss to sleep with you. In order to keep him from sleeping with other women. So that you can convince him to settle down with another woman?" Lacy was clearly horrified.

"That's about it in a nutshell. Sounded better in my head." Andy peered into the mirror. "Definitely need to straighten my hair. I bought some dye, too. He likes them dark brunette."

Lacy smacked the little cardboard box right out of Andy's hand. "Absolutely not. If you are determined to go through with this preposterous idea, *and I do think it's a bad one*, you will thank me later for not letting you permanently alter your beautiful hair."

"I know what you think. But trust me. I know this guy. He needs this, and it's going to change everything." She pulled a curl down experimentally to see how long her hair would be when straightened. Inches longer, it turned out.

"Oh, I have no doubt about *that*. It's whether it's the kind of change you hoped for that I do doubt."

"What are you muttering about, Lace? Hey, how do you use liquid eyeliner? It looks like it should be a lot easier than it is." Andy turned to her sister, a smeary black panda.

Lacy burst into laughter. "You are such a mess. I can't believe I'm helping you with this. Come here. We have to take that off. Hand me the cotton balls, I'll do it for you."

Andy obediently closed her eyes and allowed her little sister to glide the cool oil over her lids. She hummed a little under her breath, until Lacy smacked her again.

"I can't perform a seduction with a bruise, you know." She started to open her eyes, but saw a shadow applicator beginning the descent.

"You won't perform one without an eyeball, either. Keep them closed until I tell you to."

While Lacy worked her hand in a soothing rhythm across Andy's lids, Andy allowed her thoughts to wander. After she showed up and knocked Blake off his feet and into his bed, what would happen? She got warm just imagining those strong hands gripping her close. His mouth, hungry for hers, taking what he wanted. Her breasts pressing into his solid chest as he thickened against her—"Ow! Stop hitting me!"

"Stop moaning! What the hell, Andy?" Lacy swatted at her upper arm again. "I am uncomfortable enough right now without having to hear your sex noises. Okay, open your eyes and look at my shoulder. I'm doing mascara now. Don't blink. Don't look away. And *don't blink*," as Andy's lashes fluttered.

"Sorry. It's just that I think I'll enjoy it." If his kiss was any indication, Andy was going to enjoy sex with Blake *a lot*.

"That's quite obvious. Sex is enjoyable. And God knows you aren't doing it very often." Lacy recapped the mascara and flipped on the flatiron. "Speaking of which—are you still on birth control?"

"Not that it's any of your business, but I got a three-year IUD about two years ago." Back when she could afford such things. Lucky now since birth control wasn't in her budget. She'd be using a condom with Blake anyway. She didn't want to concern Lacy with the information, but his track record made STDs a real concern.

Andy leaned back into her sister's hands as they massaged some sort of serum into her curls. "And anyway, you're one to talk. When's the last time you did it?"

"Not the point. You don't see me jumping into Darrin's bed, do you?" Lacy clacked the paddles of the flatiron together threateningly. "Though I'd probably get more hours . . ."

"Does Darrin even like girls?"

"Not sure about that, actually, I can't make up my—you know what?" She paused for a moment to point the iron at Andy in the mirror. "Also, not the point. The point here is that you are making a bad business decision based on lust and not on reason. I don't want to see you lose another job because you aren't thinking beyond your own satisfaction." Back to work she went. One strand at a time flattened, lengthened, and shined.

"See, that's where you're wrong. I am starting to get a real read on this guy. Sex is the only Achilles' heel I can find on him. It's my in. I get to know the real Blake Donovan, I can figure out exactly what the angle is that I'm missing in matching him."

Lacy's tight expression said she didn't believe Andy any more than she believed herself.

"So maybe I'm looking forward to it. So what? If I enjoy myself, well. It *has* been a long time. I barely remember how to do it." How did Lacy always manage to pull confessions from her without batting an eyelash?

"The fact that you call sex *doing it* says a lot, I'll give you that. Are you sure you know what you're doing?" Lacy was making that concerned face that made Andy want to jump on her and pet her hair and assure her everything was okay.

But she knew from experience Lacy did not like the pouncy-petting. So she settled for verbal assurances. "I do. Remember, figuring out what people want is sort of my thing. Don't worry about me, or my job. This *is* me doing my job. It's always been unorthodox. I'm just taking the necessary steps now to do the best job I can." Funny how her assurances sounded a tad bit more like defensive strikes.

Lacy ran a brush through Andy's newly stick-straight strands. "You look different, that's for sure." Her voice was a bit gentler, though, as if the assurance/defense strikes had hit their mark.

Andy assessed herself in the mirror. Her hair was long, straight, and glossy. Her eyes were smoky and mysterious. A nude gloss shone on her lips, and the glow in her cheeks was all natural. She was as close as she could be to Blake's ideal woman without suddenly developing an exotic heritage and dropping fifteen pounds.

So what if she didn't look like herself anymore? This wasn't about her. If only someone would tell her body that. It was thrumming with electricity even at the thought of Blake's eyes touching her, much less the rest of him. All of her nerves were oversensitive, raw in anticipation.

Time for the coup de grâce. If Blake wanted a sweet, submissive woman, she'd deliver. Alone in her room, Andy stripped off her everyday lace-trimmed undies and donned an, okay, lace-trimmed pair of boy shorts. She skipped the bra, but only because the nightie she'd chosen was so chaste. There were sleeves, and it fell to her midcalves. It was a pure and virginal white.

She gazed at her reflection in the closet-door mirror for a few moments. She was the undeniable mix of Madonna and Magdalene—in about an 80/20 ratio—that she felt certain Blake was looking for.

Deep breath. You are about to have your world rocked. Was that too presumptuous? No, most of the women wanted to see him again. He had to be good in the sack.

She returned to her self-pep talk. *Be prepared. Put your walls up now, just in case some unexpected orgasm threatens to knock them down. Just sex. Just professional sex between two consenting and*—oh, God, didn't *professional* mean hooking? *Just unprofessional sex between colleagues.*

She was already wet at the thought.

Gird your loins, Andy Dawson. This'll be a doozy.

Feeling just as reassured as her sister—which was to say, not much—she topped her seductive outfit with a light coat she'd borrowed from Lacy. It was long-sleeved, pale pink, and gorgeous. The top was fitted like a corset, but the calf-length bottom swung freely in voluminous pleats. Best of all, it wasn't stifling in the early-summer Boston evening.

Andy splurged on a cab. The thought of the cost made her a little queasy—especially since she planned to pay to have him wait for her while she did the deed—but she couldn't call Darrin for a ride like she had when she'd delivered the puppy. Explaining her attire to her sister's boss would be quite the story. Besides, she reminded herself, she was getting some bonuses in her next check.

Anyway, a girl in a nightie and a coat could hardly hop into a subway without being mistaken for a sex worker. An available sex worker, at that. The thought of the trouble that could cause made her queasier than the taxi bill. And she was already struggling with the difference between the job she'd taken upon herself and hooker. Was it better or worse than her previous self-declared status of pimp?

She didn't dwell on the question. She also didn't pause as she swung into the backseat of the cab and gave the driver her destination.

As they drove, she gazed past her reflection in the glass and out onto the dark Boston streets. Allowing her mind to wander once again, it went back to the same thing it always did lately when allowed free rein—the wine bar. It wasn't just the kiss that stayed with her, though that was a highlight of the evening. There was more—a glimpse of Blake that had seemed almost warm and compassionate despite his self-centered behavior and egotistical nature. It intrigued her, drew her back to the memory again and again.

She had convinced herself that the man who had rescued her that night was an anomaly. That he didn't really exist anywhere but in that brief moment in time. She could have entertained dating that man. Not that she'd seen him since, but surely he must be somewhere inside the boss that she faced every day—inside the hot alpha who constantly drove her insane with his maddening personality and his irresistible form. How was it possible to be so magnetically attached to someone whose neck she wanted to wring so badly?

Swearing not to have any physical contact with Blake in the weeks that had followed had done nothing to erase the attraction she felt every time her eyes accidentally grazed his crotch. But the thought of dating someone that self-involved made her ill. Good thing sex wasn't the same as dating. In fact, for Blake Donovan, sex seemed to be the end to dating. Perhaps this planned tryst of hers would solve quite a few of their problems, including ending the crackle of energy that arced between them whenever they were in the same room.

At least, it would end it from his side. Whether she'd

also get him out of her system remained to be seen. Why did she suddenly feel sad about her impending seduction?

She shook the emotion off and refocused her gaze on the ghostly image of herself reflected back in the taxi window. *Lacy's right—that doesn't look like me at all.* She slipped out of the coat and looked again. Still not her.

A moment passed as she debated whether that was a good thing or not. If she didn't feel like herself, it would make the whole event more disconnected. That was a good thing. It made it more likely that she'd be able to walk away with her senses in order. *Plus, I'll have his missing puzzle pieces to work with.* That was the main reason she was doing this. She had to remember that. Though, truthfully, his puzzle pieces took a backseat to his other pieces— such as his hands, his lips. His . . . lower region.

The more Andy thought about it the more excited she got. Might as well admit it full on—the man made her gaga. She'd been turned on by his body since the moment she'd first seen him. She just hadn't been able to reconcile her desire with his ugly personality. But now that she'd gotten to know him better, she wondered if perhaps her definition of *ugly* was a little too harsh for the man.

Either way, she felt good about her seduction plan. By *not sleeping* with him, she was acknowledging there was a connection there. Finally. But by making that connection after hours, in well, costume, really, and by using it to lull him into answering the kind of personal questions she needed, Andy was using her horniness in a practical manner. She'd even go as far as to say responsible.

So maybe it was the biggest justification she'd ever made in her life. Second biggest—what she'd done to Max's office after he'd fired her probably still took the cake. But there was no way seducing Blake could turn out as horrible as that.

Could it?

When the doorbell rang, the sleeping puppy in Blake's lap stirred but didn't bark. He called for his housekeeper to answer it while he considered the dog. He really was a good animal—quiet and cuddly, qualities Blake would rather like to see in a wife. Of course the creature could also be feisty and playful and that was all right, too. More than all right, actually. It was sweet. Entertaining. Endearing, even.

Somewhat like Drea.

Dammit, was he growing attached to the thing?

The puppy, not the woman. Though, if he was honest, he might be growing attached to that second one as well.

He pushed that thought from his mind. Much safer to focus on his attachment to the four-legged thing than on the two-legged one that had that very day rejected his advances. At least Puppy hadn't rejected him. Maybe that was why he still hadn't gotten around to getting rid of it. Even though he'd told Drea he was going to, somehow, he just couldn't bring himself to fire it.

The bell rang again. This time he glanced up at the grandfather clock in his living room and realized his housekeeper had gone home more than two hours before. Good God, it was after nine p.m. Who would be visiting at that time of night?

With more than mild curiosity, he set down his glass of scotch and propped his detective novel open on the coffee table. He picked up Puppy with him as he stood, then set the dog in the warmth of the spot he'd just evacuated.

"Stay," Blake ordered before tightening his robe and heading for the door. "Coming," he called out to his mysterious guest.

Before he unlocked the dead bolt, he peeked out the peephole but was only met with a woman's straight auburn hair. She was facing back toward his driveway and all he could see was her backside. *Hmm.* A woman was harmless enough. And the backside was enticing. He undid the lock and opened the door.

"May I help—"

His words cut off when the woman turned toward him.

He could hardly contain his surprise at her face. It was Andrea. Completely made up. In what he could only assume was supposed to be a nightgown beneath a ridiculous pink coat-thing.

"Blake—" Her mouth gaped as if she had more to say but had gotten stuck on her next words.

He understood the feeling. Seeing her standing on his doorstep with her eyes decorated to look like she was about to go clubbing and her hair lying flat and lifeless around her face—well, it rendered him speechless. A surge of excitement raced through him as he realized the intent of her visit, enough to get his cock stirring in his pajama bottoms, but the intensity of his interest was overwhelmed by the hilarity of her appearance. She looked so gaudy. So overdone. So *not* Andy.

Knowing it was absolutely the wrong thing to do, Blake did the only thing he *could* do in a moment like this. He laughed.

It wasn't a soft chortle, either. It was full-blown, rib-bruising laughter that ripped through him. He wrapped his arms around his middle in an attempt to contain himself to no avail. It was just too damn funny to stop.

Through the tears that clouded his eyes, he noticed Drea's expression—humiliation warred with frustration for top billing on her features. He didn't want that. Not at all. But before he could gather himself enough to explain his reaction, she'd turned and stomped away.

"Andrea," he called after her, except it came out more of a muffled mess of sound. He tried again. "Andrea, wait."

He was met by silence.

Somewhat calmer, he checked to make sure the door wouldn't lock behind him and ran in slippered feet after her. He knew she didn't have a car; she couldn't have gotten far. Thoughts of her riding the subway in that getup nearly had him laughing again. And he was concerned for her safety.

No, he wasn't. No one would hit on her in that outfit. Laughing it was.

But then he rounded his garage, and found her gone, the taillights of a cab racing down the street the only sign that she'd been there. All traces of humor left him with a splat, like the air disappearing from a popped balloon.

What the hell just happened?

It was obvious her visit hadn't been business-related. Then why had she run off so quickly? Sure, his laughter had been a bit overzealous, but come on. She looked outrageous. Was he supposed to have reacted differently?

With each step back toward his front door he felt more and more certain that he'd made a grave error. And that meant he'd have to apologize. Again.

Dammit.

Chapter Eleven

Of all the ways she'd expected him to greet her, laughter had not been one she'd even considered. She was so humiliated. Her eyeliner was a smeared blob by the time she'd arrived back at the apartment. Sweet Lacy, ever the caretaker, had poured her wine and crawled into bed with her.

It took a good half an hour before Andy was calm enough to get the story out. Though she'd had every right to say *I told you so*, Lacy instead comforted Andy with alternative reasons for Blake's awful behavior. "Maybe he was simply surprised to see you."

"And that qualifies laughter? Full-on laughter, Lace. I'm not talking about a simple chuckle. He was thoroughly amused." *Humiliated* wasn't a strong enough word for how it had made her feel. *Disgraced* was more like it. Mortified to no end.

Tears having destroyed the work of the flatiron, Lacy swept the curls off Andy's face in comforting strokes. "Some people have a hard time expressing strong emotions, you know."

Andy did know. Lacy was one of those people. Unless she was singing it in a song, you only got surface emotions from her.

"From what you've said about Blake, I'd bet he's got that problem."

Wiping fresh tears from her cheek with the sleeve of her pathetic white nightie—she was burning the thing in the morning—Andy protested. "Blake has a problem all right, but that's not it. His problem is he's a complete asshole." Times ten. Times twenty, even.

Lacy reached over Andy's head to the nightstand, grabbing a box of tissues. "Is he really, though? Maybe he's just a stranger to feelings. He may have reacted in the wrong way because he isn't used to dealing. If he was completely taken off guard as well as completely turned on, maybe that would be enough to elicit an unusual response, such as laughing. And you did look completely un-Andy tonight. If you'd have shown up here looking like that, I'd have been surprised myself."

And Lacy would have laughed. But that was different, wasn't it? It most certainly was.

"You're reaching, sis." Andy sat up and blew her nose loudly then turned to look at her sister. Lacy's eyes showed such compassion and understanding that it made Andy's heart ache. Smiling past the sob bubbling in her throat, she squeezed Lacy's hand. "But thanks for that. I appreciate the try."

Lacy returned the smile. "Would you like me to sleep with you in here tonight?"

"Yes, please."

Andy chewed her lip as she rode the elevator up to Donovan's floor. How she wished it were a Tuesday or Thursday. She could use her "shopping" day to curl up in bed and cry. But it was Friday, and on Friday she was required to be in the office. Under other circumstances, she was certain she could call in and say she had appointments with potential dates. Or even claim to be sick. If she'd done that today, Blake would know she was avoiding him, and he'd know *why* she was avoiding him.

And that would mean he'd win.

The last thing Andy would let Blake do at this point was win. Not after last night.

Morning, at least, had brought clarity as she remembered that *she* had rejected *him* first. She clung to that bit of knowledge, letting it propel her as she got ready and made her way to the office. At first it gave her a smug thrill of happiness. The closer she got to seeing him face-to-face, though, the more that happiness morphed into something else—anger. Wild rage. Because, how dare he? How dare the bastard make her feel so incredibly small? Sex had been his idea in the first place, not hers. And if he was at all unclear how pissed the situation made her, she was determined to let him know.

By the time the elevator opened on her floor, she was a new woman—determined and confident. With bitter and bold steps, she made her way to his office. She stomped past the secretary without a hello and was only somewhat surprised to see Blake waiting for her inside his door with a single red rose in hand.

For one fraction of a millisecond she considered accepting his truce.

Then she shoved the idea away. Hell no was he getting off that easy. She'd been hurt. Stripped raw. A stupid flower would not appease. Especially a lame-ass rose sort of flower. How unoriginal.

Without slowing her steps, she grabbed the rose from his hand and broke the stem in two, ignoring the sharp pain from the thorns. She tossed it in the trash can next to her work space, aware of Blake's wide eyes following her as she did. Good, he could watch her all he wanted. Let him look at what he so harshly turned down.

It was after she deposited her purse in the bottom drawer that she noticed an entire vase with at least a dozen more roses sitting next to her phone. Those would have to go, too. She swept the whole thing into the trash. The sound of glass crashing and water sloshing echoed in the silence.

Andy could feel that Blake was stunned. Frankly, she was, too, but she wasn't about to show it the way his gaping jaw did. His shock only fueled her more. What did he expect? That she'd smile and nod and pretend that nothing had happened?

Well, he wasn't getting that. She wasn't one of the docile chicks she set him up with. She was stupid to ever think she could be—even for one night. Never again. In fact, this weekend she'd begin applying for another job. Until she found one, she'd work her ass off to get Blake married off. But no more niceties between them. No more trying to understand him. No more attempts at friendship.

She'd just settled in and turned on her computer, prepared to dive into her work, when he finally spoke.

"Andrea, I'm sor—"

She thrust her palm in the air like a stop sign. "Don't. Speak."

"Just let me—"

Andy didn't look at him as she delivered her edict. "I mean it, Blake. Do not speak to me. Ever again. Unless it's related to work."

"Drea, I have to—"

Slamming her hands on the desk, she swiveled to face him. "And my name is Andy. Or Andrea. When you speak to me, in relation to work only, you will use my name. My name! You don't get to nickname me."

"Come on, Andrea." He stepped toward her.

Andy popped up from her chair. "And don't come near

me." Scanning her desktop, her eyes settled on a tape dispenser. It was clear, but it would have to do. Holding the dispenser in one hand, she shooed Blake toward his desk with the other.

Surprisingly, he complied, taking several confused steps backward. When he'd crossed what she believed to be the center of the room, she got to work. Walking to the wall she fastened the end of the tape to the floor then paced it across the room before tearing the other end off. She traced her footsteps back over the line she'd made, pressing the tape into the carpet. It wouldn't stick for long, but long enough to make her point.

She finished then turned to her boss. "You see that line? That's your side." She pointed to the side of the room that Blake currently occupied. "This is my side." She circled back to her desk and deposited the dispenser in its place.

Blake scanned the line with his eyes. "You've got to be kidding."

"I'm not." She thrust out her chin and put her fists on her hips. "Do not cross to my side. Is that clear?" Perhaps it wasn't her place to make such demands, but frankly, she didn't give a hoot.

Blake, however, was not going to give in easily, it seemed. He squared his shoulders. "I'll go wherever I damn well please. It's my office."

My, but didn't he look hot when he was in charge.

Stop it, stop it, stop it! He is not hot. He's horrific. She infused her anger at herself into her next words. "I don't care whose office it is. You will stay on your side."

He folded his arms across his chest. "What are you going to do to me if I don't?"

Was that a challenge? Game on. "Try it and find out."

With blazing determination set into his features, Blake lifted his foot and slowly placed it on the other side of the tape. On *her* side.

Andy's eyes widened with rage. She wanted to hurt him. Physically hurt him. And maybe maul him a bit with her hands and her mouth as well, but mostly just hurt him. She bent to grab the first weapon that came to mind—her three-inch-heeled shoe—and chucked it at him.

Blake caught it with one hand. He chuckled. "That certainly worked the way you wanted it to."

What a pompous ass! She huffed and bent to grab the other. This time she hit his shoulder. He didn't succeed in hiding his wince. A minor victory, but a victory all the same.

Blake bent to pick up the second shoe from the floor where it had fallen. "So now I have both your shoes." His eyes twinkled with sheer evil. Why the hell did devil look so good on him? "And it's a rainy day. Good luck with your trip home this evening."

"Dammit." There were so many other things she could have thrown, why had she chosen her shoes? They were nice shoes, too. A pair of Pradas that she'd grabbed in a Filene's Basement sale before it went out of business. Several years old, but the black style was classic.

She walked up to the tape line and put her hand out. "Give me my shoes back."

"What was that?" He cocked his head. "It sounded like you were talking about something non-work-related and I'm not allowed to speak to you under those terms."

Jesus Christ, she was not doing this with him. "Give them to me. Now."

"Oh, you want these?" He held the shoes in one hand, dangling them above her reach.

Andy began to step toward him, needing to be closer to have any hope of retrieving them.

But Blake stopped her with a shake of his finger. "Uh, uh, uh," he chided. "No crossing over the line."

The damn tape line. If she stepped across it now, he

would win. She would not be defeated. That left no choice but to ask for them again. Though she didn't have to ask nicely. "Give me the fucking shoes, Blake."

Again he dangled them, too high for her to grasp without stepping across the boundary she set. But though the shoes were out of her reach, his suit jacket wasn't.

Like lightening, she stretched toward him and pulled his beloved Montblanc from his pocket. "Ah ha!" She stepped back so he couldn't immediately grab it back. Wielding it like a sword in front of her, she taunted him. "Now what are you going to do? Huh, Donovan?"

He smirked at her. "Very cute. Give it back."

Like hell, she would. "This pen? You want this?" She tossed it in the air, catching it in her palm before tossing it again.

"Would you please be careful with it? That's a very expensive pen."

Ooo, she had him. His tone was anxious and desperate. "Oh, I know what it's worth. In fact, considering I got those shoes at discount price, I think this is a pretty fair trade."

"You're not keeping my pen. Give it to me."

There was that alpha-male tone of his again. If she weren't so mad, she might consider it a turn-on. "Not until you give me my shoes."

He cocked his head, considering. "If I give you your shoes will you forget this nonsense about my side and your side and let me talk to you?"

She'd rather go barefoot. "Not a chance."

"Give me the pen."

"Give me my shoes."

Blake stuffed one shoe under his arm and studied the other. He wiggled the heel, noticing it was loose. "You know, these seem to have fairly wobbly heels. It doesn't look like it would take much to break one."

She drew in a breath. "You wouldn't dare." Not her

classic Pradas. She couldn't get a pair of designer shoes at that price again. And considering how fast she was about to be out of this job, she'd need nice shoes for interviewing.

"Give me my pen."

Yet if it came to the pen or the Pradas, she'd choose the pen hands down. "Never." She. Would. Not. Lose.

Eyes pinned on Andy, Blake pulled on the heel. With a snap, it broke free. "Whoops."

"You . . . you . . . you bastard!" Andy searched the room looking for a method to destroy his pen in proper retribution for her ruined Prada. Spying the heating vent behind her desk, she ran to it.

"Don't even think about it."

She paused, her hand poised to jam his pen in between the slats. Pen or vent, something was going to go.

In three easy strides, Blake stepped over the tape dividing line and crossed to her. Before she could react, he grabbed her arm and spun her toward him. He pulled her so close that her inhale of surprise brought with it his scent of coffee and cologne and Colgate. His lips hovered inches above hers. She could feel his breath when he spoke. "I said, don't even think about it."

Next thing she knew, Blake's mouth was on hers. He pressed against her fiercely. Without a pause to consider, she opened up to him, pressing back with equal fervor, inviting his tongue in between her lips to twist with her own.

The battle over the pen forgotten, Andy let it fall to the floor with a clunk and she wrapped her arms around his neck. One of her bare legs wrapped around his leg and Blake encouraged her to lift them both higher around his waist, his hands settling beneath her ass to help support her.

In this position she could feel what their kiss had done to him. With wild abandon, she bucked her hips against his hardness. Blake groaned into her mouth before nipping at her bottom lip. God, this kiss was fantastic. Better than fantastic. Nothing like the last kiss they'd shared—that one had been sweet and sensual. This one was frenzied and urgent and sizzling heat. That kiss was a first kiss—the type that ended. This one was a kiss that led to more.

At least, it was going to lead to more if Andy had anything to say about it. He owed her, and an orgasm would suffice as payment.

And considering the way he was entwined around her— or the way she was entwined around him, it was really hard to tell if there was a difference at this point—she had a feeling Blake wasn't in any position to protest.

Thank the Lord.

Blake could not believe this day. He'd had a sleepless night, tossing and turning as he bounced from regret to confusion to renewed amusement back to regret like a volleyball being thrown around on the sand. While he'd tried to dismiss Andrea's surprise visit without another thought, he couldn't get her obvious intentions out of his mind. Which gave him a raging hard-on. Added to the tossing and turning, it was no wonder his night had been sleepless.

So he'd come in that morning to the office determined to make things right. He'd bought roses—Drea had told him several times in her instruction over the weeks that women tended to respond positively to flowers. Her reaction to his purchase, however, had him momentarily wondering if Andrea Dawson was indeed a woman.

Then they'd argued, and hell if every furious word that came out of her mouth didn't tighten the crotch of his pants. She'd driven him from sorrowful and horny to pissed-the-fuck-off and horny. Now, through a sequence of events that surprised even him, he was making out with her and clawing at her clothing like a sex-starved maniac.

And the way her breasts pressed against his chest and her hips rocked against his pelvis, he only knew one thing for sure—Andrea Dawson was very definitely *all* woman.

He also knew this wasn't ending anytime soon. There'd been too much buildup. Now that he'd begun with her, he couldn't stop until he'd finished. Or they'd finished, rather. He'd always been a gentleman in that area.

Mouths still locked, he carried her over to the edge of her desk. He pulled away so he could slip off his jacket, half afraid that the break in contact would give her a moment to reconsider what they were doing.

He needn't have feared. Drea leaned forward and clutched onto his tie. She pulled him back to her, back to her greedy mouth. As their kiss resumed, she worked the buckle on his pants. His cock leapt against his briefs in eager anticipation. Dictated by that eagerness, his hands pushed her skirt up past her thighs. Then his fingers were dancing over the crotch of her panties.

With a great amount of willpower, he paused, stepping back to gauge her reaction and assure his venture was approved. Sure he was a man who took what he wanted, but even in his lust-filled haze he recognized the impropriety of the situation. A boss banging his employee in the middle of the office? He better at least have her permission.

With a brow raised in question, his eyes met hers.

She answered quick and sure. "Touch me, Blake Donovan." Her voice was thick with desire. He stared at her, unblinking. "I said, touch me!"

Never in his life had Blake been given orders during sex.

It was the most goddamn sexy thing he'd ever heard.

He snapped back into position, pulled like a magnet by her command. One of his hands grabbed a fistful of curls, and they were just as soft as he'd imagined. Even better was the breathy gasps she made as he tugged on them. He wanted to explore her body, cup and squeeze her breasts until her nipples hardened to twin peaks. Strip her of all her clothing and stare at her flushed skin.

But this was frantic and unplanned. And in the office. Not a time for savoring, and with Andrea now working on the zipper of his pants and the echo of her *touch me* playing in his ears, he felt obligated to return his fingers to the apex of her thighs.

Sliding beneath the crotch of her panties, he trailed his finger along the top of her cleft, so near to where he knew she wanted him yet so far away. Her hand stilled at the waistband of his briefs as he taunted her. "Is this where?" His tone was low and gravelly as his thumb settled in her nest to find her clit. "Is this where you want me to touch you?"

She didn't make him ask again. "Yes." Andrea wriggled under his touch. "Yes, please, yes."

He swirled his thumb against the swollen bud, watching her reaction as he exerted differing pressures. When her breathing grew heavier and her grip on his hair tightened, he felt sure that he'd discovered exactly what it was that she liked. And her expression—lids half closed, her face tightened into a look of impending pleasure—it was almost enough to get him off without anything else. He had to look away.

Returning his attention to his actions, he splayed his fingers like he was holding a bowling ball, one playing at her bud while he slid two digits down to test her hole. Ah, she was wet. So wet. And tight. But he was sure she was wet enough to take care of that. He could slip in now, certain she was ready to accommodate him. Yet he could sense she was close and even though he knew this wasn't an occasion to indulge, he wanted her to come apart all over him. For him.

Even in the throes of passion he recognized that this was

absurd overthinking for a quick office shag. Damn, this woman . . .

She was amazing.

In awe, he watched as she reached the edge and spilled over, her muscles tensing and quivering with her climax, her voice crying out with the sound of his name.

Crying out! What if she was heard? In a split second he wondered if his office walls were soundproof or if his secretary had left for her lunch break yet. Then simply decided the matter could be handled another way.

Gripping her behind the neck, he pulled Andrea toward him and sealed his mouth over hers, swallowing her sounds. He should have been doing this the whole time. Her kisses were incredible. She tasted like coffee and the caramels she didn't know he knew she hid in her desk for when she skipped lunch and needed a sugar fix. It was delicious.

He continued to kiss her through her orgasm, until she'd relaxed in his embrace. For one split second, he feared that now that she'd gotten her release, she'd return to her senses and push him off her. Wouldn't that be a kicker?

Those fears were quickly relieved when her hand settled on his erection and squeezed. "Your turn, Tiger."

Hell, yes.

Blake pulled his hand from Andy's core and circled his arm around her waist, intending to lean her backward on the desk. Then some small voice in the back of his head told him he should be making a bit more of an effort for this girl, so he lifted her by the buttocks, urging her legs around his waist, and carried her close against him over to the wingback chair—the same one he'd interviewed her in. *Fitting*, he thought briefly.

After all, it was sort of bad form to screw the matchmaker on top of her piles of potential matches. The voice told him that wasn't the only bit of bad form going on, but he told that voice to go to hell, because bad form had never felt better.

He sat in the chair and pulled her down on top of him. Her curls tumbled around his face, filling his nostrils with the apple scent of her. It was intoxicating. He buried his mouth in her neck and relished the way kissing her there made her squirm against him. Grabbing the top of her panties, he pulled them down her thighs. She braced herself against his shoulders, lifting one knee and then another to help him slide them all the way off. Then it was her turn to maneuver his pants and briefs far enough down to release his cock.

Finally. There was nothing left between them.

Blake pulled back and gazed into those green-flecked eyes. If they did this, there was no going back. Andrea stared back at him. The moment lasted forever, until she gave him one of those wicked grins.

"Do me," she said.

He intuitively sensed that laughing at her sexy talk wouldn't go over well, so he bent his head and hid his smile while he fumbled in his pant pocket for the condom in his wallet. After it was rolled on, he finally allowed himself to gaze at her pussy.

"Oh, that is beautiful." His thumb gently slipped between her folds to stroke the bud he'd already become familiar with by touch. Then he lined up against her opening. She let out a strangled moan and sank down, taking him into her. As he'd predicted, she was so wet, so tight around him, and Blake worried for a moment he was going to come immediately, like a teenager. He held her in place until he'd regained enough control to move inside her.

The plan, at least in his head, was to take his time and enjoy this, quickie be damned. Because there was a good possibility that when Andrea came to her senses, she'd walk out that door and out of his life. And right now, with his cock buried inside her and his lips wrapped around her left earlobe, he wanted it to last forever, to leave that eventual departure out there in the real world.

Andrea, it seemed, hadn't picked up on that plan. Her hips rose and fell, riding him hard toward another climax. Well, if that was what she wanted, he was damn well going to give it to her. He flicked his tongue around her lobe then sucked it gently as he resumed his efforts against her clit with his thumb.

He could feel the change in her as her inner muscles began to subtly tighten. He applied more pressure to her sweet spot. She clenched the arms of the chair as tightly as her walls clenched his cock and she once again came spectacularly for him. No worry about her crying out this time—her teeth were buried so far in his shoulder he almost feared he'd be the one to whimper.

The sight of her bent over him in ecstasy, the sharp pleasure/pain of her bite, the feel of her tight pussy milking him—it was enough to bring on his own orgasm. Her spasms hadn't even begun subsiding before he thickened and spilled into her. He squeezed his eyes shut as Andrea gripped the chair even tighter against the force of his thrusts. The strength of it overwhelmed him, and he felt like he was falling for an eternity.

In reality, he only fell for half a second as the gray wingback fell apart beneath the intensity of their illicit sex.

Lying there on the floor of his office in a tangle of Andrea's arms and upholstery, Blake felt his world crashing down like the chair. What had they done? Suddenly shy despite their physical closeness, he had to steel himself to look her in the eyes. He had felt something there, something even stronger than the kiss they had shared. Now the chair seemed like a metaphor for his hubris beating him over the head. He braced himself for what she would say and do.

Except, even prepared, her reaction came as a big surprise.

She was cracking up.

"Oh, my God! Can you even believe—that has never— oh, my God! I can't even!" She was laughing so contagiously that he even found himself chuckling along.

She didn't hate him after all. Maybe he hadn't just destroyed everything he had hoped she could give him by taking too much.

"Do you think anyone will notice?" he ventured, just for the pleasure of hearing her peals of laughter renew. As their laughter faded into the typical office noises, Andrea found her panties and slipped them back on. He took that as his cue to dispose of the condom and suit back up. By the time they were both fully clothed and facing each other, it was pretty clear that neither of them knew quite what to say.

"I'm thinking a sandwich from Al's. Want me to grab you one? I'm going to walk, so might be a little bit." She fidgeted a little as she spoke, not meeting his eyes.

All Blake could do was nod.

"Thank you." She crossed to her desk to grab her purse and slip into her hideous orange sneakers. "Good thing I brought my walking shoes," she said with a wink before leaving the office.

He watched after her wondering if he should have let her go. This was truly uncharted water. He hoped she'd come back soon and they could talk about it. Also, a sandwich sounded really good right about now. Maybe he could even buy her different shoes later.

Chapter Twelve

Once she left, Blake schooled his expression into his usual serious-work face. It wasn't worth thinking about while she was gone. What was done was done. He busied himself by calling maintenance to deal with the remains of the broken chair then had his secretary find him a suitable replacement. She located one from an unused office on the seventh floor. It was delivered and the other taken away, all evidence of his tryst erased in the matter of an hour.

Which was a good thing, he reminded himself. Then why did his chest feel so tight?

After the office had been set right, Blake found he couldn't concentrate on anything but watching the clock tick. Andrea still wasn't back and he worried what her prolonged absence meant.

It meant she was pissed, of course. She probably wasn't coming back. She was likely at that very moment filing a report against him with HR. Maybe he should call down and check . . .

No, he couldn't do that. He had to put some trust in her. It was only fair. He sagged in his chair letting the weight of the morning's events—or event, rather—settle on him. It didn't take long before he decided it was the worst thing he'd ever done.

Then he decided it was the greatest.

Then a glance at Andrea's empty desk across from him and he was back to thinking it was the worst.

But the sex had been so amazing.

He had replayed the entire thing at least five times, inhaling deeply to recall the last vestiges of her scent, mentally rewriting the chair situation. In his mind, he'd both told Andrea this was inappropriate and cut the whole thing off at the pass, and given her six screaming orgasms.

Blake, for once in his life, had no idea what to do or think. Every scenario he imagined seemed equally likely. If he were to ask himself what it was that he, Blake Donovan, not the CEO but the man, wanted—well, he'd tell that voice to go to hell, too. Because the truth was that he had always known what he'd wanted until the day that damnable Andrea Dawson had waltzed into his life and turned it upside down.

Now he didn't know if he wanted to kiss her or strangle her. Fuck her or fire her. No, he did know that much. He wanted her around. He wanted her close. She was infuriating and illogical and feminine and absolutely fantastic. God, his therapist was going to kill him. He made a note to fire her instead.

"Fuck!" he groaned as he scrubbed his hands over his face. *Get it together. Make a plan.*

His pulse still throbbed with the uneasiness of Andrea's long absence, but after several deep breaths, he managed to steady his nerves enough to enter his straightforward thinking mode. The B-Zone, he called it, but only to himself. *B* for *Blake*, but also cleverly for *business*. And, on particularly good days, *B* stood for *Badass*. It was his berserker mode, his karate mind-set. Everything fell into place when he could block out the world and simply problemsolve.

Today he needed to be Badass in a big way. Wasn't he a little bit already? Even with all the rules he'd broken and policies he'd violated, there was no taking away the fact that he'd totally scored. He had to give himself a high five for that. It had been hot. Fucking Andrea Dawson had been *way* hot.

He let that sink in. Let himself relish it. Let himself beam with pride.

Then, in proper B-Zone style, he made himself look to the future. Mentally he made his list of options, adding pros and cons to each. He shut out all thoughts of the carnal delights the woman elicited and stayed focused. Firing her was out of the question. Not just because of the legal ramifications but because he didn't want her gone. He needed her. To find him a bride, of course, though thoughts of matchmaking seemed foreign and unwelcome at the moment. But it was part of The Plan and The Plan would not be altered because of one feisty, albeit pleasantly curvy, female officemate. No way. Not a chance. Not happening.

Yes, he thought as he relaxed into his chair, he was definitely in the Badass Zone. He could handle this just fine.

After another several minutes of working through his options, Blake determined the best way to handle their situation was to move on. When Andrea returned, he'd acknowledge it had happened, admit that it was entirely his fault—though the blame most certainly was shared—and promise never to lay a hand on her in an unprofessional manner again. They would go forward without another thought about their attraction. Surely it was out of their system now, anyway. Right?

The answer to that threatened to take him out of the Badass Zone so he decided not to dwell on it. His plan was in place, whether she was out of his system or not.

He looked at the time again. She'd been gone nearly two hours. Where was she? Maybe she wasn't coming back after all.

The renewed idea sent him spiraling out of the B-zone and into panic mode. He stood up, ready to go out looking for her, when she meandered back into the office, sandwiches and drinks in hand. His heart settled at the sight of her. Then it quickly jolted into high-speed racing again because, well, she had that effect on him. Especially when her hair still looked tousled from earlier, and her cheeks had that glow from walking that mimicked the flush she'd had after she came.

Andrea cleared her throat. "Could you maybe help, please?"

He shook his head out of his stupor. "Oh. Of course." He hurried toward her to help with her load, stopping at the line of tape that crossed his path. Not sure how things were between them, he glanced at her with a questioning brow.

"Yes, you can cross the tape, Blake. I can't believe you'd even hesitate after . . . you know."

He had to smile at that. He finished crossing to her, taking the sandwiches and bags of chips from her hands so she could handle the sodas. He set them on his desk, planning to turn back to her and deliver his prepared speech or at least ask her how she'd managed to carry everything up.

But before he could, she was next to him, setting the sodas alongside the sandwiches, her arm brushing against his, warming him to the very bone. Wakening the parts— or rather *part*—of him that had been put to sleep by his earlier planning. He cocked his head toward her, catching her eye.

"Andrea," he began at the same time she said, "Blake."

At the sound of his name and the lusty look in her eyes that he knew had to mirror his own, his speech and plans went out the window. In a blink, he was on her again.

It had been instinct, to take her into his arms, and she submitted to him as if it had been her idea. Her lips tasted as good as they had two hours before—a little less sweet, perhaps, a little more salty. Just as frantic. His hands were already searching beneath her shirt to find her plump breast. He pressed against her, pushing her toward his desk. There were no files of dating candidates over here, after all. That made this surface completely fair game.

But just as he leaned her back against it, she put her hands to his chest and pushed him back. "Wait, wait. Stop."

Panting, he took a step back, his hands raised in surrender. "You're right. This isn't right." Leave it to Andrea to have her wits about her. As disappointed as he was with her pronouncement, he had no cause to argue. "We have to stop."

Andrea, who had turned away from him the moment he'd released her, swiveled back now to face him. "No, I was just worried about the drinks."

He looked behind her, seeing she'd moved the sodas to the floor. "Oh." That was surprising. *Pleasantly* surprising.

"But now that you've mentioned it . . ." She bit her lip.

Before he let his hopes dash, he clarified. "We shouldn't be doing this?" It was a question he hoped he didn't know the answer to.

She shrugged. "I wouldn't necessarily say that. We've already done it. Does it really matter now?"

"No, I suppose it doesn't." He tilted his gaze at her and rubbed his hand across his chin. It was obvious that Andrea's long absence had given her time to sort out things on her own. Normally he wasn't keen to listen to the opposition's viewpoint, but he liked where she was going.

She reached up to straighten his tie, reminding him of the way she'd tugged him to her earlier. "I mean, obviously this . . . whatever this is"—she peered up at him from underneath her long lashes—"isn't going to go away."

He swallowed. "Interesting conclusion you've come to there." Obvious conclusion she'd come to. And by obvious, he meant the same as his own. And if fooling around was cool with her, then why was it again that he was against it?

Not a damn good reason came to mind. He put a hand on her waist and started to tug her closer when she halted him once again.

"I'm not saying there aren't things to discuss."

He dropped his hands to his side. "You're right. Very right." What the hell was it about this woman that made him lose all sense of control? Whatever it was, he was getting it back now. And this time, he meant it.

He motioned to the chair in front of his desk. "Please, sit."

"Ah, new chair. Nice. That was fast." He tried not to notice her blush as she sat.

Blake moved to take his seat on the other side of the desk. This was good. They could talk things over while they ate. The barrier of the desk in between them should serve as some protection from their raging hormones. He scooted a sandwich toward her, indicating his intentions.

Seeming to understand, she bent to pick up the sodas from the floor and handed him one. In silence they unwrapped their sandwiches. He watched as her mouth opened for her first bite. Too many wicked fantasies flashed in front of his eyes. He had to address this now.

Setting down his uneaten pastrami on rye, he leveled his gaze. "I should apologize. My behavior as your employer has been unseemly."

She paused mid-bite. "Yeah, you think?" Did she look pissed as she bit down for another mouthful?

Blake winced, fearing she meant that bite to look as menacing as it did.

Oh, well, he was going for it. "I don't plan to apologize, however. I thoroughly enjoyed everything that happened today. I hope you did, too."

With a chuckle, Andrea dabbed at the mustard on her lower lip. "Now, there's the Blake I know," she teased. She set her sandwich down. "I enjoyed it, too, if you really couldn't tell."

His heart skipped at her revelation. "I was hoping we could do that more often." Where in the blazes had that come from? That certainly hadn't been an option in the B-Zone. But now it was out there and he couldn't deny its truth. He held his breath.

"We could definitely do that more often."

He released it. Thank goodness. Now to revise the rest of his plan on the spot. Not a problem. He'd always been good at improvisation, hadn't he? Yes, he thought. "Let's discuss how this affects your position."

Andrea gasped, her eyes wide and Blake knew instantly that he'd somehow said the wrong thing. Maybe he wasn't so good at improv after all.

"Are you going to fire me?" A tight ball of dread and hurt and pure rage formed in Andy's chest. "You can't fire me. Not after that. Oh, my God, Blake. That's not even a little bit right. In fact it's a whole lot wrong. This was two-sided. You *and* me, Donovan. Got that? I'm sure there were company policies that have been violated by both of us, buster."

She took a quick breath ready to spout off more when she realized Blake was shaking his head at her, an amused expression on his face. "Oh. Then yeah, I guess we could talk."

Intending to give Blake her full attention, Andy relaxed

back into her seat. But then, as she tried not to wonder if this new chair was sturdier than the last, a whole slew of other thoughts followed. Dirty thoughts. Delicious thoughts. Squeeze-her-thighs-together-and-bite-her-lip-so-she-wouldn't-moan thoughts. And what exactly was wrong with those thoughts anyway? She'd already decided on her walk that she would have no regrets about what had happened. In fact, she unabashedly hoped what happened might happen again. And again. And again and again, even.

It wasn't completely an absurd idea. Blake had even suggested it himself the other day. It was why she'd shown up on his doorstep, and after she'd had time to think about it, it seemed the man felt bad about his reaction the night before. At least, she hoped that's what the flowers had been for and that she hadn't been on the receiving end of a pity screw.

No, that had definitely not been pity in his eyes. And he'd just admitted he'd enjoyed it.

Plus, she noted to herself, Blake having sex was an entirely different Blake. A Blake she needed to know more about. For work purposes, of course. He was generous and unselfish. He'd given her not one, but two amazing orgasms, and truthfully, there had been a time or two in Andy's past when she had considered that she might be frigid; two orgasms in the space of one session was mighty big news for her.

The sound of a throat being cleared brought Andy back to the present moment.

"Sorry." She felt her cheeks flushing. "Go ahead. Unless you'd like me to go first."

"No. I got this." Blake's brow creased, a frown playing on his lips. "I don't quite know how to put this without seeming, as you so eloquently put it, douchey." He actually looked nervous.

Jeez, if Blake is nervous about coming across poorly,

this is bound to be bad. "Shoot." She braced herself for where he might possibly go from there. If not fired, then what? Transferred out of the office? Oh, God, was this going to affect her performance review?

Or maybe, possibly . . . was he asking for this to be more? Was her job in jeopardy because Blake Donovan no longer needed a matchmaker? The idea sent goose bumps racing along her bare skin.

Blake scratched the back of his neck. "As I said, I would like to continue doing—this—with you, and I would also like you to continue working for me in your current capacity. I realize this is a cake-and-eat-it-too situation."

Andy swallowed hard against the knot of unreasonable disappointment in her throat. Besides the failed seduction attempt, this was what she had hoped for. String-free sex with the most gorgeous man she'd ever met in real life. Just what he needed to keep his raging libido in check while he dated the women she found him. Just what she'd wanted. She'd never even considered more with the man until . . . well, until about ten seconds before.

And *more* with that man was a ridiculous idea. Crazy. Insane.

It was just that now that she'd had sex with him, truly fantastic sex at that, she didn't know *what* she wanted. She wasn't sure she even wanted to know what she wanted. But if this was acceptable to him, to continue giving her orgasms while also keeping her on staff—so be it. She'd take it. And maybe she'd slow down on the matchmaking, though that really shouldn't be a factor in this internal debate. It was separate. That was her job, and this was . . . this was Blake.

She released the lip she'd been biting, put on a bright smile, and threw her shoulders back. "I accept."

"Excellent." He winked and the glint in his eyes made butterflies stir in her stomach. "There will have to be rules."

"Yes, rules." She nodded a little too enthusiastically. Then she stopped. "Such as?"

"No fooling around in the office." Blake considered a moment, his expression seeming as disappointed with his statement as she was. "Well, just not during office hours."

That was better. "But after work is okay." It wasn't a question.

He nodded. "And before."

"And lunchtime."

"And lunchtime." His eyes grazed her half-eaten sandwich before rising to meet hers and she knew he was thinking the same thing she was—namely, that it was at that very moment lunchtime.

She forced herself to look away, grabbing her soda for a long sip. Though she'd happily spend the rest of their lunch spread across his desk, there was more to discuss.

"I'm on birth control," she announced when she put her drink back down.

"Oh?" His eyes widened ever so slightly.

"But I'd still prefer we keep using condoms. Do you mind?" It wasn't only protection from STDs, but protection from becoming too intimate. So many walls had been removed, there needed to be some barrier between the two of them.

"Of course not. It's practical." He sounded a little disappointed.

For some reason, that made Andy happy. "Exactly." She crossed her legs and drummed her fingers on her thigh. "Is there anything else?"

Blake's eyes were pinned on the newly exposed skin of her leg. "Anything else? Oh. Yes. Nothing romantic. No candlelight dinners. No overnights."

It was her turn to feel disappointed, but he was right. It was the best way to keep this . . . what? *Businesslike* wasn't at all the right term. *Simple*, maybe. "No beds in general."

He narrowed his eyes. "No beds?"

"Do we need them?"

Blake laughed. "No, we do not."

While she was certain that he was calculating all the places that were not beds in their shared office, she took the moment to stick him with the big one. Her big rule. "And I hate to be old-fashioned about this, Blake, but I need to know you aren't sleeping with your dates. Not just because of the problems I've mentioned before, but it's simply not fair to me."

It looked like Blake was going to argue for a second, but he didn't. "No, that wouldn't be fair at all." He studied her for several seconds, and she thought that she'd give up her other Prada shoe to know what he was thinking.

Finally he shook his head once as if clearing whatever thought he was having from his mind and said, "That's why we're doing this, anyway. So that I can better focus on the candidates. Right?"

The butterflies from earlier fell with a thud at the bottom of her gut. "Right."

She lowered her eyes to her fingers and tried to swallow past the lump forming in her throat. Without a doubt, she knew that Blake was as into the sex as she'd been. That it wasn't simply because he thought it might better help him find a bride. But she also knew what admitting that would mean—it would mean exposing himself. It would mean letting yet another one of his masks down. Maybe that was something he simply couldn't bring himself to do.

With that thought, she felt she understood the man a little bit better. And okay, if that was how he had to be, that was fine. But she didn't have to. So she raised her eyes to his and said proudly, "Also, we're doing it because it's fun."

His smile could have lit a dark room. "Definitely because of that."

That was all he'd needed, it seemed. Reassurance from

her. Good thing she'd spoken honestly. But she still hadn't gotten an answer to her big rule. "So, you won't? Be sleeping with your dates?"

"I can promise that I will not be seducing any future dates, Ms. Dawson." The honesty in his voice threw her for a second.

"Thank you." She stood, gathering the remains of her sandwich and her drink and headed to her desk. "Now, shall we go over potentials for next week and finalize this weekend's dates?" She sat in her chair and went decisively back to her work, suddenly anxious for the familiarity of it. She picked up a pencil.

"One moment. This conversation isn't over yet." She swiveled back. He was staring at her with the same deadly serious look he'd had earlier. *What now?*

"Your position has changed. We need to discuss your pay rate changing to reflect that." The pencil snapped in two. Just one sentence; that was all it took to turn the delicious postcoital haze into a blind red rage.

"You want to *pay* me to have sex with you?" *Last chance to dig yourself out of this hole, Donovan.*

"That sounds rather ugly, Andrea. I simply want to maintain fairness in acknowledging that you have new duties, which I do not expect to be performed gratis." She threw the pieces of pencil to the floor, deliberately, one by one.

"Ugly? Duties? *Performed gratis*?" She began advancing toward his desk. His eyes were widening with the sudden knowledge that he had really said something wrong. Good.

"Again, I feel this isn't coming out quite the way I had intended . . ." His eyes darted around, looking for an escape route. Andy continued, one step at a time.

"You mean, you didn't *intend* to call me a prostitute? Because that just happened." She was keeping her voice low and menacing, and it was working. As she stalked toward him, rounding one side of his enormous desk, his chair went sliding away from her.

"Come, now, Drea, you know that isn't what I meant." He was chuckling nervously. She rounded one corner of the desk, and his chair disappeared behind another. The soreness between her legs was reflecting the ache in her chest.

Honestly, Andy's feelings had just gotten hurt, big time. That was one of the meanest things anyone had ever said to her, and she'd worked for Max Ellis, for Pete's sake. If she were being honest, she'd say it hurt so badly because Blake was someone she was starting to care about, whereas Ellis had never mattered to her. Screw honesty, though. It was much easier to give in to her anger and cover up the hurt.

"I think you meant exactly what you said. And I also think I really missed an opportunity earlier to show you exactly how much I meant it when I told you not to cross me." She leaned over the desk to brandish his beloved Montblanc in his stupid inside-ugly face before stuffing it down her cleavage. She was fairly certain he wouldn't go after it there. Lunchtime was over. No fooling around during office hours after all.

"Andrea. Please. We can discuss this. May I have my pen back?" A note of desperation had crept into his voice. It gratified her just a little.

"I don't want to discuss anything with you, Mr. Donovan. I want a sincere apology." They stared at each other for a few moments. The silent game of chicken ended incredibly quickly when Blake stood up and strode to her. His hands gripped her upper arms as his eyes blazed into hers.

"I *am* sorry. I never meant to make you feel cheap, or bought in any way. I don't know what I'm doing here. I don't know how to talk to you. All I know is that what just hap-

pened meant something to me. It even means more than my
pen. I think. No, I know it does. I just don't really understand how we proceed from here."

That total butthole.

Now she couldn't be mad even if she tried. How did he
do that? It wasn't fair at all. Just because he "never
apologized"—suddenly when he did, she got "weak in the
knees" like a swoony romance heroine. She wanted to
scream. *Who wants to be a romance heroine?*

Still, his sincerity was undeniable, and so was his
scrumptious scent. She pulled the pen out of her boobs.
"Look. I appreciate your apology. Even though I'm not
totally ready to forgive you. Us having sex? That isn't
work, that isn't my job. That's because we just had really
good sex, and if it helps you behave on dates, even better.
There will be no change in my pay, because I am not a
whore. Got it?"

He stared into her eyes for a bit longer than necessary.
Again. That seemed to happen between them.

"Understood." He released her arms, which immediately grew cold without his touch. "Now, you said you had
things to show me?"

"I do. Here's your dumb pen." She stomped away from
him, easy to do in her sneakers, and sat in her seat. "Slide
your chair this way, will you? We're working from my desk
today."

She waited until he was sitting across from her before
she pointed at him with the end of her Bic pen. "I'm still
charging you for a new pair of Prada heels, by the way."
She let that sink in. "So, with Lia, I think there might be
a couple of issues, but she's prettier than Alice . . ."

They started flipping through the stack of folders on her
desk, both of them studiously ignoring any topic that
hinted at their earlier frolicking or the conversation that followed. Andy stopped on one particular girl, an attractive

brunette with the unfortunate name of Gertrude. She studied the profile for the umpteenth time—this chick was great, but the name combined with "celeb blogging" listed as a hobby made Andy unsure.

A prickle on her neck made her glance up. Blake was staring at her. She gave him a smile. He grinned back.

Oh, yeah, nothing was going to be the same now.

Chapter Thirteen

"You did *what*."

Andy knew that when Lacy's questions began to sound like statements, things were not going well. If she wasn't in such a good mood, Andy would be irritated by the chastising that was likely about to commence.

But she *was* in a good mood. A very good mood. So she let her sister continue.

And continue Lacy did. "After he turned you down last night? You went ahead and fucked him today?"

Andy cringed at Lacy's vulgar choice of words. Then she lost the cringe because *fucking* was exactly what she and Blake had done.

And it had been awesome.

"Am I the only one who remembers you crying yourself to sleep after that one? He humiliated you. He forced you to practically beg for him. This wasn't a seduction. It was creepy and weird and I don't like it." Lacy was not letting the matter go as easily as Andy had hoped.

"He apologized, I told you." Maybe there was good reason for her sister to worry. It had been less than twenty-four hours since the horrible failed seduction. Things had changed *so* quickly. But they'd changed for the better. Couldn't Lacy see that?

"Look, it's fine," Andy insisted. "We made rules and stuff." She topped off her sister's wine up. *So nice to be able to afford wine again for moments like these.*

"You made rules. Rules. And stuff. Did one include not treating you like a scorned escort, by chance? Rules. Yeah."

More statements that were really questions. Andy wasn't sure how to respond so she merely nodded.

"You're going to do it again, then." Lacy's eyes were narrowed over the rim of her mason jar as she promptly gulped down everything Andy had poured.

"We're going to do it again," she confirmed. "But never in a bed, no sleepovers, nothing like that. It's *fine*, sis." She did feel a tiny bit sorry for causing the concerned look on Lacy's face. That was concern, right? Or was it criticism?

"No beds. You just made rules to govern your boss's hideous sex addiction. After he treats you like trash he deigns to eventually pick up."

Criticism it was, then. Andy sighed.

"So you can bang, where? In bathrooms? In, like, the office?" A few drops of wine sloshed over as Lacy slammed her jar down on the table. She wiped them up with her finger and licked it. Clearly, Lacy wasn't yet used to being able to afford the wine.

"We don't bang in bathrooms. But that wasn't a rule." Which meant they *could* bang in bathrooms, if they decided they wanted to. Maybe tomorrow . . .

She decided she should rummage for snacks to go with their alcohol, before Lacy accidentally got too liquored up in her fury. Andy was only trying to take the edge off with all the refills, not get her drunk. Although it had worked before to calm her sister down. She poured a bit more, in case that would recur.

"So you *are* having sex in the office? You sicko!" Lacy's voice rose in equal measure to the blazing in her eyes. "Can you even *help* but self-sabotage every opportunity that comes your way? This was a good one. It's a temp job. It gives you a prestigious reference. You're even making decent money for the first time in almost a year. But that isn't enough for you?" She grabbed a handful of the chips Andy had pulled out and crunched angrily.

"It's not that it isn't enough for me. It isn't tha—" Andy began to rebut.

"Oh, my God." Lacy covered her mouth to finish chewing, eyes wide. "You don't think you deserve this. That's why you're ruining it. You poor thing. How did I not see it before? Your self-esteem is shot, so you no longer even recognize your own potential. Honey, I'm so sorry."

She stood and wrapped her long arms around Andy before continuing her consolation. "We need to look at your benefits package. Many employers offer counseling as part of a standard package these days. The stigma that used to be attached to depression really isn't there anymore. He humiliated you, and you didn't have the strength not to crawl back. It's like a country song. Why are you laughing? Dear God, are you bipolar now?"

Andy couldn't hold in her giggles any longer at her sister's complete misreading. The protectiveness Lacy always inexplicably had for her older sister was almost condescending—and way off the mark. "I'm sorry—you're being so sweet—but that's not it, either."

Lacy smiled in a way that was both sympathetic and disapproving. "I'm not convinced. It's the only way to explain your sudden fit of insanity."

Andy shook her head. Of course her sister would jump to the insanity excuse. Admittedly, the arrangement with Blake did seem a bit crazy. Or at the very least, unorthodox.

Andy would never have gone for something like that with
Max. The differences between Blake and Max, though—
well, so maybe they did share a lot of the same surface
attributes. Not looks. Blake was infinitely more attractive
than Max Ellis could ever hope to be. More than that,
Blake's inside-ugly wasn't so ugly once she'd gotten to
understand it. It was charming, in fact. Adorable, even.
Just sort of unexplainable.

After eight years of getting to know Max, however,
Andy knew his insides were still as ugly as ugly got.

The fact of the matter was that whether the situation was
strange or not, it made Andy happy. It also made her job
easier.

Perhaps it was too much to ask Lacy to understand.
"Look. Maybe I shouldn't have told you, but I tell you
everything. Please try not to be so judgey." She offered
the chips again.

After a long moment, Lacy took a few and leaned back.
"I'll listen. Doesn't mean I'll agree."

"Fair enough. What it comes down to is that I think I
was right. After we, um, did it—shut up! I don't like saying sex words." She waved a hand at Lacy's snorting.
"After it happened, he really calmed down a lot. We had a
nice talk, shared our lunch break, and he seemed to truly
relax for the first time around me. It was like I could see
someone other than Blake Douche-ovan in there."

"Douche-ovan. That's funny." Lacy was definitely mel-
lowing.

"If it's a reflection of my self-esteem at all, that should
look pretty good right now, because my theory is being
proven correct." Andy grabbed a chip for herself.

"Okay, I'll reserve my judgment for the time being. But
we are hardly through discussing it. It's possible I've had
a bit too much wine to think this through properly." She
looked at the bottle, where it stood, empty, next to Andy's

full glass. "Did you do that on purpose? Did you just get me drunk so I'd stop arguing?"

"Psych One Oh One, yo." Andy shrugged at her and took her first sip of wine. It was tasty. Her one evening as a bartender had really paid off; the quality of juice she was bringing home would no longer horrify Lacy's fancier dinner party guests.

"You're good. I forget that sometimes. Now, shall we get down to business?" Her little sister leaned across the table. "How was the sex? Don't spare any of the details. I'm living vicariously through you now."

Andy blushed. "It was good. I liked it."

"Good? You liked it? That tells me absolutely nothing. Did you . . . ? Did he give you an orgasm at least?"

Even if she were comfortable with talking about the details of a sexual tryst, Andy had a feeling she still wouldn't share more with her sister. This thing with Blake—maybe it wasn't really much of a *thing* at all, but whatever it was, it was hers. It was private.

She flashed a tight-lipped grin. "I'm taking a shower. You can finish my drink." She pushed her chair back and headed off against Lacy's protests.

"This is so not the end of this!" was the last thing Andy heard as she closed the door and leaned back against it. She allowed herself one silent squeal and wiggle before pushing the thrill of the afternoon down again.

I cannot believe we actually did it!

I can't believe we've done it, like, seven times already!

She did a mental count: the first time, of course, and then the time against the wall, the time behind his desk, the time *under* his desk, the time with the tie—a personal favorite—then the time they re-created the time with the tie, and the time with the lamp stand. She still couldn't believe she'd done that last one.

Or, wait, was it eight times?

She could never decide if the stairwell counted or not. It probably did count. She'd finished, but poor Blake hadn't gotten a chance before the sound of an open door from the floor above them had interrupted their coitus. He'd quickly tucked himself away, just in time for his head of foreign developments to pass them. Andy was still impressed how well Blake had managed the ensuing conversation about some contract snag as if he hadn't just been whispering obscenities into her ear. The two men shook hands at the end of their encounter. If only the employee knew where his employer's hand had just been . . .

It was nine times! How could she have forgotten the time when she'd played naughty secretary? He certainly seemed to like their sex to be a little bit raunchy. So did she, she'd realized with a surprise. Funny, though, there was very little submissiveness that took place on her part. She wondered—when Blake found the type of woman he'd been searching for, would he actually enjoy that type in the bedroom?

Well, that wasn't really any of her concern. If he did find a match that didn't quite live up, he could always look back fondly on his affair with Andy. She knew she would.

Andy glanced over at Blake now as he ordered their lunch. She looked away as he caught her eye, ridiculously concerned that he could read her mind somehow. Although the blush creeping up her face could have given it away.

"You *do* like uni, yes?" he verified and continued to race through the menu with their server. Andy wasn't actually sure if she liked uni, but she wasn't about to tell Blake that her sushi experience was limited to the items that cost a buck apiece during happy hour. She would bet money that Mr. Fancypants had never downed sake-bombs at two in the afternoon on a Tuesday.

Although if the sex wasn't enough to pull him out of

his shell, surely that would. She made a mental note to keep that idea on hold in case of an emergency.

Date emergency? What a ridiculous job.

On the subject of dates . . . "You have a dinner date tonight," she reminded both Blake and herself once the waiter had bowed and left them with hot hand towels. The candidate was one that Andy felt particularly hopeful about.

"Yes, yes. Eve." He delicately dabbed the towel on his strong hands. It was a dichotomy that made her smile, how he dwarfed everything around him, and yet understood fragility. Well, everywhere but the name issue, that is.

"Jane." She grabbed a towel for herself and rubbed her fingertips decidedly less elegantly than her lunch partner.

"Oh, come on, I was close this time." He flung his towel at her.

"Blake!" Andy was shocked at his breach of decorum. "You weren't even remotely close, either."

"Oh, you know, Dick and Jane, Adam and Eve. I had one half of a famous couple. It was close." He caught the towel she tossed back in midair.

"Pssh. Agree to disagree. Do you remember anything about her?" She loved the easy way he spoke when they weren't in work mode, as if they were actually friends. She relished it, but it pained her at the same time. She'd noticed that enjoying something often gave her the same feeling in her chest as missing it, as if she were always waiting for it to end.

And this—this definitely had an expiration date.

"Of course I do. She's a graduate from NYU in something uninteresting. Oh, yes. Music. She plays the harp. And she enjoys causes. Causes I approved of and not the stupid ones."

She shook her head at the *causes I approved of* remark, remembering how Blake had made her research Jane Osborne's charitable interests before setting up the date.

Also, she was glad that Blake did indeed remember things they'd gone over, even if he couldn't get a name right.

"*Jane* Osborne." He grinned, pleased with himself.

"How come you can remember her last name, but not anybody's first?" She grinned back despite herself. Maybe it wouldn't end. Maybe once he'd found his wife, they could transition to something platonic.

Though that felt weird to think about. And awkward. How could she be friends with a woman after she'd both banged her husband and arranged their marriage? Yes, there was definitely an expiration date, and not one she wanted to think too hard about.

"I don't know. I've always been able to remember surnames. It works in business, because you can use a man's last name, and the occasional woman's, and it's a mark of respect and affection, depending on the circumstance. I rarely find myself needing first names."

See, we could be great friends. Maybe his wife never had to know.

"What about your secretary?" She'd heard him use her name before, hadn't she? Come to think of it, Andy couldn't remember the woman's name herself.

Blake leaned in confidentially. "I only hire secretaries named Sarah. Don't you dare tell a soul. It's a common enough name that I can always find one qualified."

"You are *awful*," she breathed, impressed despite her words to the contrary.

"Awful, am I?" Blake sat back, a smug expression overtaking his features. "I didn't hear you complaining earlier."

"Because you were shouting *my* name."

He laughed, his eyes twinkling in that way that always made Andy have to cross her legs. "Was that what I was saying? Honestly, I think I lost consciousness for a minute there at the end."

"It was what you were saying. Over and over." Thinking about it now sent a shiver down her spine. "I think there were some *Oh, God*s and *Don't stop*s thrown in, but mostly it was my name." She was thrilled with herself for discussing their intimacy without blushing and ducking.

Well, it had been *Drea* he'd been shouting, but that counted, didn't it? Actually, now that she thought about it, and now that she understood how infrequently Blake addressed people correctly, the nickname he'd given her didn't seem quite so demeaning. It was even sort of . . . sweet.

Hmm. Blake—sweet. That was certainly never an adjective she'd thought she'd add to his character profile. Funny how initial perceptions could be so wrong once you got to know a person. Apparently even for someone who was supposed to be especially good at initial perceptions.

The waiter returned then bearing steaming bowls of miso and interrupting Andy's moment of reflection. He set one in front of each of them. "Careful, please," he warned in his choppy English. "Soup very hot."

He bowed again before leaving.

"Blake, wait a min—" Andy began when he reached for his bowl.

But she was too late. "I burned my tongue," he complained after his first slurp.

"If you had waited for a minute, it wouldn't have happened," she scolded him before blowing across her own bowl.

"I didn't want to wait." His tone had deepened, and she looked up. "I understand the principle behind delayed gratification and all, but sometimes, you have to take what you want when you want it." His eyes were dark, and she didn't think he was talking about the soup anymore.

Experimentally, she kicked off a shoe beneath the table and slowly ran her foot along his.

He didn't respond.

She moved higher, over his calf and onto his thigh. Besides a narrowing of his eyes, nothing. Her toes reached the spot between his legs and verified his arousal as he gasped.

It was Blake who quickly summoned the waiter back. "We'll take that sushi to go, please."

Chapter Fourteen

Blake couldn't stop his foot from tapping as he rode the elevator carrying the to-go order of sushi. It had been Andrea's idea to come and go separately when they dined together as to not give the wrong impression to his other employees about their relationship. Or, rather, the right impression. Besides the fact that it wasn't anyone's business, managers weren't allowed to date their subordinates. Though dating wasn't what he and Andrea were doing. Did the fraternization policy contain any wording regarding *banging*? He'd have to check.

Regardless, Blake approved of the separate entrances, but why was he the one who always had to go up last? And how did he end up carrying the food every time? He supposed it was appropriately chivalrous to attend to the baggage. The delayed arrival, however, proved to be . . . uncomfortable . . . on more than one occasion. Like when Andrea had gotten him thoroughly aroused before leaving for her trip upstairs. Like now.

Maybe it was a good thing he was carrying the food after all.

When the elevator finally stopped on his floor, Blake had to work not to run to his office. That didn't mean he didn't have a bit of gusto to his step. Especially as he got closer and saw that his door was closed. Andrea always worked with it open. What was she doing in there? Naughty things? Was she waiting for him, perhaps, undressed, spread out on top of the lateral file cabinets?

Whoops. He shouldn't have imagined that. Now his stride slowed due to, well, necessity.

Blake was so focused on his destination that he didn't notice the man sitting in his waiting room until he'd reached his office door.

"Excuse me?" The man leaped up from his chair. "Mr. Donovan, I need to speak with you, please."

Blake furrowed his brow as he tested the door handle. It was locked. His pulse picked up. Andrea indeed had to be planning something.

"Mr. Donovan?"

Blake threw a glance over his shoulder. "I'm sorry. I'm unavailable at the moment. Schedule something with my secretary." He shuffled the lunch orders in an attempt to dig in his pocket for his keys.

"Your secretary appears to be out for lunch," the man said.

Of course she was. Dammit. No, it was a good thing Sarah was at lunch since Andrea tended to get a little loud. He loved that.

"Mr. Donovan?"

Oh, yes. There was someone speaking to him. He gave another look at the bothersome fellow. It was an employee of his, he realized now. A manager in his project development department. Something or other Jennings. Bruce? No, that was the famous amputee cyclist. Or was that Bruce Jenner? He always mixed the two up. It wasn't Bruce anyway. Something like that, though.

Whatever his first name was, Jennings had been in his office only a few weeks before to try to convince Blake to give a promotion to one of his team members. It had already been in the works, but still had yet to go through. That was surely why he was here now.

"Jennings, the paperwork has been submitted for Fullman. She'll get her promotion soon enough." Blake turned back to inserting his key into the door handle.

"That's just it, Mr. Donovan." *Was Jennings always this pesky?* "I'd like to revoke my recommendation. May I come in and talk to you about this?"

Hell, no. Except he didn't have any excuse. He'd have to improvise. "Later. Right now my sushi's getting cold." He cringed. Sushi didn't get cold. God, what an awful ad lib. "I mean . . ." But he couldn't think of anything else to say. Too much blood flowing to the wrong part of his body.

"It's really important," Jennings pleaded. "Just a few minutes of your time is all I need."

Blake cursed under his breath. "Very well." He turned and set the takeout on his secretary's desk. "Talk."

Jennings looked at him skeptically. "Out here? I really think this would be best discussed in your office. In private."

In private. That's exactly where Blake wanted to be at the moment. Only he wanted to be in private with Andrea Dawson, not no-name Jennings.

Brad!

That was his name. From the expression on his face, Brad Jennings wasn't leaving until they got this over with. With a sigh, Blake opened his office door slightly and said in an overly loud voice so that Andrea would hear him, "Of course we can meet in my office. We'll go right in." He paused to give her an extra moment to scramble into her clothes if need be. Blake tried not to groan at the missed opportunity.

When he'd delayed as long as he could without seeming like he'd gone completely bananas, he pushed the door open the rest of the way and cautiously stepped in. To his surprise, the room was empty.

Well. That was a concern he needn't have worried about. But if Andrea wasn't here, where had she gone?

It wasn't the time to wonder. Blake gestured to Jennings to take a seat then shut the door behind them before he circled his desk to sit in his chair. "Now you say you want to revoke your recommendation for Fullman's promotion?" Honestly, Blake was surprised by the request. Jennings had been quite enthusiastic about his endorsement a few weeks before.

Jennings cleared his throat. "Yes, sir. Ms. Fullman is not pulling her weight. She's always late, when she comes in at all. She's distracted and unfocused. Todd, Jerry, Susan, Aaron—all of us are left to clean up her mess."

Movement across the room pulled Blake's attention. As nonchalantly as he could, he peered over Jennings's shoulder toward Andrea's area. And there she was, her head popping up over the edge of the desk from where she was hiding on the floor behind it.

On the floor behind the desk . . . they hadn't done that yet, had they?

"Does she even have approval for all this missed work?"

Blake's eyes darted back to Jennings. He blinked, trying to remember the question he'd just been asked. Oh, yes. "She does have approval for time off. I can't discuss that with you, though, of course." Fullman, he'd only now remembered, had been dealing with a mentally unsound ex-husband. She'd refused the leave of absence Blake had offered her, wanting to keep a semblance of normalcy in her life. But even though she'd been tardy and absent more than usual, he hadn't noticed any decline in the quality of her work. Was there something he was missing?

If there was, he didn't have any idea what it would be. Andrea, on the other hand, was missing three of her buttons. As in, her shirt was practically wide open, and he could see it clearly since she was now standing behind her desk. She *had* been waiting in some form of undress then. *My, oh, my.*

"No, I don't expect you to tell me what's going on with her private life"—Jennings's tone was terse—"but she shouldn't be given a promotion. Not when . . ."

Jennings kept talking, but Blake's complete attention was on Andrea. What on earth was she doing? She should stay hidden behind the desk. Or if she was trying to sneak out, she at least should be properly clothed. He wiggled his fingers in front of his own shirt, hoping she'd understand the gesture.

She did.

Jennings, however, did not. "What's that? Did you want me to keep going?"

"Yes, yes. Please." He wiggled his fingers again pretending that's exactly what he'd meant by the action the first time he'd done it.

While Jennings continued his complaint, Blake watched as Andrea tiptoed across the room to the office door. Her hand settled on the knob and Blake tensed hoping her escape was silent.

It wasn't.

Actually, what Andrea did was not try to escape at all. She opened the door, loudly, then hurried to the other side of the door so that by the time that Jennings looked toward the noise, it appeared as if she were entering, not exiting.

Blake covered his eye with one hand. Whatever she was up to, he was sure to be unimpressed.

"Mr. Donovan, I apologize. I didn't know you had company." Her voice was sweeter and higher-pitched than usual. "And I hate to bother you, but I really need to speak with you."

Blake forced a smile. "Ms. Dawson, I'm in the mid—"

"Now, Mr. Donovan." Now, that was the bossy tone he was used to. She seemed to remember herself and added a lighter, "please."

Obviously, Andrea had something to say.

Blake stood. "Excuse me one moment, Jennings. My, um . . ." He was too flustered to remember what title he'd given his matchmaker. "*She* needs to talk to me."

He hurried out after Andrea, expecting that she was upset about the interruption in their lunchtime plans. "I'm sorry, Drea, I'm disappointed, too," he said in a hushed tone when he reached her. "I'll get rid of him as soon as possible."

She shook her head. "That's not what I needed to tell you. I mean, yes, I'm disappointed, but I have something to say about that guy."

Blake looked back to the man he'd left in his office. "Jennings?" What could Andrea possibly know about him? She hadn't been present the last time the employee had come to his office, and Jennings's office was on a whole other floor.

"Yes. Jennings. He's making that stuff up about Fullman."

It was only because he suspected the same thing that he pursued Andrea's suggestion. "Why do you say that?"

"He likes her. Like, really likes her. My guess is that he recommended her for promotion thinking that would earn him favor in her eyes, but even after that she still refused to go out with him."

"No, that's not possible. He's a manager. He can't date an employee. It's against the rules."

She glared at him incredulously. "Uh-huh. And everyone follows those rules."

There was that.

"Anyway, when she turned him down he got all butt-hurt. She rejected him. He didn't like it. And this is his retaliation."

Well that was an interesting theory. A theory that might make sense. Only how could Andrea possibly know that? He asked her.

"Easy. He only referred to her by last name, while he used first names with the other employees. He's trying to distance himself from her. If he said her name, he'd probably get all shifty and nervous. What did he call her when he was in last time?"

Blake tried to recall. "Not Fullman. He must have called her by her first name. I don't remember what it was."

"Of course you don't." She winked at him.

God, she was sexy when she did that.

"Also, he's not wearing an orange tie." She must have seen that as they'd walked in. "Yes, before you protest, I know that no one wears orange but me. But that guy normally does. Like, every day when I see him at the coffee stand. He's rejecting orange now, which is usually a sign of sexual oppression. And he clicks his jaw. Another clear indicator."

"You could hear that from across the room?" He had to be careful about what he muttered under his breath.

"How could I not? It was so *loud*." She shuddered as if the sound was also an unpleasant one. "Finally, he clears his throat a lot when talking about her. So obvious that he has an emotional involvement."

Blake almost choked. Is that what she thought when he cleared his throat around her? That was a ridiculous analysis. Wasn't it? Though for Jennings, it did possibly fit. Only one way to know for sure.

Careful not to clear his throat, he said, "Thank you, Andrea. I'll take your input to heart."

He shut the door with Andrea on the opposite side of it this time, and returned to his desk. "I apologize for that." He looked his employee in the eye. "Before we get back to Fullman—what's her first name again?"

Jennings shifted uncomfortably in his chair. "Uh, Ashley."

Was that a bead of sweat above Jennings's brow? He'd daresay it was. Hmm. "You know, Jennings, that there are some people here who don't take some of the office rules to heart. Like the fraternization policy. Some employees date anyway." Did he sound guilty when he said that? He didn't let himself dwell on it. "I've fired one or two people over the years for exactly that type of violation." He hadn't, but there was nothing wrong with a good bluff.

Jennings's eyes fell to the floor.

Yes, Blake had to agree that this was definitely a case of infatuation. Andrea had nailed that analysis.

Huh.

Was this what Andrea's skills were really about? It was amazing how she could discern so much with so little to go on. He hated to admit it, but her abilities were wasted in her current position. After she was done with the matchmaking thing, perhaps he could find a better placement for her in the company. Somewhere she could use her skills to keep harmony within the company. In human resources, maybe.

Meanwhile, he still had the Jennings situation to wrap up. "There are other employees who are mindful of these policies. I would imagine that what might seem like a rejection to one person might actually be another person's attempt to follow the rules. Keep their job." There. That ought to ease the sting. Not that Blake cared much about Jennings's feelings, but he was a good employee, as was Fullman, and Blake wanted the situation over with. "That makes sense, doesn't it?"

"Yes, sir." Jennings clicked his jaw—oh, there it was! Andrea was right; it was loud.

"Now back to Fullman, are you really interested in pulling her promotion for review?"

Jennings shook his head. "No, actually. Now that I think about it, she's not that bad. She's great even." He stood. "I guess I was just having a bad day. Needed to vent."

Blake followed to his feet. "Understandable. We all have them." He walked his employee to the door and opened it for him.

Jennings nodded once. "Thank you, Mr. Donovan. Sorry your sushi got cold."

Blake stared at the floor and pinched the bridge of his nose. *Cold sushi.* Really.

"Did someone say something about cold sushi?" Andrea stood in the door frame, her hands full with the take-out bags from earlier, her expression amused.

God, she really was incredible. In a work sense, of course. How she'd completely saved him in that situation. And in a naked sense. She was incredible that way, too.

Andrea kicked the door shut behind her with her foot, set the bags on the floor, and began unbuttoning her shirt. "Then we'd better do something to warm it up, hadn't we?"

Blake had always thought uni was best served at room temperature. He had a feeling he was about to find out he'd been wrong.

Andy could not have been more pleased with herself. Keeping Blake on his toes was becoming more and more enjoyable, albeit more and more difficult. This afternoon's sushi extravaganza was a new high for her, one she was about to beat.

"Blake? Would you meet me in Conference Room Four in half an hour, please? Sarah has cleared your schedule." She used her most innocent tone. There was no way he'd agree to this, if he'd known what she was planning, but that was kind of the point. She was going to prove to Lacy and Blake both that she could still rock this job no matter what was happening in bed. On desk. Whatever.

Once she'd gotten a distracted nod from her boss, she retreated to Four to organize everything. There were sodas, tea, coffee, cookies; what was she missing? Wine. She knew Blake would make judgments based upon it. Far be it from her to keep Blake's beloved judgeys from him. She pressed the intercom and asked Sarah for a couple of bottles.

One by one, girls streamed into the room. Andy had jacked this idea from a TV show, but it seemed like an awfully good one. Gather twenty girls in one location, arrange for Blake to spend a few moments with each of them. Yes, it was a cattle call, but it would save her so many interviews. At the same time, it would give her a lot more to work on, vetting multiple candidates at once, instead of the usual one-at-a-time, no-my-boss-isn't-a-serial-killer thing.

One by one, girls walked in. Exotic girls—Mexican, Thai, a stray Scot. All-American girls, from California and Texas and Virginia. Anyone and everyone whom Blake might consider a potential spouse streamed through the doors and helped themselves to one drink or another. When he himself finally walked in, a hush fell over the girls.

It was nothing compared with the pale hush over his face. This was clearly the last thing he had expected. Andy stifled her squee. It was so fun to see him unbalanced.

"Ladies, this is Blake Donovan. Please line up quietly by the door, he'll receive you one at a time by the drink station. You will have only two minutes apiece. I understand that's not long, but do your best to impress him with what you have. Ready . . . Go!" She hopped up to sit on a folding table, whipped out her notebook, and enjoyed the show.

To his credit, he managed to resist more than one fierce
side-eye in her direction as the girls crowded around
him. Despite her words, the girls were neither quiet nor
orderly. The ones who'd been into the wine were, predict-
ably, shoving for a spot by the front. A frighteningly serious-
looking brunette managed to land the first position. She
had delivered an impressive elbow to a competitor while
beaming at Blake the whole time. "I'm Kristal Gilderoy,"
she announced, as though he should be impressed. Blake
stared at her silently until Andy kicked him. Her perch on
the tabletop put her toe just at his shin, something she
planned to take advantage of to keep him on his manners.

"Blake Donovan. Tell me a bit about yourself, Kristal."
Andy smiled and started scribbling in her notebook. *Feath-
ered bangs—not fashionable, even I know that. Doesn't
read celeb/gossip rags, clearly. Possibility here.*

"I'm sure you're kidding . . . But I'll play along . . . I'm
an indie musician . . . Very successful, I owe it all to my
fans . . . The only problem I have with them is that they
always want more of me . . ."

*She actually speaks in ellipses. I can actually hear the
dot dot dots. And I know her music. It's quite awful. I think
Lacy called her a nemesis one time. No possibility.*

"Thank you, Ms. Gilderoy. Next, please!" Andy chirped.
The girl looked disgruntled and opened her mouth to protest, but the recipient of her elbow jab gave her a shove and
launched into her own spiel.

"Mr. Donovan, I am so, so, *so* freaking excited to meet
you. I've been following your career. I've noticed a few
things, though, that you are doing all wrong. Don't worry,
I'm capable of handling that for you. Did I mention I'm a
lawyer? I am. And I am ready to go to war for you, both
professionally and—personally, if you know what I mean."

Andy didn't bother to write down what she was thinking, namely *thick-browed pompous weirdo.* She merely

looked at the woman's name tag and told Ms. Kernal they'd be in touch shortly. Luckily, those two were the worst of the bunch. By the time the numbers dwindled to four, Blake was chatting informally with all of them.

Andy already knew the raven-haired Ukrainian girl had it in the bag, but she really appreciated the way Blake was loosening up. Look at him, chatting to the Scottish girl she'd only included because she secretly hoped they could become friends.

Fiona was redheaded, intelligent, educated, and goofy. Just Andy's type. She was glad Blake was being nice to Fiona. That way when Andy called Fiona to let her down, there'd be no hard feelings. Andy could casually invite Fiona for coffee or something. She was so busy being pleased with herself that it took a moment to notice Blake himself was dismissing the ladies.

"This has truly been an unexpected pleasure. Andrea should be contacting you all shortly. Thank you again for making time in your day for this." He began to walk toward the door, smoothly hooking his arm through Andy's. It pulled her off the table and propelled her toward the door before she'd even had a chance to thank the candidates herself.

"Are you going to kill me?" she hissed through a grin over her shoulder.

"You know, Andrea, I don't believe I will."

"Really?" Andy immediately suspected a trick. "Why not? I totally freaked you out with that. I know I did. Your face was epic."

"It probably was, wasn't it." He smiled down at her as they rounded the corner and headed back into his office. "But I had a nice time. There was one girl I would certainly entertain the idea of a date with."

"I'll call Natasha," she said.

At the same time Blake said, "Please call Fiona." Andy gaped.

"But—she's not your type. Not even by a long shot. Are you sure?"

"I'm sure. Maybe you don't know my type as well as you think." With this, the man actually winked at her, and left her openmouthed as he grabbed his notebook and headed off to another meeting.

Chapter Fifteen

As Blake rattled on about his prior evening's date, Andy doodled on her notepad and internally debated whom to set Blake up with next. She'd stopped listening to his morning reports days ago, right around the same time that they'd started their new arrangement, which she considered purely coincidental. It was always the same thing—everything went horribly, the woman was all wrong, yada yada yada.

So instead of actually paying attention, she nodded and mentally went through her options of who to set him up with next. Who had it been last night? That Jane girl. Right. Cross her off. Blake had suggested that Fiona girl, but Andy was still certain Natasha would be better for him. And did she really want him to ruin any friendship she might be able to strike up with the redhead? No, she did not. Natasha it was.

Blake cleared his throat, the sign that he was wrapping up. "So all in all, it was a fairly decent evening."

Andy looked up from the row of *Doctor Who* Daleks she'd drawn. Did Blake say he'd had a decent evening? She must have heard wrong.

Except she hadn't heard wrong. Because then he said, "It was pleasant, even. I believe I will have you set up a second date with Ms. Osborne." He smiled blandly across their desks, as if everything was normal. As if he said this every day. As if she wasn't having a minor heart attack.

But then she was smiling blandly back and agreeing, as if this was just the outcome she had hoped for. And it was, wasn't it? She wanted Blake to see a woman more than once. That was the desired outcome of her job. It was the goal.

Yet this was the first time it had happened. The first time he'd said the words *second date*, and something about that bothered her to no end. For God's sake, they'd just had a naked sushi lunch the day before. Or nearly naked—they'd yet to have disposed of all their clothes while doing it, which would have given their trysts an extra layer of sensuality. As if they needed that. Andy had never in her life thought to find herself sprawled across the expanse of mahogany as her boss used his wickedly talented mouth to remove one slice of nigiri at a time from the exposed parts of her body. How on earth did someone so straitlaced bring out such naughtiness in her?

She'd never again think of sushi without recalling the sensual feel of pickled ginger on her belly button. The delicious coolness of each grain of rice she swore she could feel individually against her hypersensitive skin . . .

She was starting to get wet at the memory when he spoke and she came crashing down to earth. "What do you think we should do this time?"

Oh, yes. The second date. She stifled the harrumph that threatened to sound from her throat and pretended to consider. *A freaking second date. Really?*

She'd been okay yesterday when they'd parted after work—Blake off to meet Jane Osborne, Andy off to watch bad broadcast television on her sofa while she ate a dinner that came on a microwavable tray. It was a drab evening for her, but she'd been fine. She'd also been pretending that Blake would detest his dinner like he had every other time Andy had set him up with a new candidate. If she'd known he was actually enjoying himself, she would have been good and worked up about it last night, too.

"I think a play, perhaps, would be good. Do people still go to plays?"

She went to plays. She liked plays. She'd even considered theater as a major at one point.

She could not, though, possibly consider Blake at the theater with a woman who was a second date. No way. No how.

"No one goes to plays." She smiled sweetly. "How about a movie?" *If they can't talk, or see each other, it's basically a non-date.*

How is this even happening right now? A second date?

There was zero reason for her to have this reaction. Just because she'd begun a sexual relationship with the guy did not mean she got to be upset about this. They'd worked toward this. Together. Blake's being serious about dating was a good thing. An excellent thing.

But serious about Jane? Talk about a dark horse.

"A movie? Oh. Okay. Are there any, um, girl-type things out?"

Andy couldn't hold back her laughter, though she recognized she was using it as a substitute for that icky rage going on inside. The release felt good. When she could talk again, she asked, "Do you mean like a romantic comedy, or a drama, or a period piece?"

"A *period* piece? I would never ask—oh, my God. Is that a thing?" He looked positively shell-shocked.

Andy was dying.

"Blake! It means a historical film!" She wiped tears of laughter away, taking some mascara along with them.

Jane wouldn't have laughs like this with him. This second date shouldn't be happening. Should. Not.

"I trust your judgment. You've seen her file, talked to her. Probably more than I have."

Which was exactly why Jane was all wrong for him. He didn't even know her. She didn't even know him.

Wait, that wasn't right. Well, Blake didn't know Jane and Jane didn't know Blake, but that was what Andy was for. She'd narrowed down his interests, matched them with Jane's personality. Andy had paired them because she knew they'd be excellent together.

Why the heck were you so good at your job?

Because that was the goal, remember?

Ah, the devil and angel Andys were back. Nice timing.

"Anyway," Blake said, his shoulders relaxing in exact contrast with the knot tightening in her belly, "whatever you think. God, I'm relieved. And embarrassed. But mostly relieved. I never know about these female mysteries."

That gave her an idea. Since the date was pointless anyway, and she *had* met Jane (which was what qualified her to make that judgment), she would set up a crappy date. That bland bitch would never outright *tell* Blake that the last thing on earth she wanted to see was an action flick set in space. And yet she would have an awful time and they wouldn't be likely to go out again.

Andy surfed over to a ticketing site. Oh, even better, the movie she was thinking of was apparently a sequel. She'd bet the whole second-date bonus—her stomach dropped again at the thought—that neither of them had seen the first. The previews she recalled were laughable, but not in the campy kind of way. Just in the kind of way that made you wonder who exactly greenlit that project.

When she realized this particular movie theater allowed you to choose your own seats, she almost bounced in her chair. Front row—two clicks and the worst date ever was all set up. Between the subject matter and the inevitable migraine-slash-neckaches they'd get, she could kiss Jane good-bye.

As long as Blake wasn't kissing Jane good-bye. Good God, had he already? She couldn't think about that. He hadn't mentioned it when they'd had their before-work bump-and-grind session that morning, but they'd only talked about no *sex* with the candidates, not no kissing. Dammit, she couldn't revise the rules now. It would look suspicious.

And it would totally be counterproductive because you want him to find a match.

Well, maybe I do, devil Andy said to angel Andy, *but not this one.*

With a scowl, Andy shooed away both the imaginary representations of her warring thoughts and finished her online transaction. "Okay, you're in for a seven o'clock showing of the new Austen remake. It's opening night, so don't be late. There won't be any other tickets available, I can guarantee you. Austenites are rabid." She beamed particularly brightly. "Jane will love it. Jane. Jane Austen. Did you notice?"

The only thing Andy felt guilty about was the fact that she didn't feel guilty at all.

Blake had to admit it—he was impressed. Jane Osborne was as boring a woman as he'd ever spent an evening with, but she could certainly roll with the punches. He'd been absolutely heated when the pimply-faced kid behind the glass window had told him his tickets had gotten screwed up. He knew Andy would disapprove of him throttling the squeaky-voiced little bastard on a power trip. His most disapproving scowl and the threatening voice he used for intimidating business rivals was starting to have an effect on the kid when a cool hand settled on his arm.

"It's fine, Blake. I don't mind what we see." She smiled at him, and it seemed genuine.

"The space movie? Are you certain?" She was obviously not the space type. Or was she? After all, Andrea hadn't seemed like the *Star Wars* type, but since the initial reference she'd used enough of them he could tell she was a fan.

"I don't love space, but the lead was in a rom-com I liked last year, so it will be fine. Anyways, I tend to drift off in movies."

Ah. So not a closet space fan. He was surprised not to feel any disappointment by that. He'd made Andrea choke on her coffee last week when he'd shown her his Wookiee impression. Jane didn't seem like the type to have reactions like that. Or passions in general. Drifting off in movies— what was she, seventy?

On the other hand, the fact that she was fine with the unexpected turn of events was nice. He'd been on enough dates in his life where someone would say a change of plans was fine and then proceed to pout all night. He understood the rarity of a woman who genuinely didn't mind going with the flow.

So he painfully turned the scowl into a smile at the ticket kid and accepted the tickets to . . . he squinted. *Martian Death Squad 2*?

Good Lord. "Popcorn?" he offered to Jane. She shook her head. Again, he was struck by the contrast between the two women. Besides the obvious physical differences— Jane was nearly his height, where he could tuck Andrea comfortably beneath his arm; Jane was Chinese to Andrea's—whatever. What was her ethnic background? Dawson. Sounded British, but her coloring was Irish. German?

He sighed. These mental tangents were becoming a hobby, and all of them involved his matchmaker.

The point was, the two women could not be more

different, both physically and mentally. Everywhere Andrea was feisty, Jane was placid. It was like comparing a wildcat to a tabby. All they had common was their whiskers. Blake shook his head again. That didn't even make *sense*. Popcorn! That's what he was thinking about. Who went to a movie and didn't get popcorn? His date, apparently.

He'd only decided to go on a second date with her because he was so sick to death of first dates. First dates were deplorable. Universally, in his experience.

Especially lately. Why were all the submissive women either incredibly stupid or just plain mute? He wouldn't be the successful man he was today without being able to admit the occasional hard truth to himself, and he'd realized one about Andrea while he was on his first date with Jane.

Whatever was brewing between himself and his employee, it was infinitely more interesting than what he was experiencing with any woman she'd found for him thus far. So what was the point of continuing on with dull women? He'd tuned back in to Jane as she finished politely explaining what it was that she did. Unfortunately, he hadn't heard a word, so he still didn't know. Or actually care.

But she did a Thing, and she wasn't pushy about it, whatever it was. So he made one of his famous (in his own mind) lightning decisions. While he unraveled the tangle of feelings he was having about the matchmaker, he'd continue to date Jane. He couldn't keep doing first dates, but if he quit dating altogether, Andrea would no longer have a job to do. This was a perfect compromise. What a stroke of luck that this had occurred to him on a date with Jane, and not with Jamie, or the hyena.

So popcorn or not, it looked like he was escorting Jane Osborne to a showing of *Martian Death Squad 2*. From the front row. He sighed, and comforted himself with the knowledge that he had scotch at home.

* * *

Andy's eyes narrowed, but it was the only physical indication she was showing of her internal rage. *What kind of date was this Jane woman? She'd shown all the signs of a submissive puppy in her interview. Clearly that had carried over.*

"I'm sorry the tickets weren't what we'd planned. Was she mad?" Her voice was level, betraying no signs of her disappointment.

"She was a trooper. The shoot-'em-up wasn't as bad as I'd thought it would be. She slept through most of it. Can you imagine?"

Andy laughed politely. *No, I can't imagine.* "So you want to arrange another date, you said?" *Take it back.*

"Sure. She's game, I'm game. What do you suggest?"

A euthanizing. "A fancy dinner. Since the first two dates have gone well, I assume you'll want to spend some time getting to know her more. And girls always enjoy being pampered. Seafood, maybe?" *Haha. Jane doesn't eat fish. And I know for a fact that she has nothing to say. Game, set, match.*

"Sounds good to me. It's lobster season. We can chat over those." Blake leaned back in his chair. "I love lobster. Lobster rolls are the best, but we're farther down the coast from the good ones. Are you a seafood fan, Drea?"

"It's fine. Lobster rolls are nice." *Only my favorite!* She bit the inside of her lip until the metallic taste of blood rolled through her mouth. Why was she seething over a dinner the two mismatches weren't even having? If they went out for lobster, there would be bibs. Bibs! Nothing was less sexy.

Which got her thinking—how unsexy could a date be? Now, that was a challenge she could accept.

"Since rolls in a seaside shack aren't much of a thing here, why don't I book you a table at a nice restaurant? You

can chat over some wine and get to know each other
better." She could have sworn he'd frowned at that.

"Nice idea. A later dinner would work better for me. I
have a full day Thursday. Good thing that isn't an office
day for you, eh?"

Andy had actually booked a full spa day for Thursday
in anticipation of Friday shenanigans—massage, mani/
pedi, bikini wax. Not anymore. She had work to do.

"Actually, Thursday will be a fairly full day for me as
well. Lots of loose ends to tie up. I'm sorry I won't see you
before your big night, though." *Sorry not sorry. It's just
become a big night for me, too.*

A feeling of déjà vu settled over her as she purposely
forgot to confirm the reservations. And on Thursday, as she
removed his wallet from the suit jacket Blake had left behind during his rigorous schedule of meetings, she had
déjà vu again. Because as she settled the billfold into his
desk drawer, where he would never look before his date—
but not find it a strange place for the wallet to be found the
next day—she again felt no guilt.

The guilt also failed to materialize on the fourth and
fifth dates she sabotaged with no gluten-free menu items
and another lost reservation, respectively.

Chapter Sixteen

Andy couldn't keep from humming as she put on a final coat of mascara. Funny how getting laid on a regular basis could change a woman's outlook on life. They'd stuck to their rules, maintaining their professional relationship. But after work hours, they'd christened every surface in the office. Without ever speaking about it, they both arrived early. And stayed late. And Andy had lost ten pounds from missed lunches—or perhaps, from the extra physical activity.

Looking at her reflection, she almost didn't see the black circles under her eyes from losing sleep over Jane. Not that she would be a problem much longer.

Andy swept some lip gloss on and checked herself a final time in the hall mirror. She had to admit, sex looked good on her. Unlike the last time she'd readied herself to go to Blake Donovan's house, this time she was going as herself. She also wasn't planning any sort of seduction, though she had put on a pretty matching panty-and-bra set just in case.

"I don't get it." Lacy stood next to the front window,

looking below for Darrin's van to pull up to take her to a gig and drop Andy off at Blake's on the way. "Is this a booty call or not?"

"It's not." Which was the truth. Technically.

Lacy sounded incredulous. "You're going to his house on a Sunday night to—"

"To discuss possible evening activities for his dates. That's all." Andy walked to the coffee table to gather the files with the info she'd gathered. She really probably could have emailed them, but an in-person consult was much easier.

Lacy gave her a once-over before returning to her post at the window. "Sounds an awful lot like an excuse for a booty call, if you ask me."

"I *didn't* ask you." Andy wrapped a large rubber band around her files so they'd be easier to carry. "Not that I need to explain myself to you, but Blake has a date with Jane tomorrow and I want to make sure I get all the details settled tonight. You know, stuff comes up at work. He might not have time to talk to me in between his meetings and things." Plus, she needed time to plan her next round of sabotage.

"That sounds so wrong." Lacy turned to sit in the sill so she could face Andy. "How can you stand him dating another woman while he's banging you?"

Andy bit her lip. There was no way she was admitting to Lacy how much she couldn't stand Blake dating Jane. If she did, then she'd have to admit what she'd done to try to stop the dates. The awful, deceitful string of bad behavior. Lacy would string her up by her thong for that kind of nonsense.

Well. Hopefully her sabotage had proved fruitful. Though Blake had asked for another date with Jane after the last one, he'd been reluctant to discuss the evening's agenda. Actually what he'd said was that he was too busy on Friday afternoon, but Andy couldn't help but wonder if that was code for *not that enthused*. It was so obvious that Jane was all wrong for him, she knew he'd see it, too, soon enough. Why he hadn't already was a mystery. She was merely scooting up the time line on that by making sure all their dates sucked. Going to his house tonight was an opportunity for her to gauge the prospect of that being true.

And when she'd approached him with the idea of stopping by on Sunday, he hadn't said no. A storm of butterflies wreaked havoc in her belly at what that might mean.

Stop it, she scolded herself. She couldn't get her hopes up. Go in with low expectations and she'd have a better chance of surviving whatever happened emotionally. Tossing her curls over her shoulder, she met her sister's eyes and said words that she meant for herself as much as anyone. "It's just sex, Lacy. It's fun. It doesn't have to mean anything."

"There are some people I believe that may be true for. You are not one of them."

"Don't be ridiculous." It was true, but Lacy didn't have to call her on it.

"You're going to get emotionally attached," Lacy chided in a singsong voice.

"No. Way. Yes, he's good." Great, actually. Greater than great. "But he is definitely not for me." All lies. She was totally emotionally attached. Yet she couldn't admit that to anyone without feeling stupid with a capital *S*. Because though Blake was more than pleasing in the physical department, he still lacked in other areas. He'd improved socially under her tutelage, and he made fewer chauvinistic comments since her first days working with him, but he was still basically an ass-hat. The fact that he was serving her multiple O's while still using her to find a bride was proof of that. Totally awful.

Someone just needed to explain that to her heart.

Lacy narrowed her eyes at her. "Your expression says that you aren't so sure about that."

Goddammit, why did Lacy have to be able to read her so well? That was Andy's gig.

Andy forced a smile. "I'm fine. Stop worrying about me. *Mom.*" As if she'd have ever discussed her sex life with their mother.

Lacy ignored the crack. Or else she worked to emulate it further. "How will you get home? The train doesn't go all the way out to Rich-ville."

"I'll call a cab. Or have Blake take me home." *Or not come home at all.*

Immediately she scratched that thought from her mind.

But then Lacy said, "Or you'll stay over."

"I won't stay over. That goes against the rules."

Lacy rolled her eyes at the word *rules.* "But you might be home late?"

She was digging, and Andy knew it. Truth was, Andy wanted to be home late. Banging, as Lacy so eloquently put it, on new territory would be a definite violation of rules. It threatened to upset their carefully balanced routine. Especially when the new territory was Blake's home. It was intimate. If they crossed that line, how could Blake deny what was happening between them?

On the other hand, Andy didn't want to force it. It was one thing to ruin his dates, but whatever happened between her and Blake she wanted to happen organically. She had to be sure it was real. She had to be sure *he* knew it was real.

But what if it wasn't as real for him as it was for her?

Maybe Lacy was right to be worried. Going to Blake's home on a Sunday night under the pretense of work had the potential of backfiring big time. She could very well get hurt. Problem was, her heart was already involved. It was too late to worry about maybe getting hurt.

She glanced sideways at Lacy, who was still waiting for her answer. Andy didn't give one. Instead, having spotted the ugly pea-green vehicle pulling up below, she said, "Darrin's here."

"Lucky you. Saved by the van."

Thirty minutes later, Andy stood on the steps waiting for Blake to answer his bell. When the door opened, she was met by his housekeeper.

"Hi, Ellen. Good to see you again." Andy tossed a good-bye wave over her shoulder to let Darrin and Lacy know she was good for them to leave and turned back to the older woman in front of her.

Ellen frowned and scrunched her forehead as if trying to recall something. "Drea!" she exclaimed after a moment.

Andy chuckled to herself, not bothering to correct her. "Is Blake here?" she asked, wondering when she'd be invited in and suddenly worried that maybe she hadn't been already because he wasn't there.

"Of course he is. Where are my manners? Come on in." She stepped aside to let Andy in past her, holding the door open even after she was inside. "Is he expecting you?"

Andy tensed, fearing she was going to be kicked out without a definite invitation. "Sort of. I told him I had some things to drop off for him and he said anytime today would be fine." She bit her lip. "Is that a problem?"

"No, not at all. He's upstairs in his playroom."

Playroom? Before Andy's mind traveled too far into thoughts of red rooms filled with sex toys, she clarified. "In his office, you mean?"

"Yes. In his office." With her hand still on the open door, Ellen said, "I'm sorry I seem rushed. I'm just on my way out. Date night with the Mister. Would you mind telling Mr. Donovan that dinner's in the warmer whenever he's ready?"

"Will do." It occurred to Andy that Ellen probably always prepared Blake's meals. "Ellen, before you go—how long have you worked for Mr. Donovan?"

"Oh, gosh." She sighed with the thought. "Since he was just starting out with his business. Years. The man knows nothing about cooking himself. I've told him he needs to get himself a good wife before I retire. I planned to stay on until he married, but if he keeps dragging his feet I may have to help him find a replacement."

"Interesting." Blake's requirements for a wife who knew how to cook and clean made more sense now. He thought he was being practical—replacing his housekeeper with a bride. Silly and old-fashioned, perhaps, but somewhat understandable.

With a smile she said, "Have a good date night, Ellen."

"You as well, Drea."

"Oh, I'm not . . ." Andy let her words trail off. She wasn't there for a date, but it felt nice pretending she was. Anyway, the housekeeper was already halfway down the driveway headed to her car parked at the curb, so no use explaining otherwise.

Andy headed up the broad staircase to Blake's office. The doors were open at the end of the hall so she went on in. Only Blake wasn't there. With a frown she set the files she'd brought on his desk and considered what to do next.

Then she heard some strange noises coming from behind Blake's desk. Or from the half-open door behind the desk, rather. She'd wondered about that room before, suspecting it was a safe or safe room, but her questions about it had been blown off. Now she couldn't stop herself from looking. It was open, after all. And she did need to find Blake.

Cautiously, she paused at the open crack and called in. "Blake?" She didn't want to surprise him in the middle of counting his money or reviewing security tape or something worse. Like, what if it was a private bathroom?

When she had no answer, she pulled the door open. "Blake, are you in here?"

Blake was in there all right. But it was what else was in the room that made her gasp in surprise. "Oh, my God!"

Blake's head shot up at her exclamation. "Andrea!"

All trepidation lost, Andy walked the rest of the way into the room and took in her surroundings in awe. "This is . . . this is your playroom?"

"Um."

Her eyes stopped their exploration and landed on his fretful expression. "It is!" Again she scanned the room. Pinball machines lined all the walls. Twenty-three in total, all of them lit up and chiming with classic pinball sounds meant to lure bystanders into playing. There were many she recognized—*Attack from Mars*, *The Simpsons*, the *Star Trek Next Generation* game she'd beaten in high school. There was even a vintage *Captain Fantastic* that must have been made in the 1940s.

It was freaking amazing.

She spun to face Blake. "*PinballWizard* for your network password? That *was* you." She took a step toward him and swatted him across his biceps. Hard. "You big jerk."

"Ow!" Blake rubbed his arm. "What was that for?"

"You could have told me you liked pinball. It would look great on your profile."

He ducked when she tried to hit him a second time. "I don't need pinball to look great on my profile."

She scoffed. "You do. Trust me." Andy turned around the room once more. "This could have made up for a lot." Finally, something that showed some goddamn personality.

Of course, in her weeks working with Blake she'd discovered many other things that were interesting and endearing about the man. Little things that she could never put on a profile or explain to a potential date, like, how he insisted on drinking a full glass of water before any meal, and how he made funny expressions as he read his emails. This, though, she could have used to sell him. Why on earth had he not told her?

Blake scratched at the back of his neck, something Andy had learned he did when he was nervous. "So, it's not a big . . . turnoff? That I'm secretly nerdy?"

"That you have an awesome-ass classic pinball setup in your house?" She couldn't believe he had to ask. "Hell, no. It's a big turn-*on*." Like, really big.

"Is that right?" Blake's voice was teasingly low and seductive.

Andy swatted at him again, much lighter this time. "Stop it, you fiend." She nodded toward one of the machines, a hybrid mechanical pinball-plus-video game called *Caveman*. "Show me what you got."

He raised a brow. "Really?"

"Yes, really."

"Okay." He started to the game she'd shown interest in.

Andy followed behind. "Oh, I bumped into Ellen as she was leaving. She said dinner's in the warmer."

"Thanks." Blake paused, one hand on the side of the *Caveman* machine, his brow furrowed.

"What is it?"

"I was just thinking . . ." He hesitated, as if nervous. "Would you like to join me for dinner? You don't have other plans, do you?"

Dinner. That was decidedly against their rules. Decidedly intimate, warmer or not. And she hadn't suggested it— he had. It was happening organically after all. "I don't have other plans."

Again Blake scratched the back of his neck. "You can say no, of course. Just, I wouldn't want the food to get cold while we were fooling around up here." He swallowed, seeming to realize what he'd said. "I mean, Ellen always makes enough for leftovers. She's a great cook."

Andy smiled at the charming way he was selling the idea of a meal together. "I don't doubt she's a great cook. I've seen you bring her leftover meat loaf to the office for lunch. It smells delish."

"Oh, she's wonderful." He swallowed again. "Then when dinner's out of the way we can come back up here and beat the ball around."

It was her turn to raise a brow. "You mean play pinball, right? That's not a euphemism for anything else, is it?" She winked.

He broke into a smile—a beautiful grin that touched Andy low in her belly. "It's not a euphemism. I mean play pinball."

Andy nudged him with her shoulder, mostly because she was yearning to touch him in some fashion and couldn't stand that she hadn't yet. "Well, then. Let's get dining because I can't wait to play against you." She began to stroll out of the room then called behind her. "Blake, have I ever mentioned that I won the Beacon Hill Area Pinball Championship when I was in eleventh grade?"

She was glad she peeked over her shoulder or she would have missed his adorably worried expression.

He cocked his head at her. "Are you trying to intimidate me?"

She turned to face him head-on and shrugged. "Maybe." She smiled coyly. "Is it working?"

He leveled his blue eyes at her, his lip ticking up ever so slightly. "Andrea Dawson, there is never a moment that you don't intimidate me, and it has nothing to do with pinball. But I mean that in the very best way possible."

Goose bumps scattered down the back of her neck and over the bare skin of her arms. It was a simple statement, but so uncharacteristic of anything Blake had ever said to her that it was impossible for her not to cling to it. If she was making too much of it, so be it. She'd treasure those words for a long, long time.

Blake gestured toward the open door. "Now let's go down, shall we?"

Dinner was delightful, to say the least. Besides the spectacular meal—Chicken Cordon Bleu and glazed carrots paired with the best white wine Andy had ever tasted—the conversation and company was also very enjoyable. They'd eaten in the kitchen rather than the dining room, which was more casual, but also more intimate. They laughed and chatted, never falling into awkward silence. It was surprising, really. After the feedback she'd heard from Blake's dates, she expected him to be an impolite conversation hog. Instead, he was gracious and entertaining. Charming, even.

When they finished, Andy helped clear their plates, carrying them to the sink. Then she watched in wonder as he rinsed them and stuck them in the dishwasher.

She knew it was cheeky, but she had to say something. "Blake Donovan does dishes?"

He scowled. "No. I just wash off my dirty plates and put them in the dishwasher. That's all. They'd get crusty and gross if I left them in the sink for Ellen in the morning." He started the machine and washed his hands.

Andy folded her arms and leaned against his granite counter. "That's doing dishes."

"It's being sanitary," he protested as he dried his hands.

"Uh-huh." She crossed to the kitchen door and looked back over her shoulder. "Are you ready to go upstairs?"

"I am."

After a brief stop in the bathroom, Andy followed Blake up the stairs. At the top, he turned toward the office, but

Andy paused at a strange sound coming from the double doors at the other end of the hall. She strained her ears trying to figure out what it was she was hearing. It sounded like scratching followed by soft whimpering.

"What's that?"

Blake turned back to look at her. "What's what?"

"That noise." She took several steps toward the doors. "It sounded like . . ." She stopped herself, listening again to be sure.

"It's nothing." Blake sounded panicked, speaking rapidly. "It's nobody. Or the maid. She sometimes—has Tourette's—" He corrected himself quickly. "A mouse, I mean. Mice. Lots of mice. Big mice. Get away from there. I'll call pest control tomorrow."

With fists on her hips, she turned and narrowed her eyes at the man behind her. "Blake Donovan, did you keep the puppy?"

"I . . ." It was that or he *did* have a Mrs. Rochester in there.

The scratching creature let out a definite all-dog yap.

Without permission, Andy opened the doors in front of her, and out ran the fluffy corgi she'd left with Blake over a month before. "You did!"

She bent to hug the excited creature, who was alternately licking her face and nipping at her hand.

With a sigh, Blake knelt next to her. "I didn't *keep* him, exactly. I just haven't gotten around to taking him back yet."

"There was a ten-day return policy. You've passed that." As soon as the puppy realized that Blake's face was within his reach, he abandoned Andy and ran to his master.

"Then I'll donate him to someone." Blake rubbed the dog affectionately, nuzzling his cheek to the furball as the puppy licked his ear.

Andy's chest grew warm. "No you won't. He loves you.

You love him." If she wasn't mistaken, the man's cheeks flushed.

"Absolutely not." He wouldn't meet her eyes. He was definitely blushing.

The heat in Andy's chest spread downward toward her core. Damn, a man with a dog was hot. She *knew* she was right about this plan. "What's his name?" she asked, trying to keep her mind off what was going on between her legs.

"Puppy."

She laughed. "Of course. Creativity has never been your strong suit." She petted the dog, her hand accidentally on purpose bumping into Blake's. At her touch, he looked up and met her stare. His deep-blue eyes were softer than she'd ever seen them. They caught her up. Mesmerized her completely. Eye contact had always been their kryptonite.

"Well, you don't name things you don't plan to keep." Her sister had once had a theory like that with men. It was called "Don't Name the Puppy," in fact. She wondered what it meant that he said *her* name, even the hated nickname, with such tenderness.

When she could speak, she asked, "You are keeping him, though, aren't you?"

"We'll see." But everything about his expression said yes. He stood and reached a hand out to help her up. "Come on." When she hesitated, his forehead creased in confusion. "What?"

She might be falling in love with him, that's what. All her jealousy and rage over Jane wasn't just because she was being petty or possessive. She was falling. And she was done feeling guilty about it because the more she got to know him she more she realized he wasn't as douchey as he appeared. Actually, he was pretty fantastic.

But even if things were happening between them organically and all, she wasn't about to admit her feelings and ruin it. "Nothing. You just surprise me; that's all."

At his suspicious glance, she added, "Pleasantly." No point in rubbing this in. She was just chalking it up as a mental win for herself. It didn't bring her nearly the satisfaction it would have a few days ago. That felt weird, but nice—oh, hell. Everything was surprising her today.

"I'll have to work on that." He waved his hand, urging her to take it. "Now come on."

She laughed, slipping her hand into his. "Eager much?"

But she got it. She was eager, too. Not for the pinball war that was about to take place but for this . . . *thing* . . . that was going on with her and Blake to continue. This surprising, amazing, wonderful . . . *thing.*

And for the pinball war. That was going to be fun too.

Blake couldn't believe how great the evening had been. Better than anything he'd ever done with Andrea, and in the last month, he'd done a lot with her that he'd liked. Liked a lot. And tonight they still had all their clothes on.

In fact, he was having more fun with Andrea, as they laughed and played every pinball machine in his playroom, than he'd had on any date in months. He'd also been more relaxed, more himself, than he could ever remember being.

He didn't know what to do with that realization, so instead of dwelling on it, he concentrated on putting his all into his game playing. Turned out his employee really was a pro at pinball. She scored well, almost as well as he did. Blake had the distinct feeling that the only thing that kept him in the lead was his familiarity with the games. She was certainly the best opponent he'd had in ages. The perfect match for him.

He watched her now as she expertly batted the flippers

on the Bally Williams *Doctor Who* game, his favorite of all his machines. Damn, she was sexy—her eyes lighting up as they followed the ball around its cage, her mouth oohing and ahhing silently, her breasts bouncing in her T-shirt as she got into her playing. It was a testament to his character that he continued to win with those temptations so close at hand. *Hands. His hands. His hands covering her breasts, caressing—*

"Oh, no," Drea exclaimed, bringing him out of his less-than-chaste thoughts. "It's multiball. I screwed this up royally last time. What am I doing wrong?"

With a chuckle, Blake came up behind her. "You can do this. I'll help."

"Okay." Her voice was almost a whisper, begging him to move closer.

He placed his hands over hers at the buttons on the side of the machine. It felt good to touch her. Too good. His palms burned over the soft touch of her hands. It took all his concentration not to press into her back, not to bring his pelvis up close to cradle her ass.

Focus on the game, man.

He inhaled—*ignore the apples*—and placed himself in the B-Zone. "Instead of watching where the balls are going," he said, his face leaning in over her shoulder, "keep focused on the flippers." With her hand under his, he pressed the button as a ball came toward the exit. The flipper made contact and the ball rolled on to score another thousand points.

"Uh-huh." But Andy didn't seem to be watching the game anymore. She was watching him.

Blake tried to keep anchored. "There's no way you can watch all the movement at once, but you can zoom in on one area." His voice sounded strained, even to himself. Low, and about to burst. "When anything comes near the flippers, you hit." Another ball rolled toward the exit. He pressed both of her hands this time, and he heard her breathing pick up.

Her face was still angled toward his. So close to his. Nearly touching. She could tip up and she'd be kissing his jaw. He could turn and he'd be kissing her lips. And, God, wouldn't that be wonderful? One of his favorite fantasies began like this—spreading a woman across his pinball machine and going down on her, making her scream while the lights and the game went on underneath her.

Okay, maybe that was a ridiculous teenage wet dream, but he could so make it happen. Perhaps without the game going on would be better—just him and the woman and the pinball machine as a table. Just him and Andy.

But the idea felt off. As much as he'd love to do that, as much as he sensed that she would even be a willing participant, it wasn't exactly what he wanted from her at the moment. After they'd bonded and connected and had this wonderful almost romantic night . . . she deserved more. *They* deserved more.

What the hell kind of thinking was that? *More*? With *Andrea Dawson*?

Damn if it didn't feel so right. And that scared him.

So he did nothing. Didn't fuck her on the pinball machine. Didn't lead her down the hall to his bedroom. Didn't even kiss her.

Andrea's focus turned back to the machine. "Blake? You lost your balls."

And hadn't he.

But she meant the game. He'd lost all those balls, too. "I did."

The enormity of the situation hit him like a ton of bricks. He was bonding, and bad, with a woman who was nothing like his ideal. Not just bonding, he was falling. Falling hard.

Quickly he stepped away, unable to touch her anymore without tearing all her clothes off or asking her to do something crazy like stop looking for silly women for him to date.

Seeming to sense his sudden change in mood—and how couldn't she?—Drea rubbed her hands over her arms. "Well. Game over. It's late anyway. I should go."

"Yeah. I suppose you should." She should. She really, really should.

He didn't want her to go.

"We can go over those ideas for your date tomorrow in the morning. First thing."

"Yeah, first thing." He had a meeting that had come up for first thing in the morning, but he didn't say that. He didn't want to ruin this night with Andy by talking about another woman. He didn't want to talk about another woman ever again: if you asked him at that moment.

He was no longer scared. He was terrified.

"Um, I need to call a cab." She wouldn't meet his eyes.

"I can take you." Or was it him who wouldn't meet *her* eyes?

"You can?" Her voice sounded both happy and sad. As if she was glad that he offered, but maybe not so glad about going home.

Or was he simply transferring his own emotion onto her?

"Of course I can." He gestured for her to go ahead of him. "After you." He was confused and awed and he need- ed a minute to gather himself. Except he wasn't sure a min- ute would be enough.

What was he doing? With Jane? With Drea? All of it was a muddle. The life plan he'd set seemed off kilter. Seemed wrong. The only thing that felt right was the woman standing outside the door, waiting for her ride home.

He wasn't sure what to do with that realization. But he couldn't keep her waiting.

When he stepped into the hallway, he found her lean- ing against the wall, panic on her face as she kicked her

leg out to the side of her. Blake looked down to see the dog
was attacking her leg. At least she was laughing.

"Puppy, no. Shoo. Stop that." Chuckling, he bent down
to the floor to pry the dog off Andrea's leg. "Get out of
here." Puppy obeyed, scurrying down the stairs.

With the dog gone, he grew serious. He pinned his
focus on the gorgeous calf in front of him. "I don't blame
him, though. You do look awfully good in jeans."

Andy giggled. "So you want to hump my leg?"

He didn't answer, but he made a choice. For the first time
ever, he decided to stop thinking about rules and life plans.
He only wanted to live in this moment with Andrea, con-
sequences be damned.

He trailed his hand up her beautiful denim-clad leg as
he stood, settling it at her waist. He put his other hand on
the wall behind her, caging her in.

Her breathing sped up as she peered up at him.
"Blake . . . ?" The question trailed off as if she couldn't say
the words she meant to.

"Andy . . . ?" He suspected he knew what she was asking, but he wanted to know for sure. Needed to know for
sure. After all, he was about to break all the rules, and
though he was decided on it, her permission was absolutely
necessary.

A smile eased across her beautiful rose lips. "You called
me Andy."

That's right, he had. It was fitting for her at times, he
realized. As fitting as Andrea was at others. Both names
describing different aspects of this woman that he so adored.
This woman that he might even, maybe, love.

Hoping she didn't see the true depth of his emotion on
his face, he simply said, "Slip of the tongue." And oh,
how he wanted to slip his tongue in other places. Slide it
along the line of her jaw. Flick it across her nipples, which
he noticed were already standing at attention.

He moved in closer, his mouth hovering just inches above hers.

"Blake . . . ?" Her voice was soft and pleading.

If she couldn't say what she wanted, he'd have to help her. "If I asked you to stay the night—"

She cut him off. "I'd say yes. Are . . . are you asking me?"

"Yes." Blake closed the distance between them, kissing her jaw first and working his way up to her lips. He wanted to take his time, loving the build of anticipation. Also, he knew that this kiss was going to be important—it was going to change everything.

Chapter Seventeen

When Blake's mouth finally met Andrea's, he felt like he'd found the Force. Like he'd been searching for it his whole life and now he had it in his grasp. Though he'd kissed her before, both sweetly and frantically, this was the first time it had been with all his walls down. He was naked before her, exposed—and he still had all his clothes on. It gave the kiss a sense of newness. It was surprising. Exhilarating. The best goddamn kiss of his life.

His lips sucked at hers, teasing, tasting before he allowed his tongue to slip in and stroke along her own. For several minutes, their hands were still, letting the movement of their mouths take center stage. They had an entire conversation with lips and tongues moving in rhythm—*I want you*, they said to each other. *To get to know you. To savor you. To have* more *with you.*

Soon, though, kissing wasn't enough. Andrea brought her hands around his neck and pressed into him, rubbing her body against his like an affectionate kitten. God, that made him hot—the way she moved her tits along his chest, her pelvis pushing at his erection. If he didn't stop her now, they'd be doing it in the hall, and that was not where he wanted her.

He wanted her in his bed.

He pulled away, the confusion in her gaze lasting only until he took her hand and led her silently to the double doors on the opposite side of the hallway. Without flipping on the light, he continued past the threshold of the darkened room, steering her to his bed where he helped her sit.

She reached for his embrace again, but he stopped her.

"I want to see you." He flicked the switch on the night-stand lamp, the sudden light causing them both to momentarily blink and adjust even though the illumination was dim. The overhead was too bright, but he was aching to gaze at her when he stripped her naked.

In their trysts at the office, they'd never undressed fully. It had been almost an unspoken addendum to their rules—sex with clothes on was much different from sex with clothes off, after all. Maybe not fundamentally, but emotionally. So many times he'd wanted to unbutton her blouse, strip her of her bra, and take her naked breast into his mouth, yet he'd restrained himself. Tonight, with all the other rules already broken, there was no longer a reason to hold back. He'd feast on her with his eyes, then with his tongue. He'd make love to her with nothing between them. Hell, with her permission, he'd even forgo the condom.

When he turned back to face Andrea, he found she'd moved to a kneeling position. She reached forward to tug on his shirt. He smiled, letting her pull him toward her. She was as desperate to keep touching as he was. Cupping her hands around her face, he kissed her again, thoroughly. Then he grabbed the hem of her T-shirt and broke away from her mouth so that he could rid her of the clothing. Her powder-blue lace bra came off next, joining her shirt on the floor.

"That's better." *Much better.* Blake was amazed at how

Drea didn't try to cover herself up, but let her arms stay loosely at her sides, showing him her goods without shame. And she had nothing to be ashamed of in the least. Why had he wasted so much time on such scrawny girls in the past? Drea's breasts were magnificent. They would fill his palms, voluptuous without being showy. Absolutely perfect. He wanted to squeeze them and watch her shiver. Wanted her perfect dusky nipples between his lips.

Before he could act on those desires, however, his attention was drawn to a nipping at his toes. *Puppy.*

"Oh, no." He bent to scoop up the dog in one hand. "You are not staying in here."

"Blake, he's fine," Andrea called behind him as he escorted the creature to the doors.

"No. He's not." This was a private party Blake had planned. No Puppy invited.

He set his dog on the floor and shooed him away. Before shutting him out, though, he said quietly, "I promise to give you one of those treats you love in the morning."

"I heard that," Andrea teased, confirming again that she knew he had an affinity for the animal.

With a wicked grin, he turned back to the woman he'd left on his bed. "And I'll give *you* the treat you love right now."

"So full of yourself."

"No, but you'll be." He sauntered over to her, enjoying the blush that sparked from his naughty words and ran down her neck to the tips of her breasts. "Now, where were we?"

"You were taking off your shirt." She pulled again at his T-shirt until he took her hands, lacing her fingers with his.

"That's not where we were." Hands locked in hers, he bent down to lick along one of her perfect nipples. "This is where we were."

She wriggled under his attention. "Come on, I want to see you."

"You will. But I want to see you first." *And suck you. And taste you.*

"It's supposed to be ladies first, Blake." But she moaned, thrusting out her breasts so that he could take her more fully in his mouth.

He tugged until her nipple was standing erect. "And ladies will come first. I promise." Again, she blushed. "Now stop talking."

"But—"

He let go of a hand and placed his finger at her lips. "Stop." Turning his attention in full to her bosom, he distracted her from any thoughts of conversation. He adored her breasts completely, sucking and biting at one while kneading the other. Then switching his hand with his mouth until Andrea was gasping.

When he had his fill, he moved down, his tongue swirling along the rim of her belly button before his hands worked the button of her jeans. Gently, he pushed her back to lie on the bed so that he could remove her sandals. Then her pants. Then her panties.

Holy mother of God, he'd died and gone to heaven.

He had to stand back and admire her—her hair spilling around her shoulders, her nipples still puckered from his ardor, her thighs spread to showcase her pretty little pussy. "Andrea Dawson." His voice was thick with desire. "You are so damn beautiful."

She whimpered at his words. Or maybe from his touch as he moved in, trailing a hand down each of her inner thighs, his fingers meeting at her core. He skidded across her clit, and her hips bucked. That's when he lost all his reserve. He'd wanted to go slower, take his time teasing her with his hands. But he couldn't wait any longer. He had to have his mouth on her and now.

He fell to his knees and pulled her to the edge of the bed.

"What are you—"

He answered with his tongue on her flesh.

"Oh, my God," she cried, sitting up.

With a smile, he urged her back down and returned to his feast. He licked up her crease, dragged his mouth across her folds, skated his teeth along her sensitive nub. She whimpered and moaned as he pleasured her, her sexy sounds telling him just what she liked and how she liked it. Then he moved a hand to tickle along her opening, and she nearly screamed.

Damn if that didn't make him harder.

He was desperate now to make her come, eager to watch her fall apart from this new viewpoint. He plunged two fingers inside her, bending his knuckles to hit the spot against her wall that he knew was particularly sensitive. She was almost there. He could sense her getting near. Could hear it in the way her breathy gasps were coming closer and closer.

With his mouth and hands, he worked her until her legs were tensing and shaking, and her whimpers had turned into cries. His tongue drew letters on her clit, a trick he'd learned in college.

Then he found himself straying from the alphabet and wrote a sentence instead. "I heart Andrea Dawson." Because he did. He hearted her hard. Not just because his face was buried between her thighs, but because of everything else that had transpired between the two of them. Because she laughed at him when he was pompous. Because she didn't slap him any of the times he'd deserved it. Because she got dolled up and arrived on his doorstep in an attempt to seduce him when she was never sexier than when she was herself. Because she was feisty and outspoken. Because she gave him Puppy and could hold her own in pinball.

Mostly, though, because she was just the most incredible woman he'd ever met, and she owned him wholly—body, soul, and definitely heart.

Andy screamed and wrapped her fingers in the bedspread as she came. And came. And came. Blake Donovan was a god, she decided. A one hundred percent freaking sex god.

He was more than a sex god, though, she thought as she began to wind down from her dizzying orgasm. He was also more extraordinary than she'd ever imagined a man like him could be. He was funny and even sweet. And he kept the dog. And he had a fully loaded pinball playroom, for crying out loud. How much cooler could a person get? It was overwhelming and also really amazing in ways that she couldn't comprehend when she was still half blind from her release.

When she'd settled down enough that she could form a more coherent thought, she was no longer interested in analyzing her emotions. She was interested in the god before her—more specifically, getting the god naked.

She scrambled to her knees and pulled at his shirt. "No excuses, now. This has to go."

Thankfully, he didn't fight her.

His chest bare in front of her for the first time, she scanned every part of him, tracing along his contours with her fingers. He was gorgeous. Though not completely ripped, he had muscles. Well-defined muscles. Hard muscles, and not just the one bulging in his pants. And those sexy ridges that some men had at their hips? He had those. She had to trace those with her tongue.

Except his stupid jeans were in the way of her path. Too anxious to work at removing them herself, she simply commanded, "Off," and sat back on her knees to wait.

Blake had them shucked in no time, his briefs as well. Oh, she loved it when he responded to her like that.

Almost as much as she loved the sight in front of her—his beautiful, thick cock. While she'd spent a good amount of time in the last week with it inside her, Andy had never actually taken much time to admire it. Now it was standing boldly in her face and she could no longer resist.

"I want this," she murmured. And so she intended to have it. Circling her hand around him, she pumped his length from top to bottom. Blake's low *mmm* pushed her to do it again. He leaped in her hands and she couldn't help smiling. She brushed her fingertips over his crown and he moaned again. She loved this, too—loved torturing him. Loved having the power to make such a strong, composed man twitch at her touch.

Letting her stroke fall back down his rigid flesh, she realized that this was the component she'd been missing in her matches for Blake—she hadn't found the woman who could get to him. The woman whom he could expose himself to without fear. Not just clothes-off exposure, but everything-about-him exposure. The kind of exposure he'd shown to her tonight.

Wait. Did that mean that *she* was that woman? Was she Blake Donovan's match? She'd been into him, consumed with him, but she'd never quite believed that they were actually good together. Not long-term. But maybe they were.

Wouldn't that be something?

She ignored the tingle of hope that ran through her at the thought and tucked it away to deal with later. There would be plenty of time to analyze it further when she didn't have her mouth full.

Andy swirled her tongue along Blake's crown and then drew his shaft in toward the back of her throat. He groaned and she instinctively echoed him, her sounds reverberating along the length of his erection.

"Andrea. Drea." Blake sounded on the edge. "Please. You have to stop."

Before she could figure out if his request to end was because her actions were too awful or because they were too good, he had pulled out of her mouth and pushed her back onto the mattress. He covered her with the length of his body. Automatically, her legs fell open to him, and she felt his shaft against her opening.

"Your lips are heaven on my cock," he said in husky tones at her ear. "But keep doing that, and I'm going to come. And I already made a reservation in your pussy that I intend to keep."

Too good, then. She smiled at that. "I need you inside me, Blake."

He hovered over her, his mouth close to hers. "I need to get a condom."

He made no move to leave and she didn't want him to go, even just for a moment. Yet that wasn't the reason behind her bold decision. "No condom. Just you."

He responded by entering her with one long, slick drive. He slid all the way out to the tip and then pushed in again, seemingly even thicker and harder than he'd been just a moment before. Then he established his rhythm—a steady pulse that stroked her in all the right ways. Sent her climbing and spinning and soaring all at once.

"Blake, oh, Blake." She dug her fingers into his back. He felt so good. She was surprised exactly how good he felt because she'd had him inside her before. Perhaps the difference was the lack of condom, but she had a feeling it was more than that. So much more.

She wrapped her legs around his hips, and the new position let him push in deeper. Deeper than he'd ever been— than anyone had ever been inside her—she was sure of it. A general feeling of euphoria settled over her, even before she reached the pinnacle of her climax. She'd never been made love to like this before, and that was most definitely what Blake Donovan was doing. He was making love to her. Every touch carried a weight of affection—the way he brushed her hair from her eyes, how he cupped her face and kissed her with sweet abandon. Each thrust, even, bore the emotion of love.

Andy matched each display with sincere reciprocation. She let herself thrill in her earlier revelation that she was falling in love with the man. In fact, she'd go so far as to say she'd already fallen. Fallen as far as she suspected he had with her. The thought propelled her over the edge and then she was soaring on the crest of a relentless climax. Tears spilled and every nerve in her body burst in ecstasy as she clenched around him and all she could see and sense before her, in front of her, around her, was Blake. *Blake, Blake, Blake.* Forever Blake. She was drowning in his essence, yet she'd never felt so anchored.

Her spasms hadn't yet subsided when he joined her—pounding out his climax with each syllable of her name. Finally he collapsed beside her and neither of them said a word as they panted in unison and their heart rates returned to normal. Moments passed in the silence.

Then Andy began to fret. Would it get all awkward now? Should she go home? He had invited her to stay, but now they were barely touching and it was only at the shoulder so did that even count?

Her worry was all in vain, though, because before she had to make a decision about what to do next, Blake wrapped an arm around her and tugged her to him. He kissed and nuzzled at her neck before tucking her into the crook of his arm.

"Wow," he said. "That was . . ."

"Amazing, incredible, fantastic." She could keep going with a whole list of adjectives if her brain cells weren't numb from having been thoroughly fucked.

"I was going to say *everything.*" He tilted her chin to meet his eyes. "That was everything, Andrea. Thank you."

She nodded. Yes, that's what it had been, she thought, too overcome to agree verbally. It had been absolutely everything.

They lay tangled together, Blake stroking her arm, Andy caressing his chest, for a long while. Though they were silent, it was comfortable. Easy. Perfect.

A clicking noise broke through the quiet, coming from the direction of the TV set across from the bed.

Because it seemed time to say *something*, Andy asked, "What was that?"

Blake glanced toward the sound. "Just the DVR starting."

She stretched. "Oh. What are you recording?" Probably some boring documentary on the History Channel. No, Military Channel was probably more fitting for his business style.

"Nothing." *Wait—what?*

She adjusted so she could see his face. "What do you mean *nothing*? It's obviously something. What is it?"

His silence combined with his pained expression led her to pry. "Why won't you tell me?" She narrowed her eyes. "Is it porn?" It had to be porn. In which case, she kind of wanted to turn it on and see what kind of sex Blake was into, though she was pretty sure she already knew, what with all their recent activity and such.

But he protested. "No. It's not porn."

And her interest was piqued even further. "What is it, then?"

The tight line of his mouth said he wasn't spilling. But she'd already spied the remote on the nightstand next to her so, in a flash, she rolled over and flicked the ON button.

"No!" Blake shouted as he realized what she was doing. He wrestled her for the remote, the renewed physical contact almost distracting her completely from the DVR.

Except the sweeping music captured her attention, and when she looked up she saw a picturesque landscape and a beautiful English manor filling the television screen.

She was stunned. "*Downton Abbey*?"

With a gaping jaw, she returned her gaze to Blake, who was definitely blushing.

Then she couldn't help it—she broke into peals of laughter. "Blake Donovan," she managed to get out with a howl, "watches *Downton Abbey*?"

"Haha. Very funny." Blake retrieved the remote from her laugh-limp hand, clicked OFF, and flung it to the floor. "Thank you for your support of my tastes."

His tone said she should drop it, but she couldn't breathe. It was too freaking funny.

"Shall I pour you some more tea? Shall we have a crumpet as we watch? Where are my pearls?" Her British dialect was awful, but she wasn't going to stop.

"Keep this up and I'll give you something to laugh about," Blake challenged.

And because she couldn't stop, he started to tickle her. It was too much. Her peals escalated to hysterics. Tears formed at her eyes, and she had to grab her sides to both ease the ache and fend off her attacker. She couldn't even speak enough to ask him to stop.

With a sigh, Blake gave up his torture. "I'll wait."

It took a bit for her to calm. Then, sensing Blake needed reassurance or an apology or both, Andy pushed up to take his mouth in a sensual kiss. By the time she released him, they were both breathless.

She sat back and tapped him on the tip of his nose. "Do you know how many women you could score if they knew you watched *Downton Abbey*?"

He captured her finger in his mouth and sucked. "You mean that's what I should have used as my initial proposition to you?"

"No, not me. But other women. Chicks dig a sensitive core, you know." That sucking thing could have gotten her naked in a heartbeat, though. Sensitive core there, too.

"Not a fan, huh?" He sounded the slightest bit disappointed.

She settled back into his arms, her head on his chest. "I don't know. I've never watched it."

Blake kissed her head. "Ah, that will have to be remedied in the future."

The future. Was it totally reaching to grab onto that word as proof that their relationship would be different from now on? Proof that they had a future? She didn't think so. And for that, she was telling the truth when she said, "I honestly can't wait."

They sank back in their silence, Blake stroking his fingers up and down Andy's arm. After a few minutes, he said, "How did you end up in my life, Andrea 'sounds-like-Princess-Leia' Dawson?"

She'd actually been reflecting on just that very thing. "You posted a job opening and my sister set up an interview."

"Uh-uh. Too vague. Why were you even looking at jobs like the one I had posted?"

She drummed her fingers on his chest as she considered how to answer. "When I quit working for Max Ellis, I didn't leave on good terms. In fact, I left on very, very bad terms. Terms that pretty much ended my chances of finding a decent job afterward." She poked him playfully in the ribs. "So I was forced to take what I could get."

"Cute." He shifted her to the pillow next to him so that they were face-to-face. "But that's not cutting it. Tell me the terms. What happened?"

"Well . . ." She couldn't believe she was about to admit the truth. Though, lying naked with Blake, no covers on them even, it didn't seem as big a deal as it usually did. "Okay. The last year I was with Max, he got more and more . . . touchy . . . so to speak. Finally he out-and-out propositioned me."

"For sex?"

She nodded. "When I said no, he fired me. I could have won a lawsuit against him, I'm sure, if I'd had my head about me. But when he fired me, I couldn't help myself, I got so mad that I had to do something immediate. So I, um, burned a bunch of his employee files. I mean, like, a bunch." She kept her eyes down, unable to meet Blake's gaze. "He was the one who sued me. And he won, not surprisingly, which cost me all my savings and the little condo I owned. And my car. And the tennis bracelet I'd bought myself. Basically, he left me destitute and dependent on my sister. Pretty pathetic, I know."

"But you didn't sleep with him?"

She propped her head up with her elbow and met his gaze. "Is that all you can think about after that story?"

"No. I'm also wondering how I managed to have *my* office remain undestroyed after my own proposition." His grin suggested that he was half kidding.

But she knew Blake—or she was beginning to know him—and so she was sure he was also half serious.

"I wouldn't say it remained undestroyed." She winked at him. "There was the broken wingback."

"I've never been so happy to lose a piece of furniture." He cupped his hand behind her neck and brought her in for a brief kiss.

She shivered at his words as much from his kiss. Misreading her goose bumps, Blake suggested they get under the covers. When they were bundled up and she was snug in his arms again, their conversation resumed.

"Do you have any regrets?" he asked.

"About the wingback? No." *None at all.* "About Max Ellis? Yes. Lots of regrets."

"Such as?"

"I shouldn't have burned his files, but I really don't feel all that bad about that. That was every single bit of work I had done, for my entire career. Just because I learned what I did in kind of sketchy ways doesn't mean I hadn't worked really hard. Eight years of hard-core applied psych, that he was going to keep, and try and do me on top of. Burning it felt cathartic. If his lawsuit hadn't cost me so much, I wouldn't feel bad at all."

She pulled out of Blake's embrace and sat up against the headboard. Though she'd thought about this a lot over the last year, she'd never said any of it aloud. "Mostly, I regret the person he trained me to be. He taught me to seek out weaknesses in employees that would prevent them from doing well at his company. And I was good at that. Good at cutting people down and ignoring the best parts of them." It didn't paint the prettiest picture, she knew, and she was somewhat embarrassed to admit it.

When she glanced at Blake, though, there was only compassion and interest written in his expression. It encouraged her to go on. "But I realize now that you can't always judge a person's potential by their profile. It's a nice idea, but not very practical. And if you base a whole life or business on that thinking, you'll likely miss out on some truly amazing people."

Andy let her words replay in her head. Though she'd been talking about her job with Ellis, she could just as easily have been talking about the one with Blake. She couldn't set up a match for him because profiles didn't contain the whole of a person. There was no way they could. So she could find a woman with the right eyes, the right social background, the right goals and ambitions, but how would that ever be an indication of chemistry or emotional compatibility?

The same lesson could be applied to her initial impression of Blake. Hadn't she judged him by his "profile"? She'd decided what kind of a man he was—arrogant, self-centered, inflexible. Time together had taught her that he was so much more than that. If she hadn't been forced into his company, she'd never have given him a second look. And that would have been the biggest regret of her life.

Blake shifted so he was sitting up next to her. "Yes. I believe you may be right." He cocked his head. "So if you've lost your faith in the profile method, why is it again that you're working for me?"

She weighed her options for a moment—she could come out and tell him that her job was ridiculous, that he should fire her immediately and then date her earnestly.

But even though it was possible he felt the same, she wasn't willing to risk ruining their beautiful night. Not yet. So she gave a safer answer: "Because you begged me to."

He chuckled. "I guess I did."

"Like a desperate man." She sandwiched one of his hands between both of hers, admiring how small hers were next to his. How strong his were. "It's comical, actually. Blake Donovan, desperate?"

"Hey, I *was* desperate." He pulled her hand that was closest to him into his lap and began massaging it. "I'd tried other methods of finding potential dates. Let's just say I had my own burned-bridges sort of situation."

"You must tell me more." Also, he really must keep doing that to her hand. It felt amazing.

"Must I really? It's embarrassing."

"Tell me. I won't laugh." She paused. "Or, I'll laugh, but it will be in good fun."

His focus on his hand massage, he asked, "Have you heard of Millionaire Matches?"

Andy nodded. Who hadn't? It was the only matchmaking company that actually had any proven results. It also had a lot of notoriety since the men and women who paid for the service were generally wealthy. Many of their more notable matches made the gossip columns.

"Well, I was signed with them." Blake worked the sensitive area between her thumb and index finger. "Until I got blackballed."

Andy's jaw dropped. "What did you do? Did you accuse your personal matchmaker of having man-calves?"

"Worse." Sheepishly he met her gaze. "I slept with the CEO."

Her hand flew from his lap to her mouth. "Oh, my God." She was struck that along with being appalled, she was also rather jealous. Though she knew it wasn't reasonable, she hated the idea of Blake sleeping with other women. Even when it had occurred before he'd met her.

Blake scratched the back of his neck. "When I refused a repeat performance, she blackballed me. Then she told the other matchmaking companies in the area that I was a bad risk. That I was only using the program for easy sex."

She folded her arms over her chest. "You do have a reputation of sleeping with your dates, Blake. Or, I mean, *not sleeping* with your dates." She sounded terse, and she knew it. Well, too bad. She *felt* terse.

"Andy . . ." He trailed off, and she braced herself for whatever horrible thing he was going to say next. If he had to preface it by calling her that, it couldn't be good. "I never slept with any of the dates you set me up with."

"Of course you did," she scoffed. *Not this again.* So much for not ruining the night.

Blake took her chin and turned her head until her eyes locked with his. "No, I didn't. Not a one."

She was about to protest once more, but when she really studied his face she found that his expression was earnest and sincere. He wasn't lying. There was no way he could look at her like that and not be telling the truth.

"Oh," she said, finally accepting it. "Then why didn't you want to see any of them again?"

"Maybe your profile theory is spot-on. They looked good on paper, but in person they weren't what I was looking for." He brought a hand up to her face and caressed her cheek with his thumb. "Or maybe I wasn't ever looking for what I really wanted."

Andy could hear her heartbeat in her ears. The tone of his voice, the softness of his touch, the way he was gazing into her eyes—she had this gut feeling that if she asked him what he was really looking for, there was a good chance he'd say her. She knew it as surely as she had ever known anything. She willed herself to press him, to bring the moment to a head. As long as they were confessing, they could confess this, too.

But before she got the nerve, he threw his own question at her. "What are you looking for, Andy?"

You. Here was her chance. She opened her mouth, but the word didn't come.

"I mean . . ." He dropped his hand from her cheek. "Now that you've decided Max Ellis wasn't the place for you, and you've always been vocal about how beneath you match-making is—I tend to agree, by the way—what would you like to be doing with your life?"

Good thing she'd been silent. How humiliated would she have been if she'd answered that she was looking for him when he was asking about her career goals. Maybe she was misreading his cues. Or maybe he was dancing around the subject as much as she was.

Not knowing which it was, the only thing she could do was ride the conversation as best she could. So she pondered his question sincerely. What *did* she want to do with her life?

She had no clue.

Even if Blake was part of her future, she sure didn't want

to be a housewife. But that was about all she was sure of. "I really don't know, Blake. Is that sad? Maybe I'd go back to school if I could afford it. Honestly, I like the rhythm of going into an office every day. I hadn't realized that before. Working at Donovan InfoTech has been a much better experience than at Ellis's where everyone hated me all the time."

Instead of mocking her response, he nodded. "Something potentially in an office then?"

"Yes." She chuckled at her lame lack of ambition. "Pretty vague, isn't it?"

"Work for me, Andrea."

She rolled her eyes. "I do work for you." The urge to address that very issue tugged at her once again.

"I mean after this. In the future." He grabbed his hand in hers and squeezed. "Work for me."

She studied him. He was serious. Which was ridiculous. "What on earth would I do?"

"There are so many things I could use your skills for." He sounded excited about the prospect. Like a kid in a candy store. Or like Blake in his playroom. "You could work in HR."

Her spirits sank. Hadn't he heard her earlier? She was disgusted with her old self. She couldn't possibly do that again.

She tried to remain polite with her refusal. "Thank you, really. But I don't want to do what I did for Max—"

Blake cut her off. "Not like that. I can use your skills for good. To bring out the potential in employees rather than as something to hold over their heads. We take pride in hiring the best and brightest, but it's hard to identify special skills that could benefit other departments or positions. What do you say?"

She chewed her lip. Using her skills for good was something else entirely. It wasn't like she hadn't thought about it before. Not in conjunction with Donovan InfoTech, necessarily, but in what she could potentially do for a corporation. How she could guide and direct the promise in skilled employees rather than cut them down and crucify them for their hidden weaknesses.

"Come on," Blake urged. "Say yes."

It was awfully tempting. However, she'd also learned working for Max that her impulsive decisions weren't always the best. "Can I think about it?"

"Yes. You may." He grinned—that charming, sexy grin that had her curling her toes. "But you know how I get what I want in these situations."

She thought back to how he'd coerced her into working for him the first time. "That I do."

And finally, with all the times they'd skirted the subject, she couldn't let it go any longer. She took a deep breath. "Blake . . . about that. About the matchmaking . . ." *About us . . .*

He placed a single finger over her lips. "Shh."

His reaction startled her and she peered up at him with questioning brows.

"I just think . . ." He trailed off with a sigh. Then he pulled her to him, wrapping her in his arms. "Let's not do that tonight, Andy. Let's not profile what this is yet. We might miss out. Tomorrow we can deal with what we need to. Okay?"

"Okay." It was a weight off her shoulders, really—the admission that there were things to discuss but permission to put them on hold. She could deal with that.

Especially when Blake was kissing her the way he was. It was fairly easy to put anything on hold in favor of another toe-curling orgasm. Or four.

Chapter Eighteen

Blake woke up early to the sound of Puppy scratching on the bedroom door. It took him several seconds to remember why the dog wasn't sleeping with him, and why instead there was an arm around him and a body pressed up against his hip. Drea stirred in her sleep then and it all came rushing back to him—the amazing evening together, the sex, the postcoital confessions. The pinball.

He had to stifle the moan of pleasure that burst at the memory.

Carefully, he extricated himself from Drea's grasp and got up. The dog had probably already piddled on the floor somewhere, so he really could have stayed in bed longer. But he needed a chance to think without the sight of the beautiful naked woman beside him. Puppy was a good excuse to slip away with his thoughts.

He slipped on a robe and slippers then headed downstairs to let the dog out and pour some coffee. Ellen had set the timer before she'd left the day before, as she always did, and when he emptied the pot, he refilled it for Drea. His housekeeper had also made an egg casserole that he could just heat up. Usually he would dish a small portion and nuke it, but since he wanted to make sure his guest was fed as well, he put the whole serving dish in the oven.

By six fifteen on a Monday morning, Blake had done more domestic activities in a day than he had in a whole month before. Surprisingly, it hadn't killed him. In fact he somewhat enjoyed knowing that his actions were meant to take care of someone else. Especially when that someone else was a person he cared for.

After Puppy had completed his business in the backyard and was happily munching on his food, Blake took his coffee and headed for his office. He chose the space not only out of habit, but because it was his sanctuary, and hence the best place to get some serious contemplation in. On an average day, he'd bring the paper to read, but he didn't even grab it from the front porch. The news in his own life was enough to occupy him for quite a while.

Still, at his desk he found that he had so much to think about, he didn't know where to begin. His eyes settled on a stack of folders that hadn't been there the last time he'd sat there. They must have been the files Andrea had brought over. He'd completely forgotten about them.

Absentmindedly, he removed the elastic band that bound them together. He flipped through the files, reading the labels. RESTAURANTS, CURRENT MOVIE SCHEDULES, LOCAL THEATER. At the bottom, he found the file of the woman he'd been dating. JANE OSBORNE. It had been his first date after he and Drea had started their extracurricular activities, and honestly—Oh, who was he kidding?

Even back then every profile he read seemed flat, every picture the same as the last. For weeks he'd been more interested in gazing in the eyes of the woman who shared his office than in flipping through the head shots of attractive strangers. He'd often ask more questions than he needed just so he could listen to Drea's voice. Just so he could have an excuse to engage with her.

Continuing that string of horrible dates with the most boring woman alive was convenient. Jane Osborne—he circled the name on her file. It was nice, not having to make awkward small talk on a hundred first dates. But the slightly easier small talk he had with Jane was nothing compared with the banter he had with Andrea. He couldn't admit it at the time, too stubborn to look at the truth staring him in the face, but it was there all the same.

Now he was as desperate to shout it to the world as he was to deny it before—he was in love with Andrea Dawson.

He repeated the words in his mind, letting the statement settle in his soul. *I am in love with Andrea Dawson.* Completely, utterly, undeniably in love.

The most surprising part of the whole thing was how un-shocked he was at the revelation. He should have been reeling. Should have been tearing his hair out. Yet he'd never felt more calm.

Wasn't that something?

He sipped his beverage and thought about what this revelation meant for the future. Could he really be considering what he was considering? Andrea didn't fit any of the requirements he'd listed for a wife, yet it didn't feel like she had any qualities that were missing. He was strongly attracted to her physically—the semi he had at that very moment from thinking about her was proof. She talked a lot, but that was fine. He actually enjoyed listening to every word that came out of her pretty mouth. Well, almost every word—sometimes she could be awfully pointed with her observations about him, but only with things he needed to hear.

She didn't cook or clean. So what? They had Ellen. When Ellen retired, they'd find someone else. And if Drea wanted to keep working, so be it. He'd actually prefer having her at Donovan InfoTech where he could see her all day long. Or if she wanted to do something else, that was fine, too. It didn't matter what she did all day, just as long as she was happy and there to come home to at the end of it.

That was really what it all came down to—he wanted Andrea in his life. Permanently. And not as a matchmaker, but as his match.

Was that entirely ridiculous? No. Not entirely. He had planned on getting married, after all. He just hadn't planned on the falling-in-love part. But other people didn't plan on it, either, and all the time they were getting married and living happily ever after. That it had happened to him as well was unexpected, but not ridiculous.

What was entirely ridiculous was that he wanted to marry Andrea *now*. Well, not *now* now; even he saw the inconvenience in running away to Vegas on a moment's notice. And the talk that went around couples who eloped—it just wouldn't be fair to Andrea. But he did want to propose as soon as possible. As in today.

Blake's palms grew sweaty and his pulse ticked up a notch.

Could he do really do that? Propose spontaneously without any forethought or premeditation? Maybe he could wait. He *should* wait.

He pulled out a desk drawer and retrieved the beloved copy of his five-year plan. It was worn and faded, and, honestly, he had every step memorized. Still, he studied it now. The document assumed a six-month engagement after an equally long courtship, and then a moderate-sized wedding with a budget not to exceed one month's salary. Sure he'd been sleeping—or not sleeping—with Andrea for weeks now, but he'd say the courting hadn't officially started until the night before. Nowhere on the agenda was there an allowance for proposing after a one-night dating period. Nowhere was there an allowance for falling in love with his matchmaker. Nowhere was there an allowance for Andrea.

And that was unacceptable.

If there was no Andrea in his plans, then to hell with his plans.

Without another thought, he tore the document in half. Then in half again. And then again and again until the entire thing was nothing but shreds that he tossed in his trash can. Instead of feeling terrified or anxious as he would have supposed that he'd feel, he felt liberated. Because of her—that woman still sleeping in his bed—because of her he was a changed man. Changed for the better. He didn't need to map everything out. He could deviate and improvise. He could be his true self instead of hiding away his interests and passions. In fact . . .

He opened another drawer and pulled out the miniature pinball machine he kept out of sight and set it proudly on his desk, front and center. So long to his old self. He was a new man. A new man who could propose on a whim, if he wanted. And he wanted.

His entire body tingled with his decision, as if he'd been asleep and only now was coming to life. He was going for it, full out. Today his search for a bride would end.

He formulated a new plan—okay, so he still required strategy to his spontaneity; habits die hard, as they say. He had a meeting across town at ten, and Long's Jewelers didn't open until nine thirty. That wasn't enough time for selection, but the general manager was a member of his pinball league. Blake was sure he could call in a favor there. Was six thirty too early to phone him? He'd arrange flowers, of course. Though Drea always recommended roses as the standard, he knew she personally preferred lilies. He could order them, but he'd rather pick some up for her himself. He made a mental note to do that on his way to the office.

Next he needed to set up dinner reservations somewhere fancy. But where?

He found the restaurants file and flipped through the information Drea had gathered. Oleana was too exotic. La Campania, too casual. Hamersley's, too country. Menton, too pricey.

Wait—pricey was perfect for special occasions. It was perfect for Drea. It was short notice but it was a Monday evening, so his chances of getting in were better. He circled the number with his pen then called the reservation line to leave a message. Since he knew he'd be out all morning, he requested they call his secretary with the confirmation.

Now there was only one thing left to deal with—Jane. He debated whether he should phone the woman now, or later. Later was probably best. He could get away with an early-morning call to his league companion, but Jane Osborne would likely be disappointed by his breakup. Crushed, even. He really didn't need to deal with tears on such a wonderful day as this.

Maybe he could have his secretary handle the breakup for him . . .

Even as he thought it he knew that was wrong. Jane had been pleasant enough in all respects. She deserved a softer letdown than that. Besides, Drea would be unimpressed if he didn't behave as a gentleman. He decided he could squeeze in a quick visit to Jane before dinner with Andrea. Roses would be a nice touch. He'd have his secretary order those and have them sent to the office so he could take them to Jane personally. He shot off an email with the request. Then he opened up Jane's file and jotted down her address and phone number for later.

Now to set everything else in motion. He called his friend from the jewelers and arranged a pre-store-hours shopping trip for eight thirty. Next, he wrote a note for

Andrea. He didn't agonize over it as much as he thought he would, the words seeming to come with ease:

> *Good morning, love. I had some things to take care of this morning and then meetings until noon. Keep your lunch free—I'd like to take you out to discuss our profile. Everything's changed now, hasn't it? For the better, I believe. Coffee's in the pot and breakfast's in the oven. In case you have no cash, I've left you some for a cab.*
> *Yours, B*

It wasn't Shakespeare, but it was pretty good for him, he decided. He took the note and snuck back into his bedroom, not wanting to wake the beauty still sleeping there. Quietly, he propped the note on the nightstand on top of a stack of books. Then, noticing her phone on the floor—it must have slipped from her pocket when he'd disposed of her jeans the night before—he set it next to the note. Next, he found his wallet and left a couple of bills on the stand as well.

He had one more task to do concerning Andrea—he needed her ring size. Searching for a measuring device, he settled on the dental floss he kept in the drawer of his nightstand. He ripped off a small piece then, ever so carefully, he uncurled Drea's sleeping hand and wrapped the floss around her finger. She stirred and he froze. Fortunately, she settled again quickly and he was able to get what he needed. It might not be an entirely accurate measurement, but at least the ring wouldn't fall off when he slipped it on her finger.

He looked at his watch. He had time still before he was set to be at Long's Jewelers and a load of nervous energy that needed to be burned off. He'd love to wake up Drea to remedy that, but then all his plans would be disrupted.

A stop at the gym would be the better solution. He could shower there as well and not have to worry about disturbing her at all. It took him all of ten minutes to don some exercise clothes and grab a suit to change into. He packed his shoes and socks into his gym bag and he was ready to go.

At the door of his room, he paused to gaze once more at the woman in his bed. She was nothing he'd expected he'd ever be attracted to and yet he was more into her than anything he could imagine. His chest ached with emotion, but it was the very best feeling in the world. He thanked whatever God might exist for bringing her into his world. If all went well, after today, she'd be part of his life for good.

Andy was awoken by the ringing of her phone. Endless ringing. She tried to ignore it—too sleepy even to think— but the caller was insistent. With eyes still closed, she reached toward the sound. Instead of making contact with her cell, though, she felt her hand knock against a stack of books. And then the books were toppling over. She should probably pick them up. Except the phone had stopped ringing now, so she could worry about the books later.

That was strange—she didn't keep any books by her bed.

That's when she remembered where she was. And with who. And what they'd done the night before.

Wow. Had that really happened?

The recollection was enough to make her sit straight up. She was definitely awake now.

Then the phone began ringing again.

With a groan, Andy leaned over the bed and found Puppy chewing on something on the floor. He took off with his prize when she shooed him. Whatever he had, at least it wasn't her phone. Which was still ringing. She sifted through the pile on the floor until she found her cell. A glance at the screen told her it was Lacy. She pushed the TALK button. "What?"

"Don't *what* me. You didn't come home last night. I need to know that you're alive."

Andy should have expected full-on mothering mode. "I'm alive."

"I hear that now." There was a slight pause that Andy suspected her sister was using to calm down. "I'm guessing you can't talk right now . . ."

Andy glanced at the empty bed next to her. A quick scan of the room and she was sure she was alone. "No, I can talk." Though she wasn't sure she wanted to. Lacy would want all the details of Andy's glorious night with Blake and she wasn't ready to share just yet.

"So? What happened?" Lacy's admonishing tone from a moment before had been replaced with eagerness. "I thought there would be no sleepover."

"I was obviously wrong." *So amazingly wrong.*

"Isn't that against your rules?" There was only the slight hint of *I told you so* to Lacy's tone. Which was admirable, considering.

"It is." Andy thought about the state of things now. "Or it was. I don't really know if there are rules anymore." After last night, she had a feeling all bets were off.

"That sounds intriguing. Tell me more."

Andy opened her mouth to spill the details. Then she closed it again. Was it really fair to be pouring her heart out to her sister when she had so much to say to Blake? Even if it was, the fact was that Andy *wanted* to talk to Blake first. It was a strange feeling. She'd always shared everything with Lacy. And she still would. She just wanted some time first.

She cradled the phone under her cheek and stretched. "Look, Lacy, I just woke up. I haven't had coffee. I haven't even seen Blake yet this morning. Let me get my head functioning and I'll fill you in later." She stifled a yawn. "What time is it anyway?"

"About a quarter after eight."

"Shit!" Andy sat up straight. "I'm never going to make it to work on time."

Lacy laughed. "I'm sure your boss will accept your tardiness."

"Let's hope so. Like I said, I haven't seen him yet." There was always the possibility that Blake had decided to go awkward on her. She hoped not. After everything they'd shared it seemed unlikely. But the house was awfully quiet. Where was he?

"Well, get your pretty ass out of bed and go find him. I'm sure he's just letting you sleep in after an eventful night. Am I right?" Her subtle attempt to pry wasn't missed by Andy.

She rolled her eyes. "I'll talk to you later, Lacy."

"Fine," Lacy said with an exaggerated sigh. "I had a late night myself with my gig and another one this evening so I'm going back to bed. I'll see you for dinner?"

"You always do." A part of Andy hoped that maybe her dinner would be spent with Blake. But the thought of dinner reminded her of his date with Jane that night. Would he still go? There was no way she could know without talking to him.

"I always see you at bedtime as well, and I didn't last night so I think it was a fair question. Dinner, then. Love you."

"Love you, too." Andy disconnected the call and then noticed the red flashing light indicating her phone's battery was low. She was amazed it wasn't dead already since she usually charged it overnight. She tossed it back on the nightstand, stood, and stretched. Her body was delightfully sore. There were muscles she'd forgotten about that burned with the reminder of recent activity. And what fun that activity was.

With a smile on her lips, she bent to pick up the books and things she'd knocked to the ground. There was a Steve Jobs biography—that didn't surprise her—but the remaining three were detective novels. Not just mysteries—the old-school 1940s kind, full of chain-smoking dolls and hard-drinking private eyes. *Another Blake Donovan secret.* Her smile widened as she replaced the books on the nightstand plus a couple of twenties that must have been lying on top of the books. How could she not be completely entranced with this self-built millionaire who loved pinball, *Downton Abbey*, and noir detective novels? The answer was she couldn't.

The intensity of her adoration was what bewildered her the most. She didn't merely admire him or find him fascinating. She also felt that other emotion—the one that she'd sworn to her sister was not going to happen, and yet here it was, totally happening in every fiber of her being and not just in the middle of sex. She loved Blake. Like, *loved*, loved him. Like, could see herself married to him with children and puppies and the whole shebang.

It was a completely exhilarating feeling that warmed her from head to toe, made her giddy like a teenager. It also frightened her a tad bit. But it was the sort of frightening that she was more than willing to face.

She found his T-shirt from the pile of clothing on the floor and threw it on. Eager to be with the man she loved, to kiss him and wrap her arms around his strong form, she set about searching for him. With Puppy at her heels, she peeked first in his office. Finding that empty, she followed the scent of coffee to the kitchen, assuming that was a good place to start. No Blake. But she found a mug and poured herself a cup before resuming her hunt.

She wandered the rest of the floor, calling his name with no answer. Before heading back upstairs, she peeked in the garage. His car was gone. How strange.

With a mixture of confusion and disappointment, she returned to his office, the room she felt the most comfortable in. She curled up in the armchair by the window and sipped her coffee as she debated what Blake's absence meant. There were really only a couple of options to debate. Either he'd left because something had come up, an emergency of some sort, like he'd run out of creamer—in which case, he would have left a note or would return shortly.

But she hadn't seen a note and it had been nearly thirty minutes now since she'd awoken, which was past the *return shortly* window. And she'd found creamer for her coffee with no problem.

Which led to the other possibility—the awful, terrible option that made her stomach churn and her heart ache just thinking about it: Blake wasn't there because he didn't want to be. Because he didn't want to see her.

That was ridiculous, wasn't it? Even if their night hadn't been as incredible for him as it had been for her—a notion that caused a lump to form in her throat—even if it had just been another night in the life of Blake Donovan, he wouldn't be so rude or heartless to simply walk out on her. Would he?

No. He wouldn't. He couldn't. He'd come too far in their time together. She didn't even have a ride—he knew that. There was no way he'd leave her stranded. No way would he abandon all his social graces, no matter how miserable an occasion her visit might have been. She couldn't believe that about him.

Then she spotted the files on his desk—the date files that she'd brought with her the night before. When she'd left them there, they were still wrapped in their elastic band. Now they were spread out, a couple of them open. He'd looked at them that very morning, he had to have.

She stood and crossed over to his desk, a ball of dread forming in her gut. Without touching anything, she circled to sit in Blake's chair, to see things exactly as he saw them last. The topmost open file belonged to Jane Osborne, name circled. That didn't mean anything, of course. Maybe he was thinking about canceling his date with her or looking up her phone number or a million different reasons.

Under Jane's file, though, was the restaurant file. Menton's profile sheet was on top. The reservation number was circled in black pen. That hadn't been there yesterday. Blake must have done it that morning. It was so obvious. Oh, God. Blake was planning to take Jane to Menton's—the nicest restaurant in all of Boston.

Andy's heart sank.

When she'd met Jane all those weeks ago, Andy had been ecstatic. She'd found the perfect candidate for Blake in Jane. She had the right hair, the right eyes, the right background, the right personality. Finding her had been kismet.

Now it felt less like kismet and more like karma.

For all the shitty things she'd done working for Max Ellis, this was her reward. She now had to sit back and watch as the man she loved continued to date another woman—a woman who was perfectly picked for him by none other than herself.

A tear trickled down Andy's cheek. Another threatened, but she held it in and forced herself to calm down, to breathe and think it through. It might not be what it looked like. After their night together, Blake wouldn't treat her this way. It was a lot to assume based on two open files. There was probably another explanation. She simply had to talk to him and find out.

Using his desk phone, she dialed his cell. There was no answer. Where the hell would he be at eight thirty in the morning? If he'd seen his house number come up, he may have avoided it realizing it was her. But then he probably would have simply dismissed the call and it would have gone straight to voice mail.

She was overthinking. She couldn't know anything without talking to him.

Deciding she'd give him the benefit of the doubt until they spoke—well, as much benefit as she could muster—Andy headed back to the bedroom to get her clothes. She dressed and grabbed her phone off the nightstand, spotting the twenties that had fallen to the floor earlier. Suddenly it occurred to her that the money hadn't been there the night before when she'd reached for the remote. Had it?

No, she did not remember seeing it.

Did that mean . . . ? Was it . . . ? She couldn't formulate the thought into words, the idea was so putrid. Still, she had to take this at face value. And face value said that Blake had left her money. On the bedside table. For sex. Like she was a hooker.

Her vision went red. He hadn't even treated her as good as a hooker—a hooker would have been paid more than forty fucking dollars. They'd been through this before, with a near-disastrous outcome. They'd agreed to never talk about pay for sex again. Was leaving it on the nightstand his way of sneaking around that agreement? Or now that all the rules had been broken, was this also off the table?

God, this better be something different from what it looked like, because if it wasn't she might very well do something drastic. Something that made burning Ellis's files look like model employee behavior in comparison.

Hands shaking with fury and heart still bruised from Blake's absence, she used the remaining battery in her dying cell phone to call a cab. She briefly considered hugging Puppy good-bye—she had fallen just as hard for the little guy—but he had gone back to chewing on whatever bit of debris had his attention earlier.

With a soft, "Bye, Puppy," she went outside to wait, locking the door behind her. She didn't trust her restraint enough to be left alone in the Donovan mansion, and it wouldn't be fair to act without hearing Blake's side. Besides, Lacy would kick her ass if she got hit with another lawsuit. At this point, the latter was a bit more motivating than the former.

Chapter Nineteen

By the time Andy got home, showered and cleaned up, and then to the office, it was nearly eleven. She'd never been that late for work before. As she rode the elevator up, she considered feeling guilty about her tardiness. That idea was quickly smothered by the other emotions waging war inside her—rage, jealousy, hurt, betrayal. She kept reminding herself that she didn't know the whole story yet, but it did little to calm her. She was on the warpath and God help anyone who got in her way.

She entered the office with guns blazing, ready to accuse and blame. But Blake wasn't at his desk. His computer wasn't even on. Had he not even come in?

Immediately, she stormed back out to interrogate the secretary. "Where's Blake?"

"He has meetings all morning, Ms. Dawson," she answered. "He'll be in this afternoon."

"Dammit." She cursed again under her breath when she realized her first swear had been out loud. "Fine. Just . . . fine." There was no use taking her disappointment out on Sarah. It wasn't her fault that Blake was absent or an ass.

The phone rang and Sarah excused herself to answer it. Andy was about to turn back to the office when a delivery woman approached the desk carrying a beautiful bouquet of red roses.

Her breath hitched. *Blake isn't an ass after all!* He'd gotten her flowers. Roses, which were commonplace and lacking in character, but it was the thought that counted. It didn't exactly make up for waking up alone or for being paid like a pro. Still, it was promising.

She felt her face glowing as she accepted the vase from the girl. Then she set them down on Sarah's desk so she could sign the handheld tablet. She wished the girl a nice day and turned to admire the flowers.

"Ah," Sarah exclaimed as she hung up her phone. "The flowers for Ms. Osborne arrived."

Andy's heart skipped a beat. "I'm sorry, what did you say?" She must have misheard. Sarah didn't know the name of the candidates Blake took out. At least, Andy hadn't thought she did.

"The flowers are for a Ms. Osborne."

Apparently Andy was wrong. Sarah obviously knew Jane's name. But maybe Sarah was wrong about the flowers being for Jane. Andy scanned the bouquet for a card. "Are you sure they're for Jane? I don't see her name anywhere."

"Yes. Mr. Donovan emailed me to order them for her this morning before he went to his meetings."

Just like that the warm fuzzy feeling was gone and the rage was back. So he'd found time to email his secretary with instructions on ordering flowers for Jane, but he couldn't leave a simple note for the woman he'd screwed all night?

Fine. Just . . . fine.

Sarah stood and fake-swooned over the roses. "Aren't they lovely? This one must be special. Mr. Donovan never

lets anyone in on his private life. I had occasionally wondered if he was a cyborg."

Andy's hand tightened into a fist at her side. She'd
never wanted to hit something so hard in her life—or
some*one*. God help Blake Donovan when he arrived. For
that matter, God help anyone who got in her way before
then.

She spun toward the office when Sarah stopped her.
"Could you put this note on Mr. Donovan's desk?"

Andy spoke through gritted teeth. "Sure." She snatched
the note out of Sarah's hand. Then, because she was com-
pulsively nosy, she scanned the message before walking
away. "Blake has reservations tonight at Menton?"

"Yes. They just called to confirm. Like I said—this
woman must be special."

Then her assumption that morning had been right. Blake
had a whole evening planned for Jane Osborne—roses,
dinner at the classiest restaurant in town. So much for
giving him the benefit of the doubt. Now she'd give him
the benefit of a knee to the crotch.

Sarah's eyes flitted to a spot behind Andy. "Can I help
you?"

Andy turned to see a young man carrying a small silver bag and a clipboard. "Yeah, I've got a package for
Blake Donovan."

"What is it today? Delivery central?" She'd lost her cool
and didn't even care anymore. Too bad if she snapped at
the deliveryman—boy, really. It was Blake's fault, not hers.

The boy's eyes widened with apprehension. "Uh, I could
come back . . ."

"Don't be ridiculous. Give it here." Andy held her hand
out for the bag.

"It's for a Mr. Blake Donovan. I'm supposed to only
leave it with him." He was one of those rule followers,
apparently.

Well, rules were horseshit. What had been the point of the rules with her and Blake? It hadn't gotten them anywhere. Hadn't gotten her anything but heartbroken.

"Blake's not here. This is his office, though." She pointed to the sign on the wall. "See? Blake Donovan. If you have to leave it with him directly, then you *are* going to have to come back."

His eyes danced from Andy's to Sarah's and back to Andy's. "I'm not sure."

"Just give me the damn package." Andy was pretty sure the boy handed the bag over because of fear and not because she'd convinced him he was doing the right thing. "Thank you. I'll make sure he gets it."

"Wait, you have to—" Tentatively he held his clipboard toward her.

"Yes, yes, of course." She wrapped the bag strap around her wrist and snapped the board from him. "Where do I have to sign?"

"On the line. At the bottom."

Andy glanced over the receipt looking for the signature line when her eyes caught on the package description. *Two-carat Lucida cut, platinum band, sized.*

She almost dropped the clipboard. Her knees weakened and her breath left her entirely. All the anger she'd felt only a second before dissolved into a crashing wave of anguish. *A diamond ring.* It couldn't be. There was no way.

In a daze, she finished with the delivery boy. She couldn't say how she managed to walk when she barely had strength in her legs to stand, but the next thing she knew she was sitting behind Blake's desk with the silver bag clutched in her grasp.

She took a deep breath and peeked inside the bag. Sure enough, next to a fancy-looking pamphlet and a bottle of cleaner, there was a small, black velvet box. The kind of box that only held jewelry, and small enough that the jewelry inside was limited to very few options.

Andy's hand shook as she took the box out of the bag. She closed her eyes and flipped the top open, hoping with all her might that she'd read the receipt wrong and inside would be a pair of earrings.

But when she opened her lids again, she came face-to-face with the most beautiful ring she'd ever seen in her life. The two carats of rectangle diamond sat on top of a platinum band. Definitely worth more money than she'd ever made in a single year. It was breathtaking and gorgeous and if Blake presented it to her she'd dissolve into happy tears and she'd squeal even though she'd never been a squealer. Squee, even.

But the ring wasn't hers. It wasn't meant for her finger. And so the tears that splashed down her cheek were not of the happy variety. They also weren't of the gentle variety—her face and nose were soon a mess of snot and salt while her mind spun with the horrible soul-crushing revelation that Blake Donovan was planning to propose to Jane Osborne.

How the hell had that happened?

They'd only been on a handful of dates—how had Blake decided that this woman was the one? They hadn't even slept together—or *not slept* together—at least, that's what he claimed. It was ridiculous that he was making such a big decision after such a small amount of time. But then—Blake liked to tell Andy how his lightning decisions were famous and spot-on. Here was her proof.

Though—and this was agonizing for Andy to admit—if Blake had ever asked her to marry him, she probably wouldn't have said no. And they'd never even been on one date together. Not officially, anyway. Her stomach threatened to drop straight through her shaking knees.

It dawned on her that the way she felt about Blake could very well be the way he felt about Jane. That he could adore her every flaw and cherish the quality of their time rather than quantity. Maybe he didn't need any longer to know that he would love her forever. After all, Andy was pretty confident that she would love Blake forever.

And if he did feel that way about Jane, then there was nothing that Andy could do to convince him otherwise. She could sabotage every single one of their encounters and he'd never waver. All her efforts had been a waste. Most important—there was no reason for her to stick around any longer.

The thought was her own lightning bolt, one that seared through her, cleaving her heart in half. She thought she'd felt broken that morning. She was wrong. This was ten times that pain. There was nothing she could imagine that would have hurt more.

With no tissues in the office, her swollen eyes were still leaking when she finally cleared them enough to write a note for Blake. Instead of writing all the rage-filled insults that she'd been collecting in her brain that morning, she wrote her letter of resignation. Hopefully the tearstains that streaked the paper would fade by the time he read it.

After a long morning of meetings that drifted into lunch, Blake was eager to get to the office. To Andrea. He hadn't stopped thinking about her since he'd left her in his bed. Even while he'd finalized a huge IT contract, every thought had been on her—her eyes, her sassy mouth, the way she felt wrapped around him while he buried himself inside of her.

He missed her like it had been weeks since he'd seen her instead of hours. If he hadn't left his phone in his locker at the gym, he'd have called and texted her a million times by now. Who cared? He'd buy a new phone. He'd buy the whole company new phones if they asked, that was the kind of mood he was in.

Luckily, he had the afternoon free. They'd have lunch together, then they could spend the rest of the day . . . well, the possibilities were endless. Though he had a few creative ideas. In the evening, he'd stop by Jane's and deliver his bad news. Then it would be dinner with Andrea—a dinner neither of them would forget.

Excitement pulsed through his veins as he passed his secretary's empty desk. She must be at lunch, he decided, and noted that the flowers had arrived. That was good. In his hand, he clutched the bouquet of stargazer lilies he'd picked up on the way back from his meeting. They said *Drea* like roses never could. Roses were bland and overbred; lilies were wild and sensual.

He couldn't wait to give them to her. He wanted to see her face light up. He wanted to know she was as over-the-moon happy as he was. He wanted her to see that he saw her, Andrea Dawson, and loved every phenomenal atom for no other reason than that they existed.

Except when he stepped into his office, the place was deserted. He crinkled his forehead wondering where on earth Andy could be. His note had been clear that they'd have lunch together. *She must be in the bathroom.* Freshening up or whatever it was that women did in there.

Blake unbuttoned his jacket and started toward his desk when he heard someone come in behind him. He turned, expecting Andrea, but instead came face-to-face with his latest Sarah.

"Mr. Donovan, I'm back from my meeting."

Blake nodded. He'd forgotten it was the monthly secretaries lunch day. Whatever that was about. Gossip about him, he assumed. "Good session?"

"Some of it. Nothing worth sharing. Did you get you my message about dinner?"

It took him a second to recall that he'd asked her to make his reservations. "I just got back myself. Haven't even looked at my desk."

"Well, you're all set for seven sharp at Menton. You're lucky the manager is one of our clients. Do you know how hard it is to get into that place?"

Of course he knew. It was one of the best restaurants in town. He ignored the ridiculous question. "Please get Jane Osborne on the line for me, will you? Her number is . . ." He pulled the paper he'd written her information on that morning from his pocket. "Here. And I'll need that back." He'd noted her address there, too, so he knew where to meet her for his brush-off.

"Got it, Mr. Donovan." She took the sheet and hurried out.

When he was alone, Blake headed to his desk. On his chair he found a small silver bag. Inside was the box with the ring he'd chosen for Drea. He took it out and shoved it in his inside pocket, at once relieved and anxious. Relieved because it had arrived safely—he'd had to leave it to be sized, agreeing only if it were delivered as soon as possible. That it had made it was a load off his shoulders.

On the other hand, he'd requested it be left only with him. It had a forty-thousand-dollar price tag, after all, and shouldn't be left lying around. Also, what if Drea had seen it? That would make for a poor proposal surprise.

He tensed as he explored that idea further. *Had* she seen it? Was that why she wasn't here now? Had she gotten overwhelmed? Freaked out? Did she not want to marry him? Oh, God, what if he wasn't as good a read as he always considered himself?

The dread building in his chest was interrupted by the buzz of his intercom. "I have Ms. Osborne on the line, Mr. Donovan."

He'd have to wonder about the ring later. He pushed the

worry down with the TALK button. "Send her back." Blake removed his jacket and put it on the back of his chair while he waited for the call to come through. After letting it ring twice, he picked it up. "Jane? It's Blake Donovan."

He paused to let her respond, but also because he wasn't really sure what to say next.

"Blake. How nice to hear from you. Also, quite a surprise. Is something wrong?"

"No, no, of course not." But he understood why she'd ask since he'd never bothered to call before. "Actually, Jane, I'm sorry I haven't gotten back to you about tonight's plans."

"Are we still on for seven? I expected to hear from Andy earlier today about where to meet."

"About that. Are you free earlier? Five thirty, perhaps?" His eye caught on a note folded on his desk in front of him. It was addressed simply *Blake*, but he recognized the handwriting.

Jane *hmm*'d as though she was looking at her calendar. "I have an errand to run at four, but I could probably meet you somewhere by five. If we could do something . . ."

He'd meant to tell her he'd meet her at her house. Safer than a breakup in public. But that plan disappeared along with everything the woman was saying—he was too engrossed in the letter in his hand.

This serves as my official notice of resignation. I apologize for not giving more notice, but I believe I'm no longer needed in the capacity I was hired. You may forward my final check to my house. Please do not contact me again.
Andrea Dawson

It was short and to the point, yet it took him three times through before he registered its meaning. Andrea had left him. *Left him*, left him. Not just quit her job, but asked him not to contact her again. Everything in his body seemed to deflate at once. His lungs, his shoulders, his rib cage, his heart—sinking, sinking, sinking. Where had he gone wrong? Had she realized he was about to propose after all? Was she really only there for the sex and the money?

The idea disgusted him. Sickened him. He could barely sit with it without losing the contents of his stomach.

"Blake? Are you still there?"

He didn't know how long Jane had been calling to him before he registered it. "Just a minute, please, Jane." He placed the phone on hold and set the receiver down so he could think.

Andrea had left him.

He could call her. Or go to her house. If they talked, maybe they could work something out.

Except she'd asked for him not to contact her, and she hated it when he was a headstrong dick—her words, not his. Employing a tactic she despised wasn't a way to score points. Besides, if she'd walked away so easily, would he really be able to do anything to change her mind? He'd probably end up begging, and begging was never attractive.

So he was left with this—a note and no Andrea.

The disappointment was so great he knew there had to be another term for it. Heartache, maybe. He felt literally broken. He'd planned to ask her to marry him. Planned to spend his life with her. It was one thing if the night before hadn't meant as much to her as it had to him, but the way she'd left showed that it meant *nothing* to her. Absolutely nothing.

Whether she knew about his plans to propose or not, she'd left him. Either way, thank God she'd quit before he proposed. She likely would have laughed in his face. At least he'd come out of this with his dignity somewhat intact, even if it was at the cost of his heart.

His heart! For heaven's sake, he'd barely registered he owned one before Andrea had shown up out of nowhere. She'd found it, infiltrated it, become one with it, and then shattered it from the inside out.

So what did he do now? He was practically paralyzed. Blake Donovan *never* didn't know what to do. Or say. But right now—he was an ice statue, not just frozen, but unable to achieve motion. All he could hope for was a fast melt, not to prolong the suffering.

The phone beeped reminding him that he had a call on hold. *Oh, right. Jane.* If he'd stuck to his original plan and never broken the rules with his hired help, then he'd probably be proposing to Jane about now. He'd have the life he always intended. Now he had nothing.

Though he did still have the "ideal" woman waiting on the phone for him. Maybe he shouldn't break up with Jane. If Drea didn't want him, he might as well go to plan B. Or plan A, rather, since Jane Osborne—or someone like her—had been what he'd originally intended to end up with. He could keep seeing her. It might keep his mind off his horrid despair, anyway. If only the churning in his guts would listen to his mind.

With as much energy as he could muster, he picked up the receiver and depressed the HOLD button. "Sorry. I had a business situation come up." True enough. Ish. True-enough-ish. That was a thing, right? Andy would think it was a thing. "I'm back now."

"Not a problem. So five thirty, then?"

Jane's enthusiasm should have made him feel guilty. It didn't, but he grabbed onto it like a lifeline. If she could be happy about being with him, wasn't that better than the alternative? He couldn't, *couldn't* acknowledge the pit of despair about to swallow him like Luke Skywalker and the Sarlacc. *Star Wars.* Andy was so far in his head, he couldn't even create his own analogies!

He didn't think about it much further. He just acted. "Never mind. My plans just changed. I'll send a car to pick you up at six thirty. Our reservations at Menton are for seven."

. "I'll be ready." Her smile carried through the phone. "Menton—that's quite a fancy restaurant. Is it an occasion?"

It was an occasion. The worst occasion. The day that Andrea Dawson walked out of his life for good. The last thing he wanted to do was go out with another woman. But he'd been around long enough to learn that tough situations were best met with fortitude. After all, that seemed to be what Jane did.

"Simply dinner." He was surprised his voice came out so evenly. "The manager is a client, and I was lucky to snag a last-minute table."

"Exciting. I've never been there before."

Blake stifled a groan as he said his good-byes. It felt like a betrayal—taking another woman on a date with reservations meant for the love of his life. He'd get through it, of course. Still, the way he felt seemed to warrant at least an afternoon of moping. He gathered his things and left the office. Hopefully when he came back tomorrow he'd be able to forget all the memories he and Drea had created there. Replacing a wingback was one thing—it would be awfully expensive if he had to remodel the whole damn place.

"—or Chicken Marsala."

Blake blinked and looked from the television to his housekeeper. She was standing at the side of the couch, a questioning furrow in her brow. How long had she been there?

He paused *Downton Abbey*—he'd barely been paying attention to it anyway. "What was that you were saying, Ellen?"

She smiled patiently. "I asked what you wanted me to do for your dinner tonight. I could grill some steaks or make my Chicken Marsala."

It was his turn to be puzzled. "Those choices sound awfully fancy for just one. Besides, I'm going out tonight." More and more he regretted his decision to take Jane to Menton. Too late to back out now, though. Maybe he could say he got sick. He certainly felt sick.

He'd taken some Pepto. An hour later, he was chewing the ginger candies Ellen swore by. It turned out there wasn't really anything you could take for "heartsick." Despite his best Google searches.

"Tomorrow then," Ellen persisted. "What should the menu be for then?"

"Leftovers will be fine." On second thought, eating leftovers from the meal he'd shared with Andrea sounded dismal. "Or I'll heat a frozen lasagna."

"So you'll be having no dinner guests tomorrow?" Her expression was so hopeful that Blake had to wonder if she was losing it.

"Do I ever?"

"After yesterday, I thought . . ."

He'd forgotten that Ellen had known Andrea had visited. Actually, he had spent all afternoon trying to forget everything about the night before, though the task had turned out to be near impossible. Memories sat just under his every thought. Flashes would permeate his conscience at the most inopportune moments. Like now when he was listening his elderly housekeeper, it probably wasn't appropriate to be picturing that thing Drea could do with her tongue.

He blinked his eyes, erasing the image from his mind and returning his focus to Ellen, who was still talking. He hoped he hadn't missed much.

". . . you've been going out a lot lately. All those dates

at restaurants, what a waste of money. I thought perhaps you might invite Drea here again sometime. I'm happy to prepare a home-cooked meal. Simply tell me the date and I'll take care of it all."

"Invite Drea . . . ?" He furrowed his brow as he attempted to piece together the meaning in Ellen's statement. "No, no. I haven't been going out with Drea. It's Jane I've been seeing." *Plain Jane*. He ignored the ache of how much he wished it were Drea he'd been seeing instead. Wished it were Drea he was seeing tonight.

Ellen frowned. "Oh. I thought that . . . Drea just seemed . . . well, I suppose it's none of my business."

"I suppose it's not." Perhaps he delivered that a little too harshly, but really—discussing his love life with his housekeeper? Not a chance.

Except, if she had something worthwhile to say . . .

"I'll plan on buying you some microwave meals tomorrow, then." She started to leave. Microwave meals? Not her frozen concoctions? She must be pissed.

"Ellen, wait a minute." He paused to let her turn her attention back to him. "If it *were* your business, what would you say?"

She gave an innocent shrug. "I don't know. I hadn't given it much thought."

Blake peered skeptically at his housekeeper. She *always* had an opinion. Solicited or not. "Somehow I doubt that."

"Well." Her eyes looked upward as she pretended to consider. "I guess I'd ask you if you wish that Andrea would join you again for dinner."

Yes, he wished it. More than anything. "It doesn't matter what I wish, so the question's irrelevant."

She scowled at him. "Now, that hardly seems fair."

"Life isn't fair. I learned that one young."

"Tough talk is all that is. And you are much tougher than I, if you actually believe that drivel." Ellen perched on the arm of the couch and folded her hands in her lap. "But if speaking about Andrea is off the table, then I'd ask you about this Jane woman—do you wish that *she* would join you for dinner?"

Now Blake scowled. "I'm having dinner with her tonight, aren't I?"

"I mean, tomorrow. Here for dinner."

What was his housekeeper getting at? "If I'd wanted her here, I'd have invited her."

"I see." Ellen pursed her lips. "Then you won't be going out with Jane again?"

"I didn't say that." He hadn't quite decided about Jane, but he had a feeling he'd see her again. Not at his home, but out. Though he wasn't obligated to Ellen, it seemed she was waiting for an explanation. "I simply—don't want her with me here. My house is my space. No obligations. My time is my time."

"But if you had the choice, you'd spend your free time with Drea?" Ellen didn't wait for him to respond. "You don't have to answer. I think I understand the situation now."

"That makes one of us."

"What still confuses me, though, is this Jane woman. If you don't want to spend time with her, then why are you insisting you are dating her?"

It was a valid question, one that Blake pondered every other minute. He sighed. "She's fond of me, I believe."

"Fond of you? That's certainly a nice thing." Ellen raised a brow. "But how do you feel about her?"

"She's excellent dating material. Pleasant. Pretty. She'd make a fine wife." He'd told himself this so much that afternoon it had practically become his mantra.

Ellen swiveled to face him straight-on. "Maybe she will, but not for you, Blake Donovan. Please don't tell me that you're considering proposing to her."

"It had crossed my mind," he mumbled.

"Now, that's just downright mean." In the many years he'd known Ellen, she'd never spoken so sternly to him. "How is that fair to this Jane? If you don't love her—and I can tell by the way that you speak of her that you don't—then you're nothing but an emotional terrorist. You're holding her heart hostage. What if she could have the chance to find someone who really cared for her? Someone who adored the ground she walked on? But instead, she's wasting her time with you, when you've clearly already decided she'll never be that special to you. It's cruel."

Rarely did Blake let anyone school him as his housekeeper had just done. His immediate instinct was to defend his behavior. But there was affection in her scolding and her words were surprisingly not unreasonable.

He tried the finger steeple, but found he couldn't keep his fists from balling. "If I can't be with Andrea, why shouldn't I be with someone who is fond of me? What else do I have? You're leaving me, Andrea left me, I just want someone to be with *me*!" He was shocked at his own petulant tone and words, but his long-suffering housekeeper actually smiled.

"Just because you can't be with the person you want to be with doesn't mean you should take away the opportunity for someone else to find true love." Ellen's tone was softer now, reminding him of long years past when his grandmother would correct him on a temper tantrum or similar ill behavior.

The familiarity of her delivery caused him to really listen. To really consider her words.

"I should break up with Jane." It had been his original plan. Now he didn't trust any of his plans.

Ellen nodded. "You're being reactionary. And you shouldn't date anyone again until you're over Andrea."

"She goes by Andy, actually." Saying her name in any form caused him more heartache than he wanted to admit.

Particularly the one he knew was closest to her heart—the heart he'd thought so earnestly belonged to him. "And I'm not sure that I'll ever be over her."

"Then you'll be spending the rest of your life single." She stood and brushed down the skirt of her apron. "Either that or you could try to win the girl."

He laughed sharply. "Funny thing is that I thought I *had* won the girl. Turned out I was wrong."

There was no future for him with Andy, but Ellen was right about Jane. He'd thought that he was a catch because he had money and stability. But what about her? Didn't she deserve honesty? Fuck, Andrea had *warned* him about this. If he couldn't have her, he could accept living the rest of his life in a loveless relationship, but Jane hadn't been given that option. He had to rethink his decision to continue seeing her.

"I'll call things off with Jane." He could still break up with her tonight at Menton. A breakup over a nice candlelit dinner? It was probably a more gentlemanly send-off. He winced at the idea that Andrea would likely be proud. *You didn't order for her, did you?* Her voice was already in his head, telling him how to proceed.

"I think you've made the right decision." Ellen patted him on the shoulder reassuringly. "And will you give it a go with Andrea? I mean, Andy?"

His eyes flew to Ellen's. "I didn't say that." He didn't have it in him to explain that Andy had left him. She was gone from his life entirely. There was nothing to *give a go*.

Ellen tsked. "Your generation gives up so easily. Dinner for one tomorrow then?"

After tonight, every night for the rest of my life. I'm done. "Dinner for one."

Chapter Twenty

Menton's service was as to be expected—perfect, unobtrusive, and worth the price. The Chef's Tasting Course option took most of the decisions out of the ordering process. Even the wine was paired for them. If Blake were in a different state of mind, it would have been a very lovely evening. More than once during the evening's progression he wondered if he should have taken Jane to a less fancy location. If they'd gone to Uni, they'd have finished an hour ago, and he'd already be home with an old Dashiell Hammett novel. Wallowing. He wanted to wallow.

Notes for his next relationship-ending date, he thought. Though there wouldn't be any of those in his future if he stuck to his new plan of permanent solitude.

Blake waited until Jane had pushed away her Foie Gras de Canard before he prepared to deliver his news. His announcement would likely spoil the rest of dinner, and the meal was one price for all seven courses, so he wanted to get the most out of his dollar. Really, he'd meant to hold off until dessert had been served, but by the time he'd finished his own main course, he was too anxious to get the evening over with.

Just as he was about to speak, though, the waiter arrived.

"The check please," Blake said before the man could persuade them to indulge in another course. "We'll take dessert with us."

"You'd like me to box up the crème brûlée?" The waiter sounded horrified.

"I would," Blake answered with a straight face, but inwardly he grimaced at the thought of crème brûlée to go. What a faux pas.

The server groaned in disgust. "Yes, sir." And went on his way.

The moment they were alone again, Blake dove in. "Jane, I have something I need to say." He paused for her attention. Then, realizing she might take his statement as a more celebratory preamble, he rushed through the rest of his speech. "I've led you on. While I at one time believed that you had everything that I wanted in a woman, I've known for quite some time now that I can never have feelings for you. At the risk of sounding cliché, it's truly me, not you."

Jane took a sip of her wine, her expression showing no turmoil, no devastation, no sign of impending tears.

He must not have been clear.

"Perhaps I should say this another way—I don't think we should see each other anymore." That was too passive. "We shouldn't see each other anymore. Jane, I'm breaking up with you."

Again, no response.

This was becoming frustrating. He tried to hide the irritation as he prodded her for acknowledgment. "You do understand what I'm saying, don't you?"

She set her glass down before meeting his eyes. "I understand you perfectly, Blake."

Her eyes, he noted, were still perfectly clear. Maybe she wasn't going to be upset after all. That was somewhat disappointing to his ego though much more convenient since they were in public. A woman in tears on a date always put her companion in poor light.

Jane continued with stoicism. "You should know that I'm not surprised. I'm well aware that we lack the chemistry that is usually expected from a couple that is courting. I also don't have feelings for you. However, I don't think that's any reason we should call it quits. In fact, now that we've both admitted the truth of our emotions, or lack thereof, we can potentially take our relationship to the next level."

Blake's brow fell into confusion. "I'm not sure I'm following you." That was embarrassing. After all he'd done to prepare himself for this breakup he was the one that had been caught off guard.

Jane dabbed at her mouth with her linen napkin then folded it precisely into quarters before returning it to her lap. He liked that about her—her attention to minute detail. She really was very much his ideal woman. Or what he'd once thought was his ideal woman. Drea had chosen well for his would-be wife. The level of knowledge she had about him would be violating if it weren't so comforting. He shut that thought down before his brain could wrap around the contrast.

Jane leaned forward in her seat. "I'm saying, Blake, that I don't believe love is a requirement in marriage. I'd even go so far as to say that love should not be included at all. It can be a distraction in a successful union."

"That's ridiculous. Love is practically synonymous with marriage." Blake heard himself saying the words, wondering where in the hell they'd come from. He'd never thought much about love in romantic terms. He'd simply always assumed that once he found the *right* woman, it would follow. Yet another instance where he'd been wrong.

Jane placed laced her fingers together, careful to keep her elbows off the table. "Think of matrimony as a business contract—isn't it much easier to work with someone that you don't have strong feelings for? Sure, you want to get along—and you and I get along well enough—but anything deeper than that, your dealings become complicated and all sense of logic and judgment flies out the window."

Blake couldn't help nodding. He'd learned that lesson in the early days of his career. Going into business with friends never worked out well. Someone always got emotional, someone always lost money . . .

Oh.

He understood what Jane was trying to illustrate. Dear God, those had been his thoughts on marriage early on as well. Had been for as long as he'd considered the possibility. Jane was speaking the words he'd have written in a diary, if he'd been self-indulgent enough to keep one. When had he changed his mind?

When he'd met Andrea Dawson, that's when.

But she wasn't in his life anymore, so she shouldn't be a factor in his decision-making.

And what decision was he making, anyway? He could feel his blood pressure rising, even as his date's cheeks remained as pale as he'd ever seen them. "What are you talking about exactly, Jane?"

"I'm simply suggesting a marriage of convenience."

He would have looked for the hidden cameras from a reality prank show had Jane's demeanor not been completely sincere.

"Look, I know what you want in a wife. Your expectations were made clear by your assistant. By Andy."

Blake wondered if Jane could tell that his heart skipped a beat at the mention of Andy's name.

"My expectations are similar." The way she continued on, it seemed she was oblivious. "I'd like to have a home, a good income, one child. Two, perhaps. Security is important to me, both financially and emotionally. And the ability to spend time on the things I want to pursue. I'd like to work on a charity for Alzheimer's, for example. Head the parents' board at my children's school. Be a model wife."

He listened intently. Her dream future sounded very familiar. "That sounds like a pleasant life. And you want all of this without love?"

"I think the only way to assure this type of security is without love. Love interferes. It blinds you. It allows you to settle. I no longer expect much from love." Her expression briefly clouded. "Plenty of cultures rely on arranged marriages to build a mutual respect over time, thus creating a lasting relationship that 'love' never could." Her face hardened again.

Was that what he'd been willing to do with Andrea? To settle? To throw a log on a fire that was already on its way out? The idea left a bad taste in Blake's mouth, but it also resonated somewhere in an old part of his soul. This was what he'd always believed. Jane was making sense. *Squash* that annoying little voice inside saying his only love was gone.

He rubbed a finger along the crook of his chin. "You mentioned children. Did you want to adopt?" It was crazy that he was even asking. Where on earth did he expect this conversation to go?

"I'd prefer to have my babies the normal way. Which means that, yes, we'd have to be sexually active. With each other." Her expression remained serious. "I don't see that as a problem, though, do you? You're an attractive man. I find you physically appealing."

"Well, thank you." He'd never been complimented in such a sterile manner. He'd never been less turned on by the proposition of sex.

She shrugged. "It's fact. I'd guess you feel the same about me. I passed your initial screening, after all. Plus you've seen me for several dates. Obviously you must find something pleasing about my appearance."

Blake opened his mouth, but hesitated to respond. He was simultaneously impressed and appalled by Jane's detached approach to the conversation, and he wasn't quite sure what he should say. Was she that damaged? How far had he come on his own emotional journey to recognize that? He chose, in the end, to match her tone. "You are a beautiful woman. I'm sure very few men would disagree."

She smiled slightly. It was creepy, almost, the way it never reached her eyes. "Then the only thing we haven't explored is our sexual compatibility."

Blake raised an eyebrow. "Are you trying to seduce me?" He'd been unconventionally hit on before, but this took the cake by far. It was actually weird as hell. It made the Andy hate-fuck look downright romantic.

"I'm trying to secure the open-ended details in our potential arrangement."

"You're proposing that we sleep with each other." Or *not sleep* with each other, as he would typically stipulate.

She sighed. "I'm proposing that we sleep with each other in order to make sure that we actually are a suitable couple. Because as far as I can see, everything else about us is ideal in every way."

Blake worked his jaw as he worked the idea in his head. "I'm not immediately opposed." Something in his chest itched, but he ignored it. Jane's proposition was exactly the arrangement he'd set out to find. It was . . . perfect, actually. He didn't have to dine alone. He'd have suitable arm candy at his work functions. Someone to pose with for a portrait above his mantel.

And even if he spent the rest of his days secretly pining for Andrea, he would not be doing an injustice to his wife. Jane didn't want *more*. Which was superb since he couldn't give *more* to anyone ever again.

It was the most practical, logical plan that had ever been presented to him. He couldn't think of one good reason not to pursue it.

As he moved closer to accepting Jane's proposition, the itching in his chest increased until it was more of an ache. *Heartburn*, he decided. The meal had been rich, and he'd rushed it in anticipation for his talk with Jane. He had some calcium chews in the car he was certain would remedy the problem.

He casually rubbed at his breastbone. "You do have me intrigued. Strangely. If we pursue this, what would you suggest happens next? Do we continue to date as we have? Or do we make an appointment for the justice of the peace?" Surely a huge wedding wouldn't be expected if theirs was a marriage of convenience.

"No ceremony yet. We still have the last compatibility test to pass." She said it so matter-of-factly, it took Blake a moment to remember what the compatibility test was.

"Oh, right. The seduction." He felt his face heat. "Should we just . . ." The discussion was a bit awkward considering that he wasn't really feeling it. He was sure he could if he tried. In the proper environment. Not here with onlookers and after a bottle of wine. No, the setting simply wasn't conducive to sexual arousal.

Jane pursed her lips. "Why don't we settle up here and continue this discussion elsewhere. At my place, perhaps?"

That suggestion should have made Blake feel better, but now his wrong-environment excuse would be put to the test. It made him nervous—he'd never failed a woman in that department, and he wasn't looking for tonight to be a first. Maybe he should call it a night.

On the other hand, this was his chance, wasn't it? His last shot at the picture-perfect home life he'd imagined for himself for so long. If not Andy—no, he meant if not Jane, then who? Hire another matchmaker? Try to find another woman who didn't mind a loveless marriage?

No. This was a once-or-never deal. And even though he had no enthusiasm to pursue it, he felt somehow obligated to do so anyway. This was what he'd signed up for.

After the bill was settled, they walked to the valet stand in silence. Blake handed over his ticket, and Jane linked her arm through his as they waited for his car to arrive. He forced himself not to tense at her touch, wondering if it would be harder to relax when it was skin on skin instead of her bare arm through his jacket. He would fail the compatibility test if he stiffened at this simple junction.

What was wrong with him, anyway? He should be enjoying this. He was about to get it on with a beautiful woman—why was he so . . . turned off? Surely he was too young to need the little blue pill. It had to be stress. Yes, that was it. Stress was also playing at his heartburn. All he needed to do was get himself in the B-Zone and he'd be fine.

Deep breaths. Focus.

"It's been a nice evening, Blake." Jane's voice drifted into the B-Zone, which immediately kicked Blake out of it. "After the last few dates, especially."

Another deep breath.

Except his interest was piqued. "What do you mean *after the last few dates*?"

She shrugged. "The other nights have been pleasant as well—don't get me wrong. Tonight, though, everything went off without a hitch—for once. No lost reservations, no missing wallets, no wrong movie times. Though the valet is taking a while to get your car, so maybe I spoke too soon." She laughed. "I'm only kidding. I'm sure they haven't misplaced your car. And that's my point. Tonight there has been none of that. It's been nice. I'm . . . *happy* . . . about where we're headed."

Blake nodded absentmindedly. *Happy*. He hadn't put much thought to the series of misfortunes that had marred their previous evenings. It was almost humorous how much had gone wrong for them. Repeatedly. Another couple may have taken their bad luck as a sign that they shouldn't be together, would have assumed that the gods were out to sabotage them.

Or a person.

Something nagged at the back of his mind, a swirling whisper of an idea that began to take shape into a concrete notion. All of his other dates with Jane . . . the common thread . . . the element that had been missing in tonight's dinner plans . . .

Andrea.

No. She couldn't have. She wouldn't.

But he knew Andy, knew that she could be passionate and irrational. Knew she had a hot temper and spontaneous nature. She'd burned Max Ellis's employee files, and nearly his entire office, on a whim. She did have it in her to be subversive. And shitty. And . . . romantic.

Because, whatever motive would she have to wreck his courtship with Jane when Andrea had been hired to be his matchmaker? It made no sense.

Unless . . .

He put the pieces together and they fit perfectly, but was that because he wanted it to go that way? If there was only the slightest chance that he might be right, he had to pursue it.

With an excitement he hadn't felt all evening, Blake

pulled away from Jane and signaled the doorman. "Excuse me; can you hail a cab please?"

"Blake, your car's coming now," Jane protested, pointing to the valet who was pulling in.

"A cab, please," he repeated. Then he turned to address his date. "The cab is for you."

Jane raised her brows, but had the grace not to make a scene.

Blake was eager to be on his way, but he took a moment to do this right, speaking with an honesty he hadn't offered to anyone in a long time—anyone except Andrea, that was. "Thank you for your offer, Jane. At one point in time it would have been tempting. More than tempting. I agree with you wholeheartedly that love makes any contract risky and tumultuous. It's also the best damn feeling in the world. Not just being loved, but being in love. It's chaotic, yes, and unpredictable. And I might get my heart broken"—oh, he hoped not—"but I'd rather have the ups and the downs than security. I'd rather take the chance at being miserable and alone than say I didn't do everything in my power to nab the love of my life. So I'm sorry, but I have to end this relationship."

That was all the effort he could devote to his second attempt at a breakup. He didn't even wait to see Jane's response. Instead, he tucked a fifty in her palm and said, "This is for your fare. And maybe a value meal, because the salad you ordered at dinner could *not* have filled you up. You deserve happiness, even if you aren't asking for it. *Especially* if so."

Then he tipped the valet, climbed into his car, and headed to the woman he should have been with all along. If she thought he was too headstrong, then too bad. He was taking his chances. Somehow he managed to obey the speed limit, but only just.

* * *

Andy woke with a start, her mouth dry and her face sticky. She didn't remember falling asleep, yet she must have because here she was waking up on the couch. The light shining through the front windows was dim. Was it evening light or morning light? She sat up and tried to get her bearings.

"How are you feeling?" Lacy asked quietly.

Andy turned to find her sister sitting on the armchair, lacing up the Doc Martens she liked to wear when she went out. It must be night, then. Lacy had planned to meet up with Darrin and some other musicians at one of their favorite karaoke bars.

"I have a headache." Andy was surprised how bad it was, actually. They'd only had one bottle before she'd passed out that afternoon, and Lacy had drunk half of it. Or maybe most of it had been consumed by Andy. Honestly, it was probably the heavy crying that had hurt her head the most.

That and the heartache. *Arg*, the heartache. How was anyone supposed to know how awful it felt? She finally felt an ounce of Lacy's grief, knowing the man she loved was gone forever. Her pity had thrown her over the edge.

It had also put her in a foul mood. Though Lacy had been a great comfort to her when she'd come home that afternoon, Andy was glad that her sister had a gig that night. She really needed some time alone to sort through her ever-shifting emotions.

Lacy stood and switched on the overhead light.

Andy groaned and rubbed her temples. The light wasn't bothering her in a hugely hung-over sort of way, but just in an I'd-rather-be-mopey-in-the-dark sort of way.

"There's ibuprofen on top of the fridge," Lacy offered.

"I know where the GD ibuprofen is," Andy snapped. "I'm the one who put it there to begin with."

"Well, sorry." Lacy's tone was sarcastic instead of apologetic.

But it wasn't as sarcastic as it could have been, which made Andy suddenly feel like an apology was necessary. "No. I'm the one who's sorry." She didn't really feel sorry, though. She just felt bitter and mean. Still, taking it out on Lacy wasn't fair. "I'm just . . ." How to finish that sentence?

Lacy put a reassuring hand on Andy's shoulder. "I know. You're sad."

"Actually, I'm past sad. Now I'm feeling a little angry." Or a lot angry. "I'm getting that ibuprofen."

Andy headed to the kitchen as much to escape her sister as to get the pain reliever. When she'd come home after quitting her job, she'd been gutted. She'd truly thought she and Blake had something special. How could she have been so wrong?

Now, though, her mood brought in another kind of thoughts—the rage-filled kind. It wasn't her who'd been wrong. It was Blake. Stupid, douchey Blake. How much of an ass was he not to realize what was right in front of him? He thought he was in love with Jane? He wasn't.

Andy knew that as surely as she knew Blake hated reality television. So he'd been on more than a handful of dates with Jane. That meant shit. His reports had been pleasant but lackluster. She'd seen him more engaged when he played with Puppy. She'd seen him more excited when he'd beaten his top score on *Spiderman Pinball*. She'd seen more light in his eyes when he'd locked them on her own during a passionate round of office sex.

Apparently, personal happiness was not on the list of Blake's lifetime musts. She should have known that. He'd asked for specific qualities in a wife—not once had he said that she needed to be someone who brought him joy. Didn't he realize what he was missing out on?

And now he was going to ask his dream woman to be his bride. His *drear* woman. What a miserable existence.

Andy glanced at the clock above the stove. It was almost nine thirty. He'd probably already asked.

Goddammit. How could he?

She had to stop herself from kicking the appliance. A broken toe was no way to help a broken heart. Though it might be worth it to get some of her aggression out.

Lacy clomped into the kitchen behind her. Andy imagined she was trying to be quiet, but it was impossible in those boots.

"You should come with me tonight."

"No," Andy said, reaching for the pain pills. "Absolutely not."

"Why not? It will get your mind off things."

"I cannot be with people right now. Even you. Sorry." She was so worked up, she couldn't get her fingers to open the bottle.

"Okay. But what are you going to do? I'm worried you're going to spend all night drinking yourself into a stupor." Lacy held her palm out toward Andy, silently asking for the bottle.

"That was this afternoon. And I'm not drinking anymore." With a heavy sigh, Andy handed the medicine to her sister. "I'm actually planning to do nothing but sit on the couch and watch some sad chick flick and probably eat a whole carton of Ben and Jerry's."

"Equally destructive behavior, but I guess you're allowed a day of that." Lacy dropped two pills into Andy's hand.

Andy closed her fist around the ibuprofen and snatched her hand away. "Allowed? Damn right, I'm allowed. Not all of us can bury our heartache like you." She swallowed the pills in one gulp that she pretended also removed the horrible thing she'd just said.

She closed her eyes tight. *Stupid, stupid, stupid.* When she opened her eyes again, she looked to her sister, whose head was down. "Lacy, I'm sorry. That was really uncalled for." God, she was such a bitch. She had no reason to take her anger out on Lacy. "See? I'm not suitable company."

Lacy brought her face up, her expression blank, giving nothing away. "You know what, though? You're right. I don't deal with my emotions well. I'm working on it, in my own way, and I've so appreciated that you haven't pushed me."

Now Andy felt like an even bigger bitch. She hadn't pushed Lacy to deal with her grief because she was lazy and self-centered—not because she was trying to be thoughtful of her space. Tears pricked at her eyes. "I've been a horrible sister."

"Nope. You've been exactly what I needed. So. Whatever you need to do, do it. I'll respect your methods of dealing with this. And I'm here for you if you need me."

Andy pulled her sister into a giant hug. "God, I love you, Lacy. So much."

They held each other for several long moments before breaking away. Though it didn't fix everything—or anything, really—it did make life seem just a bit more bearable. Assuming, of course, her sister meant what she said. The guilt could almost overwhelm the pain if she thought like that.

"You're going to be good then? I could call and cancel if—"

"No," Andy said, cutting her off. "Go. Have fun. Take a cab home if it gets too late. My phone's off, but I'll check it later if you need to text or leave a message."

"Got it, Mom."

Andy stayed in the kitchen until she heard the front door shut behind Lacy. Then she grabbed a can of diet soda from the fridge and headed to the living room. Despite the heart-warming moment she'd shared with her sister, Andy was still angry. And her rage was snowballing. So much so that she couldn't sit still. She paced the apartment, wanting to punch something, kick something. The feeling was so strong, she imagined she could hear her anger taken out like hailstones pelleting against her window. *Plink, plink, plink.*

Maybe that wasn't her imagination.

She froze, listening. The sound came again. *Plink.* There actually were hailstones pelleting against her window. Or some sort of stone anyway. Cautiously she approached the windows and peered out. The sight that greeted her pulled at her heartstrings, melting her ever so slightly.

Then, she remembered . . . *everything* . . . and she hardened again. So far she'd managed to leave Donovan InfoTech with her referral intact. But Blake Donovan was outside her apartment. If he didn't leave soon, she wasn't sure she could maintain that status.

Chapter Twenty-one

Blake searched for another handful of stones from the land-scaping around the building. He knew this was a childish method of reaching Andrea, but her phone was going straight to voice mail and the front door was locked. It was only when he'd seen her pacing back and forth in the windows above that he'd resorted to throwing pebbles at her window.

If he was going to feel like a middle schooler in the throes of first love, who cared if he acted like one? Plus, there was something so satisfying about each little *ping* that he'd never gotten from an email ping.

He was preparing to pelt another round at her darkened window when he realized she was already watching him. "Andy," he called, both desperate and excited. "Andy Dawson."

She lifted the window up and yelled down to him through the crack of screen she'd exposed. "Go away, Blake Douche-ovan!"

Well, that wasn't the greeting he'd hoped for, but he

hadn't expected her to be welcoming, either. Not after the way she'd walked out on him that afternoon.

That was fine. He was in this for the long haul. "I'm not going anywhere until we talk, Andy. Let me up."

"I have nothing to say to you."

"Well, I do."

"I don't want to hear it."

"Are you sure about that?" He got his answer when she pulled the blinds down. *Dammit.* Not the answer he'd assumed. "Come on, Andrea." Then the blinds in the next set of windows went down. "Andy!"

"Hey," a voice said from the apartment below the Dawsons'. "Could you hold it down out here? Some people are trying to—Blake Donovan? Are you fucking serious?"

Blake squinted at the woman. "You!" No wonder the area had seemed familiar. It was where one of his dates lived. He *always* Google Earthed, even if it was in private. Joey, was it? Or Joy?

"I'm Jaylene," she said, with a roll of her eyes.

"Right, right." *Stupid name, anyway.* "Don't you live—" He glanced at the next building, confused. He was good with addresses, and he was sure that on the night of their horrid date he'd dropped her off one house down.

"Yeah, yeah, I'm next door. I'm . . . visiting someone."

Blake saw a man behind her. And he was missing his shirt. Ah, well, maybe there really was someone for everyone. Even though he was certain there was a *woman* for this one.

"Anyway, it's kind of late. Could you keep it down?"

He glanced at his watch. It wasn't yet ten. What was she talking about *kind of late*? City ordinances wouldn't even fine him until eleven. He was about to argue it when he realized instead that she was his key into the building. "I'll stop my shouting if you'll buzz me in. I need to see Andrea."

"Buzz you in?" She seemed confused.

He shifted his weight from one foot to the other trying to stifle his impatience. "Through the main door."

"There's no buzzer. It doesn't lock."

She was crazy. He'd tried it when he first arrived and it was most certainly locked.

"Wait there a moment, will you?" He hurried up the stairs, twisted the knob, and pushed in. It wouldn't budge. "See? Locked."

"It's a pull, not a push." She said something else that he couldn't quite hear, but he sensed it was along the lines of, *You idiot.*

Blake gritted his teeth before he let out a string of his own insults and pulled on the door. It opened. Well, that was dumb. Didn't outer doors always open inward? And why wasn't the door locked? That didn't make for a secure environment. He'd be sure to call the building's owner and get that fixed tomorrow. Whatever happened between him and Andrea personally, he still wanted her safe.

For the moment, though, he was happy to be inside. He took the stairs two at a time and found her door. He pounded loudly. "Andrea. Let me in." No sound of movement came from inside so he pounded again. "Let me in. Please, Andy."

The sound of a door creaking open drew his attention downstairs. *Great. The femi-Nazi again.* He noticed now she was clad only in a tank top and yoga pants. She leaned against her door frame, watching him, her arms folded across her chest.

The woman was infuriating even when he wasn't on a date with her. He felt sorry for the man she was "visiting." Bearding, likely. He muttered under his breath and tried to block out his audience of one as he pounded again. Still, the door didn't open.

"They have a hide-a-key box, you know."

He peered down again at the woman below, his brow raised.

"Under the railing there."

Uncertain whether to trust her—their date together had been one of the most miserable of his life—he swept his hand under the railing. Sure enough, there was a small metal box secured to the bottom. He removed the lid and out fell a key.

Well, how about that. He met the eyes of the woman downstairs, wondering why she was helping him.

As if she could read his mind, she said, "I owe Andy. Or, rather, Andy owes me. I hope tonight goes . . . exactly as it's going to." She smirked, and turned back to the door she'd emerged from.

He had a feeling that paybacks for being set up with him were the underscore of her aid. Nevertheless, he shouted down, "Thank you, JayLo."

"Jaylene, shithead!"

Right, Jaylene. But he didn't really care about his error at the moment. Right then the only thing he could think about was getting inside that apartment and working things out with Andrea. Though she hadn't seemed very warm at the window, he hoped she'd be more amiable to him when they were face-to-face.

He took the key and slid it in the lock. Then he breathed out a silent prayer, turned the key, and twisted the knob.

The minute he opened the door, an orange cross trainer came at him. He ducked and it flew past him into the hall, just missing his shoulder. He looked back at Andy. Her eyes were blazing mad, her nostrils fuming. In her hand was the matching shoe. She drew her hand back and fired it at him.

Maybe it was going to take more work than he thought.

* * *

"Why are you throwing things at me?" Blake cowered behind the front door, yelling at her through the open crack.

She had to admit she got some satisfaction from the
situation. Not enough, though. She wanted more. She wanted to seal all the cracks in her shattered heart with blood,
sweat, and tears from Blake "Fuckshovel" Donovan. She
was so mad, she'd even think that word, though maybe not
say it aloud.

"Because you're an idiot." She'd already rolled up a magazine from the coffee table, preparing to launch it next.

"I don't disagree in the slightest." He actually sounded
sorry.

But she was too wound up. Besides, she was sure he
didn't know what he was sorry for, and violence seemed
much more satisfying than explaining it to him.

She waited until he poked his head around the door to
fling the magazine. She narrowly missed his cheek.

Dammit. Why was she such a bad aim?

He flung the door open. "Jesus, Andy. That was close."

"Not close enough." She scoured the room for something
else to throw and settled on her soda. "You're also an egotistical, chauvinistic, self-centered ass-hat." She double-
checked she'd slugged down the last drop, then heaved it
across the room. It landed a whole foot in front of her
target.

A flash of a smile crossed Blake's lips, but he recovered
quickly. "You've always known these things about me. You
didn't seem to mind before."

"Didn't seem to . . . ?" She was absolutely incredulous.
She minded. She'd minded since she met him.

Hadn't she?

Considering that she fell in love with him despite all his
flaws, maybe she hadn't minded as much as she thought.
But she wasn't telling him that. Plus throwing stuff felt
really, really good. And who the hell did he think he was,

absolving her of being pissed? She had every flipping right to be pissed. And defensive.

She swiped the TV remote off the couch and readied for the pitch. "You've broken into my house. I'm defending myself."

She let the remote go.

Blake caught it midair.

Dammit all to China!

"Andrea, please stop." He held his hands up, palms out in front of him as if to halt her from further bombardment.

"Fine." She was out of things to throw anyway except couch pillows, and what kind of weapons were those? "Why are you here?"

"Can I come in?"

She shrugged, though honestly she'd rather have him come in than have Mrs. Brandy hear all her business. Also, she'd lost enough shoes to the man. Also, he was pretty even when he was groveling. She decided to stop also-ing.

Blake ventured in and shut the door behind him. He stuffed his hands in his pockets and flicked his eyes around the room. Luckily Lacy had done a quick pickup that afternoon or Andy might be embarrassed. Andy was not great at pickups. Double entendre intended.

Actually, no. She wouldn't be embarrassed. Because she didn't care about the asshole's opinion. Not everyone was lucky enough to have a housekeeper and money and a perfect, petite soon-to-be bride.

Blake's presence was certainly not helping her temper. Best to get him of her house—out of her life—as soon as possible.

She folded her arms over her chest and repeated her earlier question more pointedly. "Why. Are. You. Here. Blake. *Mister Donovan.*"

He caught her eyes and for half a moment she was falling

into him again, losing herself in the dizzy chaotic trance he always put her in.

But then he spoke. "We need to talk."

Yeah, they needed to talk at seven thirty that morning. Where was he then? Now she was past talking. "There is nothing that needs to be said."

He cocked his head. "Obviously there is. You're angry, and I'm not sure why."

That pissed her off more than anything. Not only had he completely wrecked her in every way a woman could be wrecked, but he didn't even have a clue. And if there was one thing a woman didn't do it was explain her emotions to a man who should understand anyway. "My anger is my business. It wasn't what brought you here in the first place, anyway. So whatever you came here for, spit it out."

"All right." He hesitated as if trying to decide exactly what to say. Which was odd. He'd come all that way to see her—didn't he have an agenda?

Finally he said, "I have questions about Jane."

"Seriously?" Her fury ticked up another notch. No, not a notch. It went a notch at a time, until it exploded the freaking meter. He came to ask about inane, stupid, usurping Jane? "I'm not your matchmaker anymore, Blake. You can find out anything you need to know about your *girlfriend* by asking her yourself."

He removed his hand from his pocket and rubbed the back of his neck. "That's not what . . . she's not my girlfriend."

Oh, yeah, *fiancée* was the term now. The word made her want to throw things again. Or puke. Or both. "Whatever she's called. Talk to her yourself. I'm no longer your go-between. Now get out of my house. You shouldn't be here." She started toward him, ushering him out.

"Wait!" He threw his hands out again to stop her.

She scowled but nodded to indicate he could go on.

He began pacing in the confined space she was allowing him. "It's not . . . I mean . . . There's a lot to say and . . ." He stopped suddenly and pinned her with his interrogative gaze. "All the things that went wrong on our dates—that was you, wasn't it?"

She scoffed. "No." But inside she said, *Oh shit, oh shit, oh shit.*

Blake shook his head. "The missing wallet—you took it that afternoon, didn't you? And the reservations—they weren't lost—you never made them."

"I have no idea what you're talking about." Also, she had no idea how she'd ever get a job in town again. She bit her lip. She was so screwed.

"You know you're the worst liar." Strangely, he didn't seem all that mad.

"Look, Blake, I don't . . . I didn't . . . I'm not . . ." His lack of annoyance threw her balance. How should she address this? Come clean? Then he'd want to know why and that would be one big mess of humiliation. Maybe she could just dodge the whole thing.

She plastered on the sweetest smile that she could muster. "Does it matter now? Everything worked out between you two, so no harm, no foul." *Speaking of Jane* . . . "Where is she anyway? Shouldn't you be with her tonight?"

"She's probably home by now," Blake said dismissively. "I'm not sure. I put her in a cab."

"You didn't drive her home?" It pleased her more than it should to realize he hadn't followed up his proposal with a sleepover.

It also pissed her off again. That exactly was her point about him and Jane—he wasn't even into her enough to do the deed after he popped the question. If it had been her that he'd asked to marry, Andy would have been all over him. Like the brainless sex-obsessed woman she'd apparently become reduced to in his presence.

And that just made her sad. And destructive. Wanting
to wallow in her pain, no—revel in her escape—she pursued the subject further. "You know, you don't have to keep
it in your pants anymore. You could bang her all you want
and I won't say a word."

"Is that what you want? For me to be with Jane?"

"No." It was out before she could stop it. She backped-
aled fast. "I mean, what do I care? I quit, remember?"

He took a step toward her. "And the only reason you ever
cared about that was because of your job?" His expression
was more prodding than accusatory.

She swallowed back the lump in her throat. "Of course.
Why else would I give a shit?"

"That's what I'm trying to figure out."

They stared at each other in a standstill and it occurred
to Andy that Blake might *know*. Was that possible? Did he
somehow guess that she had a massive love boner for him,
and if he did, why did he feel the need to expose it? Did
he . . . care?

No, it was probably just because of his ego.

She pinched the bridge of her nose, breaking their eye
contact. She couldn't take much more without the rage dis-
solving into tears. "Blake, I don't know what you're insin-
uating, but I have a headache. Could you please just let
this lie? Go meet Jane at her house and celebrate the occasion."

"What occasion?" He looked truly confused.

"Don't patronize me. I *know*, Blake."

"Know what, Drea?"

"About the engagement." Did he think he could hide it
from her? And why did he want to? Goddammit, was he
trying to get out of paying her find-a-bride bonus on top
of everything else? "I saw the ring. I know you were going
to propose. Are you trying to screw me on my bonus, Blake
Donovan? Because if you—"

He cut her off with a finger pointed at her. "Hold on. You saw . . . the *ring*?"

"Yeah, I saw it. So stop trying to hide the truth and let's talk about my payment. Because I *know* you proposed. Why did you *think* I quit?" If she was going to walk away with a broken heart and no referral, she'd better at least have money for groceries for a couple of months. And who was he kidding with this ridiculous late-night drop-in?

"Andy, stop talking about payment. I'm not trying to screw you out of anything. What the hell is it that you think you know about my *proposal*?"

"I know all of it. I'm not an idiot." She sighed. A deep, heavy, frustrated I-can't-believe-I'm-spelling-this-out sigh. "The ring came in while you were at your meetings. Sarah was already at lunch so I signed for the package. I was nosy. I looked. Add that to dinner reservations at Menton, it didn't take much to put together that tonight was the night you'd pop the question."

"Pop the . . ." Dawning settled over his features. "You thought I was going to propose to *Jane*?"

"Well, duh."

There were exactly two seconds of silence before Blake began to laugh. Not a simple chuckle, either, but a deep, hearty laugh much like the night she'd shown up in her nightie on his doorstep. And just like then, she felt totally humiliated and utterly confused and goddamn pissed.

Fucking Blake.

Before she could find a new item to pelt him with—this time, preferably a very hard, very damaging object—his laughter ceased sharply. He met her eyes and advanced upon her, backing her up until she'd met the wall.

He caged her in, his body so close but not touching her anywhere. God, it was just like when he'd seduced her the night before. Heat rolled off him—sexual tension and emotional tension—it took everything she had not to choke him with his tie and then rip all his clothes off. Because it was the only thought that distracted her from how she still wanted him to do that to *her*. Why was he torturing her like this?

"Why are you mad at me?" His low, husky timbre fell over her like liquid sex.

"I . . ." She wasn't sure anymore. Wasn't even sure if she *was* still mad at him. Or if she was mad, maybe she could take it out on him in another way. Like with her body, with her hands. With her teeth. Maybe one last . . . maybe they could hate-do it?

"Is it because you have feelings . . . ?" He didn't add *for me*, but it was implied.

Andy shook her head but squeaked out a contradictory "Maybe."

He settled his forehead against hers and closed his eyes, as if relishing her oh-so-tentative answer. When he opened them again, he said plainly, "I did not propose to Jane."

Her breath hitched. "You didn't?"

"No." He circled his nose around hers once, then drew back to meet her gaze. "It would be a serious conflict of interest. Considering I'm completely in love with you."

Andy swore her heart flipped in her chest. "Wh—what?"

He trailed his hands up her arms. "I love you, Andy. The ring was for you."

"For me?" Now her heart was in her throat. She had to be hallucinating because there was no way that ring had been for her. Or dreaming. Maybe she was still asleep on the couch.

Except his hands on her body felt awfully real and the scent that she'd come to know as pure Blake pervaded the space between them, filled her with all of him. Not as full as she was fantasizing, but . . .

Her eyes fell to the floor as she tried to work through

the fog that had settled around her. "But you went out with Jane tonight—"

"—to break up with her."

"At the fanciest restaurant in town?"

"I thought you'd be impressed with my considerate let-down." He took a step back. Not too far, but enough to give her a smidgeon of breathing room.

"Impressed?" He was still close enough for her to punch him in the shoulder. So she hit him twice. "It's mislead-ing! To her and to me."

Blake rubbed at the place she'd struck him, but was otherwise a good sport about the infliction. "Jane was far from misled. She was well aware I had no feelings for her before I even told her. As for you—"

She opened her mouth to ask more about the highly in-teresting thing he'd just said about Jane, but he put a finger up to shush her. "I could have explained all of it to you, if you'd asked me about it instead of quitting and running off—"

"—like how *you* ran off this morning?" That hypocrisy had to be addressed. "I may have run off, but let it be clear you abandoned me first. At least I left a note." She brushed past him, unable to stand his close proximity any longer. If he was going to play mind games with her, then she at least needed to have a fair shot at fighting back, and there was no fair shot when he was that near.

Blake spun around after her. "What are you talking about, Andy? I didn't abandon you. And I *did* leave a note."

"Where? There was no note. I know. I looked."

"There was a note, Drea. It was by the bedside with the money—" He stopped as if realizing what must have hap-pened.

At the same time, Andy remembered everything fall-ing off the nightstand. Remembered the dog . . .

"Puppy," they said in unison.

She couldn't help smiling at that. Then she couldn't stop smiling because *Blake hadn't abandoned her.*

Blake ran a hand over his face. "No wonder you were mad. You thought I'd just left you."

"Left me with a pair of twenties."

"Oh, God . . . it was for a cab to get home. You must have thought . . ."

"Let's not even go there." All that heartache, and it had just been a misunderstanding. Luckily they'd sorted it out before she'd gone and done anything drastic. Well, anything *more* drastic. How different the day would have gone if not for the damn dog.

"I told you the dog was a bad idea."

She hit him again, though a part of her agreed. "So." She leaned against the back of the couch. "What did the note say?"

"Nothing important. I wanted to save the good stuff for in person."

"Well. Here I am. In the flesh." She was flirting now. Hard-core.

"That you are." His eyes scanned down her body and she was suddenly aware she was only in a camisole and shorts.

She shivered. He acknowledged her reaction with a curl of his lip and all she wanted was to stop talking and make out already. The way he was slinking closer made her think he had the same thing in mind.

But then there was his admission of love and the ring . . . God, the ring!

Maybe he hadn't said the things she'd thought he said. It all went by so fast. "Wait, wait." She shook her hands by her head as if that would clear her head. "A lot of information has flown by in the last ten minutes and I'm muddled."

Blake halted his approach. "Understandable. What can I do to un-muddle you?"

"Let's sit. Can we sit? I think we should sit." She circled the couch and sat on the edge while Blake took the armchair. Where to start, where to start . . . "This morning—" She shook her head; she wanted to go back farther. "Last night, I mean—"

"Last night was the best night of my life, Andy."

Her lips went dry and her pulse picked up. She was dumbfounded. He *had* been as blown away as she'd been! Luckily, it wasn't her turn to talk.

Blake leaned forward, close enough that their knees almost met. "And this morning when I woke up, I realized that every minute I've spent with you has been the best of my life. I think I'd figured out that I loved you long before, but last night is when I realized you were the one I wanted to spend my life with."

Andy brought her hand up to cover her mouth. "Really?" She let her palm fall to her chest. "But I'm not your ideal." Not even close to his ideal. Her body, her personality—none of her fit the mold of the woman he wanted.

Blake reached over to settle his hand on her knee. "You're exactly my ideal, Andrea Dawson. It just took me longer to realize it than it should have."

She let out a sarcastic laugh. "Yeah, it did."

"Hey, I didn't hear any declarations from you all that time." He sat back and instantly she missed his touch. "In fact, I still haven't heard any declarations from you. Should I even be here right now?"

She practically jumped out of her seat. "Yes. You should be here. I'm glad you're here."

He looked skeptical. "Even though you threw those awful cross trainers at me?"

"Even though I threw the cross trainers at you. They are not awful, though. Don't even think I'm going to say that they are."

"Andy, I love you even though you have no taste in shoes. And don't know how to cook." He glanced at the dusty picture frames on the wall behind her. "Or clean."

She couldn't even defend herself. She wasn't good at any of those things. "Those are all requirements you had for your wife." Her spirits sank. Even if he did love her, how could she fill the role of Blake Donovan's wife? He'd never be happy with her when she lacked so much.

Blake, however, simply shrugged. "We'll just always have to have a housekeeper. There's nothing to do about your eye for bad shoes, however."

She chuckled, but immediately grew somber again. "I might want more than one baby."

"That means lots of baby making. I like baby making."

"Blake, I'm serious." This conversation was the most serious she'd ever had, to be honest.

"So am I."

She met his eyes and saw he was indeed as sincere as she was. It gave her a rush to realize they were making plans together for their future. Funny how, this time, it was her ticking off the list of requirements for his wife. "And I want to work. Even though I have no idea what I want to do."

"I hope you work for me. But even if you don't, I'll be happy as long as I can come home to you and beat your pants off in pinball."

This time when she laughed she let a smile linger after. "Do I have to be wearing pants when we play pinball?"

"I'd actually prefer that you don't."

No longer able to stand the distance between them, Andy leaped into his lap. She straddled his hips and cupped his cheeks in her hands. "Blake, I love you. I have a confession, though—I did sabotage your dates with Jane because I didn't know how to tell you, and I couldn't stand the idea of you with someone else. And that's why I quit, too. I thought last night meant nothing to you. I thought *we* meant nothing to you."

"We mean everything to me." He turned his mouth to rest a kiss on her palm. "If I asked you to marry me . . . ?"

It was an echo of the way he'd asked her to stay with him the night before, but she wasn't about to let him get off that easy. "Are you asking me?"

"Hold on. You're right. We have to do this properly. *I* have to do this properly. You deserve it." He wrapped his arms around her waist and stood. Andy squealed as he carried her out like a potato sack from where the furniture was arranged tightly to a clearing in the room. There he knelt on one knee and propped her on the other.

She giggled with nerves as he stuck his hand inside his jacket pocket and pulled out a velvet box—the same one she'd seen earlier that day. As if this wasn't happening, as if she didn't know what was going on—as if he hadn't flat-out told her. With one hand still anchored at her hip, he awkwardly used his mouth to open the box. She started to shake. Then there it was, the beautiful ring she'd held between her fingers, wishing against hope it belonged to her. And now it did.

Or, it almost did. Blake had yet to ask the question.

"Andy Dawson, you are everything I never knew I wanted. You are more than ideal—you're my perfect match. Will you do me the honor of becoming my bride?"

For the first time since she'd met him, she didn't argue. "Yes. Yes, Blake Donovan, I will."

He kissed her then. Hard and deep. She matched his passion, telling him everything in her heart through her lips, through her tongue, through her hands that she wrapped around his neck and wove through his hair. It was a kiss that spoke of beginnings. A kiss that promised the future. A kiss heavy with love. A kiss that was also the end, but the happiest ending she could dream of.

When they both came up for air, Andy pushed away. She wanted to keep kissing him all night—all her life— but she had yet to put the ring on her finger. Still on his knee, they fumbled through getting the ring out of the box and on her finger.

"I'm impressed," she said, her gaze caught up in the diamond's sparkle. "It fits perfectly."

"I may have done some measuring. While you slept."

"Clever man. And only a little creepy." She couldn't stop staring at her hand. It was so beautiful. So impossible. And so . . . *right*. "I loved your proposal, by the way. Though"—she couldn't believe she was admitting this, but fresh start and all that—"I do kind of like it when you call me Drea."

He laughed and clutched her close to him. "I knew it."

Happier than she'd ever been, she teased him as he kissed along her jawline. "Is this a good time to tell you I still want my matchmaking bonus? I did find you a wife, after all."

His mouth found her ear and nibbled. "Well, I'd hope that being married to me would be all the bonus you'd need."

"I do love you, Mr. Donovan. But I'm going to need a personal account at Macy's, too." Though she'd settle for a lifetime of that thing he was doing with his tongue. And maybe a monthlong honeymoon in St. Lucia. She *had* promised herself a tropical vacation.

Blake found her mouth again. This time the kiss was deeper, longer, more desperate. When Blake's crotch hardened against her thigh, she knew what was coming next.

"Come home with me, Mrs. Donovan-to-be," he said

against her lips. "I want to spend all night not sleeping with you. What do you say?"

And for the second time since she met him, she found herself in agreement. Because spending all night *not sleeping* was the perfect way to celebrate an engagement.

Acknowledgments

Laurelin Paige—

As with any book, this one was not born alone. There are too many people to name all the people I'd like to acknowledge, but there are a few thank-yous that are essential.

First and foremost, to Kayti McGee, my work-wife—I'll say it again and again: don't cowrite, but if you do, cowrite with Kayti. You are the wine to my empty glass. The Miss to my Match. You are brilliant and shiny in all the places that I am not. I look forward to all the places this journey takes us together.

To our editor, Eileen Rothschild—I was so nervous to talk to you that first time on the phone, and then you were absolutely everything I ever wanted in an editor. Thank you for sharing our quirky enthusiasm for this series. It wouldn't have been the same experience with anybody else.

To the team at St. Martin's Press—What a great group to

work with! Thank you for inviting us into and embracing us in your tight-knit family.

To Bob Diforio for making this deal happen and Rebecca Friedman for deals yet to be made. It's the best feeling to have wonderful people in your corner.

To Shanyn for keeping me together and KP for putting us together. It's an honor to be called an InkSlinging Author.

To Lisa—You gave me your idea. Ideas are gold. With this, you've given me the biggest gift anyone's ever given me. Thank you.

To Bethany—You fairy me through all the dark places. A particularly hard task when we both love the dimly lit moors so much. There's a well of gratitude in my heart for you that never runs dry.

To Gennifer—You named our book! It's perfect. Thank you for that and more.

The women who wrangle me—Wrahm, Naturals, FYW, and others (you know who you are): I make it through my days because of you. I also get distracted a lot because of you, but that's another story.

To my husband, Tom—Though I tease you for being flighty, you are my rock. Thank you for being so solid.

To my children—I'm so proud of all you are. I hope you see me as an example for making your own dreams come true. I love you, my babies.

To Mom—Finally, here's a book I'll let you read. Thanks for your never-ending support. Love you.

To my Maker—Praise is always in my heart, even when it's absent on my tongue.

Kayti McGee—

First and foremost—Laurelin Paige. You took me on this crazy journey, for no other reason than that you are God's angel on earth. No one can possibly convince me you aren't the best person I have ever had the honor to meet, much less call my friend. I'm inspired by you every day, to write better, be more, be better. I love you so much. You are grace and generosity and talent personified.

Eileen Rothschild took a chance on us that I could never have imagined, and then turned out to be the most badass editor ever. Bob Diforio sold her that chance, and Natalie Lakosil was so charmed by my Dream Dr. Who Team (I assume) that she looked past my horribly awkward weird-ness to become my agent. I am so lucky to have the best people in the business on my team.

My mom taught me that reading is more important than anything, and without that I would never have become a writer. Dad, Kerry, Laura, and Dann backed that up. McGrigsbys!

My friends—Sara, my bestie—my first reader and still the prettiest. M. Pierce, you redefined what friendship is for me. I'm so proud to be pub-siblings with such an incredible author and friend. Thank you for everything. The WrAHM girls, the Order, the Dirty Laundresses, Melanie Harlow,

Gennifer Albin, Tamara Mataya, my guy Tyler, my lunch buddy Jen, my late-night buddy Leah. I couldn't live without our constant contact. I have to especially mention Bethany Hagen's perfect edits, and Lisa Otto's perfect idea. You truly made this all happen, and for that, no thanks can be enough.

Read on for an excerpt from Laurelin McGee's next book

Love Struck

Coming soon from St. Martin's Paperbacks

"ADZE?" Lance looked at the word on the Scrabble board, his brows furrowed. "What the hell is an 'ADZE'? You're making words up again, aren't you?"

Lacy wrapped her arms tighter around the pillow she was holding—his pillow—and scowled in mock indignation. "Making words up *again*? I never make up words. That's you."

"I do not. Ever." But his grin would have been an admission, even if they both didn't already know full well that he often just placed letters on the board, hoping they'd spell something legitimate. "And if 'ADZE' is for real, then tell me what it means."

"It's . . . uh . . ." She was excellent at words, but not always at remembering definitions.

"If you don't know, it's not a word. I call foul." He shifted, stretching one leg out and jostling the mattress as he did.

"Careful." Lacy put her hands out to steady the board. It was the one problem with playing in bed—any movement threatened the integrity of the game.

"You be careful, missy. Cheating at Scrabble . . . who would have thought? From Lacy Dawson of all people."

"Are you officially challenging me?"

Lance dove across the board, sending wooden tiles flying.

Lacy squealed as he pinned her to the mattress. So much for the game. Oh, well, she was more interested in this new game anyway.

"Admit it. You made it up," he said as he stretched his body over her.

"It's a tool!" she said, suddenly remembering the meaning of the word she'd placed. "An adze is a kind of tool. I think."

"A tool? I'll show you a tool." Lance pressed his hips into hers and she could feel his *tool* all right.

She pretended to pout. "This tool of yours better be worth it. I mean, I was winning, you know."

He let go of one of her arms so he could pull the pillow out from between them and toss it out of the way. "I'm sure you were. But guess what? I've already won."

Lacy wiggled, positioning herself better beneath her fiancé. "Oh, really. Just what have you won?"

"You. I've won you." He lowered his lips to hers, taking her to a place where words were no longer needed, where the music she made was a duet of sound instead of a solo. Eventually he trailed kisses up her jaw and to her ear. "Lacy?"

She closed her eyes, too enthralled in the passion of the moment to answer.

"Lacy?" he said again.

"Mmhmm?" she murmured.

"Lacy?"

What the hell? She'd already answered him. Didn't he hear her?

"Lacy?" It was louder this time and the tone sounded less like Lance and more like . . .

Her eyes popped open and she was no longer underneath the man she loved, no longer on her bed with a Scrabble game in disarray around her, no longer making a duet.

Instead, she was in the recording studio, headphones on her ears, guitar in her lap, her hands shifting automatically through the chords of the song she was playing.

It was Darrin, calling her name from the recording booth. Not Lance. Of course, it couldn't be Lance. It would never be Lance again. How many months since his death and she still came back to him in fantasy every time she got lost in song?

"*Lacy Dawson.*"

She muted her strings and swallowed past the lump in her throat. "*Darrin Ortiz.* I was in the zone. What do you want?" She glared at her boss through the glass wall.

He glared back.

Dick.

They made it through almost three more seconds before he cracked up. He could never stay angry at her. She joined in the laughter, not really feeling it, but knowing it was what she would have done once upon a time.

"Get out here and talk to me and you'll find out. This recording job was supposed to be finished an hour ago."

"Sometimes jobs go long." She played a riff that suddenly popped in her head. *Yeah, that's how Lance would have liked it . . .*

Darrin rolled his eyes. "You and I both know you had this on your second take."

At least Lacy assumed he rolled his eyes. She didn't bother to look up and see, but she knew him well enough to know his mannerisms and eye rolling was one of his favorites.

She stuck her lip out stubbornly—one of *her* favorite mannerisms. "I'm fine-tuning. It's an important part of myp rocess."

"Your *process* involves spending the last hour of every workday 'fine-tuning' so you can get out of doing any paperwork."

She raised her head to see him staring her down. This time she didn't have a witty comeback. He was completely right about her fine-tuning, just not right about her reasons. She really didn't mind paperwork, but it wasn't in lead sheets and recording logs that she found Lance. She found him in the strum of her hands and the harmonic vibrations of her instrument. So with the melancholy she always felt when she returned from the music in her head—the only place Lance still lived—to the real world, she set her guitar down and exited the booth.

She followed Darrin toward the office, taking a quick moment to stick her tongue out at Kat. The other girl was polishing the cymbals on a drum set and didn't notice. Kat bugged Lacy. Actually, she adored Kat. She'd been a well-meaning friend through the last painful months. Well-meaning and reliable. Just. Sometimes Kat's perfectly styled rocker-look made Lacy want to push her into a mud puddle. Or an angry mosh pit. Or both.

But that was mostly because she had barely brushed her own hair for a year. It was surprisingly easy to resent the people who had it all together. Sometimes Lacy wondered if people used to resent her, too.

Kat looked up and grinned. Lacy blew her a kiss.

Kat held up her hand in the shape of a phone and mouthed, "Call me later."

Suppressing a groan, Lacy gave her a thumbs-up, and hurried after Darrin, who was waiting in the doorway and clearing his throat. As she walked in, he slammed the door behind her.

Which suddenly put Lacy on guard. The last time she'd been in Darrin's office with the door shut was when he'd told her that due to slow business, he had to cut her studio hours.

She didn't have many more hours to cut. *Please, oh, please, oh, please don't let it mean I'm getting fired.* She would die if she didn't have this job. Well, not die. She tried not to use that term loosely after Lance, *don't think about him, don't cry,* but it would be *near* dying. Playing around town and laying down background tracks had been the only two things that she'd lived for the last few months. The only times she could lose herself in fantasies of him without anyone questioning where she was in her head. She was able to get so few gigs these days, without the studio she'd be . . .

She couldn't bear to think about it. She'd wait until he said it outright, even if that was only seconds away.

Tightly gripping the back of the bar stool that Darrin had repurposed—aka, stolen—for his office guests, Lacy attempted to hide her trepidation. "What is it?"

Darrin slumped into his beat-up, faux-leather rolling chair, flinging a leg up on a file cabinet nearly toppling the pile of sheet music on top. "I just got off the phone with the singer from Bitchy Ether. You know, the girl band from Harvard?"

It was Lacy's turn to eye roll. "I remember them. Bunch of women's studies majors, no real inspiration except to represent women in music. I am so not looking forward to mixing their album."

"Well, that's the thing." Darrin was practically bouncing, which was sort of funny considering that he was talking about some of the most annoyingly serious musicians ever to grace the booths of his studio. Also, it was strange for a guy with such a hardcore look. His tattoos were uncountable, his hair was perfectly coiffed in a rockabilly cut, and the spikes on his collar and wristband would intimidate a pit bull. Any behavior that was giddy in nature seemed completely out of place on him.

"What's the thing? Did they actually figure out how to play their instruments? Or write a song that isn't copied from the SCUM manifesto?" Lacy giggled a little. She only knew about that particular piece of literature from her feminist neighbor Jaylene. Jay loved Bitchy Ether. She might have been their only fan.

"No, none of that. Apparently the bitchy ether is a lifestyle, and not just a name. The band has broken up, and I was forced to listen to various reasons why for at least twenty minutes. Which brings me to my point, my darling."

Dammit, she knew it. Now he was going to tell her that since the schedule was empty, he didn't need her. At least he was giving her the news gently with terms of endearment. Darrin was the only person she knew who could say things like *darling* without sounding condescending.

Well, if he was going to be graceful about it, so was she. She could save the crying for home, like she usually did, where she could bury her face in Lance's pillow. "Out with it, beloved Boss. I can take it. Tell me your point." She'd become amazingly good at false strength. He didn't even notice her knees wobbling.

"The point is, that we suddenly have an opening for studio time. And I wouldn't dream of opening it publicly without offering it to you first."

Oh.

She blinked, surprise momentarily throwing her speechless. That was definitely not what she'd expected him to say.

Maybe she'd heard him wrong. "You're offering their studio time to *me*?" With the cut back to just one operating booth, the calendar had filled up quickly. Lacy wasn't on the books now to get in for months, and that was with staff preferential treatment.

"I know you were hoping to record *your* new album, and this gets you in ten weeks out instead of after the new year. How much do you love me?" Now he actually *was* bouncing. It was so adorable, she could almost ignore that it was based on false happiness.

It was also really amazingly kind. Lacy may have teared up. Only a tiny bit, though.

"I love you the mostest, D. Thank you." She really meant it, too. Despite the pit that had just appeared in her stomach. She smiled extra big so he wouldn't notice her hand resting on it, trying to quell the sudden wave of nausea.

"You don't have to thank me. I just can't wait to hear what you've been working on. It's been a shit year for you, Lace, but I know your music is going to be amazing. I'm so proud of you. Get the fuck out of here before I get emotional." He waved his hand toward the door. "And stop pretending to fine-tune. Go grab a drink or something. Have a good weekend. Tell your sister I said, what's up!" He was practically shouting as she ran from the office.

Don't throw up, don't throw up. Lacy darted into the bathroom and leaned over the sink. What the hell was she going to do now? There was no way she'd have an album ready to record in ten weeks. She was doubtful she'd have one ready in four months. Dammit, she should just own up and tell Darrin the truth—none of the songs he'd heard her playing the last few months were anywhere near complete. And definitely nowhere near recording-ready. Hard to record with no lyrics.

But after his speech about being proud and all that, she couldn't bear to see his disappointment. Couldn't bear to admit to her total fraud-hood.

No, better not make any rash decisions. She'd talk to Folx about it first. Right now she had to get through her panic attack. Deep breaths and a splash of cold water usually helped. That and unloading on her writing group. She dug out her phone and used the group's app to send an urgent message to Folx. *Need to talk. Message me when you can?*

Lacy felt a little better already. Maybe even better enough to get through the rest of her shift.

Wait— Darrin said she could leave early. That helped her stomach subside. She'd wait for Folx's reply in the comfort of her own home. She'd probably be dragged into helping her sister, Andy, with wedding plans, though. Which was fine. As challenging as it was to hear endless conversations about linens and venue options, living with a bride-to-be was fantastic for keeping one's mind off one's troubles. Though it did make Lacy think a lot about her own wedding plans. At least it was great for keeping her troubles to herself. Engaged women, especially ones engaged to prominent billionaires, were too busy to pry. Andy's preoccupation with her upcoming nuptials was the only reason she hadn't noticed that her precious baby sister was keeping secrets.

One more deep breath. Lacy peered in the mirror. She was a little paler than normal, but otherwise looked fine. She fluffed her long blonde curls and practiced a fake smile. The trick was squinting. If you squinted just slightly when you smiled, people thought you meant it. The things learned when hiding from the world. One day she'd write a book. When she got her words back, that was.

Opening the bathroom door, she almost walked smack into Kat.

"Um, oh my God!" Kat pursed her lips at Lacy and stared meaningfully.

"Um, oh my God, what?" Of course this chick was waiting outside the bathroom. Thank the Lord she hadn't actually thrown up.

"Darrin told me you're taking Bitchy Ether's recording time! I'm so stoked for you! I'm going to do your drums.

It's my gift to you. Of course, Darrin said he'd pay me my normal rate, but I'm really doing it for you. Oh, honey, come here!" She threw her arms wide, inviting Lacy to walk into her embrace.

Lacy did, but took another deep breath first, this time not because of her nerves but because of her nose. It was her experience that Kat usually smelled like more patchouli than she was comfortable with. Some of the scent always clung to her post-hug, which was tolerable, but it was best not to do an inhale during the actual act. Inhalation led to choking fits.

And this hug was going on too long. She needed to breathe again. "I was supposed to call you?" she asked as she pushed away, using the question as a reason to extricate herself.

"Yeah! There's this band playing tonight that is like soooo good, I swear to God you will love them so much, so we have to go. Right?"

And that was another thing that sometimes bugged Lacy about Kat. She talked like a pre-teen. That was annoying as hell. Kat's taste in music was impeccable, and the fact that she was able to keep tabs on all that went on in the Boston music scene was even more annoying. Yet another area where Kat had it going on.

Lacy was torn on the invitation. She really needed to talk to Folx, but if he wasn't online, she'd just be sitting around home fretting and nodding at centerpiece options. Good music also might help resolve the tight knot in her belly. At the very least, it might be inspiring. And, man, did she need inspiration. "Fine. What's the club?"

"Tigerstripes."

Lacy sighed heavily. She'd have to change first, then. Tigerstripes was an uber-trendy place, a total "see and be seen" for local musicians. Her yoga pants and tank top might be comfortable and fine for solo studio days, but she couldn't wear them somewhere cool, somewhere people might know her. It was her least favorite part of being a musician—she really couldn't go out in public without being "in character" so to speak. Her sister usually wore pantsuits to work and then got herself casual and comfy when they went out, but Lacy didn't have that luxury.

When Lacy Dawson saw a band, she saw them as Up-And-Coming-Indie-Sensation Lacy Dawson. Which meant she needed to be in her uniform—full hair and makeup, plus trendy jeans and stylish shirt. In other words, clothes that didn't double as pajamas.

So twenty minutes later, she was at home applying copious amounts of black eyeliner and fending off her sister.

"This wedding guest list is impossible!" Andy was yelling from her bedroom.

Lacy ignored her, and started filling in her brows, but not without first glancing at her phone to see if she'd missed any notifications from the songwriter app. She hadn't. She tried not to be too disheartened.

"This process has made me realize—and don't be shocked—but I don't have a ton of close friends. Do coworkers count? Can I ignore them and elope?"

Lacy dabbed white sparkles on to her brow bone. She studied the effect, and added some more to the corners of her eyes. She told herself Andy wasn't looking for an answer. That Andy just liked to hear herself talk. That way she didn't have to feel guilty about not weighing in.

"Are roses or lilies hotter right now? We're bound to get covered in *Boston Mag*. If I pick wrong, will I be lame, or trendsetting?" It was harder to pretend Andy didn't really want answers when she kept pestering for them like that.

"Look," Lacy yelled over her shoulder. "I'll go to your meeting tomorrow with the planner. Just stop stressing tonight, okay?" She wanted to be there for Andy, but she couldn't deal with the recording studio anxiety *and* her petty bridal jealousy. It took more energy than she had.

She left the mirror and stuck her head into her sister's room. "Do you want to come listen to a new band with me and Kat? It'll calm you down." Though Andy didn't get into music, not like Lacy did, but they always enjoyed each other's company. Even when Andy was being a bit wedding-crazy, she was still Lacy's best friend.

Andy glared. "Thanks, but no thanks. The last time I went out with you two I ran into that weirdo from the Iron and Wine bar. A night at home with Netflix and a bath sounds far more relaxing. Thank you, thank you, thank you for attending my meeting, though. Be awake and not hung-over by eleven, please!"

Lacy returned the glare, but Andy was right. The strangest people hung out at the coolest bars, and the Iron and Wine guy, or Eeyore, as Andy called him, had developed a fascination with the older Dawson. He was a recovering alcoholic that dropped trou after a single Jager shot. It was weird.

Also, Andy and Kat were hard to bear when they got together. Kat got all cable-show about wedding ideas, and Andy liked it. Maybe even loved it. It disgusted Lacy. Weddings should be reflections of the couple. So why all the hassle? Andy and Blake were Type A Workaholics. They should have a courthouse ceremony followed by a formal sushi dinner and port. Ob. Vi. Us. Weddings were overdone.

She swore she didn't think that just because her own wedding had been aborted.

The doorbell rang, and Lacy was so grateful to stop the holy matrimony talk that she almost jumped into Kat's hippie-reeking arms this time.

"Hey, let's go!" she yelped. She blew a kiss to her sister and off they went.